DEFENSIVE INSTINCT

KRISTAL STITTLE

SEVERED PRESS

DEFENSIVE INSTINCT

For Margaret & Alexander 'Slim' Stittle, and Anneliese Kaufman

Strong survivors all

Section 1:
Encounter

1
Misha Labours

The soles of Misha's shoes slapped against the pavement as he ran through the early morning sun. The saw-backed machete on his belt bounced rhythmically against his leg, while the rifle over his opposite shoulder acted as a counter balance. He never went anywhere without either of them. Behind him were over a dozen footfalls. One pulled ahead of the pack, coming up fast behind Misha. Misha held his course.

The dog burst ahead of him, inches away from grazing his side, which would have thrown him off balance. It had happened before; Bullet always wanted to be the first one inside.

As Misha neared his home in the shipping container, slowing down to a walk, the rest of the dogs gathered around him. They were wagging their tails, waiting to be petted, maybe given a treat or having a ball thrown for them. Misha had nine dogs in all, an entire pack of strays that considered him their alpha; this didn't include other people's dogs who were frequently coming around to play or get attention from him.

"Go on," he waved at them. "Run time's over. Go roam."

The smallest dog, some sort of terrier mix, reacted to his hand gesture as if he had thrown something, spinning around and listening frantically for its landing. The dogs didn't understand him, not really, but they seemed to figure out that he wasn't going to give them any attention for the moment. Three of them padded over to the shade cast by the row of shipping containers and laid down in it, three others wandered away, and the terrier followed Misha, still expecting something.

Walking through the open doors of the container, Misha saw that Bullet was already inside, slurping noisily out of one of the four buckets Misha tried to keep filled with water. The terrier went to a mattress near the entrance and hopped up, lying down but watching.

Moving to the back of the container, Misha could see the contents of his unorthodox home by the light of a modification made to the container roof. A hole had been drilled through it and then plugged up by a plastic bottle that had been filled with water and bleach. Misha didn't know the science behind it, but when it caught the sun above, it glowed like a light bulb. By its light, he could see his stack of milk crates holding things like clothes, food, ammunition, tools, and dog toys. Beyond them was the mattress he slept on, and a ladder that led up to the container roof's second modification: an emergency escape hatch. Misha went to his bed to check on his ninth dog, the one who hadn't gone running with him

"Hey Rifle, how you feeling today?" Misha asked the German Shepherd.

Rifle responded by lifting his head slightly and thumping his tail against the mattress. He was the only dog that Misha allowed in his bed: the rest used a trio of mattresses at the front.

Misha sat on his mattress to rub Rifle's side and the dog lowered his head, tail still thumping. He wasn't sick, just old. He had been a spry three-year-old when Misha first met the Shepherd when they escaped the horrors of Leighton together, but Misha had been calling the dog his brother for eleven years now, which made Rifle an elderly fourteen. His muzzle had greyed, his coat had lost a lot of its lustre, and his joints were arthritic. He didn't appear to be in pain most of the time, but he didn't move with the fluid speed of his youth. Rifle spent most of his days lying on Misha's bed and occasionally accompanying him on slow walks around the perimeter.

Bullet walked over to the mattress and nosed at Rifle, then looked at Misha as if asking how he was doing. The splotchy, Australian Shepherd-looking dog could never replace Rifle, but he had taken over the duties that Rifle could no longer perform. He even wore the German Shepherd's old harness.

"He's fine, Bullet," Misha told the younger dog while giving him a scratch behind the ears.

The terrier trotted up behind him, expecting the same. Rolling his eyes, Misha scratched the little dog too. Spring responded in her usual way by wiggling her entire body, her head held up and shaking side to side making it difficult to properly pet her. Still, Spring was an amazing ratter despite her quirks, and a good ratter was vital whenever the aggressive vermin carried the disease into their midst.

"You up for a patrol, Rifle?" Misha asked.

The old dog huffed and rolled to get onto his feet. Misha helped when it looked like he was going to have difficulty today, then got his own legs under him. Bullet and Spring gave Rifle a good sniffing as he plodded toward the entrance, ignoring them. He was used to their attentions and rarely grumped at the other dogs.

Grabbing a bottle of water from a milk crate, Misha followed the pooches back out into the sun, readjusting the light-weight hood that protected his head. Sunscreen was rare these days and reserved for the children, so Misha, like nearly everyone else, had taken to wearing clothing that covered the skin yet was airy enough to allow the body heat to disperse.

The three dogs that had chosen to lie on the pavement in the shade looked up when Misha emerged. Seeing Rifle with him, two of them lowered their heads again, but the third, Barrel, got up. He was a weird mix between a Doberman and something with a much stockier body. His face was narrow and his legs were thin and a bit stumpy, but his body was bulky. Misha always tried to treat his dogs the same, but there was definitely a hierarchy amongst them, and Barrel was at the bottom of it. Rifle never snapped at him, however, so the awkward dog liked to be around him when he could, trailing a bit behind Misha and the other dogs.

Spring, not liking the slow pace, bounded off before they even reached the perimeter, hunting for rats, mice, and any other rodents stupid enough to come around. Rifle kept to Misha's side, walking along with heavy steps. Bullet tried to keep to Misha's other side, imitating the older dog, but often he would trot ahead and then circle back. As long as no one was snapping at one another, Misha let them do what they wanted.

The perimeter wasn't the edge of the shipping yard, as it was far too big to completely cover and protect. Over the five years that he and the others had lived there, dozens of shipping containers had been emptied and painstakingly moved to form a barrier some distance away from the large warehouse, which acted as their base of operations. Where the containers abutted the fence, the chain link was removed to dissuade any would-be climbers. The wall was now two containers thick all the way around, and continuing to reinforce it was an ongoing project. About a year ago, they had discovered a method to lift one container up onto another and were now making the outer layer two containers high. They left parapet-like gaps between the upper containers that could be easily barricaded with the containers' doors; this allowed them to post lookouts up there as well as use them as exit routes.

"Hey, ghost eyes!" a voice called down from the wall.

"Are you referring to me or Bullet?" Misha responded, looking up. Both he and the dog had such pale blue eyes they almost came across as white.

"The dog, obviously. He's much cuter." A teenaged girl in a battered cowboy hat was on top of the container, grinning down at him and the dogs.

"Are you supposed to be up there?" Misha asked, knowing the answer was most likely not.

Instead of answering, Dakota went to the nearest ladder and scrambled down. Bullet and Barrel went straight to her, hoping to get some treats, but Rifle stayed at Misha's side. Misha waited for Dakota to make her way back to him, flanked by the dogs.

"Well? What were you doing up there?"

"Does it matter what I was doing?" she countered in that aggravating tone that only teens testing the limits of their independence could seem to pull off.

"Yes, actually," Misha told her calmly. He knew she was trying to get some sort of rise out of him. She had been testing all of the adults lately. Misha still found it odd to consider himself an adult, but at thirty-two years of age, he couldn't deny it. He had now spent a third of his life living amongst this craziness. For the younger ones, like Dakota, it was most of their lives. She probably didn't have many memories from before the Day, if any.

"I was bringing breakfast to some people," Dakota finally sighed.

"Cameron ask you to do that?" Misha continued his walk around the inner perimeter.

"Yes. She thinks I don't have enough to do." Dakota kept pace.

"And I'm guessing you think otherwise?"

"I don't know," she shrugged.

"Are you keeping up with your studies?"

"Yes," she rolled her eyes, aggravated. It was probably a question she got asked a lot. "But most of it's boring and pointless."

"What's pointless?"

"Math."

"Okay. You have three thousand two hundred fifty-two calories of food and three people to feed. How long will it last you?"

Dakota gave him a sulky stare.

"You have to travel three miles to reach the next safe zone; how long will it take you? You have to build a wall, like this one, and need to lift heavy objects: how many pounds of force do you need and what kind of set up is required to hoist them?"

"Okay, okay, I get it, math *can* be useful sometimes," Dakota huffed. "But what about English, huh?"

"When you're out there, you'll sometimes come across notes left by other people. Sometimes they're warnings or advice about the area. You want to be able to read them. Occasionally, you'll find journals, which can contain a wealth of knowledge depending on the people who wrote them. And I don't just mean what they did right; they're opportunities to learn from the mistakes of others. You also might end up having to write your own messages one day, either to warn others coming through the area, or because you have to stay silent with someone who doesn't know sign language."

"You're no fun," Dakota grumped.

"I never said I was. Don't know where you got that impression."

"I remember you and Rifle doing tricks on the Diana."

"Well, the Diana's gone now, and so are a lot of people."

"I'm well aware of that, thanks," Dakota scowled. Loss was hard for everyone, but the young especially. "You don't like people, do you?"

"I like some people."

"I think you like dogs better," she continued. "You never smile unless you're playing with the dogs."

Misha didn't bother with a response. Her statement was mostly true after all. Sure, there were occasions he'd laugh or smile around people, particularly with Danny or Jon, but he didn't hang around with them much. He understood dogs better, plus the solitariness probably had something to do with the fact that he had been forced to kill his best friend on the day, and the closest friend he had made after that was blown up. They never did find out exactly who had made the bomb and why, or why it was planted in Alec and Misha's closet. He hoped that whoever it was had died when the Diana went down.

"Is there any particular reason why you're following me this morning?" Misha changed topics after a minute.

"Cameron said I should shadow people and start trying to learn their skill sets."

"And the skill set you're trying to learn from me is?"

"Dog handling."

Misha suppressed a laugh. "That's not a skill."

"Sure it is."

"To train a dog, you set up a reward system, you be patient, and you be nice to them. It's not hard."

"What are you doing right now?" This time Dakota changed topics.

"Walking the perimeter, same thing I do every morning after my run."

"Don't you run around the perimeter?"

"Yes, but it's harder to see and hear everything when you're running. You can't take it all in."

"What do you do afterward?"

"Go eat breakfast, say hello to some people, then head to my day's assignment. Once I'm done for the day, I'll eat dinner, take another perimeter walk, go for a swim and bathe if the weather permits, then return to my container and read until I fall asleep."

"You do the same thing every day?" She was asking out of simple curiosity.

"For the most part. I like the security of routine."

"I don't."

Another silence came between them.

"I'm going to go find Cameron. Maybe she has someone interesting for me to shadow today." And with that Dakota walked off, pausing only briefly to scratch Barrel's head when he followed her for a bit.

"What do you think, *bratishka*?" Misha looked down at Rifle. "You think she'll turn out okay?"

Rifle looked back, one of his eyes a little more grey and filmy than the other. He hadn't lost the sight in it yet, but it was going.

"Yeah, I think she'll be okay too." Misha rubbed the Shepherd's head and continued his walk.

***

"Hey, Misha. I heard yesterday that you were looking for me?" Cameron sidled up next to him in line as he waited for his morning ration.

"Yeah, I heard you were over at Animal Island." There were two islands not far from the shipping yard where they had taken to keeping the food-producing animals. "Anything we should be worried about over there?"

"No, just checking in. What did you want to see me about?"

"I think Trigger might be pregnant. She's getting a bulge around that area."

"Oh boy. I'll check her out as soon as I have time." Cameron was the one fully trained veterinarian who had decided to live in the container yard. There was another vet permanently stationed on Animal Island while the others remained in the Black Box. On occasion, she also helped doctor people alongside her twin sister Riley, but she was often too busy with things like monitoring her students.

"I don't know which boy did the deed."

"For her sake, I hope it wasn't Guard. Those could grow to be some big puppies."

"I know a few people around here who wouldn't mind some more big dogs walking around."

Misha and Cameron finally reached the front of the line where they picked up their breakfasts. Their plates were full; breakfast was the only meal that wasn't frugally rationed.

"So I hear you had Dakota up on the wall delivering breakfast to the lookouts," Misha mentioned as he followed Cameron to a table. Rifle had been lying near the line and now got up to join them by their seats. He was one of the few dogs allowed inside the warehouse.

"She came and bothered you, did she?"

"I wouldn't say bothered. She mentioned something about shadowing people?"

"Yeah, I think it's time she followed around more people than just me. I don't think she's all that interested in becoming a vet or a doctor, so she needs to start learning what everyone else does."

"Talking about Dakota?" Riley asked as Misha and Cameron joined her table.

"Yeah," Cameron nodded.

"I am not looking forward to when Hope reaches that rebellious age. She's already done enough of it growing up." Riley's eyes shifted over to the table where her daughter sat with her friends. "By the way, I'm going to visit the Black Box today."

"This is sudden," Cameron frowned. "What brought this on?"

"I've been thinking of visiting for a while. We're getting a backlog of patients that need their blood samples tested, or need scans that we can't do here. I thought I'd gather up the patients who have to go, take the samples that need taking, and head over there."

"All right. Hope going with you?"

"She's still undecided. I think she's waiting to find out what her friends are up to first. If she ends up staying here, would you mind watching her for the night? I probably won't be able to get back until tomorrow."

"Yeah, sure."

"Where's Brunt?" Misha had noticed an absence from their table.

"On the wall. He's got the morning shift for a little while."

"Your second anniversary is coming up, isn't it?" Riley enquired.

"Next week. I think it's why he's doing some morning shifts. I don't know what he's planning though."

"Well, if it's after I'm back, I can watch Dakota for you." Riley smiled but there was a subtle pain in her eyes. It had been five years since her husband, Mathias, the father of her child and a man who had saved a lot of people, had died. She still felt that loss. Misha had seen it happen and still had nightmares about it. When their previous home, the cruise ship named Diana, had sunk, Mathias ended up in the water with an injured leg. Nobody really knew how long he had been swimming, bringing along three children and a three-legged husky, before Misha's life raft came across them. After the children were scooped out of the water—one of whom was Mathias' daughter—and the dog was being hoisted up, a shark swam up behind Mathias and took him away. Misha had seen the dark shape, the tip of the fin just barely slicing through the surface of the water, but there was no time to react. Even if he hadn't been holding the husky, there was nothing he could have done. Mathias was pulled beneath the waves and that was it. Thank God that Hope had been safely inside the life raft and hadn't had to see.

"That would be great, thanks," Cameron told her sister.

"Have you checked the board for your assignment yet?" Riley asked Misha, changing the subject.

"Not yet."

"You'll be out emptying another shipping container today."

"'Kay. Whose crew?"

"I think Boyle's, although you may want to double check that."

Misha nodded that he would. "Have you checked the zombie report yet?" That word came so easily now. It used to be strange, almost laughable, but it had become a part of their daily lives. The walking corpses had taken so much, leaving behind a new world devoid of the previous one's luxuries. Medicine had basically been reduced to what they could grow, new clothes were either made of self-cured leather or dusty scraps the moths hadn't yet eaten found in shops and homes, electrical power was savoured and used sparingly, while gas had all but disappeared—no one was refining it anymore.

"The report is the same as yesterday: no sign," Cameron told him.

"We haven't seen any in a while. It has me worried," Riley admitted. "Whenever there's nothing for a few days, they always end up appearing in a bunch."

"The walls are strong," Cameron said offhand.

"It's the people outside the walls I'm worried about."

Danny, Mathias's younger brother, was one of those outside. He and a few others had gone scavenging. It used to be a simple job where they would be out and back within the day, but now they had to go farther and farther. They camped out there, mapping the land, marking locations where there were things useful to the group that they couldn't bring back with them. They had been gone for over a week now.

Misha had finished his meal and lowered his plate to the floor, letting Rifle gobble up the scraps. His tongue squeaked across the surface of the china as he licked up every bit. When Cameron and Riley were done eating, they held their plates down in the same manner.

"Well, we best get to work then," Cameron sighed as she stood up. "I'll try to find time to examine Trigger."

"Thanks. Come on, Rifle." Misha carried everyone's plates and utensils to the dirty dishes deposit with Rifle following at his heels. The German Shepherd kept out a constant eye for dropped bits of food, or people holding out their plates for him. After breakfast was cleared away, some of the dogs would be let in to give the floor a thorough once over.

Beside the dish deposit, the warehouse wall was covered in a series of whiteboards and chalkboards. On them were written everyone's name along with what they were expected to be doing that day. Although the structure here wasn't as formal or rigid as it had been on the Diana, people were still expected to pull their weight. It also helped to know where someone was at any given time. Even Danny's name was on a board, simply listed as 'out.'

Outside the warehouse, Misha and Rifle were rejoined by Bullet who had been waiting patiently. They would walk Rifle back to their home, and then go find Boyle in the usual meeting place. Misha wondered what dogs he should bring over the wall with him this time.

***

"All right, everyone ready?" Boyle asked the small, assembled group. They stood before a shipping container out in the section of yard they didn't use. In a moment, Boyle was going to open it up and they were going to go through the contents. The containers occasionally held surprises and not all of them good.

Misha nodded along with the others.

Boyle grabbed the handles, popping them up and then pulling open both doors at the same time. A sour smell washed out of the container, followed by a buzz of flies.

"Rotten bananas," Boyle announced, the first to identify the contents.

Rotted food was always the worst. It had been so long that there was nothing left but a mushy paste and a vast colony of flies that had built up in the dark. Everyone pulled up their masks. Misha wondered if one of the other three teams had found anything better.

"Let's get to work," Boyle waved everyone forward.

Misha stepped into the container alongside Harry, the Australian engineer who had designed their method for moving containers. Just because he was intelligent and innovative didn't mean he was spared doing grunt work along with everyone else. They set up step stools facing the pile.

"The wood from the boxes still looks pretty good," Harry commented as he grabbed one end, his voice muffled by his mask. Misha took hold of the other end and they lifted the box down. Two more workers took the box from them and brought it outside. There, the wood, the mush, and anything else there might be, like fruit netting, would be separated as best they could manage. Mush would be placed in deep, plastic wheelbarrows whereas the wood would be stacked on flat movers. Both wheeled conveyances would be pushed over to the wall once full, and there they would be lifted up with a pulley system to where their final fate would be decided. Mush was often put into plastic buckets that got delivered to the farms as fertilizer, whereas wood had a variety of uses.

Even if the wood was crappy and rotten, it would just be added to the firewood pile.

Misha and Harry worked at a sedate pace, allowing time for the others to do their jobs without being overly rushed. Misha's gloves soon stank, and he was glad for the full-face mask. He didn't have any filters for it, but it still helped to reduce the smell, especially with its overpowering scent of rubber.

A tiny, distant cry made its way into the container, drifting over from one of the other teams.

"White, go find out what that was about," Boyle ordered one of their lookouts while separating mush from wood.

Misha and Harry continued to do their job, waiting patiently for the news from the other team. A cheer like that was always a good thing.

When White returned, he was panting from the run.

"They found a first-aid shipment, medicine that never made it to Africa," he reported with a smile on his face.

A small cheer went up from their team. Medicine was always a great find, especially if it came with supplies such as needles and proper bandages that hadn't been used and washed several times over. Their elation was quickly cut off.

"Herd!" a shout drifted over the container yard. It was quickly picked up by the other lookouts, who began scrambling down from their perches.

Misha and Harry returned the box they were moving and swiftly evacuated the container with the others. Boyle relocked the container with the step stools still inside, as Misha ripped off his face mask. Pulling off a glove, he stuck two of his fingers in his mouth and whistled sharply. Bullet appeared at his side in an instant. A moment later, as everyone was running back toward the wall, Spring tore out from between the large metal boxes, immediately keeping pace.

"Barrel!" Misha called out as he ran with the others. "Barrel!" His eyes darted everywhere, looking for the awkward dog but not landing upon him. He reached the wall and paused beside the ladder: all of the teams were scrabbling up one of three emergency rope ladders which had been hastily lowered.

"Misha, come on," Boyle said, patting him on the shoulder. He then grabbed Spring and handed the smaller dog to the next person going up, who carried her easily to the top of the wall.

Misha tried whistling again. "Come on, Barrel." He hated the idea of leaving a dog behind, but he knew he would have to if it came to that. Zombies started appearing between the containers. They were rotted like the bananas, only more dried out. This herd looked like an old one, with mummified husks staggering along on scrawny limbs, bones poking through thin flesh while lips were peeled back or gone, revealing grimy, broken teeth. Half-blind eyes bulged from lidless sockets. It was a good sign: they were less dangerous. The fresh, juicy ones were more deadly, especially the smarter ones, the ones who could still run and climb.

"Give me Bullet," Boyle ordered. "You can be the last one up, but you can't carry two dogs if Barrel does come."

Before Misha could even give his consent, Boyle was hauling Bullet up the ladder, carrying him over one shoulder. Misha continued to wait, watching the dead get closer, watching them reach the open span between the wall and the unmoved containers.

The last of the people reached the ladders. The rope ladders were pulled up behind the final person, and Misha climbed onto the lowest rung of the metal one. He paused though; he couldn't help it. He whistled again.

"Misha!" Boyle barked at him from the top of the wall.

As Misha took another step up, resigned to leaving Barrel behind, he heard a sharp bark. Looking back, he saw the dog burst between the legs of a few zombies, knocking them over in the process. He loped awkwardly toward Misha, his tongue hanging out.

"Come on, boy!" Misha encouraged him. "Come on, Barrel!"

Above him came the sound of a cocking rifle. A few zombies were getting close to Misha, and Boyle was preparing to take them down.

Misha dropped back to the pavement as the Doberman mix reached him. Before the dog had even stopped moving, Misha was hoisting him up onto his shoulder. Turning sharply on his heel, he returned to the ladder and scrambled up. Arms wrapped around him and the dog as he reached the top, pulling him out of the way so that more hands could grab the ladder and haul it onto the wall as well.

Once he was let go, Barrel stumbled away. He looked over the far side and whined, wanting to be put back down on the ground where Spring and Bullet had already been lowered.

"You and your stinking dogs." Boyle helped Misha to his feet.

Misha just laughed, unable to control it. The joy of surviving an encounter generally had that effect. Together, they looked out into the yard, watching the diseased corpses come toward them.

"At least they're helping us move a cart," Harry commented, pointing toward one of the alleyways. Several zombies kept bumping into their flat cart of wood, slowly pushing it toward them as it scraped along the side of a container.

"How many do you think there are this time? Think we'll be able to get back to work before the end of the day?" a woman from another team wondered.

Boyle just shrugged. They would do what they always did when this happened: several people would stay on top of the wall, drawing them in from the yard, making noise if need be, and then taking them out with long, pointed objects. Sometimes it would take a few days, but other times the herd was small enough to take out in a couple of hours.

Misha turned away from the yard. He picked up Barrel again and climbed down with him. Bullet immediately gave them a sniff check.

"Looks like we have some time off," Misha told the dogs. "Who wants to throw a ball?"

He was answered by a trio of wagging tails.

2
Wycheck's In Pain

"Just a little farther. Just a little farther," Wycheck kept whispering to himself, half the time so quietly that nothing came out. He dragged his right leg painfully behind him. He had escaped the zombies, but at what cost? His weapons were gone, his supplies were gone, his ribs were in all probability broken, and his leg definitely was. Every step was agony, but to stay still was to die. He knew there were living people around here somewhere. Not only had he seen evidence of it, but the soft white smoke of a cook fire drifted lazily up in the distance. Someone had to be there; he just had to reach it.

It had been a stupid idea to come out here by himself, but he just had to get away on his own. Jasmine had been harassing him again, insisting that they were meant for one another. Wycheck knew differently, seeing as how he couldn't stand to be near her for more than a few minutes at a time. He hadn't even told Evans where he was going, or even that he *was* going. Evans would have sent out a search party, or maybe he had the whole group looking. Wycheck just had to survive until they found him. Could be that the smoke was theirs. It wasn't impossible.

"Just a little farther. Just a little farther."

It felt like the smoke wasn't getting any closer. Hauling his broken body forward a few inches at a time was getting him nowhere. There was no other option. He couldn't call out for help: the zombies could be close. There was nothing he could see that could assist in transporting him, nothing with wheels that he could move on his own. Stumble-step, drag. Stumble-step, drag. It was the only way forward.

Sweat poured off his body, soaking his already blood-soaked clothing. He fought and struggled for every motion, every forward movement. He was going to survive this. After everything he had been through, all the death and pain, all the suffering, he was going to survive. Nothing was going to break him.

Wycheck didn't get to hear the crack of the rifle or feel the sting of the bullet before it shut him down forever.

3
Abby's Tired

"Come on, Abby, it's time to get up."

Abby groaned and rolled over, burying herself deeper beneath the warm blankets of her bed.

"Up!"

The blankets were ripped away, leaving Abby exposed to a cool draft. She gasped, her eyes cracking open while her body reflexively curled tighter. Lauren stood at the end of the bed, a cheeky smile on her face as she held the bundle of blankets.

"Can't I take the day off?" Abby sighed as she sat up.

"No can do, Poker-roo." Lauren dropped the bedding and proceeded to pick out clothes for Abby to wear.

"You're very chipper this morning." Abby slid off the bed and began her morning stretching routine on the floor.

"Not all of us can wake up on the wrong side of the bed. I'll start breakfast." Lauren disappeared from the room.

Abby's bladder became insistent before she was done with her workout. Taking a break, she gathered up her clothes and left their bedroom. After relieving herself and brushing her teeth, Abby finished her routine on the tiles, skipping only one exercise that required more space than the bathroom allowed. She then showered, towel dried her thin, sandy hair, and quickly got dressed.

"Claire and Peter already up?" Abby commented on their open doors as she carried her pyjamas back to her bedroom.

"I think Claire ended up spending the night with the farmers top side; her bed doesn't look like it's been slept in."

"Again? Do you think it's because she likes farming, or do you think a boy is involved?"

"I think she just likes farming and being outside," Lauren answered with a shrug. "She hasn't mentioned a boy to me, and she's not acting like she's in love or anything."

"And Peter? Where's he off to this morning?"

"He left a note about going to the computer lab, but it didn't say why. Maybe we can ask him when we get there." Lauren served up their breakfast, which had been made from the rations delivered to their door earlier. "What are we working on today?"

"I haven't decided yet."

"Maybe this time pick a movie that I've seen. I'm more helpful with those."

"Name one."

While finishing their meal, Abby and Lauren listed off several movies to one another, picking a good one that they had both watched back before the Day. When the food was gone and the dishes were cleaned and put away, they left their apartment-like home. Walking across the blue floor, they held hands as they followed the dark grey arrows painted on the pale yellow walls of the underground building known as the Black Box. The arrows took them down a staircase and into the computer lab, which had originally been much bigger. The directions were formerly indicated by the gold arrows, but the computers weren't as useful as they had been before and so were downgraded to a smaller space. Several terminals lined the walls of the room, with fewer than a handful of people seated at them. In a back corner sat Peter.

"You're up early," Abby commented as she and Lauren walked over to him.

"Woke up, couldn't fall back asleep," he answered, more absorbed in what was on the screen than in the women standing behind him.

"What are you up to?" Lauren asked.

"Studying."

"Studying what?" Abby was looking at the screen but couldn't figure it out. Several formulas were spread across it, and half the words between them confused her.

"Math," Peter replied. He had never been one for talking. When Lauren had first taken charge of him, there had been concern because he was a baby who virtually never cried. Now, he was an eleven year old looking at complex formulas that Abby could barely recognize. And she had a near perfect memory and used to read science books.

"Dr. Guptar give you this?" Lauren asked.

Peter nodded.

"Well, we're about to start our recording. We won't bother you, will we?"

The gangly, wild-haired boy shook his head.

Abby and Lauren left him alone to go to their own computer across the room. They had in essence claimed ownership of one of the terminals by the mere fact of being down there just about every day. Lauren sat before the keyboard and booted up the system, while Abby took the seat beside her and hooked a microphone over her ear, adjusting it in front of her mouth.

"I'm glad Dr. Guptar is encouraging Peter," Lauren spoke quietly before they began. Dr. Guptar was one of the computer scientists who already lived in the Black Box before they had arrived: a brilliant man who found himself more useless than not. Teaching Peter kept him occupied most days now. "Could you imagine if we were still trying to teach him math with the other kids?"

"He'd be teaching us at this point. And probably getting frustrated."

"I sometimes wonder if he'll be the next Einstein. Or Hawking."

Abby lifted a shoulder. "Could be. Or he could get bored and move on to something else."

"I like to dream that he'll be the one to fix all of this. Make the Earth normal again."

"You know as well as I do that that's impossible."

"Like I said, I dream. And I think we can get close to normal again. Our population is a hell of a lot lower than before, and we have to treat death differently, but we could get close."

"We should get started," Abby said, gesturing to the computer. Lauren was right that humanity could probably get really close to what it had been before, but Abby didn't like to think about it. She didn't believe it was something that could happen in her lifetime, and was resigned to accepting the world as it was.

"Okay, we're recording. Go."

Abby started to recite. Having grown up with something like an eidetic memory, she could remember every book she had ever read and every movie she had ever watched. Books and movies were being found all the time and added to the massive basement library, but inevitably some would be lost forever. Fires, nature, and destructive humans were whittling away their history. Abby, with Lauren's help, had made it her personal mission to preserve what she could. Although unable to remember every word, Abby could recall all the scenes and some exact sentences from the books she had read; the same was true of TV shows and movies she had seen. While dialog was simple, Abby didn't have the imagination nor the writing skills to transfer the images to page, so that's where Lauren came in. She was more creative, better at describing things. While Abby recited, the computer recording her voice, Lauren would take notes. Afterward, they would work together to write a sort of script for the film or narrative for the book, and at the end, they would write facts about it and the people involved in its original creation. Before the Day, before the zombies came, both Lauren and Abby had worked on a television show and had a lot of experience with scripts so they were easier. The two of them felt it was the least they could do for those who were no longer around.

With her eyes closed, Abby spoke, diving deep into her memories of the movie, which allowed her to push back the memories of death.

***

"Have you heard the news yet?" Winchester plopped down into a nearby chair that rolled a few feet before stopping.

"What news?" Abby asked. She and Lauren had finished the initial recording and were now working on a proper script. The recording would be saved to a hard drive, but once the script was done, they would print it, bind it—often using something simple like string—and then store it in the library.

"I heard Riley will be coming to visit. She's got some patients who need scanning or something."

"Will Hope be coming with her?" Lauren asked.

Abby couldn't help but notice Peter in the corner, tilting his head slightly in their direction.

"Don't know, the message didn't say."

Peter's head resumed its studious position. Abby felt a bit bad. All of Peter's closest friends had moved to the container yard, and he hadn't really been able to make new ones. They came to visit from time to time, or Lauren and Abby would take him there, but it wasn't the same as getting to play with them every day like he used to. Despite his obviously superior mind when it came to math, the kids at the container yard still treated him the same: as one of them. Some days Abby felt it was her fault for separating Peter from his friends, that she should have moved to the container yard with the others. But she couldn't. So much had happened, and she felt safe inside the Black Box even if others didn't. Lauren had been willing to go along with whatever Abby wanted, but there was also Claire to think about. She was very adamant about staying at the Black Box. In the end, staying put won out, even if Abby's own group of friends—family really—got split up in the process.

"Do you know when she's expected to arrive?" Abby asked.

"No idea," Winchester shrugged. "Sometime later today is all I know. There's a very likely chance she'll be spending the night."

"She can share with us," Abby immediately offered. It wasn't unusual for Riley to sleep on their couch and Hope to take the top bunk in Peter's bedroom whenever they visited.

"Any other reason for you coming down here?" Lauren wondered.

"Other than trying to see what you two are working on, not really." Winchester leaned forward, attempting to read what was written on the screen.

Lauren quickly blocked his view with both hands. "Don't you have other things to do?"

"Probably. Do you want to help me with it?"

"What is it?" Lauren raised her eyebrow sceptically. She was much better friends with Winchester than Abby was. The two of them had survived the first few weeks together, holed up in a motel crammed with people where Lauren had somehow been put in charge of all the orphaned children. There had been quite a few, Peter among them. Since then, they had been taken in by other adults, some who were new couples willing to take on the responsibility, others were individuals who had lost their own, and still more were families that had managed to stay together through it all and were willing to expand. Lauren and Abby had kept Peter, Claire, and Jon with them, although Jon was now twenty-seven and off living at the container yard when he wasn't out scavenging.

"We've picked a new area to sow, which means clearing out the crap that's already there. Want to come do some hard slugging work? Volunteers make the workload lighter." Winchester grinned like a used car salesman.

"We should probably—" Lauren started but Abby cut her off.

"Sure!"

"Sure?" Abby's partner looked at her with suspicious eyes.

"I'm tired of sitting down here all day. I'd like to go outside and do some manual labour."

"All right, I guess. Why not?"

"Excellent." Winchester got to his feet, the movement propelling his chair to clatter away into a desk. He looked at the other six people in the lab, all hunched over their desks and working on who knew what. "How about you folks? Any of you want to help clear our next field?"

Half the people ignored Winchester; the other half shook their heads.

"All right, just us then."

Abby walked over to Peter. "You going to stay down here all day?"

Peter nodded.

"Want me to come get you if Hope shows up?"

He nodded again.

"All right. Try not to fry your brain with this." Abby kissed the back of Peter's head, breathing in the scent of his hair, then made her way to the door where Winchester and Lauren were already waiting. Abby had never imagined herself as a mother until Lauren had shown up with Claire, Peter, and Jon under her wings. Now, she couldn't imagine her life without them.

"Will Claire be joining us?" Lauren asked as they made their way toward the stairs. Even though the Black Box had a working elevator, unlike the Diana, Abby always made them take the stairs. Not only was it healthier for them, but Abby's experiences insisted that the stairs were safer.

"She up top?" So Winchester hadn't seen her up there yet. It wasn't unusual: there were always quite a number of people on the surface and a lot of fairly large fields to be tended. There was no way to tell where Claire was unless you happened to spot her or started asking around.

They exited the underground lab-turned-hideaway beside an old set of train tracks that had a forest of weeds growing up between them. The train cars were secured in place, often used as homes or a place to sleep outside in safety for those who didn't want to go below for the night. Beyond them was an old facility, presumably a chemical plant of some sort, although Abby never bothered to confirm that. Over the years, the place had been thoroughly cleared out and stripped of virtually everything. They took apart all that they could—including metal wall panels—to use as fencing material around the growing fields. Winchester led them first to the road and then down toward the barge dock. Abby squinted up at a massive crane as they walked below its overhanging arm. The distance and the sun prevented her from seeing who was up there, but she could make out at least three people, their legs dangling into nothingness. Old plastic chairs had been brought up there a long time ago and bolted at various locations along the frame. With the addition of belts and harness restraints, they made relatively safe lookout points, the only danger coming from moving to and from those seats. Abby shuddered, never having dared go up there herself.

It turned out that the new field was going to be next to the barge dock, alongside the river. On their way there, they had passed other fields, all of them being carefully tended. They were irrigated when dry, monitored for pests, defended from birds, and picked when ready. Every field was labelled and sectioned off with string wrapped around posts. Signs designated what was planted where and when. They tried to time the plantings so that they always had something ready to be harvested. It wasn't always easy, and insects were a menace. With an extremely limited and ever-shrinking supply of pesticides, they used them only if an infestation got really bad.

"This field looks terrible," Lauren commented on the one to which Winchester had led them. Several people were gathered on the cement that made up most of the barge dock, waiting for the go ahead to start on the field. They all looked to have the same opinion as Lauren.

"Some of the fields we use today didn't look much different before we decided to plant them," Winchester reminded her. "At least there aren't any trees we have to cut down here."

"Pretty sure there's more rocks though."

The trio joined the rest of the group, who handed them work gloves from a box. Only people who constantly used work gloves owned their own, and therefore had a matching set. The rest were always so disorganized that one was lucky to get a pair that fit. Abby pulled out a set that looked the same; however, the left glove was bigger than the right.

"All right everyone, I think we got all the volunteers we're gonna get," Rose called out to the crowd. "I'm assumin' you all know what to do; if not, ask whoever's next to you for help. Get to work."

Everyone headed out to the field. Only Rose, the organizer of this task, stayed at the end of the field, not because she felt she was above the work, but because she couldn't do manual labour the way everyone else could. Her left arm ended just below the elbow, and, so far, no one had been able to find a prosthetic hand that fit her. She had jury-rigged some things for herself in order to do certain tasks, but nothing had yet proved useful for fieldwork. She couldn't wield tools or grasp rocks as well as someone with two hands, and her self-made implements couldn't stand up to the stress. Instead, she found other ways to help. As well as moving people around when it looked like someone needed help, she would at regular times strap a large water barrel to her back and walk around to give everyone a drink. There were a few younger kids who were also tasked with that job, but they pulled and pushed a wagon of water barrels across the uneven terrain.

Abby was sweating in no time. Later, horses would help plough the fields, but that couldn't be done until all the large rocks and tree stumps were removed. Winchester and Lauren worked together to get them out of the ground, while Abby pushed the wheelbarrow of debris to the far end of the field for dumping. Although there were plenty of people nearby, Abby was nervous every time she went to the edge of the field. There was a fence there, one that she was reinforcing with the debris, and it led all the way to the water's edge, but still she worried. Fences had fallen in the past. Instead of worrying, she tried to focus on the salt-water river that Riley would be paddling up, but that didn't stop her eyes from being dragged outward.

"What's going to be planted in this field?" Lauren was asking Winchester when Abby returned to their side with the wheelbarrow. They were sweating just as much as she was, but Lauren seemed to be enjoying herself despite her initial hesitation to volunteer. She liked being outside and wasn't as afraid of it as Abby was.

"We're going to plant another corn, squash, and beans combination, as that seems to be working really well in several other fields," Winchester panted, straining against a particularly stubborn rock that didn't want to let go of the ground.

"I'm glad Una is with us and told us about that." Lauren worked a shovel around the rock, loosening the soil.

"She's been a real help. We're lucky she stayed with us instead of leaving with that tribe who came through here a couple of years ago." With a grunt of effort, Winchester used all his weight to pull on the rock. When it finally decided to move, it slid up and rolled onto the ground, nearly crushing his feet.

"Worms!" Lauren called out, dropping down next to the hole that had been created.

Abby grabbed a satchel hanging off the wheelbarrow, and unzipped the top as she knelt down beside her spouse. Inside the hole were several large, fat worms trying to escape. Winchester decided to take a breather, so Lauren reached into the hole and grabbed every wiggly nightcrawler that she could, stuffing them into the satchel that Abby held open and ready.

"You found worms?" Rose jogged over, narrowly avoiding being pulled over by the weight of the water barrel that sloshed on her back.

Lauren had just secured the last of them, a few having escaped into the dirt. Abby zipped up the satchel and held it out to Rose.

"Great!" Rose stuffed it into a sack hanging off her belt. "I'll empty this and brin' it back in case you find any more."

She turned to leave, but Winchester stopped her. "Water first," he gasped.

"Get that rock into that wheelbarrow and I'll see what I can do," Rose teased.

Winchester shook his head but did as she ordered, hoisting the rock up like an extremely heavy baby and then dropping it into the metal receptacle with a mighty clang.

"Your reward." Rose handed him a plastic cup that she kept strapped to the other side of her belt. While he held it, she filled it using a nozzle on the end of a hose that was attached to the bottom of the water barrel.

After Winchester had his drink, the cup was refilled again for Lauren and a final time for Abby.

"Right, so you all know what to do if you find worms and don't have a pouch or anythin' to put 'em in?" Rose questioned as she resecured the cup.

"Use a glove," all three responded, each raising a hand.

"Fantastic." Rose then turned and walked off, accompanied by the sloshing of water. She would dump the worms into a large box on wheels that sat by the barge dock, and later they would either be put to work making fertilizer, or given to the fishermen as bait.

"Break's over." Winchester stretched his muscles and moved to the next rock.

Abby kept up with the wheelbarrow until it was full again. She walked back to the far edge of the field, watching her footing, and then dumped the load.

"Help."

Abby's head shot up, quickly scanning the field. Everyone else was acting normally. The call had been so faint, she could have imagined it.

"Help," she heard again, noting a hoarse tone to it. Because she had been listening for it, she was more able to pinpoint the source. With the hair standing up on the back of her neck, Abby turned to look beyond the fence. There, stumbling across the uneven terrain, was a small human.

Abby turned to find help, but instead spotted someone running to the fence with a rifle. The man raised his gun, intending to fire.

"Stop!" Abby yelled at him.

The man paused, confused.

"He spoke! He can't be a zombie, he spoke!" Abby yelled to everyone who was within hearing range. Her words caused several individuals to come running to the fence, Winchester and Lauren included.

They all stared silently out at the boy—if he was indeed male—watching him painstakingly approach them.

"Help," he called again, his voice so quiet and stressed that no one would have heard him if they hadn't been listening so intently. The child then tripped and fell.

"Get me over this fence!" Abby turned and demanded of Winchester.

He didn't hesitate to make a stirrup of his hands.

"I'll get a boat to bring him around. Get him to the water!" Lauren called out as she took off across the field like a flash, risking a twisted ankle.

"He could be infected!" a worried bystander called to Abby as she scrambled over the top of the fence. "He could change soon!"

"Hush," a woman next to the bystander barked. "It's just a kid, we'll take our chances."

Abby hit the ground on the far side of the fence, acutely aware that she had just exited her safe zone. Her blood sang through her veins and her muscles froze, fear locking her in place.

She startled at a heavy thump next to her. It was James Brenner: he had been working in the next field over and had immediately run to the commotion.

"I figured if you have to carry him, you could use some help," he told Abby.

Abby nodded, and the two of them made their way across the scrabbly earth where long, looping grass threatened to trip them. They advanced slowly, James holding his rifle at the ready, watching for any movement in the grass. Legless zombies were a big threat anywhere the ground couldn't properly be seen. Abby kept her focus on where the boy had fallen. Her pistol remained holstered on the back of her belt, but her hands remained aware and ready to grab it or the knife alongside her right leg. She was very grateful to have James with her, finding it slightly amusing that she and others had reason to mistrust him upon their initial meeting eleven years ago. He had become one of the most trustworthy and reliable people that Abby knew.

"There he is," Abby whispered once she could see the boy. His body was sprawled across the ground.

"Is he moving?" James asked, his eyes continuing to sweep the ground around him.

"A little." The boy's limbs were moving a bit: nothing to confirm he was still alive.

Abby approached with caution, kneeling down beside the fallen form's legs, away from his head in case it was too late. A groan from the child caused her to freeze momentarily, but then she reached forward and felt the boy's wrist.

"He still has a pulse," she sighed with relief after taking off one of her work gloves to check. She quickly put it back on.

"Hold this." James held the rifle out to Abby. She accepted it and locked her hands around the grip and barrel, her awkward gloved finger resting against the trigger guard.

Pulling his own work gloves out of a pocket, James tugged them on as he knelt down beside the boy. Abby swept the area with the gun, even glancing back toward the farm fields. Quite the crowd had gathered at the fences, their work momentarily put on hold. James scooped up the boy, carrying him bridal fashion but with the child's face turned away from his body.

"Let's get him to the river." James turned toward that edge of the land. He walked carefully across the rough terrain, with Abby close at his side vigilantly sweeping her rifle.

Other than a few near tumbles, they reached the water without incident. A large canoe was already waiting for them, bobbing on the surface; its occupants held it to the relatively steep and rocky shore. James had to slow down even more to cross to the boat, carefully watching his every step. It would be all too easy to slip on the rocks and break a leg. Upon reaching the canoe, Abby put the rifle down inside, then helped James lower the boy to the bottom of the boat.

"Still breathing?" the man at the rear of the canoe asked as they pushed off.

Abby knelt along the bottom by the boy's head, while James took up a paddle by his feet. She pulled off her glove again and once more looked for a pulse, this time in his neck. Her other hand held the back of the boy's neck as a precaution.

"There's still a pulse," she announced as the canoe swiftly made its way back to the barge dock. "It's pretty weak though."

"The doctors will know what to do," the woman paddling at the prow said with confidence.

Abby wondered why Lauren wasn't in the boat, but they had reached the dock and she'd find out soon enough. The dock was a wall of cement, much too high to get up from the canoe. A smaller, wooden dock had been put together below it, which was where they tied up and got out. Already a stretcher had been lowered down the side using ropes and pulleys, and it was swiftly retracted up the moment the boy was placed on it. Abby hurried down to the end of the wobbly wooden dock where she climbed the rope ladder.

Lauren was sitting on the ground nearby, out of breath.

"I got a doctor," she panted as Abby came over to her. "I figured the kid might need one."

"Good call." Abby sat down beside her, draping an arm over her wife's shoulders. They watched as Dr. Edward Owen gave the boy a quick blood test, and then had him moved from the pulley stretcher, to one that could be carried into the Black Box.

"You think he'll be all right?" Lauren wondered between breaths.

Abby shrugged. "I want to know how he got out there, and why he was alone."

The two stretcher-bearers ran past, Dr. Edward keeping up alongside them.

"I'm sure we'll find out when he wakes up and is communicative," Lauren assured her, her arm finding its way around Abby's waist.

Abby's eyes wandered out to where he was found; she was not as sure as Lauren. There were members of their group who still refused to talk about what had happened to them, while kids were prone to forgetting it.

"Break time's over," Winchester appeared behind them, dropping hands on both their shoulders and causing the women to startle.

"Can't we get five more minutes? Did you see how much running I just did?" Lauren complained, but got to her feet, then turned and helped Abby up.

"It's not like you're doing much work anyway; I've been doing all the heavy lifting." This caused Lauren to punch Winchester's arm. "Ow! Hey! Uncalled for."

"Totally called for," both Lauren and Abby told him at the same time, then laughed together.

With a fake grumpy expression, Winchester herded them both back to the field. It didn't matter what was going on with the boy; he was with the doctors now and a field still needed clearing.

4
Danny's Alert

The crack of the rifle startled Danny even though he had been listening for it. Although guns were generally carried around at all times, they were usually used only in emergencies. Danny paused in his cleanup of their camp until he heard Jon's footsteps coming down the stairwell from the roof.

"What'd you shoot?" Danny asked as he finished tying up his bedroll.

"A lone zombie that was heading for the fake campsite," Jon told him, as he untied their bundle of rifles in order to add the new one. The familiar handle of his katana stuck up over his shoulder.

"So it works then? We've gotten really lucky with the guns this journey," Bryce commented as he oiled the wheels on their trolley.

"I wish we were finding more ammo," Larson commented from where he was holding a water bucket for their one horse named Thumper. "There are some people who need shooting lessons."

"You're thinking of Becky," Danny said, nodding. "Hope should probably start taking some, too. They've already completed all the gun safety courses."

"Hasn't your sister been using a slingshot?" Jon asked as he rolled the rifles up in the tarp.

"Basically all the younger ones are." Bryce finished with the wheels and hauled his bag up onto his back. His squat form looked even squatter once it was on. "Hey Larson, can you believe that Becky is older now than we were at the beginning?"

"It boggles the mind," Larson agreed.

Danny watched as both Larson and Bryce performed checks through the windows of the shop they were in, making sure the way out was clear. At twenty years of age, Bryce and Larson were both considerably older than Danny had been on the Day. The two of them had lived with zombies more than they had lived without them. Danny still had about three years to go before that happened. He often wondered what life was like for his niece, never knowing anything before the zombie virus was let loose. Everything she knew about normal life was from books and stories. Then again, *this* would be normal to her.

"My turn on Thumper?" Jon asked this only for clarification as he walked over to the horse, picking up his tack and saddle.

Danny confirmed it for him, then scanned the area where they had camped, making sure nothing had been overlooked.

"What do you all say to checking one more quadrant north, and then heading back home?" Once Jon got Thumper harnessed, he led the dun-coloured steed to the entrance. Thumper followed along amicably enough, probably hoping that breakfast would come soon in the form of roadside grass. Or maybe middle-of-the-road grass, as over the years more and more forced its way through the cracks.

"I don't know. If we find a big haul, I don't think we'll have enough space in the carts. They're pretty full as it is right now." Bryce held the door open for everyone. While Jon led the horse, Larson pushed the flat bed trolley, and Danny took care of a shopping cart. Bryce then ducked through the door and grabbed the last shopping cart while Danny took over the door-holding duties.

"That's true." Jon swung up onto Thumper, standing in the stirrups to get a heightened view of the area. "But I'd like to have the shopping carts one-hundred percent filled before we head back to the stash. How about just one block instead of a whole quadrant?"

"Sounds good to me," Larson told him as the other two nodded.

"Oh yeah, Danny, that zombie I took down looked pretty fresh. I think we should frisk him. Might have something useful."

"All right, where is it?"

"Right there." Jon pointed across the street to a pair of boots poking out from behind a car. Just from that, Danny knew it would be good to frisk him. They were good boots.

"'Kay, wait here." Danny released his hold on the shopping cart and jogged over to the body, his heavy bag settling into its familiar position on his shoulders. Larson followed him halfway, acting as backup. Danny would have preferred Jon, since he was the best shot, but he took whatever he got.

The dead zombie was very much a fresh one. Red blood puddled around its head, not yet muddled into the thick, putrid black of the long turned. Although banged up, especially its leg, it wasn't in bad condition, all things considered. Danny worried about where the man had come from, and what had turned him. Bumping into either the living or the dead was undesirable.

Undoing the laces, Danny stripped off the dead zombie's boots, the rubber of his tightly fitting work gloves protecting him from the risk of infection. He worked his way up the body, checking for leg holsters, and then rooting through the pockets. There wasn't much, just some empty wrappers and a photo of people Danny would never know. He left the junk behind, but took the belt, which also had on it an empty water container and equally empty knife sheath, both of which could come in handy. Patting down the torso and arms failed to reveal any other hidden treasures. Whoever this guy was, he had died with nothing left. Bundling up the belt and boots, Danny turned and headed back.

"Not much there," he commented as he placed the items in the emptier of the two shopping carts. "He was really fresh though. We better keep an especially sharp eye out; there's no way to tell if he was alone." The others understood he meant both breathers and shufflers.

"We'll stick to hand gestures from here on out," Jon commanded, turning Thumper to head north. Because he was the oldest and most experienced of their band of scavengers, he was often deferred to as the lead.

The horse's clopping hooves led the way, keeping a safe distance ahead of the three pushing the carts. With their modified wheels that were frequently oiled and greased, the carts were virtually silent as they rolled forward: only an item or two inside would rattle on occasion. If someone or something showed up, they'd locate the horse first, giving the others time to get away. It was the balancing nature of riding: danger versus having to walk.

Danny brought up the rear of the cart pusher's triangle, often checking behind himself for anything coming up on their tail. He much preferred it when they didn't have to move silently, when they felt safe enough for whispered conversations. Although the group of young men often talked about asinine things, such as girls they knew or comic books they had read long ago, it alleviated the tension. Without it, Danny was left alone with his thoughts.

As usual, Danny's mind first drifted back to the Day. He had been fourteen years old and living with a foster family, because his older brother, Mathias, wasn't allowed to live outside the secret Marble Keystone facility, from where the zombie virus had come. Danny knew his brother hadn't been involved in that—he was just a security grunt—but it meant they weren't together when everything went bad. From there, Danny's thoughts drifted to his long-dead family, all of them but Mathias killed before he had reached double digits in age. Then Mathias had died, eaten by a shark when the Diana went down. Alec, the man who had saved Danny, who had taken care of him after the zombies showed up, had been killed by a bomb just a day or two before Mathias's death. So many people Danny loved ended up dead.

He forced his thoughts elsewhere, dragging them away from the dark hole in his mind, to focus on what was still around him. Jon, for instance. They had lived in the same foster home and had basically been brothers for a while. They were even more like brothers now and shared a container-home when they weren't out scavenging. The fact that they had wound up in the same place was amazing. More than amazing, really. Danny's family had grown before Mathias was killed. He now had a sister-in-law, Riley, and a niece, Hope. There was also Riley's twin, Cameron, who had adopted Dakota, and he had become so close to various people that they were essentially family as well: people like Bryce and Larson, who had started life as cousins but became brothers when the same couple adopted them after the Day. Things kept on changing, but not all the changes were bad.

Up ahead, the clopping of Thumper's hooves stopped. Jon had reached the next block of their search and was now surveying the area while standing up in the stirrups. After a moment, he turned and gestured to the trio behind him, pointing to where they would check first. His arm movements seemed pretty enthusiastic.

By the time the cart pushers reached the spot where Jon had gestured from, they found him already dismounted outside a store and waiting for them. Looking across the small parking lot at the store's name, Danny grinned and understood why Jon looked fairly excited. It was a small place that sold paint and painting supplies, easily overlooked by less-thorough scavengers but capable of holding a surprisingly good haul.

Taking out a notebook, Bryce peered through the dark windows between the advertisements and hastily sketched as much of the layout as he could see. Based on that, Jon put together a quick plan, using jotted notes and several hand signals, to which everyone agreed.

Turning to the door, Danny pulled on the handle only to find it locked. That was something he loved about being in Texas. Down here, they had had enough of a warning to pack up and bug out, but still hadn't known enough about what was going on to bring the right stuff. Occasionally, the scavenger team would come across areas that had been turned upside down or completely picked clean, but there were also a lot of locked doors elsewhere. From his back pocket, Danny withdrew his lock picks and set to work. It would have been easier just to smash in the glass door, which is what they would have done in an emergency, but the shattering glass could draw unwanted attention. It was always advisable to take the quiet approach whenever possible.

Danny focused on his work, closing his eyes while feeling for the movement of the tumblers. Locks like these weren't particularly difficult to pick when you knew what you were doing and had practice, but they could still be stubborn and take time. With the other three at his back, Danny was unconcerned about anything sneaking up behind him.

The tumblers finally slid into place, allowing Danny to turn the lock as though he had a key in it instead of thin strips of metal. Pulling open the door, he squeezed inside. There was a gate there, not far from the door. The cross work of metal bars travelled from one end of the store to the other, protecting the windows as well as the door. Still holding it open, Danny reached back through the door and tapped Jon's shoulder. Jon and Bryce both turned and slipped through, moving to the left and right, squeezing up against the bars. Larson remained outside with the horse and carts. Using his fingers as a countdown, Danny co-ordinated those inside to turn on their flashlights simultaneously. The lights were strapped to their wrists, and pistols were closely held to the beams as they tracked their way around the store. Dust covered everything, pleasing Danny. The dust indicated that it had been a long time since anyone had been in there. Danny pulled up his cloth mask to cover his mouth and nose, not wanting the dust that his movements had kicked up to cause a sneezing fit.

Looking over at Jon, he saw the more experienced man nod. Danny nodded back, then did the same with Bryce. Removing one hand from his pistol, the one with the light strapped to it, he grabbed the security gate and shook it as hard as he could, releasing a shower of dust from the bars. In the still, stale air, the rattling echoed across the displays in front, travelling past the cashier's desk and down the dark aisles beyond it. The three scavengers held still, flashlights trying to pick up every dark corner, searching for the slightest hint of movement. There was nothing.

Holstering his pistol, Danny brought out his lock picks again and set to work on the security gate. When it finally opened, Jon pushed one side in one direction while Danny pushed the other in the opposite. As soon as there was room, Jon stepped through the gates and Danny signalled the others. This place was likely to be a treasure-trove where they would spend a bit of time, so Larson and Bryce were going to bring the carts and Thumper inside for safety.

Having already planned ahead, Danny fanned right while Jon went left. They kept pace with one another, scanning behind and between all the displays before moving forward. Neither of them were focused on the items that adorned the shelves, their goal being to make the place safe first. The shelves were lined with large paint cans in a variety of types and colours, their metal sides weakly bouncing back the light. Finally reaching the back of the store, Jon and Danny came across no threats, just a bathroom door, an office door, and a paint-mixing machine. The bathroom was checked first. Danny pointed to the pile of plastic-wrapped toilet paper before he backed out. Toilet paper was a constantly shrinking commodity that everyone loved to have; the stack alone was a great find. Jon approached the office and tried the handle but it was locked. This one they couldn't pick as it was a number pad.

"No back door," Danny commented as soon as both he and Jon assumed relaxed positions.

"I'm guessing it's through the office."

"If something is in there, it can get out here pretty easily."

"I'll watch the door while you guys pack up," Jon volunteered.

Danny nodded and returned to the front of the store.

"Shop's clear," he told Bryce and Larson who were in watch positions. "Possible incursion point at the back that Jon's keeping an eye on. Nothing much to take back there except toilet paper and, if we have room, maybe a few cans of weatherproof paint." They used paint as a sealant on occasion, especially around the holes they made to put bottle lights in the shipping containers. Some people also liked to paint their doors to distinguish them from their neighbours making it easier to find their way around. Danny kept waiting for the day they gave the aisles between containers names, like streets.

"I'll get that stuff," Larson said as he headed for the back.

"Bathroom's on the right," Danny called after him.

He and Bryce then turned to the displays in front. Danny went straight to a corner where he had spotted a bunch of masks. They weren't just simple paper masks, but full, solid face shields with a piece of clear plastic to cover the eyes. He grabbed all of them off the rack, stripping them of their plastic packaging. Bundling the masks as tightly together as possible, he fit them into a cart. He then went to another display consisting of straps and harnesses that he also took out of their boxes. Next to them was a bundle of tarps and drop cloths. Bryce was on the other side of the store, gathering up scrapers, gloves, and tape. Larson returned from the back carrying an armload of toilet paper, which he deposited in a plastic bin that was strapped to the front of one of the shopping carts. It wasn't long before every gap in their carts was filled, with additional items hanging off the sides. It was decided that no one would ride Thumper, and so the horse was loaded up with as much gear as possible. The place had been a gold mine of supplies.

"We'll meet up with the others and head home," Jon confirmed as he picked up Thumper's reins. The horse bumped his shoulder with his nose, eager to go back outside.

Once everything was out the door, they headed back the way they had come.

Not one of the young men had noticed that they had been spotted.

***

They reached the secondary camp by sundown. The carts felt like they had gotten three times as heavy before they were pushed through the rollup door.

"Good job, guys." Lenny slapped Danny on the shoulder as he entered. The door then rattled shut behind him.

Inside the mechanic's shop attached to the car dealership, Lenny and Shaidi had been left in charge of guarding their temporary forward-operating base. In one corner stood three other horses. In the opposite corner stood a pair of large horse-drawn carts. One of the carts was already loaded up with supplies from previous days.

"I'm going to take care of Thumper. Can you get the map?" Jon asked, already starting to remove items from the horse's back. The beast of burden looked excited to see his fellow horses, and kept inching his way toward them.

Danny was grateful to release his cart and let Lenny take over.

"Shaidi outside?" Bryce asked as they moved toward the larger carts. The gear would be unloaded and made ready for moving out tomorrow morning.

"Yeah, she found a way up onto the roof," Lenny answered as Danny made his way further into the garage.

Against the back wall was where they had set up a sort of living quarters. Every time Danny saw the seat that had been removed from the back of a van, his heart gave a lurch. The first night after the zombies came, he had spent it in a garage similar to this one but much smaller. It was there that his brother Mathias had found him, but it was also that same night he had seen five-year-old Alice for the last time before she was killed. Although the van seat was the comfiest place and they took turns sleeping on it, Danny wouldn't take a turn. He couldn't.

Why do I always find myself in garages? he thought as he approached the tool bench beside the little living area. Even on the cruise ship, he was often in a makeshift garage that had been set up for the helicopters. Danny had wanted to be a helicopter pilot growing up and got to live his dream for only a short while. Thanks to a complete absence of fuel, their helicopter had eventually been stripped down for parts to be used elsewhere.

On the tool bench was spread a map of the area. The garage and its immediate surroundings were marked with a red circle, while larger blue, green, yellow, and purple squares jutted out around it like dandelion petals. Danny followed the coloured blocks to their outer edge, where he located the quadrant they had finished searching. Picking up the next coloured pen in the sequence—purple—he drew a box around the area. He then picked up green and placed a tiny dot on the painting supply store that was in the next search area. The grid around the garage had been paying out quite a number of supplies and they might return to it on their next hunt. Looking at the rest of the map, Danny scanned the areas where they had already been. Unfolding the map would reveal dozens of red circles in the middle of colourful squares that spiralled out from them. They liked to stagger their scavenge sites this far out, so that other humans couldn't just follow the emptied places back to where they lived. Checking the map, Danny figured it would take at least two days but more likely three for them to get back home to the container yard.

"Map's been updated," he told the others as he walked over to help them move the supplies from the smaller carts to the larger ones. It didn't take long before it was all ready to go, the shopping carts themselves strapped to the backs of the large carts while the flat bed trolley hung off the side of one. The next morning, the horses would be harnessed together to the carts and they could head out.

"I'm going to check on Shaidi," Danny said as he headed outside. The others were settling around the living area, spreading out their sleeping mats once more.

Outside, the streets were quiet and dim. The sun had sunk below the horizon, but still threw rays of coloured light onto the few clouds drifting by overhead. Garbage clung to the curbs, but not much. The place was a ghost town. Small animals skittered about, often just out of sight. Insects droned as they always did, only they were more noticeable not having to compete with the sounds of traffic, TVs, and conversations. Danny knew it wasn't safe to stand around on the street by himself for too long. Zombies and dangerous humans weren't the only threat out there. A wild pack of dogs could easily be deadly, and they once spotted a pride of lions that must have escaped from a zoo and had managed to survive. There was no telling what other animals had escaped. Then there were the rats. Rats were carriers of the disease, and it made them extra aggressive, more prone to biting.

A deep hiss drained the blood from Danny's face and drew his attention behind him. A block away, a long flat snout was making its way around a corner.

"Danny," a voice whispered from above.

Danny looked up and spied Shaidi staring down at him with her cat-like eyes.

"The way up is over there," she pointed toward the far side of the car dealership, thankfully away from the scaly beast that was lumbering into an intersection. It would spot Danny soon enough.

Dashing in the direction that Shaidi had indicated, Danny didn't bother to look back. He knew well enough what was coming. Just around the corner was a ladder. The bottom had formerly had a cage locked over it, but the lock lay broken on the ground having met Shaidi's bolt cutters. Scrambling up, Danny reached the roof in no time. He quickly made his way to Shaidi's side and looked back down on the street.

The alligator had made its way into the intersection and seemed to be deciding on which way to go next. A small handful of animals acted strangely when infected, their behaviours changing but not in typical ways. Alligators, for instance, suddenly shunned the waterways, and instead took to walking about in search of prey. They weren't any more aggressive than normal, but then they didn't need to be to threaten the humans.

"I hate alligators," Shaidi mumbled as they watched it make a decision and lumber off down another street. Danny didn't really hate them, but he had a healthy fear of the reptiles.

As the sun continued to plunge farther and farther into the west, the day became so much darker. Gone were the human-made lights to keep the darkness at bay, to reveal the monsters lurking within it; monsters like infected alligators, who loved to hunt in the inky black of night.

"Have a good time out there?" Shaidi whispered, relaxing now that the alligator was out of sight.

"Probably a better time than you, spending all day up on this roof," Danny whispered back.

Shaidi gently elbowed him in the ribs. "I have a great time up here. Get to watch all the animals who usually run away from you stinking lot. I spotted a twelve-point buck this morning."

"And you didn't shoot it?" Danny pouted. Everyone had grown to enjoy the taste of venison, as it had become a common meat source. They had even captured a few deer and were trying to create a sustainable herd on Animal Island.

"I didn't know how long you boys would be out, and I didn't have anything to pack the meat in. Not to mention that Lenny and I don't have a good place for a fire of that sort. Oh, and that alligator is not the first I've seen in the area. There's a bigger one lurking about."

"Okay, I get it." Danny grinned and put up his hands in surrender.

"I also thought he was too beautiful to shoot," Shaidi added as an afterthought.

Danny nodded, understanding. There were just certain animals on which you couldn't pull the trigger when they were in your crosshairs. He wondered why that was.

"We should probably go inside while we know the streets are clear," Shaidi recommended, pulling away from the edge of the roof.

"Sounds like a good idea to me."

Before he followed Shaidi back to the ladder, Danny looked up at the sky. It was a moonless night, but the stars were coming out in ever increasing multiples. Back at the container yard, where Danny knew he was safe, he would spend hours watching the twinkling points of light so very far overhead. Now was not a good time or place however, so he quickly looked away and scrambled down the ladder after Shaidi. Once at the bottom, she closed the gate back over the lower rungs and hung the broken lock from it. It would discourage other things from climbing, but a human could easily figure out the lock was broken.

Back inside, the other four were gathered around a tiny cook fire, putting together a late dinner. Its smoke gathered against the high ceiling, while the group of battery-powered electric lights threw a cheery glow about the garage. Even the horses, whose movements were limited by their tethers, clustered as close as they could to the solar lanterns. Danny quickly located his pack where he had left it, and unstrapped the bedroll from the top, rolling it out on the floor near the others.

"What's on the menu for tonight?" Shaidi asked Lenny who seemed to be the boss of their makeshift kitchen.

"Stew," he answered simply as he stirred a large pot. It felt like they were always having stew.

Danny sat quietly on the floor, leaning against a thick square post, and waited for dinner to be ready. He pulled off his boots and rubbed his feet while waiting. Even after years of spending days on his feet, they still got sore, as did his hips and knees. Despite knowing this, he still went out scavenging every time there was a call for it. He couldn't relax if he was in the container yard too long.

Once the food had been eaten, and all but one of the lights turned off, the group of six made their way into their sleeping bags. Bryce was given the van seat that night, as well as first watch. Danny's was in the middle of the night, his least favourite time, but then no one liked taking the middle watches and so they rotated. Curling up, Danny held the corner of his pillow with both hands, remembering an old stuffed animal he had lost when the Diana sank. As he closed his eyes, he tried to think of bright sunny days in the container yard, as opposed to the pitch-black murk of the sea.

In the moonless dark outside, things moved in the shadows. This was the case every night, but something was different. Something stayed still, its eyes upon the garage where the scavengers rested inside. The watcher's gaze was filled with intent.

5

Riley's Concerned

While the canoes were being loaded, Riley sifted through her packed bag again, making sure she had everything she needed. She wanted to go through the coolers as well, but once they were pulled out of the cold water of the large bay, it was a bad idea to open them.

"Mom, did you grab my hair brush?" Hope asked, going through her own bag.

"It's in the side pocket," Riley said, gesturing to her daughter's bag. She watched as Hope found the brush and packed it in a different pocket. Although she still left the bag packing to her mom, Hope had begun having her own ideas about what went where. Riley was glad her daughter had decided to come with her.

"Five more minutes!" Karsten called out in his German accent. He was in charge of the canoe voyage, currently making sure that all the supplies they were giving to the people at the Black Box were properly loaded. All along the end of the large cement dock were people making last minute preparations. Riley had intended for this to be a small journey, but apparently Karsten had other ideas. He had been overdue for a shipment, and when Riley had requested some boats, he thought now was as good a time as any. Riley couldn't begrudge the man for doing his job, for turning several trips into one, but it did mean they were leaving considerably later than she had wanted.

Hope didn't mind the delay at all as it meant she got to spend the morning with her friends. Her hair was still damp and soaking the back of her shirt from their swim that morning.

"Once your hair is dry, remember to put your head gear back on," Riley reminded her offhandedly.

"I know, Mom," her daughter responded with a roll of her eyes, a habit she had no doubt picked up from Riley herself: those eyes that were the exact same as her father's.

"Are you excited to see Peter?" Riley changed topics.

"Yes!" Hope grinned at her, showing all of her teeth which were a mix of adult and baby, with a gap along the bottom where one had recently vacated. "It's been years!"

"It's been four months, actually," Riley told her.

"Which is like years when you're not an old fogey," Hope retorted.

"Are you calling your mom an old fogey?" One of Riley's patients was sitting nearby and overheard the conversation. "Because I don't know what that would make me."

"You're a cool old dude, Mr. Bill," Hope told the white-haired man who liked to tell pre-zombie stories to the kids.

"I'm a cool old dude," Bill said to Riley in a proud voice, yet lifting his eyebrows in a knowing way that made Riley chuckle.

"All right, gear's packed up. Everyone prepare to board," Karsten called over everybody's heads.

Riley performed a quick head count of her patients, making sure she hadn't forgotten anyone and that no one had run off to grab a last minute item. They were all present. Forming orderly lines, those that were taking the trip to the Black Box began to board the canoes. The cement dock was very high, which meant they had to climb down ladders into the boats. It was a wobbly affair, but from experience and with assistance from those already in the canoes, no one fell overboard or had any other sort of accident. Riley helped Hope off the ladder, then took the seat behind her once she sat down. The canoes were very long, able to hold several people each along with the gear. All who boarded picked up paddles that lay strapped to the outside of each seat.

"Everyone aboard?" Karsten called up to the woman on the dock. She would pull the ladders up once they were gone.

She replied with a thumbs up.

"All right, canoes, push off."

Together, the passengers placed the ends of their paddles against the cement wall—which had been studded with ringbolts so that the canoes could be held against it while loading—and pushed out into open water. The paddle blades were then plunged through the surface and everyone worked together to move forward. It wasn't long before a simple song started up amongst the paddlers to help them keep in time with one another. Hope sang along, but Riley kept quiet. She had never been one for camp songs.

On either side of the canoe train, a person in a single kayak kept pace: one out in the front on the left and one at the back on the right. The kayaks were more manoeuvrable and acted as lookouts for the convoy. They also carried high-powered rifles secured in waterproof bags. Although the canoes were armed as well, all hands would be needed if they had to escape to safety. Had Riley been travelling alone, she would have taken one of the kayaks, but unfortunately this couldn't be a solo trip.

It wasn't long before they were away from the shipping container dock and heading for the gap between Animal Island and a somewhat smaller island that they used to quarantine potentially sick creatures. Between the container yard and the larger island spanned the most precarious bridge that Riley had ever seen. Nearly all the lifeboats from the Diana, along with a hodgepodge of barrels and large, plastic, dock floats, had been strapped together in a line with innumerable wooden boards attached to the tops of them. The thing bobbed and wiggled with the current and waves, its unsteady motion having bucked many people off into the seawater, earning it the name Bitch Bridge. There were plans to complete a rope railing along one side, but so far it only stretched about a quarter of the way. Riley hated that bridge and refused to let Hope cross over it, allowing her daughter to visit the island only via boat. It would be too easy to get a leg caught between its many shifting parts and have it snap. She didn't know how her sister Cameron managed to cross it as often as she did.

On the far side of Bitch Bridge, the rest of their water transports lay pulled up on the shore. The canoes and kayaks would get damaged if they were kept tied up to the cement dock, and so they rested on Animal Island until they were needed. It was the one advantage Riley could think of having Karsten turn her trip into a convoy: she didn't have to cross Bitch Bridge herself to get the boats.

Beyond the overturned canoes and kayaks stood the only true structure on Animal Island. It was half-shack, half-tent, and housed the only veterinarian who had become a permanent resident of the place. Riley didn't know how he could stand it there, especially when the wind picked up. Maybe he had crossed Bitch Bridge once and decided never again. Along with the shack were a few simple board and wire fences, but the surrounding water made the best barrier for keeping the animals contained. As Riley watched the island begin to slip by, she saw a lonely cow looking back. Cameron appeared on the hill above it, carrying a halter and clearly searching for the wandering cow. When she spotted the flotilla paddling by, Cameron raised her hand and waved. Riley, Hope, and several others who saw her waved back. On the other side of them, Quarantine Island remained empty.

Beyond the pair of islands, they crossed the larger half of the great bay and entered the wide river. The speed of the canoes slowed down at that point, with inexperienced paddlers becoming weary on the long journey as the current worked against them. That was all right though. The river water was always much calmer, and therefore safer than the rough waves of the bay.

Riley remembered the first time she and Hope had travelled these waters. It had been only a couple of days after Mathias had died. His loss still felt like an empty place in Riley's heart, but back then it had been so much more. It had been a freshly ripped wound, tearing her in half and hollowing out her guts and mind. She suspected that her grief was the reason she had eventually left the Black Box with the others. The place held no memories for her beyond terrible ones. Cameron and Danny had also decided to leave, and Riley still needed their support: not just for herself, but for Hope. There had been days when it took everything Riley possessed just to get out of bed. There were days when even that hadn't been enough. How was she supposed to take care of a five-year-old child when she could barely manage to take care of herself? The answer was that she couldn't. Cameron took care of both of them, as well as Dakota, and Danny helped where he could. Others did as well, but they weren't family and weren't sure how to act in such a situation. Riley had been born to a family who prepared for every physical eventuality they could think of, but no one had prepared her for what depression was truly like. It had been easier to abandon the hospital she worked in on the Day, than to deal with the loss of her husband. If she hadn't had Hope to worry about, Riley would not likely have made it through that dark period of her life. The Black Box only reminded her of it, which was why she didn't visit all that often.

Before they even reached the barge dock, Riley spotted people. Their fences had been extended since the last time she had been there, and it appeared a new field was being worked. It was difficult to tell for certain from her low angle. As the workers spotted the canoes, they waved enthusiastically. Most of the paddlers stopped at one point or another to wave back. Hope, who had grown weary of paddling and hadn't dipped her blade the entire time they were in the river, waved to all of them. Riley thought she might be looking for Peter, but she doubted the boy would be among the farmers.

By the time they reached the wooden dock and started to double park against the Black Box's canoes, a welcome party had formed. Several of them climbed down to assist them.

"I want to go find Peter, Mom," Hope stated rather than asked as she and Riley made their way up to the top of the barge dock.

"I don't want you running around here by yourself. Wait until someone can take you to find him."

Hope huffed. She was usually given free rein within the container walls, but she didn't know the Black Box as well and neither did Riley, so she had to stay put for the moment.

Once Riley's patients had assembled, she began to lead them to the nearest entrance by the train tracks. Back on the barge dock, Karsten would finish unloading, then take on a shipment of food and return to the container yard.

"How come no one's here to greet us?" Hope asked, holding her mom's hand like a good girl, which was unusual. In Riley's other hand, she carried the cooler of blood samples.

"I'm not sure." Although there had been a welcoming party, Riley knew what Hope meant. Usually someone they knew well would be waiting for them, like Abby, Lauren, or Josh. Where were they?

As they neared the crane tower, Riley spotted the shape of a person climbing down from it. He or she must have started climbing down the moment the convoy had arrived, because the individual was near the bottom now. Riley couldn't tell who it was owing to the distance and shifting layers of clothes, but once the person hit the ground, he or she began to run. Whoever it was, was coming toward Riley's little group instead of heading for the dock.

"Wait a second, guys." Riley held up a hand to stop her little troop. Those who hadn't already followed Riley's gaze did so now, picking out the person coming toward them.

The smiling face beneath the wide-brimmed hat became clear as it got close.

"Claire!" Hope released Riley's hand as if she realized she had been holding a poisonous snake.

"Hey, Hope, you here to see Peter?"

"Yeah. Mom, can Claire take me to see Peter? Please?"

"I don't mind taking her," Claire added.

"*Pleeeease?*" Hope stressed.

"Do either Lauren or Abby know you were up there?" Riley asked, gesturing to the crane.

"Umm…no," Claire spoke a little sheepishly, but then straightened up. "I'm twenty-one years old, you know, I don't have to tell them how I spend my days."

Riley paused momentarily, briefly distracted by the thought that Claire had been the same age Hope currently was when the Day occurred. She had been just a little girl when she watched her family and friends get killed, barely surviving herself.

"No, you don't, you're an adult and can make your own decisions," Riley agreed, "but don't you think you should tell them in case they're ever looking for you? It would be better to hear it from you than to find out during some sort of emergency." Riley didn't want to think about that emergency being Claire splattered below the crane, but didn't say as much.

Claire sighed.

"She's right, you know," Bill added. "This isn't a time to be keeping secrets; your parents should know how to find you."

Claire gave him a scathing look for speaking up, but it quickly softened. She knew they were right, of course.

"Can I go find Peter now?" Hope whined, tired of standing around and perhaps worried that Riley would find something about which to lecture her.

"All right, you can go with Claire to find Peter."

"Yes!" Hope jumped and pumped her fist. "Come on, Claire! I bet I know where he is!" She wrapped her hand around the older girl's and pulled her toward the entrance.

"Remember what I said, Claire!" Riley called after the pair.

Claire raised her hand in response as the duo dashed on, reaching the entrance and disappearing inside.

"I don't envy you," one of Riley's female patients commented as they resumed their more leisurely pace to the entrance. "I can't imagine trying to raise a kid amongst all this."

"It's not so bad," a man who was a father of now grown children responded. "I mean, it's different, yeah, but at least we don't have the internet to compete with. And it's not like you have to worry about someone kidnapping your kid and taking them to God knows where."

This started a discussion amongst the patients about what had changed and what had stayed the same when it came to kids. Riley tuned them out. She had other things on her mind, the least of which being where her friends were currently hiding themselves.

***

When Riley entered the first of the rooms that made up the medical suite, she was surprised to find so many people she knew lingering on and around the plastic chairs. Abby and Lauren sat side by side, their heads together in conversation, their hands and faces covered with smears of dirt. Crichton sat ramrod straight beside the door to a recovery ward, while James Brenner paced back and forth nearby. Just as Riley registered them, and they registered her, Josh and Robin strolled in. Back before the Day, Josh had been a medical resident under Riley in the ER, and on the Diana, Robin had been her medical student. It was nice to see them working together now.

"Riley, you're here." Josh sounded a little surprised to see her.

"Did no one tell you I was bringing some patients by for testing?" she gestured to the people gathered behind her while also lifting up the cooler.

"No. I mean, yes someone told me, I just forgot is all."

"What's going on?" Clearly Riley was missing some important information given the lack of the usual greeting. People's minds were preoccupied with something else.

"Can we have a status update on the boy, please?" Crichton cut Josh and Riley's conversation short.

"He doesn't have an active infection," Robin told the room. "However, Abby and James, we'd like to run your blood as an extra precaution. Sorry for dragging you away from your duties like this, but you know how paranoid some people get."

Abby nodded and got to her feet, Lauren's hand lingering in hers before she walked with James and Robin down a short hall to one of the exam rooms.

"He's grossly malnourished," Josh continued where Robin had left off, "but we've been giving him some liquids. Unfortunately, he's still unconscious so he can't feed himself or answer any questions. We've cleaned him up and assessed that he has no injuries besides a few on his hands and knees that are consistent with stumbling and falling. There was nothing in his clothes to give us any idea who he is, and he had no weapons of any kind."

"May I sit with him until he awakens?" Crichton asked, pushing up onto his feet.

"You're welcome to, just let me know the moment he does."

Crichton nodded and then disappeared through the doors behind Josh.

"New arrival?" Riley guessed based on the bits of conversation she had heard.

Josh nodded. "Yeah, a kid, maybe somewhere between seven and twelve years old best I can figure. He showed up outside the fence and nearly got mistaken for a zombie. Luckily, Abby had heard him cry for help before he collapsed."

"Poor sod," a patient behind Riley mumbled. They had begun to disperse about the room, finding themselves seats.

"You should have seen how quickly Abby was over that fence," Lauren added. "She and James went out there to bring him in."

"Hence the blood tests," Riley nodded.

"So," Josh clapped his hands as he changed topics, "how are you? Need any help with this lot?"

"I'm fine. Are some of you okay with Josh running your tests?" Riley asked her group.

"I'd prefer it," one man answered. He was here to get a strange discolouration of his testicles looked at. It had originally been examined by one of the male doctors at the container yard, and the man had been acting a little squeamish about the idea of Riley taking a look.

Shrugging out of her backpack and opening it, Riley took out the patients' medical files. They were similar to what they had been pre-zombies, only now everything was hand-written. Several doctors wrote too fast, or too illegibly, to the point where they had 'hired' a former nurse whose job it now was to go through everything and rewrite it all in a much neater print.

"I should tend to these first," Riley told Josh, indicating the cooler while she handed over the medical files.

"Of course. You know where the lab is. We can catch up later." Josh looked at the man who had spoken up about preferring him. "What's your name? I'll start with you."

Riley picked up her backpack and the cooler and left the medical suite. Although there was some equipment in there, the mini lab across the hall was better stocked for what she needed to do. The lab was currently occupied by only one other person, Dr. Edward Owen. He waved to Riley as she entered, then returned to his work. Riley wondered what he might be up to. He could be running similar tests to those Riley was about to perform, or he could be doing a more extensive work up on the blood of the boy who had shown up.

After placing the cooler on a table and hanging her bag off the back of a chair, Riley located a pair of gloves to snap on over her hands. Then she set to work. There were blood samples to examine for things other than the zombie prion-virus hybrid, as well as a blood sample from a newborn that she needed to type. Without being able to keep a supply of blood on hand in case of injury, the doctors filed everyone's blood type so that they all became potential donors. Along with the blood were some Pap smears, and a couple of tissue samples, one from a persistent rash and one from a persistent sore throat. The scariest thing that Riley had to exam was a biopsy. It had been performed on Bill in the shipping container they had made sterile and covered in plastic. A growth had been discovered in his lymph nodes. His reason for coming along on the trip was to get a full work up, but this biopsy might be all they needed. If it turned out to be cancer, there was nothing they could do about it except maybe give him a rough estimation of how long he had left. Riley tried not to let her worry show, even after Edward had completed his own tests and left her alone in the lab.

Getting inconclusive results for the rash and sore throat was annoying, but not unexpected. When there was nothing left to do but monitor the machines, Riley crossed the hall and examined and ran additional tests on her patients. Robin and Edward assisted. With four doctors, it didn't take long to get people the x-rays, scans, and various examinations they needed, including an endoscope of a woman's stomach. It all provided more data for the lab to process.

Josh walked into the lab, carrying the last of the x-rays, and found Riley sitting on a stool with her face propped up and buried by her hands.

"Everything all right?" he asked, pausing on his way to the light table.

"Bill has cancer." She moved her hands away from her mouth to speak clearly but continued to cover her eyes, not wanting Josh to know that she was crying. "It's inoperable."

"I'm sorry," Josh spoke sincerely, then continued on to the light table where he proceeded to examine the films. Riley took the opportunity to clean up her face. After some time, Josh leaned against the computer-laden table behind him and asked "So how are you? I know you said fine earlier, but you know... You're not always honest."

Riley thought for a moment that she had failed, that it still looked like she had been crying, but then realized that Josh was just trying to make some light conversation.

"Really, I'm fine. Same old, same old, I guess. You? Still seeing Anne?"

"We're living together now, actually." Anne used to be the girlfriend of Tobias, a member of their group. When Tobias was killed, their little extended family had agreed to look out for her. Apparently, Josh started looking out for her more than most, and after an appropriately respectful amount of time had passed, they began seeing each other.

"Congratulations," Riley told him. She really was happy for him. Josh used to have a crush on Riley, which had sometimes made her feel guilty about being with Mathias. She was glad he had found someone who could return his affections.

"We're not married or anything, we haven't even discussed it," Josh was quick to add. Quick enough to make Riley think he wanted to marry Anne, but was still unsure about how she would respond to the idea. "I don't suppose you have any prospects?" he changed topics, managing only to strengthen Riley's idea.

Riley gave him a look to remind him that she had no interest in other prospects. She had loved then lost and was okay with leaving it at that. She didn't think she could handle another love in her life.

They continued to chat about other things, like what Hope had been up to, how the crops were growing, and who had decided to leave their respective colonies. Riley personally hated that word, colony, because it made it sound like they were in some newly discovered land, but there were times it was the best description despite that.

"Anyone new over there?"

"Nothing but zombies showing up at our wall. What do you know about the boy?"

"Barely anything. You heard what I told Crichton, right? That's pretty much it."

"You said you were giving him liquids?"

"Not an IV if that's what you're thinking. We still have enough supplies for one, but it's not necessary. No, Robin and I just boiled a watery broth, which we've managed to trickle down his throat a little at a time. His swallow reflex is still active."

"You think he might be faking his unconsciousness?"

"If he is, he's very good at it."

"Well, I should get back to work. I'd like to have all my data collection done before tomorrow morning." Riley pushed off the desk they had been leaning on and walked around it.

"Let me know if you need anything. I assume you're spending the night at Lauren and Abby's?"

"That I am."

"All right, I gotta go deal with this," Josh decided, tapping on the x-ray. "See you later." He exited the lab with a wave.

Riley waited a few minutes, then exited after him. Her tests were already complete, but there was someone she had to find.

The hallways branched off one another like an erratically grown tree, but Riley knew where she was going. Even in her depression, she had managed to study and memorize the layout of the Black Box and its colour-coded walls and floors. Despite her good sense of direction, she was delayed when she turned a corner and literally bumped into Rose.

"Hey, Riley!" she smiled brightly.

"Hello, Rose. How are you?" Riley did her best to return the smile. She had been one of the doctors to save Rose's life when she lost her arm, and had sat with her beneath the smoke while the Diana burned and Rose waited to be evacuated.

"Not too bad, not too bad. Yourself?"

Riley shrugged, tempering it with a fake smile.

"Yeah, yeah, I get 'cha." Maybe she did, maybe she didn't. "How's Jon?"

"He's out scavenging right now."

"Oh." A funny little look crawled its way across Rose's face. Riley knew what that look was. She hadn't been the only one depressed upon arriving at the Black Box. Rose was the kind of girl who would jump at the chance to be a scavenger, but lacking a hand made it too dangerous for both her and the people she would be out with. She didn't even move to the container yard because of her disability, although it was probably safe enough for her to come now.

"He should be back anytime during the next week and a half. Do you want me to tell him to come visit when he shows up? He should probably visit Claire and the rest of his family anyway."

"Yeah, yeah he should visit them." Rose clearly wanted to see him too, but jumped on the chance to hide that. She could be very similar to Riley at times, which made it easy for Riley to talk to her.

"By the way, I'm looking for Dr. Haily, have you seen her recently? I wanted to go over your medical supplies with her."

"Yeah, I think she's in her room right now. She's been doing night shifts and might still be asleep."

"Good to know, thanks."

"I'll let ya be on your way." Rose grinned and stepped around Riley. "I think I might try to jump scare your daughter."

"Good luck with that. She's become very aware of her surroundings ever since you started doing that whenever we visit." At first Riley didn't like that Rose would deliberately try to scare her daughter, but now she was glad. Constant awareness was a skill Hope needed to have in this new world.

Rose gave Riley a cheeky wink and then headed off down the hall. Riley watched her go for a moment, noticing how Rose always seemed to stick close to the wall, keeping her shorter arm away from anyone who might be passing by.

Continuing on her own path, Riley felt a little bit sorry for lying to Rose. She wasn't going to see Dr. Haily, but couldn't think up a good reason to go see the person she was hoping to find.

Riley made her way into the hydroponics lab, where rows and rows of troughs sat beneath the glow of sunlamps, a variety of greenery flourishing within each one. Some of them were fruits and vegetables, usually the more exotic kind that couldn't be grown outside, but most of the plants in here were for medicinal purposes. As they ran out of premade resources, they fell back to the source. Both camps were still hurting for things like vaccines—Riley was just waiting for tuberculosis to rear its ugly head once more—but at least they still had painkillers, soothing ointments, various antibiotics, and penicillin. It was unfortunate that the zombie virus didn't wipe out other diseases and infections, but such was life.

"Freya?" Riley spoke in a normal voice, not calling out the name as she wove around the greenery, searching for the woman. There were others in here taking care of the plants, but that's not why Riley kept relatively quiet. There was something about the hydroponics lab that gave it a library-like quality. Beyond the hum of machinery, the hiss of the mist sprayers, and the leaves rustling in the fabricated airflow, it was silent. No one in here held conversations louder than a whisper, and most of the words were spoken to the plants. Riley speaking in a normal tone of voice was as good as yelling, and it drew a few glances her way. It was the perfect place for Freya, who had been a mute for as long as they knew her.

The woman appeared ahead of Riley, emerging from between two giant, leafy monster plants that Riley couldn't identify. When Freya had first arrived at the Diana, she had essentially been feral. Although she had cleaned up and socialised since then, Riley could still see that other woman inside. Her hands were filthy, as she never wore gloves like the others when she worked, smudges of dirt having made their way to her cheeks. Her hair was kept brutally short, forever mindful of the zombie threat outside, while her dark skin was covered by long, tight clothing for the same reason. However, Freya also wore larger, looser clothes over top, around her torso and hips, deliberately hiding her woman's curves. Riley didn't know the whole story, but from what she did know, she understood the impulse. Around Freya's waist was tied a band of leather, while on a belt below it hung a small pouch. The leather was a sling and the pouch contained stones, more or less useless against a zombie when compared to the long machete slung across her back, but effective against humans when combined with her deadly aim. Freya was not a woman to be trifled with.

Upon seeing Riley, she used the signs for *hello* and asked her what she wanted. By now, nearly everyone had learned sign language: being able to communicate in silence saved lives. It certainly made things easier for Freya, yet she still carried a small chalkboard and chalk for when she had to communicate with those few people who still didn't know sign or weren't completely fluent.

"I need your help with something," Riley whispered.

What?

Riley looked around at the other people. Freya understood immediately, and gestured for Riley to lead them somewhere. Once they reached an empty hallway, Riley took a stabilising breath before continuing.

"I need your help running some tests."

What tests? Why me?

"Because despite not knowing you very well, I trust you to keep a secret."

What tests? Her expression had become impatient.

Riley looked around one more time, confirming again that they were alone. "I'll walk you through them, but the tests are on me. I found a lump in my breast."

6

Evans Is Annoyed

Evans was aware that Wycheck was missing almost the instant he got up that morning. He knew because Jasmine was shaking him awake, telling him that Wycheck was gone. She was practically hysterical about it, and if he hadn't quickly picked up on her words, he might have thought there were zombies roaming amongst the party.

"Jasmine. Jasmine, calm down. Jasmine."

She wasn't listening, and continued to tug on his arm, wailing about Wycheck, garbling most of her words too much with tears to be understood.

"Jasmine," he said more sternly, gripping her shoulder with his free hand. "Stop this right now. You're not helping anything. Stop it."

She didn't stop.

With no remaining course of action, Evans removed his hand from her shoulder and then slapped her across the face. Jasmine gasped and released his arm as she fell over. It wasn't a very hard slap considering Evans' size, but it was enough to shock her.

"I get it, Wycheck is missing and you're worried about him. Crying all over me only hinders me from doing something about it, so shut up and let me find out the facts," he spoke quickly, getting everything in while she still lay curled on the floor.

Standing up, Evans first checked on everyone sleeping with him in the living room and adjacent kitchen. They were all quietly sitting up on their mats, having also been awakened by Jasmine. The light coming through the windows suggested that the sun had only just risen.

"Any of you see Wycheck head out?" he asked.

A lot of shaking heads and sleep mumbled 'no's responded.

"All right. Since you're all up, someone might as well start breakfast, yeah?"

A few of them began stirring.

Stretching as he walked, Evans headed to the front of the townhouse where his party had slept the previous night. The front room was the same size as the living room in back, but fewer people had stretched out in there and all of them had taken a shift during the night, guarding the front of the house. They were also awake and waiting to hear from Evans.

"Any of you see Wycheck last night?" he asked. "Apparently he's missing."

"He—" Jasmine, who had followed along behind him, started to speak but Evans held up his hand to silence her. She could never be objective about Wycheck.

"Didn't see him. Although *she* was badgering him all day yesterday," Arman nodded his head in Jasmine's direction. She scowled back at him.

"Let me know if you remember anything else." Evans next stuck his head out the front door and questioned the two guards sitting on either end of the porch. They hadn't seen anything either.

Walking upstairs, Evans could hear Jasmine padding up behind him. Three quarters of the way up, he stopped and turned to face her.

"You're going to keep your mouth shut up here, alright? You've probably already scared the hell out of them with your caterwauling."

Jasmine nodded, her eyes urging him to hurry up. She knew who he should be talking to about it, but Evans needed to check on the others first and make sure none were panicking.

On the top floor were three bedrooms. Evans first headed to the largest one at the back of the house, as it contained the most people. Inside were three couples with their kids, some from prezombie relationships, some born afterward, and a few adopted. The youngest were clustered on the king-sized bed, while the parents were on mats near the door, all of them alert and waiting for Evans. Some of the older kids stood by their mats on the bed's far side, ready to open the window and throw out a rope. The others were clustered by the bathroom door where they had slept.

"It seems Wycheck went off by himself in the night," Evans told the parents, but speaking loudly enough for the kids to hear as well. "Jasmine here just had a panic attack about it is all." He quickly turned his head to look at Jasmine, giving her a cold glance that reminded her to keep her mouth shut.

"Will you be sending someone after him?" one of the parents asked calmly.

"I haven't decided yet; I'm still collecting information about what happened. He may have just gone for a walk and could be back shortly."

The parents nodded, understanding that he had just gotten up like they had. As Evans turned to go to the next bedroom, he could see Jasmine itching to say something, most likely to beg for a search party. He didn't give her the chance.

In the next small bedroom, an elderly, grey-haired, wrinkle-faced trio shared the double bed. They didn't appear alarmed in the slightest, and were dressed neatly, ready for the day. Evans bet they had all been awake before Jasmine's freak out and were alert enough to have heard every word. Still, they waited politely for Evans' explanation.

"Wycheck's wandered off. He say anything to any of you?"

They all responded in the negative.

"Well, everyone's up now and someone downstairs should be starting breakfast soon if they haven't already."

Moving to the last room at the front, Evans expected more negative answers and he got them. The room had no bed and was shared by another six senior citizens—or close to—but they weren't nearly as advanced in age as the other three. They were all right sleeping on mats and in sleeping bags like those downstairs. They even took shifts at the window during the night, providing a higher look out for the street below. Leaving them with orders to help the older three down the stairs, Evans returned to the main floor. Jasmine continued to dog his every step, her impatience all but radiating from her skin as he went into the basement.

Down there, on the carpeted floor and a few couches, slept the most rowdy of their group. The teenagers and twenty year olds who didn't have parents were the fittest of the group but also the most likely to do something stupid. There had been a few mornings when Evans was woken up to be told that one of them had had some sort of accident. As he descended the steps, he saw that not all of them had been awakened by Jasmine's screaming.

"What's up, chief?" Elijah met Evans at the bottom of the stairs. He wasn't the oldest, but he was the most responsible of the group and did his best to keep them safe from themselves.

"Wycheck's gone off, and I'm wondering if anyone knows anything."

"Oi! Wake up!" Elijah clapped his hands together.

Those who had still been asleep raised their faces toward the sound, their eyes blinking and squinting, while the words 'five more minutes' hovered on their lips. There were wild hair and limbs tangled in sleeping bags everywhere.

"Chief here wants to know if anyone has seen or heard about Wycheck going off on his own last night," Elijah spoke loudly.

Some gave answers, mostly those properly awake, while others just put their heads back down or returned to whatever it was they were doing. Lately, cards had been a popular pastime.

"Think that's all you're going to get out of them," Elijah said, turning back to Evans.

"Thanks," Evans patted him on the shoulder then retreated back up the stairs. He had to pause halfway up to wait for Jasmine to turn and get out of the way. He tried to be nice and patient with everyone, but she was just one of those people who made it awfully difficult. Sometimes she reminded him of a small, yappy dog, often trembling about one thing or another. Thinking of that comparison now, he thought she might pee her pants as he finally moved to the back door.

Outside, the small backyard was wedged between a pair of fences, with the townhouse blocking the front and a garage corking the back. A quintet of tents had been erected on the grass, filling the backyard, and as Evans looked at their wired and prepared occupants, he realized he should have come out this way first. The tent sleepers had been close enough to hear the disturbance in the house, but the walls were solid enough to muffle the details.

"It's all right, just Jasmine," Evans told them, holding up his hands. He showed them that he hadn't even brought his weapons with him, that's how safe they were at the moment. Well, he wasn't completely unarmed: there was the always-present knife strapped to his thigh, but everyone knew that Evans frequently carried much larger weapons.

The occupants in three of the five tents had been travelling with Evans' party for only a few weeks now, as opposed to the months and years of the others. They were still jumpy, and Evans couldn't blame them. Everyone in his party had been part of one group or another before joining him. A few had been wanderers like himself, but most had been settled somewhere. They ended up with Evans when their camps were destroyed and they were forced to flee for their lives. Evans had been wandering since the start, before the zombies actually, and was well adapted to living on the road, but others weren't.

"Wycheck has apparently wandered off. You know, the guy with the crooked nose who this one is always hanging around?" Evans hiked a thumb back at Jasmine: everyone knew who she was thanks to her loud and social nature. "She got a little upset about it. I'm looking for information. Old Salt? You were sharing a tent with him last night, what do you know?"

Old Salt, so named for his sea dog looks and nature, stepped forward. "He got up maybe an hour or two before sunrise. I thought he was takin' a piss and went back to sleep. Didn't wake up again until she poked her head in lookin' for him. I guessed that maybe he was hidin' from her. Told me she had been botherin' him more than usual the last few days."

Jasmine looked ready to strangle him. "You crusty old bastard."

Evans held a restraining hand out toward her, making sure she didn't try anything stupid for her own sake. Old Salt could be a bastard, but he was observant and honest. He would also defend himself, should Jasmine actually make an attempt at anything, which would end very poorly for her.

"Anyone else see or hear anything around that time?" Evans asked the other tent sleepers.

A few mentioned having woken up to hear someone outside, but when they heard that person go into the garage, they went back to sleep. Evans thanked them and apologized for not having come out and explained the situation quicker. Later, he would encourage Jasmine to go around on her own and apologize to everyone for the rude awakening.

Evans' last stop was the extended two-car garage. Old Salt was now following him as well as Jasmine. No doubt he was cursing himself on the inside for not realizing sooner that Wycheck wasn't just relieving himself. He would want to help.

The garage was filled with the smell of horses. Two large, predominantly wooden, supply-laden carts took up the space against the wall nearest the house. On the other side, nearly a dozen horses were crowded together against the wide rollup door. The space wasn't really large enough for the horses, but they were put in there only at night and the large beasts were used to it. The party had been lucky to find the place; the garage, to which someone had added an extension for storage, was the only one in the area that could fit both the horses and the carts once the junk had been cleared out. From a wide shelf beneath the peak of the roof, the eyes of Leo peered down at the trio who had just entered the cramped space. Somewhere up there, Nathan, Leo's partner in crime, was also hiding in the shadows, unseen.

"Yes?" Leo asked.

"Wycheck come through here? Over an hour before sunrise?"

"He did."

"Know anything about it?"

"No."

"All right. Well, breakfast is cooking if you want any and the horses can be let out whenever you're ready. Don't take any of them too far, though. We might need a couple to go looking for Wycheck."

"Okay."

"You didn't try and stop him?" Old Salt grunted up at Leo.

"Why would I? He left the horses alone."

Jasmine made a loud scoffing sound that wasn't too dissimilar to the scraping of the horses' hooves on the cement floor.

Evans turned and ushered Old Salt and Jasmine back outside before anything could get started. Leo and Nathan were weird: they didn't think like other people did. They were more concerned about the horses than about any of the humans. Some of the other party members suspected they were actually a gay couple, but Evans didn't think so. They certainly didn't show any kind of affection for one another. In Evans' mind, Leo and Nathan were the same person split into two bodies. As far as Evans knew, they weren't related, but it was possible. They acted like brothers at times and had their own way of communicating with each other.

"We'll have breakfast, and if Wycheck doesn't show up in the meantime, I'll hold a meeting to decide what to do."

"A meeting? We have to go find him now!" Jasmine whined.

Evans didn't bother to respond. Someone had lit the barbecue and was placing what remained of their meat upon the grill. They had come across some cows who had somehow managed to survive on their own and shot a pair for the meat and leather. The other cows they let go on their way, knowing that they had no more room for animals. The cooking beef smelled heavenly. If Wycheck didn't come back for this, then he was definitely out of the area.

***

"So it all boils down to one question," Evans sighed, attempting to sum up the meeting. "Whether Wycheck intended to come back or not, do we go looking for him?"

He and six other members of the party had gathered around a table in the townhouse next door.

"It's his own fault for leaving, I say we leave him," a woman mumbled. She was one of the new people and had insisted on attending. Evans was fine with that, but she hadn't said much, and when she did, she always mumbled.

"I'm goin' to go look for him, no matter what you decide," Old Salt declared for the umpteenth time. Evans knew him well enough to know his words were hollow. He'd do what the group decided.

"Wycheck wouldn't just leave," said a mother who had volunteered to speak for the families. "He might have gotten annoyed and gone off by himself for a day, but he'll come back. We shouldn't send anyone out until at least tomorrow."

"Tomorrow might be too late," Arman reminded her. "We've been seeing quite a bit of activity lately. More of the dead have been showing up every day, wild animals too. Wycheck hasn't been truly alone for a long time. I can understand the need to get away every now and again, but he's gone too far. Salty said that some of his personal supplies are missing, over a day's worth, and he's not in any of the nearby houses. It's very dangerous to be alone right now, more so than usual."

"If we do go looking, I know a bunch willing to make up a search party," Elijah volunteered.

"You've been quiet, Ki-nam." Evans turned to the former North Korean. He had spent the meeting listening quietly, sitting perfectly still except for his silver hair which got caught in a slight draft. "What are your thoughts?"

Ki-nam remained silent for a moment longer before speaking. "I suggest we send a small team after him. As Arman stated, the dead have been finding us more frequently. We need to move on from this place. A scouting team will go ahead, following Wycheck's trail, if they can. The rest of the party will follow at a safe distance, perhaps a day or more behind."

Evans nodded. He had been meaning to get everyone moving again, but searchers kept coming across good finds, like the cows.

"What if we can't find his trail? If he doesn't want to be found, he won't be marking the way," the mother worried.

"If he doesn't want to be found, then he doesn't want to be found," Evans said, shrugging. He would never force someone to remain with the party. "However, we'll also inform the searcher teams moving with the party to keep an eye out for anything the forward team might miss. Are we agreed?"

They were, albeit unenthusiastically. While Evans was perfectly happy on the move, most of the others were not. They liked taking breaks in places like the townhouse, where they could settle and rest up for a few days, maybe even a couple of weeks. But in the end, Evans always kept them moving. He understood peoples' need to settle, and the advantages of it like growing crops, but he believed in movement. The number one reason he lost party members was their desire to cocoon. Often, when they came across a friendly camp, a large swath of people would stay behind. Whenever that happened, Evans just reminded himself that most of the people who had joined him had done so because their camp had fallen due to one threat or another: zombies, raiders, illness, or inner turmoil; Evans had heard it all.

Lately, however, he'd been losing more party members to death. He couldn't find any signs of them being followed, and it didn't feel like they were moving through someone else's territory, but someone had been picking off his searchers when they were alone. He knew that's what Arman really meant when he said it was especially dangerous to be alone these days. The party hadn't been informed, because they were safe all grouped together, but they knew something was amiss. Far too many searchers had had 'accidents' lately. Evans and Arman both knew that they weren't accidents; the men and women had clearly been stabbed. It enraged Evans that he hadn't been able to do anything about it, that every few weeks or sometimes only days, Arman would come to him and mention that another searcher was dead. Every time they moved, Evans hoped they had gotten away from the perpetrator, but so far they had had no such luck. Maybe this time he would take his party a very long distance before stopping. If someone was stabbed again, then they were clearly being followed, or else someone within the party itself had snapped. Either way, Evans had protocols for such events. The only reason he hadn't done anything yet was because of the infrequency of the deaths. He prayed they were merely within the roaming territory of a cowardly band of raiders.

All of the meeting's participants rose from the table and headed for the door. Evans exited last, making sure there was no one who wanted to linger to ask a private question. No one did: they all knew what to do when it came time to move, even the new folks.

Back in the townhouse where they had spent the last week, a flurry of activity filled the hallways and rooms. Backpacks were refilled with personal items and bedding, while supplies that had been brought in were carried back out to the carts. In the backyard, tents were carefully disassembled and the last of the meat was eaten off the barbecue.

Evans went to his own corner of the back room, picking his way through the couch cushions and other items that still littered the floor. There had been two couches around a TV when they had first arrived. Since then, the party had taken the TV and its stand, as well as a coffee table, and had chucked them over a back fence to make more floor space. The couch cushions had been pulled off for some people to use on the floor; others set up their sleeping mats on the denuded couches. Evans personally didn't know how they could sleep with the springs so uncovered like that, but to each his own.

Picking up his pack, Evans proceeded to carefully go through his personal stash of supplies. If he got separated from the party, a possibility that had happened before, he could still survive on his own. He encouraged all party members to pack their kits with the same items. Inside his bag were a few packages of dried goods, two water bottles he always kept filled, basic first-aid supplies, water-proof matches, a lighter, flint, shotgun shells, both empty and ready to be used, a sharpening block, some rope, a flashlight with an extra set of batteries, at least one other set of every article of clothing he wore, a tarp, a couple of maps, and a few personal hygiene products. Taking most of the stuff out in the process, he repacked it all in the order he liked best while travelling, then rolled his sleeping mat and blanket, and fastened them to the straps hanging from the bottom of his pack. Unlike most of the others, he didn't use a sleeping bag or carry a pillow. They tended to stick to warmer climates, so he often used the blanket as a pillow.

While he was packing, Arman came back with a forward scouting party prepared to head out. Evans accepted the walkie-talkie from him, then let the party be on their way. They would communicate back to him their whereabouts and anything they might find.

Standing up, Evans hoisted his bag onto his broad shoulders. At six feet, four inches, he was easily the tallest member of the party. His size, at one time making people wary of him, now drew them toward him. They felt safe in his presence, as opposed to threatened. His choice of weaponry matched his size. Across his back, beneath the backpack, he slung a large broadsword, the handle sticking up behind his head. It had been given to him by an old woman in a friendly camp, as if he were some great knight. Evans thought the woman was crazy, but liked the weapon and accepted it, secretly leaving behind a tin can filled with oil in exchange. Hanging against his thigh opposite the knife, was his pistol grip, twelve-gauge shotgun. Although not the most accurate, and not very good for distances, it was chosen by Evans because he seemed to find the most ammo for it. Also, he knew how to repack expended cartridges, dismantling and using the powder even from non-compatible ammo. Besides, he rarely fired the thing anyway; ammunition was a precious commodity these days.

Walking around the house with his full kit, Evans offered his assistance to those who were taking longer to pack. Whenever they stopped for a few days, people somehow managed to misplace things they simply couldn't leave without: personal items like photos, teddies, books, various trinkets, odds and ends. Evans had no such items. The closest would be the small, leather-wrapped notebook kept in a side pocket of his pants, but even that he wouldn't be too upset about losing. Unlike a few others, he didn't keep it as a journal. Instead, he wrote down tidbits of useful information: names of people in his party, various important notes about them, locations of camps along with apparent leaders, attitudes toward travellers, trades that had occurred, what plants were edible, what was good to pack in a shotgun shell, and so on.

The fact was that Evans didn't make attachments. He seemed incapable of them ever since his father had butchered his mother and then turned toward him with the knife. Evans, at thirteen years of age but already growing big, had defended himself against the larger man, finally delivering a killing blow and saving himself. The people around him now weren't there because he needed them to be. They were there because he understood about safety in numbers, shared knowledge, and shared workload. If they were all to suddenly die, he'd be sad, but no more than if the horses died, or if all the food was stolen.

"Here, Annabelle, your doll ended up in the closet."

***

Evans walked along at the head of the column, like a Viking with his short blond hair and equally short blond beard. The dull blue colouring of his eyes masked their sharpness as he kept alert for threats. Behind him rattled the two large supply carts, each pulled by a team of four horses. The smallest children and the eldest of the elders sat along running boards on their sides, whereas everyone else walked beside them. The riders mounted on the last three horses brought up the rear, occasionally trotting up next to the column, or ducking down side streets and alleys to check on the small teams running parallel to them.

A small furry bit of movement drew Evans' eyes down to the pavement. A black and white cat was trotting alongside him.

"So you decided to stick with us, huh?" Evans mumbled to the cat.

The cat meowed at him.

Evans didn't mind there being pets in the party, but he made sure that whoever brought them understood that the animals were their responsibility: they were never included during the rationing process. Every now and then, an animal would start following the party on its own. Evans treated it the same. If it wasn't hostile, it could stick around, but he certainly wasn't going to feed it any of his rations. This black and white cat had shown up at the townhouse the first night they spent there and immediately made itself at home. It took to rubbing against legs and sticking its face into people's food, suggesting it had been fed by people before. While Evans wasn't a cat person, not even an animal person really, with most creatures ignoring him as much as he ignored them, this one black and white cat decided to cuddle up against him every night and follow him around during the day. Evans had no idea why.

After acknowledging the cat's presence, he returned to scanning for threats. From the edge of his vision, he noticed the cat continuing to keep pace with a light trot. From what Evans knew about cats, it was an odd behaviour, but he figured the stray would soon get bored or tired, and either leave the party or convince someone else to carry it.

"Evans?" a voice called out from behind him. "Arman's on the walkie for you."

He slowed his pace and dropped back until he was next to the cart where the driver was holding out the walkie-talkie for him. One of the party members had been a mechanical engineer and had rigged up a system so that the turning wheels of the cart could charge their few walkie-talkies and one hand radio. As Evans accepted the black box with its slightly mangled antennae, he found himself checking for the cat. It was keeping its distance from the horses and carts, but still keeping pace with Evans. He wondered if the cat would stop if he did.

"Go ahead," Evans said into the walkie as he depressed the side button.

"Is there a good place for the party to stop near you?" Arman's distorted voice broke through the static.

Drifting sideways, away from the main column, Evans lowered his voice. "There are some potentials, why?"

"We found Wycheck. You may want to see this for yourself, but the rest of the party probably shouldn't."

"Give me your location," Evans sighed. He knew this meant that Wycheck was dead.

Arman gave him rough directions to where he was.

"All right, I'll be there shortly."

Returning to the cart, Evans handed the walkie-talkie back to the driver. He then turned to the rear of the column and waved one of the horsemen forward.

"What is it?" Ki-nam asked as his horse came up alongside the tall man.

"I need to go meet up with Arman. That store on the corner there looks like it has sliding doors large enough to fit the carts through. Think you could clear it out and get everyone to hold up there until I get back?"

"Not a problem." Ki-nam quickly rode off and started giving orders.

Several people asked Evans questions, but stopped when they realized he was going somewhere else. It wouldn't be the first time this had happened, and those who had been in the party longest knew exactly what it meant.

"I'm coming with you." Jasmine ran up beside Evans.

"No, you're not," he replied without breaking stride.

"It's about Wycheck, I know it is. I have to know he's okay."

"Stay with the party."

"You can't make me."

Evans stopped and wheeled around to face her. "Stay with the party." He hadn't lowered his voice or put on a threatening tone, but Jasmine saw it in his face. She shied away, taking a few careful steps back before turning and retreating toward the other party members.

Turning around again, Evans ran a hand across his face and kept walking. He didn't want to have to deal with Jasmine's grief while looking over the body. She was going to get hysterical when she found out.

On his way to Arman, Evans walked out in the open. Being by himself, he didn't want to risk turning a blind corner only to bump into something with teeth. By strolling down the middle of the road, he'd see anything coming his way. Although ready to draw it with twitch-like reflexes, Evans kept his sword on his back. He wanted to show confidence to any cowardly humans that might be in the area.

The moment he spotted Arman, he knew something was up. Only two of his team members were with him, the other three off someplace else.

Not only that, but they were agitated, pacing around the body that lay on the broken sidewalk between an old stripped car and the side of a building. It seemed they had come to their own conclusion about what had happened here.

Evans waved in greeting, and Arman responded by stepping out of the way, letting him see the body. Evans stepped up beside it, quickly confirming that it was Wycheck, and that there was no way he was alive. The hole in the side of his head was hard to miss.

"Bastards robbed him. They beat him, shot him, and robbed him," Arman grumbled.

"They tricked him and ambushed him," one of Arman's team members, Justin, spoke through gritted teeth.

"Tricked?"

"Fake cook fire in the distance," Arman pointed. "Helen and Mike are over there now with our other walkie. Wycheck must have seen it and started heading for it when he got jumped. Broke his leg, beat him a little. I don't know whether they took his stuff before or after they shot him." Every word Arman spoke was peppered with anger.

"They even took his fucking belt, man," Chuck muttered.

Evans had noticed. If he were going to strip a man of everything, he would have taken the belt too. Hell, he would have taken Wycheck's jeans as they weren't that bloody, but he definitely wasn't going to say any of that; not around these men who were chomping at the bit for someone to lash out against. Everyone else who had been killed recently had died quickly, but Wycheck looked like he was in some pain before he got taken out. And a bullet was different from a knife. If Evans had to guess, he would say that this murder was committed by a different person, or persons.

"They've gone too far this time," Arman seethed, not coming to the same conclusion.

Spotting something fluttering near the tireless axle of the car, Evans bent down and fetched it. It was a battered photograph, one Evans had seen Wycheck looking at before. It was a group of happy, smiling people with their arms around each other, possibly siblings or maybe just friends. Evans put it in his back pocket. Later, he would toss it when no one was looking. It had no value to anyone anymore, but it would only stir up the team members more to see him treat it callously.

"If Helen and Mike went to investigate the cook fire, then where is Elijah?" Evans knew the young man had volunteered to go with Arman.

"He went to check out the buildings in the area, should be back soon."

It was no sooner said, than he returned, running as quickly as he could. Evans and the others waited for Elijah to reach them, his face bright red and his voice broken by ragged panting.

"I found…" he gasped. "I found the fuckers who did this."

"Where?" Arman and the others straightened up, hands moving toward weapons.

"They just left a paint supply store. They must be stripping the area. All the buildings around here are pretty much cleared out. They have a horse and some shopping carts."

"If they're stripping, they probably have a camp somewhere." Arman turned to Evans, knowing he understood that. "We've reached the bastards' home territory."

Looking around at them, Evans saw the same glint in their eyes. They wanted revenge. They wanted to direct their anger at someone, and that target had presented itself.

"Follow them," Evans gave the order. "Don't interact with them in *any* way, but follow them. Let's see where they go."

7

Nessie's Calm

When Nessie awoke that morning, her pop bottle light was only a faint glow, letting her know just how early it was. She remembered the days when she could sleep past noon, but they were long ago and buried in memory. There was no sense in trying to fall back asleep now; years of early mornings had taught her it would be impossible. At least she wouldn't have to worry about her bladder for a little while, as she had used the potty in her container roughly an hour ago.

Easing herself up, Nessie swung her legs over the side of her bed and allowed gravity to help her get to her feet, which slid into a pair of battered slippers. With her hand wrapped around the familiar carving of a bear on the head of her cane, she made her way over to her dresser and got dressed. From there, her slippers now replaced by the rubber wading boots she always wore, she went to the front of her room and turned on the little electric kettle. After a series of trades, she had managed to secure herself a solar panel, a big, high-end one that let her make her morning tea provided she didn't run anything else at the same time. While the kettle was heating up, Nessie removed the iron bar from the brackets that kept her doors closed and swung them open. She breathed deeply the fresh morning air, enjoying the scent of the sea. In her younger days, she had dreamed of living by the ocean, but never had she imagined it in quite this way.

The influx of light drew a rattling from behind her. Turning around, Nessie saw her parrot waiting for her, hanging on to the door of her large, makeshift cage.

"Polly want a cracker?" she asked.

"Fuck Polly," the parrot gave his usual reply. *"I'm a dragon."* He then imitated the T-rex roar from *Jurassic Park*, which Nessie had played for him several times. *"Dragon. Dragon."*

"That's my boy," Nessie cooed at him. She walked over to the cage and opened the door, letting Dragon side step his way up her sleeve and to her shoulder. He could fly, his wings hadn't been clipped, but being raised in a small apartment never gave him much room and so he had learned to walk and climb more often, with only an occasional flutter from one spot to another.

As the water in the kettle began to boil, Dragon copied the sound. This kettle didn't have a screaming whistle on it, but the one she used to have did and if she let it boil too long, Dragon would whistle for it.

As she sat down and steeped her tea, Dragon moved to his customary spot near the table edge that butted up against a wardrobe. He poked a tin kept there, trying to get it open on his own. When he couldn't get the catch to release, he turned to Nessie.

"Pellets?" he asked. *"Dragon wants pellets?"*

"Ask nicely."

"Please, pellets?" He then rumbled like a car for no reason.

Nessie picked up the tin, with Dragon gently nibbling her hand in anticipation. She opened it carefully, making sure to hide the trick of the latch from Dragon's watchful eyes. Once the lid was off, she took out a few pellets and placed them in Dragon's bowl. They'd hold him over until breakfast.

"I'm going for a walk to the bathroom," Nessie told her parrot.

He made the sound of a toilet flushing.

"You've been good lately so I'm letting you stay out of your cage, but I'm closing the container doors."

"Darkness," he then laughed maniacally, yet with the bottle light it wouldn't be dark.

Nessie got up and exited the container, leaving Dragon preoccupied with his pellets.

"See you later," he croaked as the doors were swung shut.

With her cane and a mug of tea carefully held in one hand and her nighttime potty in the other, Nessie made her way toward the toilets. It was embarrassing having to carry the children's potty, especially with its *Dora* pictures, but her bladder, and the limited number of commodes the scavengers brought back, didn't give her much choice. Not many people were up at this hour, mostly just the wall guards, but she spotted Misha on his daily run. He wasn't hard to miss with that pack of dogs trailing behind him. Nessie used to run, but now her aching joints could only manage a swift hobble or maybe a light jog for a short period of time if the situation demanded it. Most days she could get along just fine without the cane, but she always had it with her anyway. Not only was it useful on the days the arthritis in her right knee flared up, but it was practical in this age of walking corpses. With a twist of the bear-shaped handle, she could unlatch it from the ebony shaft, allowing her to draw forth the metal blade within. When her knee had started to go bad, her niece had bought her the cane knowing Nessie would think it was cool. She had not only been right, but the sword within had saved her life on a few occasions. Nessie wished she could have returned the favour, but by the time she and Dragon reached her niece's home, the entire family was either dead or gone. That's where Marble Keystone had eventually found her, sitting on her niece's bed and watching an electronic frame as it ran through a hodgepodge of photos.

The outhouses came into sight along the water's edge. Nessie had since learned to trust them, but when they were first completed she wasn't so sure. Just because a man said he was an engineer didn't mean he knew shit about building a shitter. Turned out that this man did.

Along the river's edge, a string of wooden structures had been bolted into the concrete, with guy-wires providing extra hold from their upper edges. While half of each structure was on solid ground, the back half hung out over the water. Nessie made her way into the box she thought had the best seat, her tea mug now empty. Placing the mug on a small shelf within and leaning her cane against the wall, Nessie emptied the potty through the opening, and then dropped her drawers and placed her bare fanny on the seat. It was just like using an outhouse, except instead of their waste accumulating in a reeking pile, it dropped into the salt water river, which carried it out into the large bay and then the sea.

The toilet paper supply was getting low again. Nessie prayed that those out scavenging found a whole lot to bring back. They had run out of the stuff a few times before, and it wasn't fun using a rag that you then had to wash by hand.

The doctors said that Nessie had a strong bladder for her age, but she wasn't so sure she believed them based on how often she found herself emptying it. Once done, she then carried the used toilet paper back out of the box with her and deposited it through the flap in a large, plastic bin. Later, it would become compost. With that done, Nessie turned to the large basin of salt water kept next to the bin and washed her hands. This batch of soap wasn't very well made and caused her hands to itch. She used the same water to rinse her mug and potty, dumping it back into the river when she was done with it.

Cleaned up and ready to go to breakfast, Nessie first took a moment's pause. Looking around the container yard, she could see more and more people waking up and opening their doors. A small group of women were heading toward the toilets, while a few men made for a space next to them, preferring simply to pee out in the open. After a handful of good mornings were exchanged with these relatively early risers, Nessie headed back to her home to get Dragon, and to shove the potty back into its hiding space under the edge of her bed.

"Bright light! Bright light!" Dragon greeted her as the door was opened, repeating a line from a movie that Nessie enjoyed. She had taught Dragon to say a lot of useless things, but they were entertaining every now and again, especially when other people weren't expecting them.

Once the bird was in his customary place on her shoulder, the mug returned to its place beside the kettle, Nessie headed back out, leaving her container doors wide open. She wasn't afraid of anyone stealing anything: why would they? There wasn't much she had that others didn't or couldn't get with ease, except for maybe the solar panel, but it would be pretty obvious if someone took that. Besides, she left a power bar hooked up to it at the edge of her container, free for anyone to use. It was obvious to anyone looking in that she wasn't home, but a cardboard sign hanging from the bracket on the inner side of her door confirmed it with one word: out.

Inside the community centre building, the cooking of breakfast had only just begun. That was all right: Nessie was used to waiting. She took up her usual seat. Dragon fluttered over to the back of the one next to her, his talons having left several scratches and pressure marks in the plastic over the years they had been there. On the board, Nessie's name was listed under its customary task: clothing repair. While she waited, she took the battered notebook out of her pocket and wrote in it. Pages upon pages were filled with her cramped, tiny handwriting. Virtually her entire life had been recorded in point form by her own hand ever since she learned to put words to paper. Her house had been filled with all sorts of notebooks, every one dense with her written words. She often wondered if those notebooks and journals still existed, jammed together in boxes in the basement storage unit of her building, with more recent ones stuffed into the cupboard of her nightstand. How odd they must be for someone else to find. While waiting for breakfast, Nessie summed up the previous night's dreams and her morning activities, including things that Dragon had said. There had been a few occasions when he managed to surprise her with words and sounds that she hadn't taught him. Most of those were later forgotten when she didn't reinforce them.

"Good morning, Nessie," Bill greeted her as he sat down. "Morning, Dragon."

"Morning, Bill," Dragon croaked.

"Good morning, Bill," Nessie said at nearly the same time, not looking up from her writing.

Bill grinned at the bird, patiently waiting for Nessie to complete her writing. "You are one ugly bird," Bill told the grey parrot.

Dragon ruffled his feathers as if he knew what that meant. Maybe he did. Nessie finished with her writing, and then the book disappeared from the table and into one of the large pockets of her coat. Even in Texas she found herself cold half the time and was almost always wearing her faded blue jacket with its large pockets and oversized hood.

The pockets and hood were great, but she especially loved that the collar zipped up all the way to cover her neck.

"I saw Dr. Riley outside just before coming in here," Bill said.

"Oh? And what did she have to say?"

"She's planning on taking a trip to the Black Box to run some tests. Wants me to go with her."

"You better go then."

"I suppose if the doc says I should, then I guess I should."

"You saying you don't want to? Don't want to sit around in comfort with the electricity on, running water all the time, and where you don't have to worry about what the weather is like before you go anywhere?"

Bill smiled at her, realizing that Nessie was teasing him. "We came out here for a reason. Besides, that's not why I'm not keen on going."

Nessie waited silently for him to say more.

"I'm not sure I want to know what's wrong with me."

Nessie nodded, as she understood completely. If you were dying, it might be better not to know.

"Looks like breakfast is ready. Shall we?" Bill rose from his seat and held out a hand to Nessie.

She accepted the unneeded assistance to her feet, holding out her arm for Dragon to crawl up the coat's sleeve. Another advantage of the jacket was that it was made of a tough fabric that could withstand the abuse from Dragon's talons, although it still had to be repaired on occasion.

As Nessie and Bill stood in line together, the rest of their breakfast mates found them. They customarily sat at one of the larger tables, and while most of their group consisted of older folks like Nessie and Bill, there were some from the younger generations as well. Conversations were always light and entertaining once they were all together, Bill not mentioning to the others what he had told Nessie.

While Nessie ate, adding bits to the conversation every now and again, she picked out pieces of her meal and gave them to Dragon. He gobbled up each morsel gratefully, occasionally even squawking a thank you. All the while, Nessie thought about what it might be like to know you were going to die soon. The way the whole world was now, living until a natural death of old age was a luxury most people wouldn't have.

***

The sewing machine whirred as Nessie worked the foot pedal. It was the only thing in her container that she had hooked up to the solar panel beside the kettle and power bar. Even then, on darker days or when the solar charged battery ran out, it could be worked by turning a hand crank. She had been at it for a while when she noticed a shadow near her door. The cardboard sign was turned around, now reading 'in,' and she had been receiving visitors all day. People who had clothing that needed mending were always stopping by, adding to her pile of work.

"Don't just linger, come in if you'd like," Nessie called out without looking up after the shadow hadn't moved for a while.

There was a hesitant shuffling, and then the shadow moved inside. Nessie glanced up to see that it was young Becky who had shown up at her door.

"Do you have something for me to fix?" she asked the child.

"No." Becky looked over her shoulder like she thought she had made the wrong decision and was thinking of running away. "No. I came to see Dragon, but I can see he's sleeping."

The parrot was on a perch within his large, chicken wire cage, his eyes closed and feathers slightly poofed.

"Come sit down." Nessie gestured to the office chair near the straight-backed one she was sitting in. She liked the different chairs depending on what she was doing.

Becky shuffled her feet once more, but eventually walked all the way over and sat down.

"This from your solar panel?" Becky asked, pointing to the light on the sewing machine.

"Indeed it is." Nessie depressed the foot pedal slightly, the machine chugging a few more stitches through the jeans she was repairing with a small, thin patch of leather. "I don't normally see you alone. Your friends all busy?"

"Yeah," Becky nodded. "Hope's gone with her mom to the Black Box, I think Dakota is on Animal Island right now, and Adam is helping his dad with that car project thing."

"Adam, he's the dark-haired boy you three are usually with, right?" A few more chugging stitches. She'd talk to the girl, but Nessie wasn't going to stop her work outright.

Becky nodded. She wiggled slightly in the seat, so that it turned partial rotations back and forth, her feet dangling over the edge and not quite reaching the floor.

"Doesn't his dad usually help out with the wall? He's the engineer that started the whole thing I thought."

"He did. A bunch of zombies showed up, so everyone searching the containers and stuff had to retreat." Becky started to warm up a little, but still spoke like she didn't know why she was there

"Anyone hurt?"

"No. At least no one has said that someone got hurt."

"That's good. Why aren't you learning from your folks?"

"They don't have any school lessons for me right now."

"And you don't want to help them out with their jobs? I thought that's what you kids do sometimes."

Becky sighed, bending at the waist to prop her elbows on her knees and rest her chin in her hands. "My dad mans the radio, scanning the frequencies every now and again. It's really boring; he mostly just reads books all day. My mom cooks. I usually just get in the way when I try to help."

"So your mom was responsible for today's flavoured potato mash, huh?" Nessie then leaned toward the girl conspiratorially. "Not her best work."

Becky actually smiled in response. "She doesn't decide what we eat though, she just helps make it."

Nessie shrugged and pressed the foot pedal some more, finishing up the last of the patch. Carefully snipping the threads so that she saved as much on the spool as possible, she removed the jeans from the machine.

"There, what do you think?" Nessie held up the jeans for Becky's inspection.

"That's a lot of patches," she observed. There was one on each knee, another on the right thigh, and still one more along the left shin.

"Uh huh," Nessie nodded. "Some people wait until they absolutely need stuff patched before bringing it to me. In this case..." She turned the jeans around and showed Becky a patch running along the seat of the pants.

Becky smothered a giggle with her hand. "That must have been embarrassing."

"I hope it wasn't a windy day for him, 'cause then it might have gotten a little chilly too."

This time Becky laughed openly, finally relaxed. The noise woke up Dragon who said something garbled, but the girl didn't pay attention to him. She seemed more interested in talking to Nessie now, and Nessie was okay with that.

"You know, I can teach you how to knit if you'd like. It'd give your hands something to do."

"What's knitting?"

"What's knitting?" Nessie put on an obviously fake flabbergasted tone, hiding her honest surprise that Becky didn't know. "See that blanket on my bed?"

Becky couldn't, so she got up and walked over to it. "This one on the top? Made of wool?"

"That's the one," Nessie nodded. "I made it myself, using a knitting technique."

"It looks really warm," Becky commented as she returned to her seat.

"It is, it's very warm. How about I teach you how to knit one yourself, and you can keep the result?"

"Really?"

"Maybe we'll start with a headscarf instead of a large blanket, but why not? Knitting is a useful skill to have."

"Okay, I guess."

Dragging out her basket of yarn, Nessie plucked out a set of knitting needles for each of them. Using her own as an example, she set to work teaching Becky to knit. Once the girl seemed to have the hang of it after a few rows, Nessie returned to her patchwork.

"Where do you get all this stuff?" Becky commented, staring intently at her slow work. It would be a long while before she got comfortable enough to knit by touch alone, or to pick up any sort of speed.

"All what stuff?" Nessie's machine chattered on before her, as she sewed a cloth patch along the belly of a T-shirt.

Becky shrugged. "Any of it."

"Well, some of it was supplied to me as basic necessities, just like in your container."

"We have a bunk bed in ours, with a bigger bed along the bottom."

"I think most containers with a kid and parents have that."

"Yeah, but we don't have a dresser, or that big standing cupboard thing." Becky carefully put down her knitting to point to the wardrobe. "And you have two desks."

"I requested these things. When it comes to furniture, you just put in a request and your reason for wanting it, and then, if there's time, someone will go get it from one of the nearby houses." *Although they don't always get exactly what you want*, Nessie silently added, thinking of the *Dora* potty.

"So I don't have it because my parents don't want it?"

"That's right."

"What about this other stuff? All those scraps you're using as patches and this wool?" Becky returned to her careful knitting.

"Most of the scraps are given to me. People who don't sew have no use for them, so they donate them here with the understanding that one day they may be used to patch up their own clothes. As for the yarn, it's rationed out just like food. There's probably some in your container if your parents haven't bartered it away."

"What's barter?"

"It's another word for trade."

"What do people trade for?"

"I don't know, various things I guess." Nessie finished the shirt, folded it up, and put it on her pile of completed clothing. She then picked up the next article, which was a pair of holey socks. Although needing patches around the toes and heels, one also required some stitching along a run up the back of the ankle. "I'm usually the recipient of a wool trade. That means I'm getting the wool."

"What do people want from you?"

"I usually knit the wool into clothing or blankets they want, but most of the time, people give me things to move their clothing up the line. Sometimes it's their last pair of pants I'm fixing, or their favourite shirt, and so they want it repaired sooner than the usual time it takes. They give me wool or sometimes larger pieces of cloth and leather to get bumped up the line. I then take what they give me, turn it into new clothing or what have you, and trade it back to other people for other things or more clothing supplies. That's how I got the solar panel. It was actually one of your brothers who traded it to me, if I'm not mistaken. Does one of them have a long leather coat?"

"Yeah, Larson does." Becky sounded excited about this revelation.

"I made that for him along with several other high-end items in exchange. I believe he still wears the coat, although he might have traded the rest for other goods."

"Why did Larson have the solar panel anyway? Shouldn't it have been with the others on the community building?"

"Honestly, what do they teach you if you don't know this stuff?"

Becky shrugged. "Math and junk. How many calories to eat each day. I know how to cook a bunch of things even if I'm not very good at it."

"Well, first of all, the community centre currently has all the solar panels it needs. Mind you if that changes, or one breaks, they can take mine. It's more like I have it on loan in that way. The reason your brother got it was because he goes out scavenging."

"That's where they both are right now." Becky sounded a little sour about this, either missing them, worried about them, or most likely both.

Nessie nodded, remembering seeing their names on the away board. "I won't sugar coat it, it's a dangerous job they do. But, because it's dangerous, they get to claim part of the loot they bring back as a reward. Basically, they get first dibs on anything the community centre doesn't need."

"I think I'd like to do that when I get old enough. It sounds exciting."

"What? More exciting than a swarm of zombies showing up at our wall?"

"Yes."

"Well, you're not old enough yet, so keep knitting." Nessie thought she might have a talk with Becky's parents later, or maybe even talk to the girl herself. More exciting? It was deadly out there. Sure, it wasn't as bad as when the outbreak occurred—Nessie refused to call it the Day like everyone else—but it was still the most deadly occupation. They had lost a few scavengers over the years, while others had been injured, and one team had been completely lost. They went out for a search and not one of them made it back. No one knows what happened to them; could have been any of a number of things. There were zombies to worry about, but there were also animals, unfriendly humans, unsafe terrain, and even basic illnesses. As structures aged, they weakened, becoming more prone to collapse. Even if the whole thing didn't come down, enough scavengers had returned with cut-up legs and broken ankles to attest to the dangers of even one weak spot in the floor. It's why Nessie decided to move to the container yard. She could see and trust the structures here, whereas the Black Box's supports were buried beneath painted drywall so the place looked good. Who wanted to live somewhere that looked nice when your life was at stake? Nessie thought that Becky didn't understand the world yet and that somebody should talk to her about it. Then again, when do young folk ever listen to the advice of older generations?

The sewing machine whirred as she moved on from the socks to a jacket.

A skittering of nails on metal drew the attention of both Becky and Nessie to the front of the container. One of Misha's dogs stood there, the tall skinny grey one who was mostly Great Dane. Powder was her name.

"I don't have any treats for you today," Nessie told the dog.

Powder's head cocked to the side upon hearing the word 'treats,' her tail making a single swish back and forth in anticipation.

"No, not today," Nessie said again, avoiding the trigger word.

This time Powder took another step inside. When Nessie turned away, ignoring the big dog, she listened as it circled the front of her container and lay down.

Nessie sighed. "People don't like bringing me things when there's a giant dog blocking most of the entrance."

"I can take her somewhere. I think she just wants attention." Becky carefully placed her knitting on the table beside the sewing machine and dropped out of her seat.

"That would be lovely, thank you, dear. Anytime you're bored and would like to knit, this will be waiting for you." She patted the beginnings of a headscarf that might one day shade the girl from the sun, or hold back her hair depending on how large it became.

"Come on, Powder," Becky called as she walked toward the Great Dane. "Let's go find you something to play fetch with."

The dog raised her recently lowered head, inspecting Becky as she approached. Upon determining that the girl was indeed talking to her, Powder quickly scrambled back up onto her feet. Dragon barked at Becky's back as she left with the lanky beast.

Nessie sighed and shook her head once she was alone again. She had never had any children of her own, never wanted them, but she worried about the future generations all the same. It wasn't just that they were growing up in a changed world, it's that their parents hadn't, and so didn't know the proper way to raise them. What should be taught? What could be ignored? On average, how did kids react in certain situations? No one really knew, because no one had grown up in this world. Most of the teenagers had grown up to be clever, helpful individuals, ready to step forward and assist at a moment's notice, but the ones even younger? What would they be like?

As she moved on to the next item in her 'to do' pile, Nessie thought about starting a sewing class. She could teach the kids not only how to use a sewing machine, but also basic hand stitching, crocheting, knitting, and even embroidery. Although they were still finding and repairing machine-spun fabrics, there might come a day when all clothing had to be made from scratch. Nessie felt it was up to her to make sure the younger generations knew how to when the time came. The scavengers had been told to look for looms and spinning wheels, but these items weren't easily found and none of the teams had had any luck so far.

The sewing machine whirred on.

The next interruption came with an odd-sounding knock on the side of her container that usually meant whoever was there was holding something and couldn't use their hands to create the sound. Nessie looked up and saw a young man standing in the sunlight. He was carrying a fair-sized metal box and kept shifting his weight from one foot to the other. Nessie had seen the scrawny, greasy man around but had never interacted with him directly. It appeared he repaired his clothes on his own and used duct tape to do it, which was a waste of useful tape in Nessie's opinion. She thought his name might be Venti, but wasn't sure.

"Can I help you?" she asked, watching as he continued to shift left and right.

"I hear you're willing to trade for high-value items?"

"Provided I want what you have. Come inside." Nessie got up from her chair as Venti stepped into the container. He was a loner of sorts, often out fishing by himself. Nessie wasn't sure he had any friends.

Venti placed his box on the floor, metal striking metal, sounding heavy. "What kinds of things do you usually offer in return?"

"Clothing and blankets, usually made of leather or wool. You can request something, and I can make it special for you. I also have some other odds and ends in my wardrobe, but again, it depends on what you're offering. It's not just the metal box is it? Because, as nice as it is, I don't need another box right now."

"No, no. It's what's in the box." Venti sounded nervous, like he shouldn't have whatever he was offering.

"Tell me what it is then."

Glancing over his shoulder, Venti made sure no one was going to see them. Nessie doubted anyone would. Her container was at the end of a row, and the one across from it was used as a storage depot to stockpile junk for which they had no immediate use. There was no reason for someone to come down here unless they were looking for Nessie.

Satisfied, Venti bent down, flipped up the latches on the front of the box, and raised the lid, allowing Nessie to see what was inside.

"How on earth did you get these?"

8
Doyle's Restless

Doyle sat in the plastic chair, flipping through a battered collection of short stories in an attempt to find his favourite one to reread, with his fire axe leaning against the side of his leg. The scar on his face was itchy again, but there wasn't much he could do about that. The itching sensation was lodged under the skin, and no amount of scratching or rubbing seemed to make it go away. He'd just have to ride it out as usual. At least it didn't bother him as frequently as it used to; it was especially bad in the days after he sustained the injury when the Diana sank. A bullet had grazed his face, tearing the meat off his cheek, just inches away from killing him.

The door opened and Robin stepped in, startling somewhat when she spotted Doyle. She hadn't been expecting him there.

"Doyle, what are you doing here?" she asked as she moved toward the boy on the bed.

"Crichton asked me to sit a spell for him while he takes care of some things. Wants me to let him know if the kid wakes up before he gets back." Doyle held up the walkie-talkie that Crichton had given him; it was already tuned to the man's channel.

"You can help me then. I'm going to pour some more liquid down his throat and could use your assistance."

As Doyle got up to help, he tossed his book onto the seat and readjusted the axe so that it leaned against the chair. There were only a handful of times that Doyle had separated from that axe since the Day. It had saved his life on countless occasions. When the zombies had first broken out, he had been at an outdoor concert providing extra security along with some other firefighters. He had no idea where his buddies, Jim and Cillian, were now, just that they weren't here. There had been a disturbance at the concert, now known to be caused by the zombies, and Doyle had reacted quickly. He didn't know why he grabbed the axe off the side of the truck, just that he did. Jim had followed him; neither of them had thought to wake up Cillian who had fallen asleep in the front seat. In the crowds, Doyle and Jim had become separated, and Doyle found he could no longer help anyone but himself. Fighting his way across the park, he managed to get behind the stage where all the band buses were kept. He boarded a bus that happened to contain the mega band, Gathers Moss, and drove their asses out of there. Later, after he had left the bus in order to find help, he got together with a small group of strangers. Eventually, the group stumbled into Gathers Moss again, but by then, the band's numbers had reduced to two, and one of them was trying to kill Robin and her friend. Hearing the screams, Doyle reacted to his fireman's instincts for saving people by using his axe to cut through the hotel door, despite the risk to himself. He and Robin had been fairly close friends ever since, locating the Diana together with the rest of their group. Before that, Doyle would never have thought he could be friends with someone so much younger than him. The Day changed a lot of things.

Going over to the bed, Doyle helped hold the boy's neck and head steady while Robin carefully poured some discoloured water into his mouth. Doyle assumed the water had a strange colour due to some dissolved nutrients in it. He was glad to see the kid swallow it on his own, that he wasn't so gorked out that they risked choking him. Once Robin determined he had had enough, Doyle repositioned the boy so that he looked comfortable.

"I wonder what happened to him," Doyle spoke over the prone body.

"Really?" Robin raised her eyebrows at him. "Looks pretty obvious to me. He was alone and couldn't take care of himself."

"Yeah, but I'm wondering how he ended up on his own. There are a lot of ways, but which one did he have to go through?"

"We'll find out when he wakes up. If he even remembers." Robin listened to the child's heartbeat and carefully checked his blood pressure. Since she didn't need his assistance anymore, Doyle returned to his seat.

Robin continued to perform a few checks on the boy and made chit chat with Doyle. Eventually she finished and Doyle was once more alone with the mysterious child. He wouldn't admit it to anyone else, but he didn't particularly like this job. Something about the kid was creepy, although he couldn't put his finger on what. Maybe it was because, right now, he seemed no different from a corpse. And, these days, you didn't want to be in a room with a corpse for too long no matter how the person had died. It had been quite a shock when they discovered the virus had gone airborne. Everyone had always been afraid of that happening, because then they couldn't do anything against it; they couldn't fight. It turned out to be not as terrible as they had feared, however. Instead of instantly killing everyone and turning them into psychopathic pathogen spreaders, the airborne crap stayed dormant. Robin made a habit of updating Doyle with what was known about it. While the active stuff attacked your organs and shut you down, the new and improved airborne junk waited until something else did the job for it, whether it be illness, injury, or active zombie virus. What it all boiled down to was that everybody would become a shuffler once they died, save those taken out by a massive head injury, say for example, a bullet to the brain. The boy lying in the bed looked dead, which meant he could be a larger threat than if he were alive. It was creepy and unsettling.

Doyle's walkie-talkie crackled. He stopped watching the kid and looked down at it, waiting to see if anyone was going to say anything. It had already emitted a few bursts of static that turned out to be nothing. That was not the case this time.

"Doyle?"

He picked it up and pressed the button. "I'm here."

"It's Crichton. I'm coming back now. Has there been any change?"

"Robin came in, performed some checks and poured some watery stuff down his throat, but that's it. The kid's still out of it."

"Thank you. I'll be there shortly."

This time Doyle didn't hold down the button when he spoke, talking only to himself. "I look forward to it."

He didn't know why Crichton was so absorbed with this kid; why he, personally, had taken it upon himself to be there when the kid woke up. Doyle suspected it was because it was something to do. For the most part, Crichton took care of their defences, but lately those had been running themselves well. The farmers knew how to build fences when they expanded, the lookouts were always in place, and only the smallest of children didn't know what to do if a threat showed up. This kid was their first visitor in months. With Brittany and James handling the smaller day-to-day operations, Crichton found in the boy something on which to focus his attention.

Doyle didn't bother flipping through his book again. He knew that even if he found the story, he wouldn't be able to read it in time before Crichton showed up. Studying the cover instead, Doyle began to suspect he had grabbed the wrong book: he wasn't sure now that this was the anthology containing the story he was remembering. Sighing, he put the book in one of the large pockets on the side of his pants and once again wished they had found a copy that hadn't had the table of contents ripped out of it. Books were not a high-priority scavenge item.

Maybe I should go out with a small team for a day trip just to get books? Doyle thought. If the guys at the pre-Day firehouse knew he had those thoughts, they would think he had been replaced by a body snatcher. Doyle reading books? Unheard of.

When Crichton finally entered the room, Doyle was more than happy to vacate his seat, picking up his axe and sliding it into the holster he had made and wore on his back.

"You going to be down here all day?" Doyle asked as he moved toward the door, changing places with Crichton.

"Until he wakes up, yeah. Why? Something on your mind?" Crichton paused before sitting in the plastic chair.

"I was thinking of grabbing one or two people and making a run to the nearest bookstore. It's not too far; we should be able to get back by tomorrow, two days at the latest."

Crichton thought it over for a moment, looking at the boy. "We don't know where he came from, or what dangers he could have lured this way."

"Has dual purpose then," Doyle shrugged. "We can see if anything's amiss while we're out there."

Crichton's expression rarely changed, but you could always tell when the gears were turning in his mind. "Very well. But you explain exactly what you're doing and what the dangers might be to those who volunteer to go with you."

"You got it. Oh, and what should I do with this?" Doyle held up the walkie-talkie. He didn't usually carry one around; Crichton had just given it to him when he had shanghaied Doyle into babysitting.

"Take it for now. Radio me before you leave and tell me who's going, along with what your supplies are. After that, hand it to anyone watching the fences and they'll get it back to me."

"You got it."

"Anything else?"

"That's it."

"Get going then. The sooner you're out there, the sooner you can get back. And try to take a good runner with you if you can, just in case you need to send a message back to us."

"Will do." And with that, Doyle slipped out of the room containing the creepy boy.

He thought to look for Freya first. She was an avid reader and would probably enjoy having more books on hand, as well as being a great person to have watching your back. Unfortunately, she also proved exceptionally difficult to locate. He thought about asking Robin, but it was probably best that all the doctors stay home, especially with the appearance of the boy and all the patients visiting from the container yard. Doyle tried to find the rest of the people with whom he had survived the Day; he trusted them the most. Like the majority of people who had survived without Keystone's help, he felt closer to those people who had endured with him. Unfortunately, a good portion of them had moved to the container yard, including Harry, Elizabeth, and Cynthia. Quin, the old rock star, was still here but he wasn't a good candidate for this mission. Not only was his body failing him because of his age and rough treatment, but he had never been all that well equipped to handle the zombies in the first place.

It took a while, but Doyle finally found his first volunteer: Canary. Her real name was Ophelia, but she had never been fond of it. When Robin admitted that she used to think of the young woman as the canary, thanks to her blonde hair and willingness to go into places first, she had jumped at the chance and had encouraged the nickname's use. Now, more people knew her as Canary than those who knew her real name.

"I'd love to come," she replied to Doyle's request, even after being told what all the risks were. "It'd be nice to see something outside these fences again."

When they had first moved to the Black Box, several scavenging teams frequently went out, but since then, there wasn't as much of a need. People from the container yard were always giving them found goods in exchange for the crops they grew, and everything else they needed was inside the barriers.

While Canary went off to get her gear, Doyle searched for one more volunteer. He was a bit surprised when it turned out to be James Brenner.

"Crichton told me what you were up to," he said with shrug. "I'd like to come, if that's all right."

"Sure. Any particular reason for wanting to come?"

"I'd like to see for myself if there's anyone else out there. Also, being honest, I'd like to get away from some of these people for a bit."

That surprised Doyle even more. "I thought you liked everyone here?"

"No, I get along with everyone, there's a difference. It's just…" James paused, considering what words to use next. "Since the Day, I've been helping people survive. Every day for eleven years. Trust me, it wears on you. This will be like a mini vacation for me. With fewer than a handful of people, and all of them capable of taking care of themselves? It'll be nice."

Doyle nodded and agreed to let him come. How could he not? James was right when he said he took care of everyone. He got people to safety on the Day, organized a rebellion against Marble Keystone, helped get loads of survivors to the Diana, ran the off-shipper teams once there, and now directed their internal defences; their pseudo police force, fire teams, and doctors, all reported to him on roughly a daily basis. And despite that, people still came directly to him with various questions and problems. He had never been at the very top of the command chain, but was always right beneath it, keeping things running smoothly and doling out advice.

"It'll be great to have you," Doyle told him honestly. "Based on my current luck finding a volunteer, it'll probably be just us and Canary. Pack as light as you can and we'll meet by the truck."

"Thanks for this," James clapped him briefly on the shoulder and then turned away to get his gear.

Having two volunteers he could both trust and find, Doyle went to prep his own gear. He would bring food and water for four days, just in case, but not much else. He wanted as much room as possible in his rucksack for books, as well as any other useful items they might find. Once he was ready to go, he headed out.

The truck was a broken down long hauler, with busted tires and all sorts of detritus piled up underneath. It hadn't worked since the day they positioned it as part of their fence, siphoned out the remaining gas, and deliberately crippled the massive vehicle. Even the gap between the trailer and the cab had been filled with old bricks and rocks removed from the planting fields. Still, it continued to be useful in that it made a distinguished marker along the fence, and was also the easiest place to pass through. As Doyle approached the truck, he spotted Rose sitting on the footboard. There was a backpack at her feet.

"Um," he pointed at the bag.

"I'm comin' with you," Rose told him as she stood up.

"You really think that?"

"I know that."

Doyle looked directly at her shorter arm, the one that didn't make it out from her long-sleeved shirt.

Rose sighed, annoyed. "You're just goin' to the bookstore for a day or two. I understand all the dangers that might be out there, and I can take care of myself. I used to do this job all the time, remember?"

"Isn't that how you lost your hand in the first place? Isn't your accident why you decided to stay here instead of going to the container yard? Because it was safer?"

"I feel useless here."

"I see you helping out all the time."

"Kids can do what I do," she snapped angrily. She shuffled and turned in place, her eyes darting around as she tried to find something to focus on. It looked like she had more to say, but was trying to figure out how to say it. "I know it's not safe out there," she started tentatively. "I know that better 'n most." For emphasis, she raised her short arm, the sleeve flopping over her scarred stump. "But you're goin' somewhere that people have been before, right? There won't be any surprisin' terrain, no climbin' or nothin'. I have a pistol and a hammer, both of which I can use one-handed should somethin' come up. The fact is, even if it's been years, I know what things should look like out there. I've done this a lot more than you have. I'll be able to spot dangers before you can."

"Just let her come."

Doyle startled to hear the voice right behind him. James stepped around and stood near Rose.

"She does have valuable experience. And although she can't communicate in sign as thoroughly as the rest of us, she can still gesture the most important stuff."

Doyle studied James' face, trying to determine his reason for letting Rose come with them. In the end, he couldn't find one, but chose to agree with him.

"Fine, she can come."

A bright smile lit up Rose's pixie face as she quickly grabbed her bag and slung it over her shoulders. They had to wait only another minute for Canary to show up.

"Sorry I'm late," she beamed, sweeping her hair back from her face and expertly tying it up in a bun. "I was getting some book recommendations from a few people."

"All right, then I guess we're all ready to go." Doyle brought the walkie-talkie to his lips and relayed the information Crichton wanted. Crichton gave him the go ahead, and wished them luck.

Stepping up on the footboard, Doyle knocked on the passenger side window of the cab. After a few seconds, a sleepy bedhead appeared in the window, looking out at him. Upon seeing Doyle's face, the man nodded, unlocked the door, and backed away. One by one, Doyle's party climbed up into the truck, passed over the front seats, then climbed out on the other side after unlocking the door. Doyle hung back for a moment to drop off the walkie-talkie.

"Any book requests, Clive?"

"No." Clive took the walkie-talkie from Doyle without looking directly at him and placed it on a charger in the back of the truck. The rear of the cab accommodated a small bed and a hot plate that ran off of solar panels set up on the trailer's roof, same as the chargers. There were also several small compartments carefully packed with various items. Clive lived in the back of the truck's cab, away from the general population. Doyle didn't know what was wrong with him, or whether it was something that had affected him even before the Day, but he understood not to look directly at Clive. The man seemed to be afraid of all people and could interact with them for only short periods of time. He kept an odd sleeping schedule—if you could even call it a schedule—and left the truck simply to relieve himself in a hole near the back of the trailer. Working as a gatekeeper allowed him to be useful, while respecting his need to be alone. He scarcely interacted with people; on occasion when someone dropped off food and water, he'd make an appearance, but mostly he let him or her just leave it outside.

"We should only be gone for a day or two. I'll knock four times when we're back, okay?"

"Okay."

And with those few words spoken between them, Doyle exited through the driver's side, its window reinforced with chicken wire. As he stepped onto the road beyond their fences, he felt a gust when Clive swung the door shut behind him and heard the thunk of the lock sliding into place. Doyle found he couldn't quite remember the last time he had been beyond the fences.

***

Nothing really looked like it once did. Some of the same lines still existed—the edges of buildings, roads, street poles, signs—but they had all been softened. Grass and weeds forced their way up through the cracks, widening them. Trees and bushes grew out of control where once they had been trimmed back, swallowing power lines that had managed to hang on and obscuring street names. Here and there ivy had managed to take hold on a brick wall, and other walls had crumbled under one force or another. A surprising number of windows had managed to remain intact, becoming cloudy and obscure with the dirt, dust, and sand that was repeatedly blown into them. Others had given up, cracking and shattering into jagged points. Old trash and masses of leaves filled the gutters, while still more clung to the bases of buildings and filled doorways. Large branches from storm-battered trees, and occasionally entire trees, remained where they had fallen. There was no one left who cared about cleaning it all up.

"Highway or railroad?" James asked as they headed along a road leading away from the fences.

"Railroad," Doyle told him. "The highway is too dangerous for a group this small, and we don't have any carts."

"Sounds good." James seemed quite content to let Doyle make the decisions. No doubt he would step up if Doyle were to make a stupid one, but Doyle liked to think that that wouldn't happen.

A couple of minutes later, they arrived at the train tracks and peeled off the road to follow them. Doyle felt more comfortable on the old rail lines than he did on the roads. Abandoned, weed-choked rails had been a staple in several communities even before the zombies screwed everything up. Unlike the roads with their decaying vehicles, they felt more natural. They had become part of the landscape far quicker; even animals used them as trails to get from place to place, wary of the roads. Doyle felt they should learn from the animals in that regard. The chances of running into a gang of humans was hopefully lower in the woods or on the rails, because people often followed their road maps when they didn't know the area. Zombie encounters had also proven to be less likely. Some of them probably had just enough intelligence left to understand that the roads were easier for them to shuffle along. Those in the woods were often discovered well in advance due to their constant tripping, falling, and snapping of dead branches. That's not to say the woods were completely safe. They hid dangerous animals, and zombies who weren't moving weren't easy to spot. Their rot provided a sort of camouflage against the pebbled tree bark. The ones who had proven to be the most dangerous were the zombies who had somehow wound up beneath a car, or lying on the ground where a drift of leaves concealed them.

"How long has it been since everyone's been outside the fences?" Doyle wondered, keeping his voice to a whisper. In the quiet, it easily reached all the ears within the small group who stuck as closely together as they could.

"Last time you went out, I think," Canary whispered back. "What was it, seven months ago?"

"Something like that."

"I was technically outside the fence earlier today," James told them, "when I went to help Abby bring in that kid."

"What about before that?"

"A couple of weeks ago. Some of us went to a nearby building to strip it for fence material, although we weren't gone long, just a couple of hours."

"Rose? What about you?"

"I've never been outside the fences here," she admitted. She sounded sad, but thankfully unafraid. Although she was in new territory, she clearly trusted the team she was with and didn't seem nervous.

Doyle nodded, thinking that maybe they should start sending parties out more often. It would be good if everyone knew the area outside their fences, and not just what it looked like on a map. He decided he'd bring it up with Crichton once they returned to the Black Box.

They proceeded slowly along the old rail line, taking their time. This wasn't an emergency trip and so they could proceed as cautiously as they liked. Doyle and James stepped on the slowly rotting wooden ties, the tall weeds that had pushed up through the gravel brushing against their legs. Canary and Rose were more elven-like, balancing along the rusting, metal tracks, both of them looking younger, closer to the age they had been when this all started. Watching her smile over at Canary, revealing all her teeth and a lot of her gums, Doyle was glad he had consented to bringing Rose along.

After some time, they reached the edge of the forest, where the ground sloped away through a marshy patch before reaching the river and the bridge that spanned it. The girls stepped down off the rails that changed from being laid on the ground, to being held up by beams. The whole group paused as Doyle pulled out a pair of binoculars with which to scan the far side of the river, especially the swampy bit of land that mirrored the one before them. Zombies were often spotted stuck in bogs.

"Mind if I take a look when you're done?" James whispered.

"Not at all." Doyle handed the binoculars over. "I didn't see anything, but it's always good to double check."

James took longer scanning the area, perhaps searching for some small sign of the boy's path. Doyle didn't think he'd find anything. Based on where the kid was found, he hadn't come from this direction.

"We good?"

James nodded, but kept his eyes pressed to the rubber eyepieces a moment longer. Doyle pulled his axe out of its carrier and started crossing the bridge. He moved even slower than he had through the woods. He tapped the butt of his axe against each board several times before he moved onto it. They were always worried that the bridge would give out one day, and so Doyle proceeded with an extra modicum of caution. The others followed closely behind him, keeping a constant look out. Unlike the highway bridge just up the river, there wasn't really anywhere to hide along the railway bridge's length. It was entirely open to the middle, where a metal structure that raised and lowered a section of the bridge for ships to pass under offered a little bit of protection. The openness worked favourably in that if it looked clear, odds were it was; however, it also meant there wasn't any place for them to hide should a threat appear. Their options were to go forward, backward, risk taking a swim, or worse, getting stuck in the marsh, so they had to remain alert.

"Can we pause for a second?" James asked when they were halfway across.

Doyle didn't particularly want to, but he could see that James was going to stop no matter what. He still had the binoculars and was now pointing them up river, scanning the other bridge. Doyle could've kept going and let James catch up when he was done, but he didn't want any gaps in the party as they crossed. Instead, he pressed himself up against one of the metal support beams they had reached, it being the only thing that might provide any sort of cover. Snipers were always a worry.

"See something that caught your eye?" Canary wondered.

"A few zombies. Fresh ones, by the looks of it. They all have backpacks on."

"You sure they're zombies?" Doyle asked, worried.

"Pretty sure. Take a look." James handed the field glasses back.

Following James' guidance, it didn't take long for Doyle to find what he had been looking at. James was right: they looked an awful lot like zombies from what he could make out. There were maybe a dozen of them, weaving, shuffling, staggering around the few cars over there, occasionally bumping into them. Their backpacks looked heavy, threatening to push the zombies onto their faces, or pull them over backward.

"If they are humans, they're insanely drunk," Doyle commented.

"Should we intercept them?" Rose wondered. "There's probably some good stuff in those packs."

Doyle actually waited for James to answer, before he realized it was his decision. "If we do, we'll lose the rest of the day and have to set out again tomorrow. The rotters will probably find their way to the fences, and then the guards there can take care of them and loot their stuff. We'll press on to the bookstore."

"You got it," James accepted his decision easily, pressing on across the bridge and using the butt of his rifle in the same manner that Doyle had been using his axe. Still, Doyle caught him glancing toward the other bridge several times.

"What are you thinking about?" Doyle asked him.

"I'm just wondering what happened to them. What would cause several people to die together, backpacks still on their backs? If it were an illness, they wouldn't likely be geared up. If it were a zombie attack, the horde would have had to be fairly big to have kept them all together, but then where did they shuffle off to? If another human had taken them out, why didn't he or she take their stuff?"

"Could've been gas," Rose volunteered. "You know, poisonous gas? Or maybe they ran out of food and collapsed close enough together for their corpses to stick by one another. Also, people are crazy. Someone may have killed them for purposes other than takin' their stuff, you know? We came across some odd stuff when I was an off-shipper."

"I know, I read all your reports." James smiled at her, reminding her that he had been her boss back on the Diana. "I'm just curious is all."

They continued to cross the bridge, coming to the marshy section on the far side. Doyle had to admit that he was curious now, too. It did seem odd for so many zombies still wearing packs to be clustered together, but then Rose was right, stranger things had happened.

Reaching the far end of the bridge, they were able to pick up their pace again, the trees closing back around them. They followed the tracks for a while longer, but eventually split away from them, heading into the trees.

"Watch your footing," Doyle reminded the others. The ground could conceal many things, some deadly while others would just break your ankle.

Staying in their close formation, the group moved stealthily through the trees. Cresting a hill, the forest suddenly gave way, and nothing but suburbs filled the land before them. Somewhere within the cluster of buildings was the bookstore that Doyle wanted to reach. They paused to look over the houses they could see.

The air was still and quiet. An area of densely packed houses like this was one of the most dangerous places to go. Although this area had been evacuated, there was no telling who had returned to their home to die. Sometimes the evacuation sites weren't that far away, and when they had become overrun, they released their deadly occupants back out onto the streets, creating a super horde.

"There's the hole in the fence," Canary pointed to the gap in the boards that allowed them to officially enter the housing development.

Doyle continued to pause. He thought about the zombies on the bridge, wondering if maybe they should go back and check them out. The bulging packs would surely have something of interest inside, maybe even a book or two.

Stepping forward, Doyle went to the gap in the fence and peered into the backyard. It was empty, just as it had been the last time he came this way, although the shadowy interior of the dog house was always suspect. As he squeezed into the yard, he hoped he was making the right choice, that nothing would happen to make the books not worth it.

9

Dean's Thoughtless

Standing in the middle of the horde, Dean felt no fear of the moving corpses pressed up against him. What was there to fear when you were one of them? And yet, he was different. He was smarter, *much* smarter than the rotting, singularly purposed minds around him. Like them, his one desire in this second life was to spread his contagion, to find something living, and infect it. But he could do so much more. Whatever it was that Roy had forced into him was different from the usual blend of madness. He infected things the same way, but for whatever reason, his mind remained more intact than most. It was probably why other zombies were drawn to him. Unless something else properly alive drew their focus, they gathered as close to him as they could, sensing he was closer to the living than they were.

Dean didn't mind. He had learned early on that meat kept him from rotting. By taking bites out of his brethren, he was able to maintain his body far longer than they were. A couple of the brighter bulbs had learned to imitate him, chomping on dead flesh whenever he did. In this way, Dean was able to separate the smarter ones and keep them close in case he needed them.

There were other things that Dean had done in order to keep himself together. Wearing body armour, for instant, not only prevented the humans he had run across from wounding him, but also protected him from rocks, branches, and other natural elements that tore at the others. He wore goggles filled with water to maintain his dry eyes. Although the view was always distorted, it was better than going blind. The helmet secured to his bullet-shaped head, with its retractable visor, was the best touch, as he had seen enough zombies go down to understand that his head was his weak spot. Still, he did get injured from time to time, causing sludge-like blood to ooze out due to gravity as opposed to a heartbeat. After those instances, he wrapped the area in tape, not even removing the body armour to do so. The taping was the most complex physical job he could still accomplish; his body was not as responsive as it had been when he was alive.

There wasn't much he could remember about living, no specifics anyway. There was a lot of muscle memory packed into the former mercenary, but not a lot of emotion. Every now and then he got flashes of things, a few managing to be retained in his limited memory, most being forgotten again minutes later. The strongest was Roy and the needle he had stuck into Dean's arm. Dean remembered Roy and his nametag more often than he remembered his own name. The needle had turned him into what he was. Although unable to understand things like fear and anger, Dean had wanted to infect Roy the moment he turned. He never got the chance.

After managing to teach a bunch of zombies outside his place of confinement—a school he sometimes remembered—to start battering the windows, more people in white coats came and locked him inside a box. Dean was in the box for a long time. After a while, he remained perfectly still. So still, that one of the white coats worried that their precious specimen had been lost, somehow. A woman had foolishly opened the box just enough for him to bite her. She must have hidden the wound from the others, because the next time Dean's box opened, it was because of a helicopter crash, and her mangled body was still twitching and flailing in the wreckage. The box meant to contain Dean had protected him, and, ever since, he had wandered the Earth, looking for things to infect while the horde around him grew and grew.

The only other memory that hung around was that of sitting in a classroom, maybe in the same school, with desks piled up. He was with a group of people, all adults save one teenage boy. Sometimes Dean remembered that this was his mercenary squad, and that the boy had been sort of adopted by them, but most of the time he had no idea who they were. For whatever reason, his infection kept focusing on them, making him want to find them and infect them. He hadn't found a single one, but it was for that reason that he kept moving. A few times he had stumbled across a heavily fortified base with some living humans inside. There were ways he knew to get in that the brain dead didn't, but on most occasions he moved on, preferring to keep searching rather than waste a lot of time and resources for only a few infections. That's often how he considered the dumbest of the zombies: resources. The more he had of them, the greater his defensive wall of flesh, and the more bodies he had to throw at the larger compounds, the ones that held more than a dozen people.

A body moved past, bumping into Dean's shoulder. Dean turned his goggled face, peering through the slightly murky water. If he could remember, he should change the water soon. The zombie who had bumped into him was saggy blue shirt, a smart one who still moved with grace and ease. Dean couldn't remember individual zombies unless he was looking at them. Now that saggy blue shirt was within his line of sight, Dean recalled that the zombie had been around him for a long time, eating enough protein and managing to avoid dangers so that his body had barely rotted. He still had his motor functions intact, a valuable asset. If something interested him enough, saggy blue shirt could still run, a skill many had lost upon turning, or else were no longer capable of due to stiffened muscles or various injuries. Dean was once able to move like that, but he hadn't consumed enough protein to properly maintain himself for it. Saggy blue shirt was even now chewing on what was no doubt a piece of the horde.

Dean was not in the center of the mob. He continued to move in a single direction, chosen for unknown reasons. A group stayed closely around him, able to head in the same direction without looking at him, or else being pushed along at the front. The rest trailed behind in an amorphous column, new zombies joining all the time, while others wandered off or became too injured to keep up. They trampled the land flat as they moved from one place to another, searching for humans or the odd animal. The travelling humans were the best, when they slept in exposed camps. Their guards and defensive warnings were no match for the sheer size of Dean's horde. Lately, however, Dean actively wanted to find a large group. Something was telling him that maybe the people from his memory were in a complex somewhere. He wanted to know where.

And so Dean kept walking, kept hunting, his horde following along obediently: his army of corpses.

I
The Boy

The boy had been awake for some time, but continued to remain still, his eyes closed, letting these people think he was asleep. He didn't know what to make of them. They had saved him and given him watery soup, but would they want something in return? New people were always such an unknown. Some were obviously destructive, some genuinely cared, while others were sneaky. They made you think they were the 'good guys' only to turn on you and reveal a hideous underbelly.

Knowing that he couldn't pretend to sleep forever, the boy assessed what he managed to hear. He knew there was a man in the room, that he had been there most, if not all, of the time. He had left only once, and some other man had sat in. That second man was now apparently going to a bookstore, and he was going to see if the boy had drawn anything to this place when he had staggered toward their fences. The bookstore might just be a bookstore, but it could also be a nickname for some other place.

The boy would have to risk opening his eyes at some time, it might as well be now.

Section 2:
Infiltrate

10
Nessie's Unsure

Usually by the time the sun had set, with the last of the light leaving the sky and her pop bottle light bulb, Nessie would be in bed attempting to sleep and frequently succeeding with ease. Tonight, however, she lay on her back and stared into the darkness. It wasn't a full moon night: the pop bottle was unable to pick up much light, but it did show as a faint speck against the ceiling that could easily be mistaken for the imagination or an after image.

Nessie was thinking about the metal box beneath her bed. She knew she should turn it in, and either brush off their questions or perhaps even answer them. Something held her back, though. This wasn't like finding a box of fishing lures; even Venti had understood that. He obviously couldn't handle the stress of keeping it himself, and had decided that Nessie was the best person to hand it off to.

Sitting up with a sigh, Nessie slid out of bed, her feet finding their way into her slippers. She shuffled around in the dark with practised ease, locating a candle and matches. Entirely by feel, she opened the box of matches, plucked one out, and ran its head along the striker. With a pop and a hiss, the match ignited, surrounding Nessie's hand in a glow of light and heat. She quickly applied it to the candle's wick, where the flame burned a little larger and would last a lot longer. This particular candle was already halfway melted, but that was fine; Nessie didn't think she would need it for very long.

As she made her way back to her bed, carrying the candle in the tin holder, she heard Dragon change places in his cage. The light had woken up the bird, or at the very least had caused him to stir. Nessie ignored him as she knelt on the floor beside her bed, resting the candle on the nearest flat surface above her. Stretching her arm beneath the bed, she groped around for the metal box. Her hand encountered dust, along with a few blankets she intended to trade, and a pair of shoes she had stopped wearing since acquiring the rubber boots. At last, her fingertips bumped into the hard surface of the box, quickly roaming about it until they found the handle along its side. She had pushed it deep under her bed, and it took an unexpected amount of effort to pull it back out.

Once the metal box was sitting before her, Nessie paused. There really was no reason to look inside again, yet something told her she must. In the dead of night, one often had to confirm things a second time. Popping open the clasps, Nessie gently raised the lid of the box.

Inside, nestled within sculpted foam, were a dozen hand grenades. Nessie knew if she lifted up the layer of foam, there would be two more layers underneath. Thirty-six explosive devices sitting under her bed; what was she thinking?

Running her hands along the vaguely egg-shaped items, Nessie thought about the story that Venti had told her, the one about how he had found them. Apparently, he had been fishing in a spot he liked to go to of late, somewhere along the shore closer to the open waters of the Gulf of Mexico. He had spotted a large rabbit on shore, and thought he'd try his luck at catching it; not killing it, but catching it alive to add to Animal Island, where they bred rabbits like cattle for a source of meat. It seemed that Venti was fine with killing both zombies and fish, but he said no when it came to doing in mammals. The rabbit got away, no doubt with ease, as Venti was no trapper. As he was returning to his boat, he tripped over something hidden in the grass. It turned out to be a corner of the box, which Venti then proceeded to dig up. When he saw what was inside, he knew he had to bring it back to the container yard, but from there, didn't know what to do. He had the same reservations about turning them over to the community leaders that Nessie had.

Grenades had the sole purpose of killing humans. If the container yard were inhabited by the kind of people who were landscapers, needing to blast away at a boulder or something it would be a different story, but they weren't. Other humans had come to the container yard with bad intentions before. A few had even been shot and killed, but most had been left alive. To shoot someone was one thing; there was a chance you could then save them. But with a grenade, that chance dropped to nearly nil. Nessie thought of the movies where she had seen grenades used and pictured the mess left behind.

No, there was no reason to hand them over. Even if Nessie could completely trust that, without any doubt, the grenades wouldn't be used, then what would be the point? They would just be placed in a storage container somewhere. At least this way, only Nessie and Venti knew about them, meaning no one would be tempted to take one, or two, or the whole damned box.

Sighing, having convinced herself for the third time that she was doing the right thing, Nessie closed the lid and snapped shut the latches. She pushed the box back under the bed with both arms, wiggling it around any objects that may have drifted in the way after she had pulled it out.

From his cage, Dragon made a loud chattering sound that caused Nessie to flinch and lie flat on instinct. It took her less than a second to identify the bird as the culprit and not real guns. He never got that sound quite right, never put enough power behind it, for which Nessie and everyone around her were grateful. Since the Day, Dragon had heard more than enough gunfire to try to repeat it, but Nessie never encouraged his efforts, hoping that one day he'd stop trying.

"Go back to sleep," she hissed at the large bird, looking over to where his big, round eye reflected the candle light, becoming luminous as he watched her.

"*Sleep. Sleep,*" he whispered in the near dark, and then made obnoxious, exaggerated snoring sounds.

Rolling her eyes, Nessie got back up on her feet. She returned the candle to its usual place and blew it out with a puff, the resulting black immediately swallowing up her container. Licking her fingers, Nessie used them to pinch the wick a few times, making sure that even the embers were smashed out. Wiping the worst of the resulting soot on her nightie, she made a mental note to add it to her wash pile tomorrow.

Sliding back out of her slippers, Nessie crawled once more beneath her blankets.

"Goodnight, Dragon," she whispered.

"*Goodnight,*" he whispered back with a soft whistle.

Although warm and comfortable, Nessie continued to stare into the darkness.

***

Despite her restless night, Nessie was up and following her usual morning routine at the regular time. The only change was that she made her tea extra strong.

At breakfast, she observed that Dr. Riley and her patients hadn't returned yet, and therefore Bill was still away. Making note of this in her book, she avoided looking at the entry about the metal box. While the others chatted as usual, Nessie found it hard to focus on their conversations, often withdrawing into herself. Despite her efforts, the metal box continued to occupy her mind.

"Are you all right, Nessie?" the woman sitting next to her asked.

"I'm fine, thank you. I didn't sleep well last night," she forced a smile.

"You should think about taking an hour or two off today to take a nap."

"Maybe I will." She knew she wouldn't. Not only was there too much to do today, but she had never been one for naps; she didn't want to waste her life sleeping. Besides, she'd probably only think about the box again, and lie awake.

After breakfast, she left her sign in the 'out' position and gathered up her laundry. Once she had made sure that everything was in the basket, she placed the basket into a sort of harness she had acquired through a trade. It allowed her to carry the basket on her back, leaving her hands free for various things, including holding her cane. Dragon perched on the side of the basket, ready to ride. As she exited her container once more, she felt like she should close the doors; she now had something she wanted to keep hidden, but she managed to override the urge by convincing herself that closing the door would only make people more suspicious.

"Do you need any help, Nessie?" a young man on his way to the wall stopped to ask. He must have noticed that she was using her cane more than usual today.

"I'm all right, thank you." She gave him the same forced smile that she had given her breakfast companion.

The young man nodded and trotted off to whatever job he had been assigned. Nessie sighed and looked up at the sky, wondering if some outside confirmation about what to do with the grenades could be found there. There wasn't one; instead, she spotted some ominous-looking clouds in the distance out toward sea. Although the sky overhead was bright and sunny now, a storm was going to roll in off the Gulf in the near future. Ocean-born storms were always the worst. Without satellite imagery and a bunch of meteorologists pouring over complex data, they never knew how bad the storms would be. They never knew if it was just a lot of rain coming in, or if they were going to have to deal with a hurricane. So far, they had gotten lucky during hurricane season and hadn't been directly hit by one. Some people in the group believed that if they ever were, their entire camp would be wiped out. Precautions were taken, such as keeping loaded and therefore heavy storage containers pressed up against the community building for stability in the wind and protection from flying debris. Living containers were lined up side by side in rows in the hopes that it would be easier for the wind to funnel down the aisles this made. Each container was braced by those next to it, provided the wind didn't change course. Everyone knew the drills, knew where the safest places were, such as the dozen containers that had been painstakingly bolted deep into the concrete where the ends of the rows were closest to the community centre. Of course, if a big enough storm surge came along, there wouldn't be much they could do beyond pray, as everything, themselves included, got swept away. Water was a powerfully destructive force.

Nessie was thinking about the strength of storms when she reached the wash basins. As with the barrel for washing hands, the water here was frequently reused, and consisted only of collected rainwater. The sudden influx of fresh water was the one reason to look forward to a storm.

A few other men and women were already at the basins, which were really a series of deep troughs, and Nessie found a place among those at the first one. Several washboards rested along the sides of the trough, ready to be used in the murky water. There wasn't any soap in this water; it was for scrubbing off clumps of mud and other such stains before moving onto the next one. Kneeling down next to the trough on a padded mat she carried with her laundry, Nessie slid out of her carrier and set to work, with Dragon perching on the trough's edge to watch. As she scrubbed the worst of the grime away, her mind began to relax, her tension leaving with the dirt. By the time she was ready to move onto the next trough, she felt like her old self again.

At the second trough, the water was frothy with soap; there was more soap sitting on a ledge just under the outside of the lip. Here was where most of the cleaning would be done and the most time spent. Down at one end of the basin, a trio of men were laughing and making jokes as they scrubbed their clothes. At the opposite end, a young girl was softly singing, a mountain of articles to be washed beside her; probably the laundry for a whole family. The atmosphere was lovely, and Nessie soon found herself humming along with the girl, while Dragon shuffled about, inspecting what everyone was doing, making the occasional remark, and drawing out more laughter from the men.

"Hi, Nessie."

Surprised, Nessie managed not to startle when Becky settled herself beside the old woman. She wasn't alone today; her older friend Dakota stood behind her.

"Good morning, Becky. Dakota," she nodded at them both as she continued to wash.

"I went by your container, hoping to do some more knitting. Dakota said she wants to learn too."

"I figure it's better than shadowing a wall guard, or a blacksmith all day," Dakota shrugged, as if she needed a good reason to be knitting.

"Well, you're going to have to wait awhile. As you can see, I've already started my laundry."

"Maybe we can help," Becky offered.

"That's very kind of you to offer, but I'd rather do this myself. Under garments, you know?"

Becky grinned, a chuckle nearly escaping from between her teeth.

"Come on, Becky. Maybe Adam is doing something with his dad today." Dakota gestured for them to leave, not knowing the woman very well and feeling a little uncomfortable in her presence.

"We'll find you later then?" Becky asked Nessie as she got to her feet.

"Once you see my laundry hanging outside my container, you'll know I'm in."

"Thanks. Bye, Dragon."

"*Bye-bye,*" he squawked, not necessarily knowing who had spoken his name.

As Nessie returned to her laundry, she looked back toward the sky. From this angle, she couldn't see the storm clouds, which hopefully meant they'd stay away until her laundry had dried. Although it was possible to hang them inside, things dried quicker when out in the sun, picking up any sort of wind that came along.

With the young girl singing, Nessie soon found herself completely absorbed in her work and humming again.

***

Outside her container, Nessie's laundry waved in the breeze. She had rinsed it in the last of the three troughs, and waited in line to send it through one of the two presses. Then she had hung it on three clothes lines she had erected with the help of a footstool between the upper edge of her container and the one across from her. Becky and her friend hadn't shown up yet, so Nessie was free to sew in peace. Her machine's humming was nowhere near as nice as the young girl's singing, but it was equally distracting.

After an hour went by with still no Becky, Nessie found herself getting unexpectedly worried. There was no reason for her to feel that way; Becky was young and could've easily found something elsewhere to distract her. Still, Nessie thought something might be wrong. As more time dragged by, she found herself looking out the front of her container more than at her sewing. Eventually, she gave up and snapped the machine off.

"Come on, Dragon, we're going to look for her," she said as she got up onto her feet.

The parrot cocked his head sideways. He had been climbing up and down the outside of his cage, agitated, and not likely for the same reasons. The bird sensed the coming storm, in that way that animals had. He had never liked heavy rain.

Once Dragon was on her shoulder, Nessie turned her sign around and stepped out amongst her laundry. The wind had picked up with the approaching storm, billowing her pants and shirts and in the process drying them faster. The wind was also good for loosening them up, for it had been a long time since anyone had any good fabric softener.

With the tip of her cane clacking along the concrete, Nessie set off in search of Becky. She had no idea where to start looking, and knew there was a risk the girl would show up at her container while she was out, but it made her feel better to be active. Maybe the storm was agitating some primal instinct within herself as well as Dragon.

Walking along the aisles formed by the container homes, Nessie looked into those whose doors were open. There were a wide variety of arrangements inside. Some were over-crowded with bunk beds, while others were Spartan. A few had very homey layouts, with curtains separating the sleeping areas and art hanging on the walls. All sorts of shelves inhabited the containers, from bookcases, to metal tool racks, to boards resting on milk crates. People used what they could get, some coming up with ingenious solutions. One container contained a hammock strung up near the ceiling, leaving the floor space open. Another had a rebuilt exercise bike to generate power, while yet another had modified their upper escape hatch with a funnel and trough system that brought fresh rain water to a large barrel they kept inside. People were constantly finding new uses for various items, resulting in containers that were all different from their neighbours. Nessie didn't spot Becky in any of them, and the few people she asked hadn't seen her.

After walking down every 'street,' Nessie went to the community building, thinking that maybe she was trying to help her mother cook, despite the fact that she hadn't seen the girl there when she popped in to pick up lunch on her way back to her container, with her soggy laundry on her back.

"No, she hasn't been here today. Can I ask why you're looking for her?"

Nessie assumed the woman she had asked was the girl's mother, based on the defensive tone.

"She said she'd come by and do some knitting with me," Nessie explained, playing up her age in an attempt to keep the cook from worrying. "When she didn't show up, I thought it would be good exercise to go find out why for myself. I assume she just found something more interesting to do with her friends."

The woman nodded. "Try the dock and the rocky shore. Although Becky doesn't like to swim much, she'll be sitting there if her friends are."

"Thank you. Dinner smells delicious by the way."

The woman laughed and made a shooing gesture at Nessie. The food almost always smelled the same, as they were always using the same rotation of ingredients. So much corn, and there always seemed to be potatoes.

Nessie left the community building and headed for the dock per Becky's mother's suggestion. She could tell the girl wasn't there just by standing at the head of it. Not only was there clearly no one on the dock, but there also wasn't any splashing or giggling to suggest someone was swimming around the big concrete structure. It was possible they had gone to Animal Island, so Nessie made her way to the end of Bitch Bridge, which jutted out from the rocky shore. She had never crossed it herself, too dangerous, but could see a large chunk of the island from the end of it. The water was rougher than it had been when she saw it last, another effect of the on-coming storm. The bridge rode the waves, tugging at the moorings on either end. On the island, she could see several adults running about, gathering up the animals and bringing them to various, small shelters. It was unlikely that the kids were there, and they clearly weren't swimming. They might have been on the island earlier, but as the ocean got rougher, they would have been sent back before it got too dangerous. Once the animals were safe, everyone over there save one would return across the bridge, and then the far end would be disconnected so that it wouldn't be torn apart. If the storm was expected to be really bad, then it would be hauled in and dragged up on shore, piece by piece. Nessie wondered which one it would be today as she moved on, deciding to follow the outer wall next.

Where it met the rocky shore of the bay, the wall was only one container high, still waiting for some more to be emptied out, moved over, and hauled up; a long and strenuous process. There were a few other containers lying around haphazardly within the confines of the wall. These had been emptied, cleaned, and were in various stages of modifications to make them habitable. With less than five hundred people in the container yard and all them having a roof over their heads, it wasn't a priority to finish these with any sort of haste. The smooth logs that were used to roll them from one place to another weren't even sitting under any of the containers anymore; they had been brought nearer to the higher wall, ready to be hoisted over after another outside container was emptied. Nessie was surprised to find Becky and her friends there.

Up on one of the incomplete housing containers, the girl stood with Dakota and a boy who must be Adam. They had been talking in low voices, but when they spotted Nessie, they fell silent and attempted to drop out of sight. Clearly something was going on. Walking straight to the container on which she had seen them standing and going around to the far side, she found the wooden ladder they had used to climb up. Someone was evidently trying to pull it up onto the container with them, hoping they hadn't been seen. Nessie took hold of the bottom rung before it could get any higher.

"Leave that down here, please," she said, tugging it free of the younger hands above.

The tops of three heads appeared over the side.

"What are you doing up there?" Nessie wondered.

"Nothing," Dakota instinctively responded.

"Uh huh, then you won't mind if I come up?"

The eyes all looked at one another, clearly not liking this idea. Obviously, this meant that Nessie *had* to go up there. Tucking her cane under one arm, she tested the sturdiness of the ladder, and then proceeded to climb up.

The kids scrambled up onto their feet and backed out of the way as Nessie reached the top. Dragon fluttered off her shoulder to sit on the container's roof, his head twisting to look up at Dakota.

"Git along, little doggie," he commented at her hat.

Once standing, Nessie looked around for anything suspicious. After she had walked around the container, she saw that the doors hadn't yet been modified, the outside latches still securing them. Up top, the hole for the light hadn't been cut, but the emergency hatch had been installed. She couldn't see anything suspicious.

But then a soft sound came out of the container beneath her feet. Nessie looked at Becky and her friends, who all looked nervously at one another. Walking over to the hatch, Nessie bent down to open it.

"We were going to tell someone, honest." Becky's voice trembled.

It caused Nessie to pause. She had thought that maybe they had locked one their other friends inside as a joke, but such a cruel prank wouldn't have elicited those words. This was something else. Carefully gripping the edges of the emergency hatch, she raised it up and looked inside. The container was dark, only a small patch lit up by the sunlight streaming in through the opening. Dragon croaked, and quickly scuttled away from the hole, fluttering to rest on the highest rung of the ladder. Nessie had heard him make that particular sound only a few times before. A rattle drew her attention back to the hole. It was the rattle of a chain on metal. A shadow came into the light and Nessie found herself looking down into a pair of dead eyes.

"We didn't do it," Adam quickly said. "We just found it like this."

The zombie had a collar around its neck, with a dog chain attaching it to something inside the container. The thing was silent, no groans escaping its diseased lips, the only sounds coming from its shuffling feet and the louder scraping of the chain. Pale, bony fingers raised up, as if to catch Nessie were she to fall. A mouth full of blackened teeth popped open, a silent gasp of awe for what its discoloured eyes were showing it. Nessie didn't look long before carefully lowering the hatch back into place.

Secrets. More secrets. Although the box of grenades was one she could keep to herself, this one would have to be brought to the leaders. Someone in the shipping yard was keeping a zombie. He or she had either captured one and locked it up, or else had locked up a live human until that person had died. Nessie found herself hoping for the former, although neither option was good.

"You kids are going to come with me," Nessie told them as she got back on her feet and headed for the ladder.

"We didn't do anything, we just found it before you showed up," Becky hastily explained.

"And I believe you." Although Nessie thought that maybe the kids had spent more than just a few minutes up there, wondering what to do. It was possible they had known for a few days, and didn't want to risk getting into trouble for one thing or another. Besides, they had never really gotten to look at a zombie up close, not really. Nessie wouldn't be surprised if one day they started throwing rocks at it, or opening the front doors and daring one another to get as close as possible had she not gone looking for them.

Once everyone was off the container, Nessie took the ladder down and instructed the kids to return it to where they had found it. She followed along behind them. Along the way, Dragon fidgeted on her shoulder, frequently bobbing and twisting his head, and nibbling on her hair. He was even more agitated than earlier, having smelled or seen the zombie before Nessie had. The bird hadn't made a sound since his initial croak, fretting that more might be in the area. Nessie looked at the other containers around her and hoped that wasn't true.

The ladder was returned exactly to where the kids swore they found it, between two other partially modified containers. It had either been left there and forgotten by those doing the modifications, or someone had deliberately placed it where it was unlikely to be seen. No one ever really bothered with these containers; no one but a small group of bored kids.

"All right, we're going to go tell the community leaders now," Nessie instructed.

All six shoulders on the three kids slumped simultaneously. They didn't complain though; they knew this was something that had to be done. Nessie didn't think they'd get into trouble; she didn't know of any rules that forbade them from climbing up onto the containers, and they obviously had nothing to do with the zombie. Still, she let it worry them as they walked, figuring they'd learn some sort of lesson in the process.

The sky cracked and rumbled with thunder, causing the little group to pause and look skyward. The storm was almost upon them. Great big black thunderheads were rolling across the sky, soon to swallow the sun. Beneath them would be torrents of rain and dangerous lightning.

"Your laundry is still out." Becky pointed to where they could just see the end of Nessie's row, her laundry flapping with the increased winds.

Nessie looked back to the community centre. People were scattering from it, carrying early dinners to various containers. They would rather ride out the storm in their own home as opposed to the drafty building.

"Come on, kids, let's go save my laundry," Nessie guided them toward her container. "The leaders won't be gathered in one place right now anyway, and we need to get to cover."

The kids ran ahead while Nessie power walked, the situation not quite dire enough for her to risk more speed. Becky was quick to locate Nessie's stool and hand it to Dakota, still the tallest of the three. Adam might shoot past her when he hit his growth spurt, but for now he was a bit of a shrimp. Instead of trying to take down each piece of laundry, Dakota undid the end of each line and handed it down, the other two bundling it all up to keep everything off the ground. It made Nessie smile to see them problem solving so well. The world might have gotten fucked up, but the next generation seemed to be handling it well, considering their parents had no idea what to teach them.

When Nessie reached her container, the kids had finished and were piling her laundry on her bed. The first droplets of rain struck her back as she entered the safety of the container. Dragon fluttered off her shoulder ahead of her and landed on the side of his cage with a clatter. Nessie was wondering if the kids would have time to dash to their own homes when the skies truly opened up, a cascade of rain crashing down. The wind suddenly howled, throwing one of the container doors shut and pulling the other further open.

"Help me get this closed!" Nessie shouted over the wind as she grabbed the open door, getting soaked in the process. The three kids rushed to her aid, and together they hauled the slab of metal shut and slotted the bar into its brackets. Nessie went to the back of her container and pulled two beams out of the corner. It was pointless to use them on a regular basis, but this wasn't a regular storm. The kids helped her slot those into place as well, having to work in virtual darkness.

Once the doors were secure, Nessie located her candle and matches as she had the night before and brought light into her home. Becky, Dakota, and Adam were huddled up against the doors, dripping wet from closing them. Nessie located her towels and handed one to each of them, grabbing a not fully dry one from the bundle on her bed for herself. Hopefully the kids' parents didn't worry too much about their absence. It wasn't uncommon for people to end up in containers that weren't their own when storms hit, as most people headed for the nearest shelter.

"Make yourselves at home, there's no telling how long this storm will last." Nessie busied herself finding places to drape her laundry, while the kids awkwardly shuffled, not knowing what to do with themselves. Becky was the first to move, taking a seat on the edge of Nessie's bed. Adam soon followed her lead, and then Dakota sat down in the nearby desk chair that Becky had occupied the other day. It seemed they believed that the hardback chair beside the sewing machine was Nessie's domain and should be left alone for her. Perhaps it was the carefully centered seat cushion and ergonomic backrest that told them this. Nessie didn't care where they sat, but took the remaining seat.

Secrets upon secrets, she thought, looking at the kids. They had no idea about the box of grenades beneath the bed they were perched upon. Nessie wondered what else would happen, as bad things had a tendency to cluster together. She hoped the storm would pass quickly, both the literal one and the figurative one.

"So, who would like to learn how to knit?" Nessie asked the three children as she located the headscarf Becky had already started.

11
Danny's Anxious

From the roof of the garage, Danny watched the dark clouds in the far distance and tried to estimate when they would reach the scavenger party. The distance made it nearly impossible to judge their speed, and the fact that the group would be heading toward them only added to the difficulty. His only certainty was that clouds that dark coming from the direction of the ocean would eventually reach them. Looking down at the map in his hands, he figured out where they would spend the night if nothing slowed them down. From there, he worked backward to locate several other safe places along the route. Their best option, from what he could figure, was to press on, and each time they reached a safe spot, to check how close the storm was and determine if they could get to the next one. As plans went, it wasn't exactly elegant, but it was the best one he could come up with. Folding and rolling up the large map, Danny tucked it into one of his cargo pockets where it took up all available space. He headed back to the ladder and climbed down to street level, where the others were just finishing readying the horses.

"How's it looking?" Lenny asked, checking the tightness of Thumper's harness. The horse seemed annoyed about being back on cart-pulling duty after the freedom of their searching. His partner, Potato, stood serenely beside him, not minding at all.

Danny took the map back out and spread it as much as his arms would allow. Lenny then held a side flat, freeing up one of Danny's hands for pointing while the others gathered around. Danny told them his plan, pointing out the locations he had picked out. The others agreed, all nodding their heads in approval and making a quick study of the stops. Lenny took the map when they were finished and placed it in a waterproof baggie that was then tucked into a large pocket of his backpack. They probably wouldn't need it again until their next outing.

"All right, let's head out." Lenny climbed up into the first cart, pulled by Thumper and Potato, and picked up the reins, while Jon headed for the second cart. Danny was first in line to spell Lenny, so he stayed close as they started rolling forward. The horses were certainly strong enough to pull the loaded carts with the additional weight of people, but not knowing what lay ahead kept some humans on the ground. At least Danny didn't have to carry his bag; it sat strapped to the side of the cart where he could get at it. On the other side, Shaidi kept the same pace, while Bryce and Larson flanked the second cart.

As they walked, Danny found himself unusually jumpy. He was used to having a lot of threats around him, but he specifically felt watched this morning. Constantly glancing around, he could see nothing that validated his unease. Everything was the same as it had been the whole time they had been out here. It seemed he was just having a twitchy day.

They reached the first stop without trouble. Bryce climbed the nearest available structure and informed them how far the storm was. They could get to the next shelter easily.

Danny rotated into the driver's seat of the cart, Lenny now walking along beside it. It felt nice to sit on the simple wooden bench, his eyes now nearly twice as high as they had been and able to take in more. Thumper and Potato walked on effortlessly, needing very little guidance or monitoring. The reins lay in his lap, one hand curled gently around them, while his other hand held a rifle propped up against his shoulder. If someone *was* watching, he wanted him, her, or them to know that they wouldn't be easy pickings.

Thumper suddenly stopped short with a heavy snort and a head flick. Potato then danced as much as she could in her harness, attempting to force the cart backward. The horses were clearly agitated. Behind them, the second cart had stopped at a minimum safe distance, its horses also agitated although to a lesser degree. As soon as the horses had stopped, Lenny and Shaidi moved in on either side in an attempt to calm them.

Danny slipped off the board and was quickly joined by Bryce, who had been driving the second cart. Jon and Larson were keeping those horses calm. Everyone knew what was going on and what to do. Bryce and Danny walked forward, their eyes sharply trained on every recess, shadow, and corner. Whenever the horses suddenly became agitated without whinnying, it meant that they had sensed a zombie somewhere in the vicinity. Danny was impressed by how quickly animals had learned to keep quiet and avoid zombies; they were a new predator that had taken over the top of the food chain. Even carrion eaters avoided the moving corpses, swooping in only once they were put down for good. Maybe elsewhere in the world, where there were different animals, some of them actively hunted the zombies, but so far, here, they had only seen the dead attacked when an animal was cornered.

Reaching an intersection, both Danny and Bryce raised their rifles, pointing them down both sides of the street while keeping their backs close together. When nothing was spotted on the roads, they both looked up, scanning the rooftops.

Bryce patted Danny on the shoulder, and when Danny turned to look, he tugged on his own ear. Danny nodded, because he could hear it too. From somewhere nearby was the gurgling, rattling groan of dead vocal cords. It was too loud to be inside, and it sounded close, but they couldn't see anything. Spotting a storm sewer half-buried in leaves, Danny walked over to it while at the same time pulling out his flashlight. He clicked it on and pointed the beam of light down. There, standing in some stagnant water and adding to the stink, was not one, but three bloated and decaying zombies. Their flesh was swollen and pale, while places of it were split and hanging free of the water-logged muscle and bone. Upon seeing Danny and his light, they got a little more active, the water around their knees sloshing and releasing more stench. Danny backed away from the sewer, a hand pulling up his facemask. He checked up and down the street, but couldn't see an open storm sewer anywhere. They had seen zombies fall through open grates before, becoming trapped and getting pushed farther along the system with each storm. It was also possible someone living had deliberately herded them into the storm grate and then closed it. Whatever the reason, they weren't dangerous.

Back beside Bryce, Danny waved the carts forward. With one person next to each horse and leading it, it was possible to move the frightened beasts past the perceived threat. Once they were calm, Danny and Bryce climbed back up onto the driver's platforms, and took up the reins, the horses now eager to press onward away from the zombie sewer.

At the next safe spot, they had to debate whether to press on or not. The storm was visibly closer, giving them a better sense of its speed. After a brief discussion, it was agreed they would go to the next stop and then stay there. Danny started keeping an eye on the clouds whenever they were visible between the buildings. The carts were now driven by Shaidi and Larson.

"Shit," Lenny hissed from the far side of the horses as they began rounding a bend. Up ahead, a large, modified bus had crashed into a building, blocking most of the street. It hadn't been there on their way out, which meant someone had been in the area recently. Whether that person was still alive was unknown. Danny remembered the recently turned man that Jon had shot, wondering if he had come from this bus.

"Looks like we might be able to squeeze around the back of it." Shaidi pointed to where the rear end of the bus didn't reach the buildings opposite the one in which it had become wedged.

"It would be quicker than going around these buildings if we can," Lenny nodded, his voice a little hesitant about the idea.

Jon trotted up beside them to join in on the conversation, Bryce staying back with his brother.

"I remember this area," he said, nodding to a still-recognizable sign for a nail salon. "Over that way there's a wooded hill we can't get through. We'd have to go around it, but it's a decent distance and we'd be walking through a valley. With a storm coming, that might not be such a good idea."

"And the other way?" Lenny looked at the building in the other direction as though he could see through it.

"Remember all that debris we passed on our outbound trip? That's what's over there."

Danny recalled what Jon was talking about and realized it would be a long trip to go around it. Their outward journeys from the shipping yard were always longer than the homeward trips because of the unknown road conditions. In the case of the blocks next to them, there was a ton of debris on the road. Somewhere, a building must have exploded for one reason or another, sending bricks, mortar, and who knew what else scattering every which way. There was possibly an area they could pick their way through, but the main danger lay in other buildings suddenly collapsing from weakness caused by the initial explosion. Danny hadn't been with the team when it happened, but an unexpectedly weak structure had nearly buried a man. Since then, they were always cautious, keeping the carts to the middle of streets just in case things weren't as stable and secure as they looked.

"I think it's worth spending the time to see if the carts can go around," Shaidi voiced her opinion from her higher position. "I can start checking the map for the quickest route to and through the valley just in case."

"I agree," Danny said, nodding.

When Jon headed back to inform the guys of their decision, Lenny went to their cart to get what they called the width stick. This wouldn't be the first time they were unsure if the carts could fit through somewhere, and so they always carried a length of wood that was slightly longer than the carts were wide. If the stick got jammed anywhere, then the carts would and they couldn't risk the passage.

Danny volunteered to investigate the bus with Jon, strapping his flashlight on as he walked, while Lenny and Bryce headed for the rear with the width stick. Larson had brought the second cart forward to stand beside the first, where he could guard both of them plus Shaidi while she checked the map. These were all things they had done before, in different variations of the same situation.

The door to the bus was closed, the glass missing from it and replaced by plywood. The rear door looked like it had a sheet of tread plate welded to it. The windows were covered in chicken wire and bars, their lower halves also boarded up. From where they stood on the street, Danny and Jon could only see the ceiling through the upper halves, which told them nothing about what they might find inside. The front door was actually within the building the bus had smashed into, but was surprisingly clear of debris. Danny thought this meant someone had likely gotten out of the bus at one point and signed his thoughts to Jon. Jon nodded in agreement, and signed back that it was possible whoever had exited the bus, also could've returned to it. Bypassing the door, Danny and Jon investigated the very front of the bus. Brick debris had piled up in front of it, maintaining a shockingly well-preserved, wall-shaped chunk. The bus must have smashed into several displays that also remained clustered there. Danny couldn't get past the wall of junk to see through the windshield. He couldn't help thinking that, based on the bus's position, it had to have been travelling pretty damn fast when it smashed into the wall. The building was probably what saved it from toppling over onto its side, because there was no way a bus like this could take that sharp of a corner and remain upright. They would probably find some very dark skid marks marring the road on the other side.

Moving back to the front door, Jon and Danny took up positions flanking it. Danny pressed his ear to the wood, listening for any sounds they might not have heard while outside. There was nothing. Nodding to Jon, he stepped back and levelled his pistol at the door. Jon crouched below his firing line, and tested how easy it would be to get into the bus. It turned out to be surprisingly easy. By digging his fingers into the soft rubber seal of the door's edge so that he could yank sideways and by pushing on the center hinge at the same time, he opened it with a scrape and a slight squall that put Danny's teeth on edge. Jon immediately rolled out of the way once it was open, while Danny prepared to fire at anything that might charge its way out. Everything remained still, the only movement coming from the back of the bus where Lenny and Bryce peered around the corner to check on them. Danny flashed them a thumbs up, then quickly returned his hand to his pistol and stepped through the door. Jon was up and following him within seconds, leaving just enough space for Danny to quickly back up an arm's length if need be. In tight places like this, one never knew when a hand was going to reach out of the dark.

The first sight that greeted Danny's eyes was a gross, yet oddly comforting one. His flashlight found the driver slouched dead in his seat, held there by a non-standard harness. A clear circular hole marred the side of his skull, possibly from a gunshot but it could also have been from an ice pick. This told Danny a few things: someone had survived the crash, had the wits about them to make sure the driver wasn't going to turn or to put him down if he already had, and that that person left without a plan to return. If someone living had planned to stay here and use the bus for shelter, they would have moved the rotting disease factor for health purposes. If whoever had left thought to put down the driver, odds were they thought to put down anyone else left on the bus as well, so presumably it was safe. Still, Danny proceeded with extreme caution, understanding that every situation was different, and a broken mind was impossible to read.

Danny stepped farther into the bus. It was obvious to him that people had lived here before it crashed. At the front, where seats once clustered, were a pair of folding cots pressed up against either side, with hammocks hanging above them. This arrangement was then duplicated allowing for eight people to have lived on the bus, assuming they didn't time share the beds, and that none of them were children who could double up. Danny took a few steps forward, his eyes constantly scanning for threats, and then paused. Behind him, he heard Jon give the first set of cots and hammocks a more thorough going over, looking underneath and poking around everything that remained. Danny stepped forward again, and Jon repeated the process with the next set. Just beyond the cots and hammocks was the rear set of doors. Two beams held in place the metal pressed up against them. As his flashlight quickly crawled over the arrangement, Danny saw that it could be dismantled without difficulty from the inside to provide escape. Across from the doors was a metal rack of shelves. They were cleared out, but based on the wires dangling from the ceiling above them, it was likely they had once held the occupants' only electronics.

Danny took his time climbing the few steps at the back of the bus, pausing on each one for a few seconds before continuing. There was a warren of boxes and shelves back there, disturbed and thrown about from the crash. With his heart hammering, Danny made his way through the debris one slow step at a time until he reached the rear wall. Nothing jumped out at him.

"Clear," he breathed out slowly, giving his heart a chance to settle.

"Watch my back for a minute." Jon holstered his weapon and started to scale the metal shelves, bolts having kept them secured to the wall during the crash. At the top, he was able to reach the bus's emergency hatch in the roof. It was meant for passengers to be able to escape should the bus roll onto its side, but now that Danny was looking right at it, he saw that the wiring disappeared out around its edges. Soothing sunlight pierced the darkness of the bus as Jon got the hatch open, only to be blocked off again when he stuck his head and shoulders out through it. After a satisfying look, he came back inside and dropped to the floor of the bus.

"What'd you see?" Danny asked, as the smack of Jon's boots hitting the floor vibrated the bus slightly.

"Nothing, just the other end of the wires. My guess? These people had at least one other vehicle. I'll bet there were solar panels or some such up there, which people forced to walk wouldn't have bothered to take. Also, there's nothing but trash around the beds, no personal items, not blankets or anything. Did you see anything that wasn't junk up there?" Jon gestured to the back of the bus with his head.

"No, just toppled shelves and empty boxes and crates. Someone could have picked over this place before us."

"Maybe. Come on, if we have time, we can take the hammocks and the cots."

Back outside, Danny and Jon swiftly explained what they found, then Lenny and Bryce gave them the good news that they could squeeze the carts around the back.

"If we grab the hammocks and cots, we definitely have to stop at the next safe place," Shaidi told everyone.

"I think we should take them," Jon voted.

Danny agreed, and one by one the others followed suit. Walking to the back of a cart, Danny opened the tool box hanging there and selected a socket wrench he thought would work on the bolts holding the cots to the floor and the hammocks to the frame work. Just in case, he grabbed a few similar sizes so that he wouldn't have to walk back out if he was wrong.

With Bryce joining him this time, Danny returned to the bus, while the others started the process of walking the horses and carts around the back of the bus.

"Think I should grab his boots and check his pockets?" Bryce asked about the driver as Danny set to work. He had selected the right socket wrench the first time.

"Can you do so safely? It looked like there was a lot of blood all over that harness and stuff."

"Maybe not his pockets, but I think I might be able to snag his boots."

"If you think you can, then go for it."

In the end, Bryce managed to get the boots, which were clear of blood, and took the man's socks while he was at it. The hammocks came down without a hitch, consisting of nothing more than fabric cocoons held by chains on either end; they didn't even have spacers on either end to stop the hammocks from curling up around their occupants. Once they were down, Bryce took them and the boots out to the carts while Danny set to work on the cots.

The sound of sliding pebbles caused Danny to pause.

"Bryce? Jon? That you guys?" he spoke hesitantly. His earlier thoughts of being watched came back, so he pulled out his pistol and laid it on the floor beside him, within easy reach, and then locked his eyes on the door as he continued to loosen the bolts. Even if there wasn't a stranger out there, pebbles shifting on their own was a cause for concern when the building the bus had smashed into could collapse at any moment. Danny worked even faster, bruising his fingertips by turning the bolts with them as soon as they were loose enough, his other hand moving onto the next bolt with the socket wrench. When Bryce came back, Danny told him what he had heard. Bryce began using his own fingers to help out, and the two of them hastily freed the cots. Folding them up, they each then carried out a pair and made their way to the other side of the bus where the carts were waiting.

"We better get moving ASAP if we don't want to get hit by that storm," Larson warned them as the cots found places amongst the rest of their haul.

Danny could feel that the wind had picked up and knew what he meant. He climbed up onto the board seat with Larson; Bryce plopped down on the other side. Jon and Lenny were already sitting in the lead cart with Shaidi. With everyone onboard, the horses were encouraged to move at a brisk trot. It was faster, louder, and more dangerous, but they decided to risk it with the thunderheads rolling in. Zombies generally got confused during storms, so they weren't too worried about leading a bunch of them to their next hideout. By sticking to the middle of the road, it was unlikely they would get surprised by something popping out without one of them spotting it before it reached the carts and horses. Other humans were the only real concern, but then they always were, no matter what the circumstances.

They reached their next safe spot ahead of the storm, but only just, as the black clouds became visible from ground level. The sun was still out-racing them, but not by much; it would soon be overtaken, leaving everything in darkness.

"Let's get them inside!" Lenny called out over the increasing wind, moving from the seat to Potato's head.

Danny slipped from his seat as well and grasped the halter of Soot, a drab grey horse who was old and almost deaf. Shaidi had already dropped back to take hold of Spark, the young, energetic buck who stuck by Soot's side like a grandson helping his grandpa. With Jon by Thumper, it was left to Bryce and Larson to go in first, to make sure their space had stayed safe in their absence. Danny watched as they headed a short way down a wide alley to a large shipment door. An easily removed bolt held it closed in place of a lock, and its presence suggested that there was nothing inside. Throwing the door up, Bryce and Larson moved boldly inside, pistols and flashlights clearing the way. The space they were searching didn't have any places to hide, and so they cleared it without delay and waved the others forward.

Danny stood impatiently beside Soot, watching as the other cart was led in. As the sunlight was swallowed, day became night. The wind was roaring now. Soot leaned his old head into it, his barely functioning ears flat against his skull. Beside him, Spark struggled in his harness, wanting to follow the other horses immediately; only Soot's stubborn obedience to the people around them stopped him. Then the sky split open and Danny found himself waterlogged before Jon appeared in the doorway to wave them in. Walking the eager horses into shelter, Danny was not looking forward to their wet stink reeking up the place.

Their safe spot was the back of a furniture store, where display models had at one time been put together and where the boxes of disassembled items were stored. Some time ago, on a previous scavenge, they had moved all the large boxes from the back room to the display floor, leaving a wide, open space. Only a few shelving units remained, pushed up against one wall, and half a dozen couches they had pressed up against the other.

"Let's dry off what we can," Lenny spoke loudly over the hammering rain, his words punctuated by distant thunder. The lightning hadn't reached them yet, but it was on its way.

An assembly line of sorts was created to go through the contents of the second cart and dry off what they could using a stack of towels from the first cart. Only Shaidi neglected to join the line as she dealt with the horses, first freeing Thumper and Potato from the lead cart, and then brushing and to some extent patting dry Spark and Soot as they were released. Danny didn't get to dry himself off until after the second cart had been checked. He had used his damp hands to go through the soggy items, causing the flashlight attached to his wrist to throw erratic light patterns whenever he moved. Anything that needed to be kept dry was bundled up, but with that much rain falling that heavily, it was wise to go through it all and dry off the bottom of the cart to protect the wood.

The horses were free to walk around the space, but they grouped together against the far wall, beside the door that led into the store's front, where they no doubt believed they were the farthest away from the storm.

Once everything was finally laid out to air dry, the flashlights were replaced with lanterns. Danny and Shaidi dried off as best they could with the now damp towels, and then laid their guns down and started stripping them. They wouldn't be able to tell if the powder in their bullets had gotten wet and gone bad, but there was no point in letting any dampness sit in the pistols or rifles. Danny hoped the bullets were fine. Although the Black Box had the necessary equipment to make more, they didn't produce a lot, and it wouldn't do them any good if the bullets were needed before getting home.

With their tasks completed, and the storm roaring overhead with sharp cracks of lightning, there wasn't much to do in the back of the furniture store. Bryce and Larson were playing cards, Jon had placed some pots outside to gather rainwater and was waiting by the door for them to fill, Lenny was lying on a couch, reading a book, while Shaidi plucked some horse-friendly food from their supplies and fed it to the huddling beasts. Danny drifted around for a bit, then helped Jon lift the door and snatch the pots. The water would be used for cooking, drinking, and mopping up horse urine if it got too bad. Once that was done, Larson and Bryce invited them over to play Hearts. Danny wasn't particularly fond of the game, but that was probably because he wasn't very good at it, unlike Bryce. Still, he sat down and joined them to pass the time.

Eventually, Danny found himself on a couch, sprawled out as much as he could be, his eyes closed and his mind drifting. He kept thinking of the bus and wondering what had happened it to. More importantly, he wondered where the people from the bus had gone.

***

The pressure in Danny's bladder and the hunger gnawing at his stomach woke him up. There was a moment of blindness before his eyes picked up the light from a single lantern, burning low near Shaidi and Lenny's couches. Everyone else was asleep. Danny had slept through dinner—no one had bothered to wake him—but near the light he spied a container that held his share. His bladder had to come first, however.

Easing up off the couch, Danny tiptoed his way over to the door that led into the front of the furniture store. It was quieter than the delivery door, and even though the room already smelled of horse shit, Danny preferred it to foul a room where he wasn't sleeping and eating. As he registered the calmness of the horses, still huddled together by the door, he listened for the storm. The crash of thunder had moved on, and if it was still raining, it was no longer hard enough to be heard from inside. Tomorrow they could get moving with the sun, spending some time to cover the carts with tarps and themselves in rain ponchos if needed.

Danny had to feel around for the door handle; the small light was not bright enough. When he did find it and pulled the door open, there was nothing but an inky darkness beyond. With some form of clouds still overhead, there was no light to come in through the front windows, nothing to illuminate the space. A small shudder ran its way up Danny's spine. The front had been barricaded when they first decided to make this a safe spot, but barricades weren't invincible. The others would have checked out the space when they came to relieve themselves, but Danny still found his small hairs standing on end. Stepping part way through the door so that it blocked him from the others should they wake, he unzipped his pants. Normally, he'd relieve himself farther in, but whatever was making him jittery kept him close to the door. When he finished, Danny decided he needed to check out the space in order to make himself feel better. He reached for the flashlight on his wrist and clicked it on, revealing what he had feared and foolishly brushed off.

A man was standing just out of arm's reach, so close that Danny could see the startled expression cross his face, just as, no doubt, one was crossing his own. The man was no one he knew, and as that thought fired through Danny's brain, he yelled at the top of his lungs. As he tried to back through the door, the mysterious man rushed at him, grabbing his shirt and pulling him toward the store's front, past his puddled urine. Shadows moved all around, not all of them cast by the erratic flashlight on Danny's wrist. At the same moment he learned that the man was not alone, the man drove his knee into Danny's stomach, knocking the wind out of him and cutting off his shout of alarm.

It was impossible to know what was happening in the back room as Danny fell to the floor, grappling with the interloper and throwing punches. Horse hooves clattered on the cement floor, people began yelling and screaming, their voices overlapping. There were no gunshots, but was that a good thing or bad? Danny could barely hear himself grunt when his assailant landed a blow against his ribs. He reached for his knife, but someone, not the intruder he was fighting with but someone else, kicked it out of his hand. The pain was sharp, like having a door slam on it, followed by a more crushing force, pinning down his entire arm. Danny heard the roll up door rise; was it his friends escaping, or more attackers getting in? Flailing and struggling against the weight of two men now, Danny tried to get a better look at his assailants, hoping to spy a weak spot. Before he could make out any detail however, a cloth bag was pulled over his head, blocking out what little light there was. Something, probably a fist, struck the side of Danny's head, stunning him.

Is this how I die? Fighting in the dark? Danny thought during the haze. His mind sharpened before his body was ready. Not only was he struggling against the men, but he was struggling against uncooperative limbs. Whoever had attacked him was taking advantage of Danny's current ineffectualness. He felt hands flip him over onto his stomach, and then his arms were wrenched behind his back and roped together. His legs finally started to obey him, but from his belly he couldn't get much kicking force. They were soon tied up as well and Danny felt that he was trussed up like a hog. Shaking his head, he attempted to throw the bag off of it. Light was seeping through the fabric now, as more lanterns and flashlights were lit somewhere. One of his attackers, seeing his attempt to free his head from the bag, bent down and tightly secured some sort of blindfold over where Danny's eyes were, completely blocking out the light.

Things were calming down now. The attackers were panting nearby, talking in whispers that were muffled by Danny's own harsh breathing within the bag.

"Put him with the others," were the first words spoken loud enough for him to make out.

Others? Danny had hoped his friends had escaped, but it appeared not all of them had. Unless these people had kidnapped someone else before him? It was a possibility. Danny wished he could do something, anything, as he was hoisted off the floor, his bound limbs crying out in pain. Had he managed to get the bag off, he might have been able to bite someone, but as things stood, the tightness of the blindfold kept it snug over his face. He was deposited on the floor with a thump, his captors not exactly dropping him, but they weren't being gentle with him either. Danny listened to the sound of a door closing behind him and guessed he was in the employee bathroom based on the smell. It would stink worse in the back room with the horse waste, and there were no other doors in the place, so he was definitely in the bathroom.

"Who else is here?" Danny whispered.

"That you, Danny?" Bryce's voice came from the other side of the room.

"Yeah."

A soft, muffled groan filled the space between them.

"I'm pretty sure that's Lenny," Bryce answered for the groan. "I think I saw him being gagged."

"What about the others?"

"I think they escaped. Jon and Shaidi for sure got outside on horses, but I lost track of Larson. Since they're not in here, I'm betting they got away."

"That's good. Larson wouldn't leave us behind, and Jon is good at planning. He'll figure something out."

"I hope so. What do you think they want with us?"

"Our stuff. What does anyone want these days?"

"Yeah, but why grab us? Lenny kept trying to negotiate with them, and they seemed upset that some of us got out."

Lenny made an indecipherable response.

Danny could think of two reasons off the top of his head, neither of which was good: enslavement and cannibalism. As he lay in the dark, he wondered if he'd see his family again, either those back at the container yard, or the ones who had passed on before him.

***

Danny didn't think he had slept on the bathroom floor; his limbs were far too uncomfortable for it, but his mind had certainly wandered. He had no sense of time, and his arms and legs had gone from being painful, to a strange sort of tingling numbness. A few times he had heard Bryce or Lenny shuffling about, but they had ceased speaking to one another. There wasn't anything more to say for the moment. Beside him, Lenny breathed slowly and heavily, able to use only his nose due to the gag in his mouth. Danny worried about him suffocating. At times, he found himself startled into a more wakeful state, particularly whenever there was sound near the door. Every now and again, one of their captors would walk past, or a few snatches of conversation would drift over, none of it intelligible enough to make out.

When the door finally opened, Danny's heart rate jumped from a resting pulse to that of a racehorse within the span of a few beats, all his senses becoming hyper alert.

"Could you take his gag off?" Bryce asked from the far side of the bathroom. "Please? He's clearly having some difficulty breathing."

Danny heard a grunt in response from whoever entered. More than one set of boots came into the bathroom, and Danny was painfully hoisted up again. He clenched his teeth as hard as he could to keep from crying out, the tingling numbness replaced by shooting stabs. As he was brought out of the bathroom, it didn't sound like the others were coming with him.

After being lowered to the floor again, Danny's binds were cut. His limbs flopped outward, bringing a whole new pain from the sudden release of stiffness and the return of proper blood flow. He was so startled by it, he didn't have time to react before hands were wrapped around his limbs again, and he was placed upright in a chair, probably a dining room chair from the display floor based on the feel. Danny felt his ankles get bound to the legs, while his upper arms were strapped to the back. His lower arms were left oddly free, giving him a chance to rub his sore wrists after his captors were done manhandling him. His fingers traced the grooves left in his skin from the rope and where his flashlight used to be. The sound of footfalls retreated, but Danny got the sense he wasn't alone. He kept his mouth shut, waiting for whoever it was to speak first. In the silence, Danny wondered if he'd be able to remove his own blindfold and suspected he might, but wanted to wait before trying.

A scrape of chair legs on linoleum tiles before him confirmed Danny's thoughts. It also let him know that he was on the display floor somewhere, as it was tiled whereas the backroom was not. Hands untied Danny's blindfold, then pulled the bag off of his head without ever touching him. The sudden light was harsh, making Danny squint as he struggled to adapt as quickly as possible. By the time he could see, the person who had removed his blindfold was sitting down across from him. He was a large man, very tall with broad shoulders, his short blond hair and beard covering unmoving features that included a pair of dull grey eyes. The man's eyes reminded Danny of the storm as it had been rolling in. The light that had blinded him was a lamp sitting on a shelf beside his captor, but there was also a soft grey light from elsewhere. It was morning, and the storm had left behind a blanket of clouds, which now dulled the sunlight coming through the furniture store's windows. Danny and the unknown man stared at one another, waiting for the other to react first.

"What do you know of the bus?" the man finally asked, his voice deep and without emotion.

It was a strange opening question. Had he asked it purely to throw Danny off guard, or was there another purpose behind it? Were his captors the people from the bus? He had already decided the sound he had heard while inside it must have come from these men. How long had he and the others been followed before that?

"Only that it wasn't there the last time we had been through," Danny decided to answer. He gave the man no indication as to when that was, or what destination they had in mind.

"What's your name?" was the second question.

Danny chose not to answer that one.

"Telling me your name will only give me something to call you. I'm Evans."

Danny thought for a moment, but decided he was right. It wasn't like there were databases that could be searched to find people based on things like names. "Danny."

"And your friends?"

"Bryce, and the black one you *gagged* is Lenny."

Evans nodded slowly. "Lenny already told us his name, so thank you for not lying."

The small hairs stood up on the back of Danny's neck, no doubt the desired effect. By telling him he already knew Lenny's name, and by mentioning the bus, Evans was trying to unnerve Danny with a show of knowledge. He was letting Danny know that lying might not be a good idea.

"Where were you going?"

No answer.

"Where were you coming from?"

No answer.

"Why did you kill Wycheck?"

No answer, but this time it was because Danny had no idea what the question meant. It must have shown on his face.

"Oh, right, you wouldn't have learned his name, not from shooting him in the head with a rifle."

"I have no idea what you're talking about," Danny retorted, breaking his silence again.

There was a shuffling of feet behind him. Danny turned his head to look, but couldn't see anyone. Whoever it was, must have been listening from beyond one of the shelving units that flanked them. Evans didn't bat an eye. The man's focus was completely on Danny, to the point where it was unnerving. His voice maintained the same emotionless monotone as he told Danny about someone being shot as it had when asking Danny his name. When Danny returned his full attention back to Evans, the man reached beside him and picked up a pair of boots from the shelf, dropping them at Danny's feet without a word.

Danny studied the boots, trying to make sense of what was happening. Had the boots come from one of their supply carts? It seemed likely, based on the way they were presented to him. But they had gathered several pairs of boots during their scavenging run; what made this pair so special?

"Allow me to jog your memory," Evans continued in that calm tone of his. "Two nights ago, you, with three others and one horse, spent the night in a shop, the kind with the owners' residence above it and a stairwell to the roof. At some point, you decided to beat up and gun down a man as he made his way along the street toward your fake camp a few blocks over. Very clever, the way you laid out the fire so that it would burn and smoulder all night. Tell me, how many others have you fooled with that trick?"

Danny had to reel back his memory to the time Evans was talking about. He remembered the crack of Jon's rifle, the one he was testing, as he fired it from the roof. Jon had shot a zombie in the street, and they had taken its boots afterward.

"I see you remember now," Evans commented on some change that must have occurred on Danny's face or in his eyes.

"We didn't shoot a man, we shot a zombie," Danny defended their actions.

The scuffling happened beyond the shelves again. Whoever was listening, was upset. Evans still didn't acknowledge it, but was shaking his head at Danny.

"We know that's not the truth."

"But it is!" Danny didn't like being accused of murder and found he couldn't hold his tongue. "We had recently found a rifle that needed to be tested, so we tested it on a zombie that was shuffling down the street."

"Liar!" a pissed-off voice shouted from beyond the shelves.

This time Evans responded by turning his head toward the outburst, shifting his weight so that his chair creaked. There was some more scuffling from over there, and another voice or two shushing the one that had cried out. Danny had no idea how many people were listening in and found himself frightened by the prospect of being lynched.

Evans returned his gaze to Danny. "Tell me about the others."

"What others?" Danny assumed he meant Jon, Shaidi, and Larson, but he wasn't going to say anything about them.

"Carol, Hector, Lee, Moore, Millia. Of course, I wouldn't expect you to know their names either."

"I have no idea what you're talking about." Danny was now even more confused. It sounded like he was being blamed for more murders.

The scuffling and murmuring behind the shelves got worse. The small hairs on Danny's arms stood on end as gooseflesh crawled along his skin.

"You stabbed them."

"What?" Danny would have stood in outrage had he been able. "We would never do such a thing!"

Someone from the group of listeners had finally had enough. Danny had no chance to defend himself, before the back of his head was struck. He was stunned, and the world spun as he held tightly to consciousness, darkness creeping into the edges of his vision. The last thing he saw before the black bag and blindfold were returned, was Evans' expressionless face.

***

Danny had been returned to the bathroom, still bound to the chair, and Lenny had been removed. Someone stayed in the bathroom this time, so that when Bryce tried to ask Danny what had happened, he received a threat about his teeth being kicked in. Danny's head pounded as he sat there. Again, he might have been able to remove his blindfold and the bag, but decided against it. Not just because of the guard who was present, but if the blow to the back of his head had broken the skin, the blindfold felt like it was in the right spot to be applying pressure. Later, Lenny was returned, now also strapped to a chair by the sounds of it, and Bryce was removed. Lenny no longer breathed heavily around a gag, but that was all Danny could tell about his condition.

Time passed in darkness, with Danny doing his best not to throw up. He still felt dizzy from the strike and hoped that no permanent brain damage had been done. It was possible he had a concussion.

Bryce wasn't returned to the bathroom. Instead, he and Lenny were hauled back out. The jostling movement as he was carried on a crooked angle, made Danny feel even more nauseous. He wanted to focus on where he was being carried, but not puking required all his attention. Had he actually eaten last night, he probably wouldn't have been able to hold it in.

Eventually, he was stopped, upright, and potentially outside. The air smelt like outdoors, and there was a sense of space. With a rattling jerk, he began moving again, and once he identified the sound of horses' hooves, he realized he was on the back of a cart. Unable to sit in darkness any longer, Danny reached for his blindfold and bag. Tucking his head down so low made his mind swim dangerously for a moment, but Danny was able to grasp both pieces of fabric and pull them off. The bright, white sunlight passing through the overcast sky stung his eyes, but again he adjusted to the light as swiftly as he was able.

Looking around, Danny assessed his situation. He, Lenny, and Bryce were all strapped to chairs facing backward on the rear end of a cart that was much larger than their own. Behind the cart, facing them, was a scarred mug Danny hadn't seen before, watching his movements without comment. The horse he rode was unfamiliar, as were the two to either side of the cart's rear, with still more strangers riding them. Lenny started to remove his own blindfold; Bryce didn't have one. It seemed Bryce had taken the brunt of these men's anger to his face, which was swelling and turning various shades of purple. His lip was split and bleeding, and as he looked back at Danny across Lenny, his tongue darted out to lick the wound. Behind the unknown horseman, Danny saw the front of the furniture store slowly receding. He had no idea where they were going. Twisting in his chair, he attempted to look ahead. The cart he was in was definitely larger than the ones he and his group had brought along, and was loaded down with supplies, all packed in a way that kept the contents safe from the weather. It seemed like a more permanent packing job than their own carts, and contained nothing that suggested the supplies were being brought to a camp. On either side of the cart, elderly sat upon running boards, a few of them eyeing Danny and the others suspiciously. It was hard to see beyond the front of the cart, but Danny suspected that one of their own was ahead of them. There were also more people walking along up ahead.

"Danny," Bryce hissed, drawing his attention back around to him.

Lenny was already leaning toward the younger man conspiratorially. Danny did the same, eyeing the horse riding guard behind them, but the scarred man didn't seem to care.

"They have our map," Bryce told them.

Suddenly, Danny knew where they were headed. As vertigo struck him again, he looked back at the guard, this time specifically focusing on the rifle he carried.

12
Abby's Worried

Stretching her sore muscles, Abby took a brief break from her work to look at the storm heading toward them. They hadn't been able to finish the field the day before and were now trying to complete it ahead of the rains. If they didn't, it meant working in the mud later on, which would cause a severe drop in their volunteer numbers. Abby suspected that Lauren would be one of the dropouts, although Abby found herself enjoying the exercise and wouldn't mind getting dirty.

They worked for hours, the storm clouds moving closer and closer, until they could see the sheets of rain pouring out of them. All the other field workers had packed up and moved inside. Most of the guards who didn't have sheltered watch spaces had abandoned their posts, with a few remaining to watch over the volunteers. Several had even pitched in to help, everyone working like mad beasts to beat the rain. Working near the fence now, they ditched the wheelbarrows; the close proximity of the fence made it faster to carry the rocks as soon as they were pulled up.

Finally, Abby's row was done and she turned to help the people in the row next to her. As that one was finished, she and those volunteers looked for any other rows where they could assist. When no more rows appeared in need of help, Abby finally took a short pause. She gazed out through the fence, toward where she had picked up the boy in the field. Throughout the day, she had thought about him, wondering how he was doing and whether he had woken up yet. Crichton was managing that whole affair, which meant that rumours were many while facts were few.

When every row was complete, the volunteers rushed to gather up their supplies and headed as fast as they could for the nearest entrance. The wind was at their backs, hurrying them along just that much faster. The guards who didn't have trains, or cars, or shipping containers to watch from kept pace at the back, making sure no one fell behind. The rains were nipping at their heels, and by the time everyone had crammed into the stairwell, several people were completely drenched: specifically those who had to drop off the supplies in a nearby storage shed. Most of the volunteers flooded down the steps, but Abby joined Lauren and a few others who were taking a brief break on the large upper landing. The door was still open, protected from the wind in an alcove and under an overhang, so that they could watch as the water pummelled their hard work and attempted to drown their crops. In no time at all, it became too dark to continue watching, and so the door was pulled shut, cutting off what wind had been getting in.

"Well that was fun," Lauren laughed.

"I've got bruises on top of bruises," Abby commented as she pulled off her work gloves. Labouring at what felt like break-neck speed, she had stopped being careful, frequently scraping her knuckles or stubbing her fingers. Looking at her hands now, it appeared the gloves had done their job and none of the skin was broken.

"Yeah, I got a pretty good scrape," Lauren held up her arm to show Abby the angry red welt along her forearm.

"Oh," Abby made a sound that was half-distress and half-sympathy as she inspected her partner's injury.

"It's not that bad," Lauren told her, gently removing her arm from Abby's hands once she had had a long enough look. "It's not like I did this or anything," she playfully swatted the scar on Abby's forearm.

"I pray you never do." Abby smiled as they turned to head downstairs. They joined the trickle of stragglers, most of whom were people who had gotten wet and had paused on the upper landing to wring out their clothes and hair. Both Abby and Lauren held onto the railings as they walked, being careful to avoid the puddles left behind by those ahead of them. Slipping and falling on concrete steps would make their work-related injuries look like nothing.

When the pair reached the landing to their floor, Lauren opened the door but Abby stopped, looking farther down. Lauren noticed her pause and, while standing in the open doorway, figured out what she was thinking about.

"I'm sure the boy's fine. Crichton's watching him like a hawk, and the doctors are taking care of him. He's probably already awake and just being questioned before he's allowed to join the rest of us."

"That's what I'm worried about." Abby turned to her with a small, forced smile. "Crichton can be a little intense."

"He has to be, what with all that's happened to us." Lauren took her hand and guided Abby into the hallway, continuing to hold it as they walked along.

"I know. It's silly of me to worry."

"It's because you saved him, you feel responsible for him. I understand. Remember how I was, once we got all those kids with foster parents on the Diana? I kept hovering, making sure they were okay, that they were happy and that their new caretakers were doing their jobs right."

"I remember you wondering if you should set up a program, where you'd go to visit each kid at their new place once a week. You thought they'd all be miserable without you." Abby laughed, although it wasn't the unkind type. Lauren and she had frequently laughed about it in the past, as it was the best way to deal with it.

"Of course, once the kids were settled, they got annoyed with my constant popping up. Remember Robbie telling me to get lost?"

"Of course I remember. You kept checking to make sure he was eating all right."

"Well, he wasn't a very good eater when I had to take care of him. He pulled the 'you're not my mom' card, and that's when I knew the kids weren't my responsibility anymore. At least not those kids."

They had rounded a bend, reaching the hallway where their living quarters were situated. Ahead, in front of their door, Claire was sitting on the floor with some of her friends, gabbing away. They fell quiet once they spotted Abby and Lauren. It was nice to know teenagers never changed, even if it was annoying as hell at times.

"Did you get caught in the storm?" Claire asked as they approached.

"Some did, but we managed to get in just ahead of it," Lauren told her.

"Is it as bad as it looked?"

"It's pretty bad, yeah. We're going to have to do a lot of clean up tomorrow."

"Did you get the field done, though?"

"Sure did, and I think our clothes paid for it." Abby looked down at herself. Not only did she have several dirt and grass stains, but a few new tears as well. An especially big one had her right knee exposed. "We should probably clean up."

"You going to be in for dinner?" Lauren asked Claire.

"Yeah." And with that confirmed, it was obvious Claire was done talking to them and hoped they would disappear once more. She was old enough to consider moving out on her own now, but having people cook for her and clean up after her were so far keeping her home. Abby was only too happy to head into the apartment space, looking forward to a nice hot shower. All her muscles were sore in unusual ways and starting to stiffen up.

Entering the suite of rooms, Abby immediately spotted Riley sitting on their couch, slouching forward, and could tell by the sounds that Hope and Peter were playing in his room with the door closed. Even Peter was at an age where he preferred the adults to not completely know what he was up to with his limited number of friends.

"Who's showering first, you or me?" Lauren asked.

"You go ahead," Abby told her, casting a quick look in Riley's direction. Lauren understood with a nod, and disappeared into the bathroom. It took only seconds for the sound of rushing water to seep through the door.

Abby made her way over to the couch and perched on the armrest, so as not to get any dirt on Riley's bedding.

"Hey, Riley," she opened with, prepared to gauge the other woman's response. Abby knew there was something wrong the moment she had walked in and Riley didn't turn to see who was entering.

"Hi, Abby, do you need something?" It took her that entire sentence to turn her head and look up at Abby's face.

"Just wondering how you're feeling. You look a little distant."

Riley nodded. "Just thinking, is all. We were supposed to be home by now. Not that I don't like visiting you, and the hot water is especially nice." She tilted her head in the bathroom's direction.

"It's just not home, anymore," Abby finished for her. "I get it. I mean, you guys left here for a reason. Is there anything else on your mind? Maybe I can help."

"Have you read many medical papers?" Riley asked with a weak smile, already betting she knew the answer.

"Sorry, no. I can tell you about the history of Spain, if you'd like." That drew out the more genuine smile that Abby had been hoping for. "There a patient you're worried about?"

"Always. I've been wracking my brain trying to remember everything I learned, all the papers and studies I've read. I feel I'm missing something, that there's more I could be doing." Riley flopped backward against the back of the couch, her head coming to rest on top of it so that she stared up at the ceiling.

"Have you talked to the other doctors?"

Riley dipped her chin several times. "I wish I could talk to Dr. Anderson."

"Who's Dr. Anderson?" Abby wasn't sure she had heard that name before, which likely meant she hadn't.

"He was the lead attending when I worked in the ER: my mentor. He got bitten on the Day, before we knew what was happening. I don't know what happened to him after that. He probably evacuated with Lauren and the others, but I don't know what they would have done once they learned he was bitten."

Abby didn't know if she should tell Riley or not, but after a moment's hesitation, decided the truth was better than several things her friend could imagine. "Lauren told me that when they discovered someone was infected, they put them outside the walls and wouldn't let them back in. Some fought and had to be driven farther away, while others stayed nearby, crying to be let back in. But apparently, most of them accepted it and walked off, or at least thought they were fine and that there was somewhere better to go."

"Anderson would have walked off," Riley decided instantly. "He would have gotten as far away as he could, so that when he turned, he wouldn't be near anybody."

Abby watched as her friend continued to stare at the ceiling. She remembered Riley's depression, when she would lock herself away for days. Only her daughter, her sister, and her sister's recently adopted daughter were allowed near her, and that was only because they were sharing the room with her.

"What would you like for dinner?" Abby changed the subject, adding a lightness to her voice as she playfully swatted Riley's arm.

"You know, I've forgotten what having meal choices is like." Riley lifted her head and turned to Abby with a smile. "I'm so used to community food."

"Come on, then. We don't have much of a selection, but it's better than nothing. Whatever you want, we'll cook."

"Mind if I cook, actually? I haven't done any cooking since God knows when."

"Yeah, not at all."

"Just let me know what portions of your rations I should use. Actually, you should probably just monitor the whole process, as I was never much of a cook to begin with." Riley laughed at herself.

Getting up off the couch, the two of them walked over to the little kitchen area. As they looked through the cupboards and fridge, the sound of the running shower was replaced by a hairdryer. Riley picked out what they would have for dinner, and the ingredients were laid out. It was still too early to start dinner, but that was fine because Abby really wanted to shower first. As soon as Lauren had vacated the bathroom, her wild hair having taken a considerable amount of time to blow dry, Abby ducked in. As she stood beneath the hot cascade of water, she wondered if Riley had told her the entire truth. She also found herself wondering about the boy again.

***

"I am stuffed," Hope declared as she leaned back in her seat.

"We definitely cooked more of your rations than we should have," Riley said while giving Abby a bit of a frown.

"It's fine. We just prepared a new field, remember? We're going to be growing even more food soon. Besides, you're our guests; we're allowed to spoil you."

"We should have guests over more often," Claire joked. "What do you think, Hope? Want to become a permanent guest?"

"If we can always eat like this, yeah!"

"But I don't want to share my room *forever*," Peter grumped, his social awkwardness causing him to miss out on the joke.

"Hope's not moving in permanently, love," Lauren consoled him, rubbing his back.

"I don't think we'll be staying too much longer," Riley told everyone at the table. "If it weren't for the storm, we most likely would have left by now."

"Well, you're going to be stuck with us a bit longer." Abby got up and began clearing away the dishes. "After a storm like that one, we might need to repair the dock again. Hopefully, the boats were properly secured on shore this time. Remember the last big storm, when they either washed out to sea or got scattered across the fields?"

"I remember having to slog through muck to get a bunch of paddles that were sticking up out of it," Claire said, nodding, a look of disgust on her face. "I lost a shoe that day."

"Well, you did volunteer for it," Lauren reminded her.

"Only because Leelo dared me to. It makes a good argument against volunteering."

"But we're all going to volunteer tomorrow," Abby told her family as she returned to her seat. "Right?" She looked specifically at Peter, who so rarely helped out with physical tasks.

"Well if we're stuck here, we'll volunteer too, right mom?" Hope looked to Riley.

"Of course we will," Riley nodded.

"We can find something to volunteer for together, Peter." Hope turned back to her friend, getting him to nod his consent. Abby had enjoyed having Hope over. She was able to bring Peter out of his shell in ways that she, Lauren, and even Claire couldn't.

A knock at the door interrupted any further conversation.

"I'll get it." Claire shot to her feet, nearly tipping her chair over backward in the process. She didn't exactly run to the door, but she didn't walk at a normal pace either. By opening it only a crack, Abby couldn't see who was there or hear what brief words were exchanged. "It's for you." Claire turned away from the door. "Abby," she clarified.

Claire still didn't hold the door open enough for her to see, so Abby had to get up and walk over to find out who was there. She had no idea who would come by at dinner. Taking the door from Claire, she pulled it open enough for the others at the table to see as well, Claire taking the opportunity to return to her seat.

"Crichton," Abby didn't so much greet him as express her surprise to see him. What was even more surprising was the boy standing shyly at his heel, staring at their feet. It was the boy that Abby and James had rescued. Abby couldn't see much of him around Crichton, but she could see how frightfully thin he was. The clothes he wore were newer than what he had come in wearing, the shorts and T-shirt hanging off his bony frame.

"I'm sorry to bother you at dinner," Crichton apologized, glancing past Abby at those gathered around the table.

"That's all right, we already finished and were just talking. What's up?" Abby couldn't stop looking at the boy. One of his shoes, also recently donated, was untied. She felt an urge to bend down and fix it.

"I've been informed that the storm has abated enough for us to go out and assess the damage. It's too late to do any actual cleanup, but we can task what needs doing and check on the guards who remained out there. I was hoping that in the meantime, you could give Journey here, a tour of the Black Box."

"Journey?"

"That's what he told me his name is."

Abby knelt down so that she was level with the boy. "Journey is certainly a unique name."

His dark eyes darted up to her face and then returned to the floor just as quickly. He mumbled something that Abby couldn't quite make out.

"Pardon? I didn't quite catch that."

"Some people used to call me Jo," he mumbled slightly louder.

"Would you rather be called Jo?"

The boy shrugged, and then after a second's hesitation, he nodded.

"It's nice to meet you, Jo, I'm Abby." Abby held out her hand.

The boy looked at it, but didn't offer his in return.

Still smiling for him, Abby returned her hand to her side, understanding he must be afraid. "How old are you, Jo?"

He didn't give any response to the question.

"We don't think he knows," Crichton answered for him. "As much as I've been able to get him to answer, I don't think he's been educated or even knows what 'age' is. He knows seasons, but not years."

Abby nodded in understanding. Since the beginning, the people she'd been with had done their best to educate the younger generation, but even they had their difficulties with what they should be teaching. Other groups out there could easily be having it rougher, education forced to take a backseat to pure survival. Abby guessed that, based on his name, he had been born post-Day to a group that kept on the move, although she accepted it was possible he was older and that the name had been given to him, in much the same way that Lauren had to name Peter.

"So what do you think, Jo? Would you like it if I showed you around?"

Jo shrugged again and this time didn't add a nod.

Abby stood back up and faced Crichton. "Just give me a minute to let the others know."

"Go ahead."

Abby returned to the dining table; meanwhile, the door attempted to swing shut until Crichton put his foot in the way.

"What's going on?" Riley asked first.

"The boy that showed up outside our fences the day you got here is awake now. Crichton wants to go topside and check out the storm damage, so he asked me to show him around in the meantime."

"What do you know about him? Do you want me to come with you?" Lauren asked this time. She had dealt with all sorts of children in shock and suffering from various forms of abandonment issues after the Day and had learned a thing or two about handling them.

"No, I think I'll be all right on my own. He might remember me helping to bring him in, and I don't want to surround him with too many people too quickly. His name is Journey, although he's usually called Jo. Outside of that, Crichton didn't tell me much. Poor kid doesn't even know how old he is. Crichton thinks he might not understand what years are."

Lauren shook her head sadly, while Claire lifted her legs up onto her seat and pulled them tight against her chest. After being the lone survivor of her family, thanks to Abby, Lauren, and Jon, she was sympathetic towards all kids.

"Is he expected to stay here overnight?" Riley wondered.

"He could share with Peter and Hope or he could share my room with me," Claire immediately volunteered.

Abby smiled at her. "I don't think so; Crichton didn't mention anything like that. I should get going."

Lauren got up and walked around the table to her partner. They embraced, and briefly pecked each other on the lips.

"Yuck, grown-up stuff," Hope commented, which set her and Peter to giggling with one another.

"Be careful, okay?" Lauren whispered. "We don't know anything about him."

"When has anyone not been careful these days? But I understand," she whispered back, then turned to the table. "I should be back before bedtime," Abby spoke directly to Peter. Abby always tried to be in when Peter went to bed. It was when he was the most willing to talk, telling both Lauren and Abby about his day or how he was feeling. He kept a notebook in his room in which he always wrote first—his script both tiny and neat—to work out his thoughts, and then relayed his findings to his parents.

"Bye, Mum," he answered quietly.

Abby separated from Lauren and returned to the door.

"You ready?" Crichton asked when she pulled it the rest of the way open.

"I think it's better to ask Jo if he's ready." Abby smiled for the boy.

He glanced up at her and then back down at the floor. He gave a mumbled, unintelligible response.

"I think that means he is," Crichton commented as Abby left her apartment, letting the door swing closed behind her. "I'm going up top now. I'll come find you afterward."

"All right. Hopefully it's not too bad up there."

"Hopefully." With that, Crichton headed for the nearest exit.

"So, Jo, where should we start?" Abby didn't expect him to answer and was proven right. "How about right here, then? This level, as well as the two levels above us and three levels below us are all apartments. Here, they consist of a main living space that includes a kitchen, and three bedrooms with one bathroom, while on some other levels they may have fewer bedrooms. I don't know if you know this already or not, but we have hot and cold running water here. Have you ever taken a hot shower?"

The boy didn't answer.

"You'll probably get to check out an apartment more thoroughly later. Let's go look at something more exciting." Abby led Jo toward the stairwell. Always thinking about what Lauren said, she never let Jo drift behind her, keeping him in her peripheral vision at all times.

The hallways were noisier than usual. With everyone kept in because of the storm, several people had propped open their doors to wander between their apartments and their neighbours'. A few groups had formed on the floors, mostly kids and teenagers who didn't want to hang out near adults. Some looked up as Abby and Jo passed by, recognizing that there was a new face in the facility, but none of them reacted fearfully, just curiously.

"So, this is one of the stairwells," Abby told Jo as they stepped into it. "There are three throughout the Black Box. I'll try to show you where all of them are, although it'll probably take you awhile to get a handle on the layout. Two stairs reach the surface above, while the third only makes it to the top level. There is also an elevator not far from that staircase, and it goes to the surface. Now, we try not to use the elevator too often so that those who need it, aren't waiting forever, but if you get tired, let me know and we'll use it."

Abby decided to show Jo the upper levels first, so that if he got tired, at least they'd be heading down.

"You may have noticed the coloured lines and the arrows in here as well as on the walls of the hallways," she spoke as they climbed. "Each level has a different coloured floor, and the lines and arrows help you get to where you're going. Of course, you have to memorize the floor colour of where you're trying to get to in order to use the system, but even if you don't, it'll help you find a stairwell."

On the very top level, they came to the hydroponics labs. Abby smiled when Jo's eyes widened at the sight of all the plants. Abby always enjoyed visiting the hydroponics labs, as they reminded her of the greenhouse back at Riley's cabin, which was the first place she found herself able to think clearly after the Day. The labs were a little more crowded than usual, with people trapped inside because of the storm who came here to enjoy the false sunlight. Abby led Jo into the nearest lab, letting him look at the special light fixtures, troughs, and plants.

"What's this one?" he'd ask as they passed certain plants, seeming to take a genuine interest. Abby would smile every time she answered him.

After leaving the hydroponics, she took Jo all throughout the Black Box. They entered the computer server farm that was pretty much useless these days, but didn't stop long as there wasn't much to see. Next came the large space used for meetings and for when large groups wanted to dine together, followed by the extra food storage that was still without a completely functional cooling system; every time one thing was fixed, something else broke, and right now it was basically just an ice block. Several people thought that the server farm's air conditioning should be turned back on so that they could use that space as cold storage. Past the apartment levels, Abby showed him the medical centre, which he had probably seen already but took a bit more of an interest in anyway. Farther down was the small computer lab where Abby often worked, and below that were some classrooms that doubled as a day-care centre. The classrooms were used infrequently, mostly by children who were being taught one-on-one by their parents and guardians, but they were good for small meetings, like discussing planned expansions. On the next level down was the security office, where video feeds from some cameras were monitored, and their extra weapons and ammo were locked up.

"Why are some floors larger than other floors?" Jo observed.

"Do you mean the spacing between them or the square footage?" Immediately after she said it, Abby wondered if Jo even understood what square footage meant.

"Both," he replied whether he knew or not.

"No one here was involved in building this place, so we don't know. Best guess? They built whatever space they needed. I guess that's an advantage to digging through solid rock, if you need a floor to be bigger, just dig outward more. There's also a lot of buried wiring, pipes, and ductwork that we can't see. I'm not an engineer, so I don't know much about it. Speaking of which, we've reached the water treatment facility."

Jo was curious about the water treatment, but Abby didn't have much information for him. She had never taken the time to learn about it herself. Based on what she knew aboard the Diana, the Black Box probably ran much the same way, in that it cleaned and recycled the water that was used, while desalinating water brought in from the river.

"Last level," Abby announced as they reached the next door.

"But the stairs keep going," Jo observed.

"All you'll find down there is a heavy, metal door. It's where our power is generated. Only a few people have a key, and I'm not one of them."

"Does Crichton have a key?"

"I'm not entirely sure who has a key, as there aren't many. Come on." Abby led the boy through the door for the floor they were on.

Beyond it was a large cement room supported by several pillars along its length. A few people were jogging around the vast room, and a group of kids were playing soccer in the middle. Some teenagers were gathered around a Ping-Pong table, the sound of a small plastic ball being swatted back and forth echoing off the ceiling and floor, joining the calls of the soccer kids, and the many slapping of many running feet.

"This used to be a garage, but now we use it as an exercise and games space, as well as a library." Abby pointed out a bunch of equipment stored at one end, a few card tables and a pitiful stack of games and puzzles next to their bookcases. "It gets the most use during rainy days like today, when it's better to stay indoors."

"There are no cars." Jo frowned.

"This place was almost abandoned when we got here. There are a few though. If you come this way, you might be able to spot them beyond the pillars."

"I like cars. Can we go see them?"

"I don't see why not." Abby led Jo across the space, avoiding the joggers and the kids' soccer game. When a goal was scored between two of the pillars, the cheers of the team ricocheted around the space, becoming even louder than normal. The goalie that had been scored on then had to chase down the ball. Any nets that would have been large enough to span the distance between the pillars, were either used on Animal Island or as fishing nets.

Jo ran over to the cars once they were in sight, his small hands slapping onto the dusty hood of the nearest vehicle. When Abby caught up to him, she noticed he was out of breath. Although he hadn't said anything, the tour was clearly wearing him out.

"Is that how they got down here?" he asked, pointing to a massive, gated elevator shaft that all the cars had been pushed up against.

"Yes. We don't use that elevator though, as it only goes between here and the surface. Maybe if we had to bring in something large we would, but we've never needed to."

"Do you know who owns these cars?"

"Most of them, I think." Abby began to tell him what she knew about the cars, answering what she could and giving him the names of people who would know the answers she didn't have. She was fairly certain that all the cars belonged to the people who had been living in the Black Box before the Diana residents arrived and that they were all still here, none of them choosing to move to the container yard.

What Abby didn't notice was that Journey wasn't really all that interested in the vehicles. He had tons of questions, but wasn't paying that much attention to the answers. Whenever Abby wasn't looking at him, Jo's eyes were locked on the giant elevator shaft, studying its size, and trying to estimate where it might come out on the surface.

13
Doyle's Bored

The storm pounded on the shingles overhead; the wind howled through every crack and crevice. From out in the hallway came the *spat, spat, spat* of a leak in the roof dripping onto the carpet. Doyle sat on the bedroom window's wide sill, looking out into the rain. It had become dark as night out there, and by the time the storm abated, it probably would be. He hadn't counted on this rain when he decided to make this trip to the bookstore, and he hadn't counted on the zombie horde they had to make a detour around the day before. Both had certainly slowed them down.

Behind him in the room, James was cleaning his weapons by candle light, Rose was doing yoga, and Canary was playing with a yo-yo she had found in the kid's room next to this one. She was pretty good at it, doing various tricks and practising the ones she screwed up. Doyle turned away from the window and watched her for a bit; the little plastic thing whizzed through the air.

"Did you happen to see any board games or anything like that in the kid's room?" he eventually asked.

"Didn't really look," Canary shrugged, her eyes never leaving the yo-yo. "I just checked that the room was clear and happened to notice this on the desk by the door."

"I'm going to go look." Pressing his hands on his knees, Doyle heaved himself up onto his feet.

"Scream if you need anything," Canary joked.

Doyle went to the door and squeezed his way out past the bed. To create more room, they had upended it, and leaned it against the wall near the door so that they could use it as a barricade come nightfall. Based on the simple décor of the room in which they were squatting, it had formerly been a guest room. Seemed fitting, although they weren't really guests.

In the hallway, Doyle avoided the ceiling leak and went into the kid's room. He assumed it was a boy's room based on the faded blue walls and scattering of robot toys that his flashlight illuminated. Over the bed, which hadn't been occupied by the boy in a very long time, a poster had come loose at the top and flopped down over the headboard. Out of curiosity, Doyle went over and lifted it, checking out what image it bore. The poster was for *The Night of the Living Dead*. Doyle shook his head and let it flop back down. It was strange to remember that people used to get enjoyment out of this stuff. Living it was vastly different from watching it on some screen. It was painful, stressful, disgusting, and, occasionally, deathly boring. Things weren't wrapped up after two hours, you didn't get to go back home with a belly full of popcorn, talk about what the characters should have done, and sleep in your nice, cozy bed, feeling safe and secure. Instead, you did things like search a boy's room—one who was probably dead—for a game to pass the time, and if something happened, if you fucked up, there were no rewrites or alternate endings to save you. Just because you're the most important person in your own life, doesn't mean you survive until the end. There is no end.

Doyle managed to locate some boxes that looked like board games in the dark gloom of the kid's closet. Banishing his thoughts to the recesses of his mind, he pulled out the oldest and most beat up looking one in the hopes that it wasn't some newer game that no one had heard of, forcing them to read the rules before they could play. Careful not to topple over anything else, he pulled it from the pile. He chuckled when he read the name of the game he had chosen and carried it back to the spare room.

"Did you find something?" Canary asked, her eyes darting to the box in Doyle's hand.

"Yeah. This seemed oddly appropriate." He held up the box so that everyone could see. In his hands, was *The Game of Life*.

Rose read the box and laughed hard enough to wobble out of her tree pose.

"I figure none of us can live a life like the ones found in this game, so why not play it?" Doyle moved to the center of the room and sat down on the carpet, where he was swiftly joined by Canary and Rose.

James took a little longer, first drawing the curtains so that when he moved the candle from the corner in which he had been working—a corner he had carefully set up to block the light from reaching the window—nothing outside would be able notice them. While Doyle and the women set up the board, James reassembled his weapons and stowed them away.

They had barely started the game before everyone agreed that the spinner in the middle was uncomfortably loud, even with the storm outside. Doyle returned to the kid's room and picked up all of the game boxes this time. Back in the guest room, they pilfered some dice from another game, which were much quieter when rolled on the carpet. They also chose a few games they could play after this one. James seemed pretty keen on *Monopoly*.

As the darkness of the storm gave way to the darkness of night, the group ate some rations from their packs while they played. Despite having to whisper, everyone appeared to have fun with the board games,

Rose and James forming a rivalry in everything they played, while Canary just couldn't seem to win, but frequently came in second.

"We should bring some of these back with us; we don't have nearly enough games back home," Canary suggested.

"That's a good idea," Doyle nodded. "We should try to reduce the number of boxes we end up carrying. We should check the kitchen to see if there are plastic baggies we can put the pieces in, and maybe some rubber bands to hold down the box lids."

"Once we're done this; I'm about to win." Rose rolled the dice, then groaned quietly when she still didn't land where she needed to.

The game continued for several more rounds until Rose finally got what she needed and put everyone else out of their misery, as they were all doing terribly.

"All right, I'm going downstairs. Who wants to come with me?" Doyle got to his feet, his knees popping unexpectedly.

"I'll come with you," Canary stood as well.

"I think I'll stay here and set up our sleeping mats." James looked over at their nearby gear.

"I'll keep James company," Rose spoke as she began to clean up the game they had just finished.

"All right, let's go then." Doyle stepped over the board and headed to the door, taking his fire axe in hand along the way. Canary stayed close to his back as they exited the guest room.

Hugging the wall to avoid the leak, they made their way down the hall in the darkness. At the top of the stairs, Doyle reached for his flashlight, but was stopped when Canary's hand tightly grasped his wrist. Facing her, Doyle could just make out her facial features beneath her nearly luminous white-blonde hair. She had the index finger of her other hand pressed to her lips. Doyle hadn't heard anything, but trusted her judgement, gripping his axe tighter.

He descended the stairs, pausing each time his foot was planted until Canary tapped his shoulder for him to continue. Three steps from the bottom, Canary took longer to tap his shoulder. Doyle strained to hear anything over the pattering of light rain upon the roof, but couldn't. There was only the breath in his lungs and the lighter breathing from Canary behind him. He could also make out a few shuffling sounds from Rose and James back in the guest room, but knew that Canary wouldn't mistake those for anything else. Then she tapped his shoulder again and they continued to the ground floor. Their slow descent gave his eyes plenty of time to adjust to the gloom.

At the bottom of the stairs was the front door by which they had entered, with a couch shoved across it to make up for the now-broken lock. Doyle studied the darkness of the nearby sitting room, as well as the hall that led to the kitchen, dining room, and living room at the rear of the house. Canary perched on the couch at Doyle's back, looking out into the rain through the door's glass panel.

This time Doyle heard it. He couldn't identify the sound, but he heard something that hadn't come from them or from the two upstairs. Whatever it was, it came from the rear of the house, not the front. Using hand signals, Doyle and Canary agreed to split up momentarily. Canary headed down the hallway, with an iron grip on a long, sharpened screwdriver in her left hand and the rifle she had borrowed from James in her right, while Doyle drifted into the sitting room. His eyes scanned the windows, confirming they were all closed and intact. Nothing looked like it had been shifted, and he couldn't see any damp spots an intruder would have left coming in from the rain.

At the back of the sitting room, he pushed slowly through a swing door into the kitchen. The only window in there was a hole cut through one wall that looked into the hallway. Doyle and Canary made eye contact through it, nodding that each was okay. Canary carefully finished closing the door to the closet under the stairs, which she had just poked around in, and moved forward toward the opening that led into the dining room. Doyle circled the large kitchen, checking out both sides of the island. He was no longer thinking about finding plastic baggies and rubber bands. At the end of the kitchen, a wide breakfast counter abutting a pillar separated it from the giant living room. Doyle waited at the end of the counter, next to the pillar, watching Canary's fair hair move about the dining room across the hall. She walked all the way around the table, sweeping beneath it and the chairs with the end of her rifle, then gave Doyle another thumbs up.

Doyle stepped into the living room from the hallway; Canary pushed through another swing door at the far end of the dining room. They entered the large space together, hastily scanned all the hiding places and scoped out the windows, then jabbed at the deeper shadows to make sure they weren't concealing anything. Everything looked fine. Canary pointed to the door that opened onto the basement steps, her eyebrows raised in a question. Doyle was about to nod that they should investigate it, when they heard the sound again. It had come from behind the house.

Keeping to the deeper shadows, Doyle made his way toward the sliding glass door, while Canary headed for a long, skinny window next to the TV on the other end of the room. Even with his face pressed to the glass, Doyle couldn't see much of the backyard; almost no light was able to penetrate the cloud cover overhead.

They heard the sound again. It was some sort of rattle, definitely coming from outside. Doyle gritted his teeth, frustrated that he couldn't tell if it was a soft sound close in or a louder sound farther away.

Canary slithered up beside him, tapping his shoulder and gesturing for them to move away. Doyle followed her back into the hallway.

"I don't think we have to worry about it," she spoke close to his ear, and in such a gentle whisper that Doyle wasn't sure she believed her own words.

"Did you see something?" he whispered back, his eyes focused on the darkness toward the rear of the house.

"No, but I'm pretty sure the sound came from beyond the rear fence."

"Pretty sure?"

Doyle could just make out her expression of pinched lips and furrowed brow, a few seconds of silence passing between them.

"Well, it's definitely outside," Canary continued. "Either we go out there, in the dark and the rain, to investigate, or we don't." She had a point.

"All right. Let's just move some furniture in front of that sliding door first. It'd make me feel better."

Canary nodded her agreement.

Working as quietly as they could, Doyle and Canary picked up the chairs from the dining room and placed them in a line along the expanse of glass. They hadn't bothered to do it earlier when they decided to spend the night here, because anything trying to come in that way would have to shatter the glass. It gave Doyle peace of mind to have this little bit of extra security. Canary then went to the couch that faced the flat screen TV. Pushing it along the carpet, she jammed it up against the basement door. Once they were both satisfied, Doyle and Canary headed back upstairs.

Returning to the guest room, they found Rose and James standing in the middle of it, weapons at the ready, metal surfaces flashing in the flickering candle light.

"You heard it too?" Canary dared to speak a little louder in here.

Rose nodded. "That, and it was certainly takin' you guys long enough."

Doyle remembered his original purpose for going downstairs, and feigned slapping his forehead. "We'll look in the morning, when it's not so dark."

James stepped around him to shift their blockade and cover the door completely.

"Did you see anythin'?" Rose asked.

Canary shook her head. "I think it's coming from beyond the fence. You?"

"We blew out the candle for a bit and looked, but nah. Neither of us could see anythin' out there."

"It could just be something catching a bit of wind," Doyle offered.

The others nodded, but they all knew it could be something else. If it was something capable of motion, then the repeating nature of the sound suggested it was being caused by a zombie. And frequently, where there was one, there were many, as the horde yesterday had reminded them.

Rose had not finished laying out their bedrolls, and now there was no point. Those that had been laid out, were re-rolled and packed. A sound outside like that made them tense, made them more worried about being attacked in the night. Without a word, the group unanimously decided to sleep on the bare carpet, using their packs as pillows with one arm still hooked through the straps. If they had to leave, they could leave in an instant.

"I have first watch," Rose declared, sitting against one wall, squishing her bag between her back and the drywall.

Doyle settled down next to the window, assuming he wouldn't be able to sleep much and deciding to keep his ears open for the strange rattle. As Canary blew out the candle from where she was lying, Doyle found himself hoping the sound would continue throughout the night. If it did, then he would know that whatever was making it was staying put.

***

The sun rose in the early morning, rising from the east as it presumably always had and presumably always would. It slowly turned the overcast sky into a sheet of white light. As soon as it was bright enough to see clearly, Doyle and the others were up and ready to go. He led them out of the room, across the mouldy carpet, and down the stairs. In the middle of the group, James carried a small stack of board games, ready to drop and abandon them if a moment called for it. Moving along the first floor hallway, Doyle eyed a water stain that, over the years, had spread along the ceiling and down parts of the walls. They were lucky that the wood hadn't yet rotted to the point of collapse and should have been more cautious when choosing where to spend the night, but the storm had forced them to make a hurried decision. Upon reaching the kitchen, James and Rose immediately searched for plastic baggies and rubber bands, while Doyle and Canary continued on to the back windows, where they moved the dining chairs out of the way.

The noise had stopped at some time in the early hours, causing just as much worry as when it had started. Now, Doyle's eyes scanned around the long grass of the uncared-for backyard, trying to spot anything amiss.

When he didn't, his eyes moved beyond the fences, trying to see through them into the other yards and scanning the backs of the houses he could see. It was almost disturbing how normal it all looked. Beyond the wild grass, nothing appeared wrong. This neighbourhood looked mostly untouched; the people who lived here had been evacuated a long time ago, most never to return. Looking along the houses out back, Doyle could imagine these people just showing up one day and resuming their lives like nothing had happened, as if they had all just been on an extended holiday.

"Okay, the games have been packed up," James whispered from the kitchen.

"I think we should check out that house," Doyle whispered back without turning, his eyes still locked on the windows that faced the one out of which he was peering.

"Not that I mind, but are you sure?" Rose queried, stepping up beside him to stare through the glass door.

"With that kid showing up the other day, I think we should."

"Agreed." James reached between Doyle and Rose and flipped open the lock.

Doyle opened the door himself, wincing at the crack and whoosh as the rubber seal let go. He stepped carefully out onto the small porch, thinking of the water-stained hallway and rot. Several boards creaked as he made his way to the steps; the others behind him tried to avoid those spots, only to find their own noisy wood. Doyle felt relieved once he got his booted feet on the grass and dirt, but that didn't stop him from immediately turning and scanning beneath the porch. James, who had been following closely behind him, joined in the investigation, clicking on his flashlight to banish the murk in the far corners. They found gravel, spider webs, a few hardy weeds struggling against the limited light, and nothing else.

Everyone moved slowly across the backyard, watching their every step. Considering that there were no major depressions in the yard, no one expected there to be a zombie in hiding, but snakes and rodents weren't so easily spotted. Long grass like this was perfect for infected rats; it was why, no matter how hot it got, the group wore long pants tucked into their boots for the entire journey.

At the fence, Doyle peered through the cracks, seeing nothing more than another unkempt yard. Using hand signals, he gestured for Canary to bring over the plastic slide that stood near to her. Once it was set against the wood, he used it as a step, getting just enough height to peer over the top of the fence. Nothing moved in the grass on the far side. While the yard he was in had a few weather-worn kids' things lying around, the next one was barren. A bush huddled in each corner, having grown to nearly the height of the fence, and a small tree stood long dead, in the middle of the space. Looking straight down, Doyle could see a few stones that had once marked off an area, most likely a garden, but it had been overrun by grass and weeds, choking out whatever used to be there.

He gestured what he saw to the others and then hauled himself over. One by one they followed; Rose had to concede to James' offer for help when she struggled to climb over on her own. Once she was over, she gave her shortened arm a disgusted look, as though it were a subordinate that constantly failed its assigned tasks. In Rose's mind, it probably was.

There was nothing in the yard that could have made the noise they heard last night, and so the group approached the house, checking under a porch once more before stepping onto it. This porch was far more rotten than the other one had been, and Doyle had to test every placement of his foot before putting his full weight on it. Some of the boards were disturbingly spongy. Canary followed him, and the two peered through all the windows they could reach, while Rose and James waited on the grass.

When Doyle and Canary still couldn't see anything that might have made the sound, they returned to the dirt and signed their lack of findings to the others. They all agreed there was a possibility that the sound had come from deeper in the house, or even upstairs, but no one really believed it had. They all thought it had originated from the yard, and the fact that they found nothing that could have created it was disturbing. Just in case, James and Doyle peeked into the other nearby yards, but there was nothing obvious in them either.

Signing slowly, often having to spell out words because she couldn't make an accurate sign, Rose said they should forget about it and move on. They were already being extra vigilant in watching out for themselves; this wouldn't change much. Doyle nodded his agreement, and then led the group around the side of the house.

The street was virtually empty, with only a few cars remaining in driveways. They were probably abandoned by two-car families who needed only one to get to the evacuation centre. There weren't very many trees on this street either, just a few out of control bushes here and there. On the plus side, it meant there wasn't much to hide anything, but unfortunately that also included themselves. Sticking as closely as he could to the fronts of houses, Doyle led his little team. He had begun to think this was a stupid trip, that he had put himself and others in danger for a dumb reason. He refused to turn around, however. For him, this was no longer just about books, but about proving to himself that he could still survive outside the Black Box fences; that people didn't have to remain so scared and huddled together. As he dashed across a street, he hoped he wasn't going to be proven wrong.

***

The four of them lay huddled together in the shade beneath a long-haul trailer, peering out around the rear wheels. Doyle could see the bookstore, a small, one storey, boxy-looking structure they should have reached either their first day out, or at least by the morning after that. There were faded signs hanging from a few windows, and no security measures could be seen beyond them. One of the windows had already been smashed, whether deliberately or from a storm it was impossible to say at that distance. Between the trailer they hid beneath and the bookstore, fourteen zombies had been counted.

"Fifteen," Canary breathed. "There's another over by that large fallen tree branch."

Doyle looked for the branch she meant. He squinted, not knowing what she had seen, until a small flash of yellow resolved itself. A child zombie was entangled in some smaller branches on the far side, partially hidden by the larger section of tree limbs.

"We have two options," James sighed. "Either fight our way through, killing them all, or continue to lie here and wait for them to stagger away."

"I don't think they're goin' to stagger away," Rose huffed. "Most of them ain't even movin', just standin' there, and those that are, keep followin' that damn bird."

Along with the moving corpses, there was one completely dead person lying facedown on the pavement. A bird, some sort of hawk or osprey, kept alighting on the poor individual's back, taking a few pecks at his flesh, and then taking off again when the zombies tried to grab it. The bird would circle a bit or land nearby, the zombies that had been able to track its movements, shuffling after it. Once they were far enough away from the corpse, the bird would swoop in for a few more bites and then repeat the process. Doyle had to admit, it was a fairly clever bird.

"Maybe we can lure them off," Doyle suggested.

"That would require someone to be bait." Rose was shaking her head as she whispered. "In my experience, unless the runner knows exactly where they're goin' and knows the route has a very high chance of being clear, such plans don't work so well. You have to pre-plan a really good hidin' spot, or some sort of barricade to stop the zombies. It's doable, but we'll need to start plannin' now."

"I think we should just take them out," Canary decided. "There's not *that* many of them, fewer than that herd we bumped into, and none of them are acting like they're very smart or fast. I know you can't always

140

tell that just by looking at them, but I figure the bird would have caused it to reveal itself if there were one."

Doyle continued to weigh the options in his mind, conscious of the fact that everyone was looking at him. This was his mission; he had to call the shots. He scanned the area again, counting the zombies, then turned and looked behind them at the way they had come.

"Okay, we'll take them out. But first, I want to see what's through that doorway behind us. We should have an escape route, just in case."

The others agreed, and they all crawled backward out from under the truck and then dashed back into the alleyway from which they had entered the street. On the right side of the alleyway, a metal door with no handle led into the one-story building. James dropped his bag and removed a slim piece of metal from it, which he used to jimmy open the door. Doyle entered first, his flashlight sweeping the corners and his axe at the ready. The small group made short work of searching the space, which appeared to be some sort of trash room. Several trash bins, just small enough to fit out the doorway, stood gathered along the walls, a few of them at capacity with garbage that had been thrown away long ago. It had either lost its stink during that time or was weak enough that Doyle didn't notice it.

"All right, so this is our fall-back position. We'll prop the door open, and if we're forced to retreat, we'll duck in here, shut the door, and barricade it with these trash bins. Everyone agreed?"

The other three nodded. Doyle hoped they weren't forced to run away. He took a cursory glance through the other door that led from the trash room into the rest of the building, a coffee shop based on what he saw, but pursuing zombies could easily get in through its broken front windows if they missed the alley.

"Okay, Rose, I want you to borrow James' rifle."

"Why?"

"You're going to be on overwatch, on top of the truck."

"James should do it, he's the better shot."

Doyle gritted his teeth, trying to figure out how to say what he wanted to say without pissing her off.

"It's 'cause of the arm, isn't it?" Rose interpreted his expression. "All the more reason James should do it. I'd need help to climb up on the truck and would get stuck up there if no one could help me down. Besides, it's been far too long since I used a rifle."

"She has a point, I really should be the one up there," James sided with her.

Canary tentatively nodded her head in agreement.

"Fine, James is on overwatch then."

Rose slipped off her bag. "Canary? Wanna help me get this on?" She pulled a bundle of straps and metal out of the bag.

"What is that?" Doyle's brows pinched together. He knew Rose was constantly making things to help her with her handicap, but this one was new to him.

Rose slid her short arm through the straps, all the way up to her shoulder. Canary helped her tighten them. A chunk of metal, shorter than a baseball bat, but rounded on the end like one, became attached to what remained of her forearm.

"Wouldn't a knife be better?" James wondered, clearly never having seen the device either.

"Nope," Rose shook her head, flexing her arm to test the tightness. "This is more to hold a zombie back," she explained, placing the end of the metal against Doyle's chest as an example. "I don't want it to be sharp. I don't want to stab a zombie with somethin' that's attached to me in case it gets stuck."

"Have you ever tested it?" Doyle asked as it was removed from his chest.

"Not really. I haven't been outside the walls since I made it, and I could bruise someone pretty bad if I tested it against them."

"I'm sure it'll work great." Canary smiled and patted Rose's shoulder, nothing about her suggesting she was lying. She seemed to think Rose's contraption was actually useful.

"Okay then. Everyone put your masks on."

A variety of masks were taken out of bags and secured over faces. James didn't put his on completely, letting his bandana hang around his neck and his ski goggles sit on his head. Since he would be up on the truck, he wouldn't be in much danger from spraying blood. Canary wore a white painting mask with a pair of swim goggles over her eyes, and Rose wore a full-face mask, her expressions completely visible beneath the Plexiglas. Doyle had a firefighter's mask, the upper half transparent, while the lower half was covered by a breathing apparatus, minus the connection to an oxygen tank. Because of his former profession, he never found himself uncomfortable in it.

Once packs were returned to backs, and everyone nodded that they were ready, they headed back outside. James went straight to the truck, easily scaling the side of the cab and reaching the top of the trailer, where he lay down with his rifle in a position where they could see his hand signals.

Doyle, Rose, and Canary went around the front of the truck where they would be making their stand. Canary stood closest to the truck. Her screwdriver was the shortest weapon and needed the least amount of room to wield; her other hand gripped her pistol as back up. Doyle took the outside, giving himself quite a bit of room to swing his axe, while Rose was in the middle where the other two could watch out for her.

A trio of zombies noticed their appearance right away and began their awkward shuffle toward the three humans. Doyle set his feet and gripped his axe with both hands, ready to swing it like a baseball bat. One clean hit was always the best.

The first to arrive went straight for Doyle, its long, bony fingers reaching for him, completely oblivious of the threat to its being. This one was old, its skin grey and peeling, revealing its innards. The moment it was close enough, a distance Doyle knew well from years of practice, he swung the axe. It thunked into the zombie's skull, nearly cleaving off the entire top of it. The dead thing went down instantly, not a twitch remaining. Doyle ripped his axe back out, the blade drooling thick, dark blood behind it. He turned just in time to see Canary put down one of the zombies with a lightning quick jab to the side of the head. Her screwdriver was in and out of the thing before it had finished taking a step, only to collapse at her feet, a small round hole now in its temple. The third zombie was just about to reach Rose.

"Don't help," she demanded, spotting Doyle taking a step closer.

Doyle hesitated, thinking he should help her anyway, but his pause was just long enough for the thing to reach her. Rose thrust with her self-made prosthetic, not hard enough to knock it over, but enough to cause it to stumble back a step, a chunk of loose skin sliding off the top of its head like a bad wig. She continued to hold the thing at bay, letting it paw at the metal against its bony chest, the thing too stupid to realize it wasn't actually a part of her. Rose swung the hammer then. She must have built her arm extension with this in mind, as the zombie was at the perfect distance. The thing's skull cracked, its legs giving out beneath it. While it was crumpled but still moving, Rose swung again, her aim perfect as she smashed the exact same spot. Her hammer broke through the skull and flattened the brain beneath, ceasing the zombie's movements for good.

Rose turned and grinned at Doyle, the blood spotting her mask seeming to spot her face.

"Pretty good," Doyle complimented her, his voice muffled, "now let's see you do it several more times." He pointed to where the rest of the zombies were now coming for them, having heard or seen their fellow rotters go down.

The zombies came at them in uneven clumps. Some reached them alone, while others were in bunches. Doyle didn't bother to count how many. There were definitely more than they had counted while under the truck, several of them appearing from around corners and out of broken shop windows. None came from behind, however, which was the real worry. James kept an eye out, but didn't have to fire. With each zombie the trio on the street took down, they moved back a step, keeping those that had fallen out from underfoot. The fallen bodies worked to their advantage, as the next wave of zombies found themselves tripping over the sprawled limbs and torsos. It was a chaos of blood and sweat, Doyle's arms eventually tiring from the constant swinging. Rose tired even faster, having to haul around her prosthetic. By the end, she was accepting help, often using the punt to move a zombie either Doyle or Canary's way, depending on who wasn't currently occupied. She frequently swatted them to the ground near Doyle, where he could chop into the zombies with gravity's assistance.

When at last his eyes could perceive no more immediate threats, Doyle looked up to James, who held up one finger and pointed. The last zombie was making its painfully slow way toward them. It was the boy that had been tangled up in the tree branch. He was young, too young to have been born before the Day. He must have been freshly turned, his skin not yet sagging. Now that he was heading toward them, Doyle could see that he wasn't tangled in the tree branches, so much as he was pierced by them. The boy's little legs were straining to haul the large tree branch behind him, suggesting he was a smart one. The regular dummies never used strength. Over the past few years, a number of interesting facts were learned about the undead, such as the smart ones were created only by bites from other zombies, not by dying of other causes and then turning because of the airborne infection that lay dormant within their systems. So the boy had been born after the Day, recently bitten, turned, and then impaled on a large tree branch.

"I got this one," Doyle told the others, stepping through the killing field to meet him. Behind him, James climbed down off the truck, but undoubtedly readied his rifle again once his feet were planted.

Doyle approached the zombie carefully. If it suddenly slipped loose of the tree, it would become very dangerous, very fast. Tiny growls and snarls issued from the dead boy's throat, his teeth snapping punctuation. The branches made it a bit difficult for Doyle to get into a good position. When he was finally ready, he swung for the boy's forehead. At the last possible moment, the boy lunged, one of the branches holding him snapping. This caused Doyle to catch him in the neck instead of the head, his axe slicing through his weak flesh and becoming buried in the largest part of the branch. The head continued to snap as it fell and rolled toward Doyle's ankles. Doyle responded by squawking and stumbling backward, tripping over his own feet and landing painfully on the pavement. The head stopped out of reach, its teeth still gnashing.

"Yeah, you got this one," Rose teased, stepping up beside him. She used her prosthetic to jab the head away from Doyle and the large tree branch. Once in the open, she held it as still as possible while Canary bent down and stabbed her screwdriver through it.

"Smooth," James chuckled as he helped Doyle to his feet.

Doyle didn't bother to dignify their friendly taunts with a response; he just walked over to the branch and set to work pulling out his axe. It was wedged in pretty good and took several tugs to come free; Doyle stumbled backward again when it did, although this time he kept to his feet.

"Looks like we're good to go to the bookstore," Canary commented as she scanned the area. The bird seemed delighted that it had more bodies to pick at and fewer to flee from. Somewhere nearby, a crow was cawing loudly, smelling the carnage and calling his friends.

As the group moved on, they did their best to wipe off the blood using street trash: things like really old paper, the rare rag, and a lot of leaves. It was unfortunate that there wasn't a stream or river close at hand in which to rinse off, but at least the street litter was wet from the storm. For the first time, Doyle found himself cursing efficient storm drains. Flooded streets wouldn't be so bad.

Upon entering the bookstore, they split into two pairs to search the place for threats.

"Clear," James called out, and received a similar response from Rose.

Once safe, everyone split up to look for their favourite genres. Doyle went straight to the mystery section, and was greatly disappointed to find it was next to the broken window. Most of the selection was heavily water damaged from not only the previous afternoon's storm, but from several before it. Still, Doyle managed to find a few that had escaped enough harm to be readable. He checked out the books in the surrounding categories, not caring about their sun-faded covers as he added them to his pack, even surreptitiously sneaking a book from the erotica section. He wanted to include books for more readers than just himself, and that meant taking a few books he wouldn't dare have touched in his previous life.

When he heard Canary and Rose giggling nearby, Doyle wandered his way over to see what was up. The women were in the magazine section beside the register, huddled closely together, with a large swath of formerly glossy covers scattered about their feet, knocked there by intruding winds. Rose had removed her prosthetic, some of the straps hanging out of her pack.

"Can I know the joke?" he asked, coming closer as he spotted a collection of bookmarks to loot.

"We're just imagining what some of these actors would be like today," Canary told him, a bright smile on her face.

"Yo, she totally still wears high heels," Rose chuckled, pointing to a cover Doyle couldn't see.

"Oh no, my shoe!" Canary mocked in an excessively girly voice.

Doyle didn't get their amusement and moved on, spotting a few pens and notebooks that might be good to get.

In the middle of the store, where it was surprisingly bright thanks to the skylights scattered overhead, James was taking his time reading the back covers of some general fiction novels. Doyle hadn't bothered when he had selected his books; he'd read anything these days.

"I already picked out what I think are the most useful ones to us, but the science section is over there if you want to take a second look." James pointed without even glancing at Doyle, his attention completely absorbed in the back cover of the book he held.

Doyle decided to take his advice and went to the science section. There were a lot of books about space and theoretical physics that he completely ignored. If future generations ever got to the point where they were comfortable and settled enough for that kind of stuff, they'd probably have to recover a lot of ground. Adjacent to the science section was history. Doyle thought preserving some of those books was more important, so he chose a few that covered different eras. His bag was quite heavy now, so he decided he had enough.

As he made his way back to the women, curious about what they may have helped themselves to, his blood went cold as one of them swore loudly. His leisurely meander among the stacks, turned into a sprint. James reached them seconds before he did, the group now all together by the front windows. It didn't take long for Doyle to figure out what the cursing was about. A substantially large horde was shuffling toward them, quite possibly the zombie mob they thought they had avoided.

"Check the other sides!" James ordered.

Doyle was already moving along the outer wall, peering out through the windows. Everywhere he looked, more and more zombies were filling the surrounding area.

"How did so many get around us like that?" Rose called out from the far side of the store.

"They're coming toward the back door too!" Canary shouted, appearing from the stock room.

"We're surrounded," James relayed, oddly calm. "Start pushing the shelves against the windows.

Doyle obeyed immediately, no longer caring about how well the books left behind would fare against the weather. Several mystery books fell out of the broken window as the shelf he pushed up against it tipped over slightly.

"Skylights!" Rose called out from the middle of the store. She and Canary began dragging a bookshelf directly beneath one of them.

The closest zombies hit the outer walls and windows and began trying to push their way in. The air was filled with their groaning and moaning.

Canary screamed in frustration as she tried to open the skylight, balancing on top of the bookcase, but it appeared to be the sealed type.

"Just break it!" Rose shouted at her.

As the glass from the skylight cracked and rained down, so too did the glass of several of the windows. Doyle ran around the edges of the bookstore, battering back any zombies that appeared close to getting in.

"I'm on the roof!" Canary yelled down.

The bookcase James had dragged in front the door was slowly sliding, threatening to tip over with the concentration of zombies there pushing against it hard enough to bend the hinges backward. Doyle ran and threw his weight against the shelves. The glass in the door was broken; dead arms were squeezing between the frame and shelf backing to get him, scraping off their own skin in the process.

"Doyle!" Rose shouted.

Looking up, Doyle saw her on top of the bookcase beneath the skylight as James' legs disappeared up through the opening. Lower down and beyond them, some zombies had gotten the shelves out of the way and were now pouring in, their already battered bodies becoming further cut up by the broken glass.

Doyle dashed away from the door; the bookshelf toppled over behind him as more zombies forced their way in. He reached the shelf that Rose was upon and began scrambling up, disturbed by how much the thing shook beneath him.

Once on top, he helped Rose by hoisting her up high enough that James could grab the loop on the top of her pack and haul her the rest of the way onto the roof, her stump arm seeking out whatever leverage it could to help the rest of her.

The zombies hit the bookshelf beneath Doyle and it wobbled precariously. His arms pin wheeled as he attempted to stay upright.

"Hurry up!" James called from the opening, sticking his arms through it, ready to assist.

Doyle reached up and gripped the lip of the skylight. Just as he got a hold, and James' hands latched onto the shoulder straps of his backpack, the bookshelf below over balanced.

"Fuck!" Doyle cried out, his feet now swinging in the air. The toppling bookshelf caused a slight domino effect, knocking over several others. On the plus side, they crushed a bunch of zombies.

"Pull me!" James called over his shoulder at the girls.

Doyle did the best chin up of his life, assisted by the others, trying not to think about how close some zombie hands might be to his boots. Once he got his elbows over the sides, Canary and Rose reached down on either side of him and grabbed his belt beneath his pack. With everyone hauling together, he was quickly dragged up onto the tar paper roof and free of the skylight.

Lying on his stomach, Doyle panted, James doing the same in front of him. They looked at each other and started laughing. Doyle didn't know why, probably just the joy of not being dead.

"I never thought a bookstore could be so excitin'," Rose commented as she huffed down next to them.

"Let's hope the roof is less exciting, shall we?" Canary responded. She had gashed her hand at some point and was now carefully tending to the injury. It didn't look too bad, just painful.

"Come on, we've got more to do." James sat up and brushed himself off. "We need to check out our options up here and make a decision as to whether we try to escape now, or wait them out. If we wait, we best inventory our supplies again."

As Doyle sat up, his belly hurting from the scraping along the edge of the skylight, he was glad that he wasn't in charge anymore. James was good at this stuff; he would probably get them out of this mess that Doyle had gotten them into. At least, that was the hope.

14
Riley's Scared

Cancer. She couldn't believe she had cancer. Her parents had trained her to face everything—earthquakes, tsunamis, plague, war, alien invasion, *zombies*—except for cancer. All day, while Riley helped clean up the area above the Black Box, she found herself stopping and staring at nothing. Abby knew something was wrong; she had asked several times if Riley was feeling okay. Riley always said she felt fine, got back to work, worked hard for a while, and then found herself staring into nothing again. Even Hope realized that something was wrong. While she ran around with Peter, she frequently looked over at her mom, her little face lined with worry.

Riley had just hauled a load of fallen branches to the collection pile when a hand fell on her shoulder. She expected it to be Abby again, but instead she found herself faced with Freya.

Do you need to talk? Instead of signing, Freya had handed Riley her small chalkboard that she had written on. Riley appreciated the courtesy. She understood that writing things down was more tedious and frustrating for Freya than signing was, but it was also more private. Since everyone had been taught sign, they could figure out whatever Freya was saying from a distance.

Riley found herself getting unexpectedly emotional. Tears threatened. She took a deep breath, looked down at her feet, and bit her tongue until it passed. Freya waited patiently until Riley got herself under control, and then gently took hold of the other woman's arm to guide her somewhere more private. They went between a pair of train cars, sitting down on either side of the coupling mechanism, facing one another. Several seconds of silence passed between them.

Still respecting Riley's privacy, Freya wiped clean her slate and wrote on it again, taking out a piece of chalk from the stylized tube-pendant she wore on a necklace. Riley listened to the tapping and scratching as she wrote, accepting the chalkboard when it was handed to her again.

Do you know what you're going to do?

Riley nodded. "There's really only one thing I can do. I need to tell some of the other doctors I trust and have them perform a double mastectomy."

Freya gestured at her own breasts, miming cutting them off.

"Yes. Thankfully, it's been caught early. I don't think it's spread. There's no other option though. We don't have radiation and chemotherapy treatments. All we have is surgery." Riley knew she was speaking in a stilted, unemotional tone, almost as if she were talking about someone else. It was the only way she could talk about it.

More tapping with the chalk. *When?*

"As soon as possible. Once everything is cleaned up here. Waiting would only put me in more danger."

Would you like me to get

your sister and bring her here?

Freya had to write this in two parts, her little chalkboard not large enough to fit it all in one go.

Riley teared up again at the offer. She was unable to answer vocally, having to nod her head in response while biting her tongue again.

It is okay to be afraid.

Riley took a deep breath and steadied herself. "I know. I know it is. I just..." she didn't know what she wanted to say. Her thoughts kept jumbling up, getting tangled together.

I will go and get your sister today.

We'll be here tomorrow at the latest.

Riley wasn't going to say anything, but she liked the pauses in their conversation that Freya's writing created. It gave her an extra few seconds to try to extract a reasonable thought, or secure her emotions.

"There's no dock, though." Riley had seen what used to be the little dock attached to the barge dock, down river and caught on some rocks on the opposite shore. As they spoke, some volunteers were trying to free it and bring it back. There was no good way to connect the wood to the cement wall, but they were always coming up with new methods. While helping to gather the fallen branches, Riley had heard the latest suggestion was to drill more eyebolts into the cement to use as anchor points.

I do not mind the rocks. Freya made a waving off gesture as Riley read her message. Most people avoided the cascade of rocks beside the river, as it was easy to break an ankle or leg between them. Riley could picture Freya among the rocks, moving calmly across them, no hesitation. She had a dangerous sort of grace to her.

"And they'll just let you take a boat?" From what Riley understood, boats from here were only taken in groups or during emergencies, and Riley definitely didn't consider picking up her sister an emergency.

Freya shrugged in an offhand manner as she wrote. *Someone should check on their storm damage.*

This was true. Although they had the radios to communicate with, it was better to have someone go lay eyes on the situation personally. Riley looked at the damage that had been done here, and hoped that the others hadn't been hit as hard.

"All right, if you're sure you won't get into trouble or anything. Make sure you have permission."

It'll be okay.

Riley's heart squeezed in tandem as Freya gently gripped her shoulder. The other woman was about to get up and leave, when she clearly had another thought and sat back down.

Do I tell your sister? Or will you?

"You can tell her." Riley was going to have enough trouble telling the doctors she wanted operating on her. She had no idea what to say to Hope.

Would you like me to wait?

Riley frowned, not entirely sure of the meaning behind Freya's question.

Help you here, first.

With others, she wrote as Riley still didn't quite catch on.

"Oh, no. That's okay." Riley actually would have liked her to stay, but then it would take longer for her sister to get here, and therefore delay the surgery more. Every moment the cancer was in her was another moment it had a chance to spread.

Freya completely cleaned off her little chalkboard, using some dampness from the surrounding surfaces. She got up and patted Riley's shoulder, the same one she had squeezed earlier, then walked off to get permission to take a boat. Riley watched her go, admiring Freya's self-confidence. Thinking back on her life, Riley felt that she had used to be like that. She used to know what she was doing, what she wanted, but now? Even before the cancer, she always felt like she was drifting from place to place, job to job. Ever since Mathias had died.

She never talked about it, but Riley hated being this upset over him. It had been years since he was killed, and yet her throat still locked up whenever she overheard someone telling some story that involved his name. How had she become this person? How had her happiness become so entangled with the life of one man that she completely fell to pieces once he was gone? She had never wanted to be that woman, but there was no going back. Although she found happiness when she could, there was always this cloud of depression overhead, never letting it last.

Riley got up off the train car and made her way back over to the pile of branches. She grabbed a pair of gloves from the nearby bin, picked up a small handsaw, and started cutting limbs down into smaller, more manageable sizes. The small bits would be burned, while the larger, more useful pieces were separated into another pile. They would be woven into the fences, used as posts and markers in the fields, or carved into canes or other implements. Riley set herself to this work with a will, imagining her sickness sweating out of her; both the cancer in her body, and the darkness in her mind.

***

When the day was done, and the workers had all dragged their weary bodies back inside, Riley debated whether she should go find her doctors first, or sit down with her daughter. Both options were extremely unappealing. Her feet made the decision for her, carrying her to the medical centre as opposed to Abby's for dinner. She realized that the doctors she wanted were most likely eating their own dinners right now, but maybe one of them was still on duty, as there was always at least one person at the ready, usually more.

Riley lingered outside the doorway. There was no turning back from her decision. Freya had already left, gone to assess the damage at the container yard and to bring Cameron back with her. With every person who was told, it became more real. Cameron would know that Riley would have no other choice than the one she was taking. The doctors as well. Right now, it felt like she had options, but once she opened her mouth, they were gone. It was a trick of the mind, causing her to hesitate. There were no other options. If she said no to the surgery, the cancer would spread, and she would die a slow and painful death, a drain on the resources meant for those who would survive. That, or a quick bullet to the head.

Suicide was not an option, not with Hope around. After the Diana sank, Riley had seriously considered it. Her husband was dead and she was just so exhausted. She was tired of running, of fighting, of losing people. But in the end, she couldn't do that to her daughter. Hope had just lost her dad, not to mention her Uncle Alec, right after her first funeral for her friend's dog, Shoes.

Riley wished Milly were still around. Her three-legged husky had died about a year and a half ago. It wasn't anything traumatic that had taken the dog, just the wear and tear of old age.

Maybe I should get another pet, Riley thought as she stood in the empty hallway. Milly had really helped her with her depression. She would never tell Cameron, but it was more the dog than her sister or her daughter that got her back to even ground. Although Hope prevented her from killing herself, it was Milly for whom she got out of bed, to walk, and feed, and throw a ball so that she got proper exercise, watching her act just like all the other dogs, as if she weren't missing a limb. That's what it had felt like to lose Mathias: it had felt like losing a limb.

Her thoughts about getting a new pet led to Cameron. She always knew which animals were pregnant and expecting. Riley would probably want a dog again, but she'd ask Hope what she would like. Maybe they could get two: a dog and a goat, or something unusual like that.

Of course thinking about talking to Cameron reminded her what her next conversation with her twin would be about. Riley wondered if Dakota or even Brunt might come with her. Dakota had been family for the past several years, and it was looking strongly like Brunt was going be sometime soon. Too bad Danny was out scavenging somewhere. It would have been nice to have him nearby, his face so similar to his brother's.

"Riley?"

Riley startled, so deep within herself she hadn't noticed Dr. Haily Guiles begin exiting the medical centre, only to pause in the doorway, a look of concern on her face.

"Are you all right?" she asked, unsure if she should step closer or not. They had worked together since before the Day, both of them residents of the same ER. She had been a student in the year between Riley and Josh. Riley had watched her develop her skills over the years, skills that were already sharp to begin with.

"No." Riley hadn't meant to tell the truth, but it was the first thing her stormy mind was able to get out of her mouth. The admission threatened more tears, and Riley hated herself for it. She didn't want to cry, not in front of someone she had helped train, not in front of someone who had always seen her as a leader and advisor.

"Come in, tell me what's wrong." Haily was gentle and understanding, not touching Riley, but simply stepping out of her way to let her pass.

They moved through the thankfully empty waiting room into a small, office-like space. Both female doctors ignored the one tiny chair to lean side-by-side on the edge of the desk.

"Do you need me to get someone? Abby, Josh, Robin?" Haily asked after a moment of Riley saying nothing.

"Yes. No. Later," Riley shook her head, an attempt to rattle free what she had to say. "Can you tell Josh and Robin after I tell you?"

"Of course. What's this about?"

"I have cancer."

Riley expected a gasp of surprise, a pitying look, confusion. She did not expect the sagely nod, as if Haily had already known. Had Freya told her?

"What kind? How far along?" she asked. Freya hadn't told her then.

"Breast, and early stages. There's a lump here," Riley pointed to the offender within her body.

"And you want a mastectomy." Haily didn't ask.

"A double mastectomy, to be sure."

Haily nodded again. "I understand. I'm assuming you want me, Josh, and Robin to do the surgery?"

Riley nodded. She liked how straight forward Haily was being, not asking questions about how she was feeling, or coping, or whatever. It let Riley slip into her own doctor's mentality, to speak as if they were talking about some other patient that wasn't her.

"Yes."

"We should bring Dr. Lewis on board."

"I don't know him that well."

"Yes, but he's the best surgeon we have. He's done this exact operation before."

When the Leighton hospital had been evacuated, it was mostly the ER doctors who had escaped owing to their proximity to the evacuation point. Dr. Lewis wasn't the only surgeon to be evacuated, but he was the only one who then survived long enough to be mentioned now. Riley had worked with him only a few times, most of their shifts set at opposing hours. One of those times they worked together, however, was when Rose was brought in missing a hand. Riley had gone in early while Lewis stayed late, all hands on deck to save Rose's life.

"Yeah. Okay. He can help," Riley agreed.

"How many other people know right now?"

"You, me, and Freya."

"That's it?"

"Freya only knows because I got her to help me run the tests. She's on her way to the container yard right now to tell my sister. After this, I plan to have a sit down with Hope."

"You should tell your friends, Abby and Lauren, and the others at the container yard. I'm sure they'd like to know."

Riley shook her head. "I don't want more people than necessary worrying about me. They can find out after it's done and I'm okay."

"All right, that's your choice I guess. You should talk to Brittany. She's been through this procedure and can tell you what to expect from a patient's perspective."

Brittany, who had become a general counsellor and type of manager at the Black Box, had survived two forms of cancer before the Day. She had also had a double mastectomy, but the difference was that she had been in a proper hospital, fully equipped, and had been able to get implants later. Riley would have a flat chest forever afterward. She had never really cared before, never thought of herself as womanly or sexy, or whatever, but it was strange now to know that her breasts would be gone. They were the most outwardly female aspect about her.

"Maybe," she lied to Haily about talking to Brittany. She definitely wasn't going to say a word to the woman. When Riley had been depressed, Cameron had brought her in. The two women were very different from one another and saw eye to eye on nothing. Her good-natured attempts at bringing Riley out of her funk ended up with Riley screaming at her. They hadn't spoken since, and Riley had no intention of ending that silence.

"All right, well, the others are most likely having dinner right now, but I can find them afterward. Where did you leave your test results?"

"I hid them across the hall." Riley led Haily back out of the little office. They crossed the hall into the lab, and Riley retrieved all her test data from the back of a dusty cupboard, behind oddly shaped beakers for which no one had discovered a use and then forgotten.

Haily kept nodding to herself as she looked over the data, coming to the same conclusions as Riley.

"I'll show this file to the others, but we may need to perform some of the tests again."

Riley watched as Haily unconsciously wrapped one of her arms just beneath her breasts, her other hand still flipping back and forth through the test results.

"We should head to dinner," she said suddenly, closing the folder. "I assume you're staying with Lauren and Abby as you usually do? They'll be wondering where you are."

"You're right." Riley knew that, but at the same time wasn't sure she could face them just yet. Unfortunately, she couldn't stall any longer, as Haily also needed to go to dinner.

"When do you want it scheduled?" Haily asked as they both stepped out into the hallway.

"Freya only said she'd be back tomorrow, not when. I'd like to do it as close to when my sister arrives as possible."

"Then hopefully our load is light tomorrow. I'll go over your findings with the others tonight, and in the early morning we can run any other needed tests. You sure you can handle not eating for that long? What if they're late?"

"I want my sister here when you operate."

Haily nodded, maybe understanding, maybe not. Riley was always considering worst-case scenarios, which frequently meant death. If she died on the operating table, she wanted Cameron to be here for Hope.

As Riley trudged to Abby's apartment, she thought of Hope and what to say to her. What words should she use to tell her ten year old? She didn't want Hope to worry too much, but she didn't want her to be unaware of the dangers either. How to inform her, without scaring her?

"Riley, there you are," Abby called out, standing up from the table as she entered the apartment.

"Sorry, I had to help someone out." A lame, vague excuse, but one that would work.

"I hope you don't mind that we started without you." Abby gestured to the food on the table as she sat back down.

Riley made her way over, and took the empty seat. The food was still warm; clearly they hadn't been waiting long. "It's no problem."

"Mom, look what I did to my hand today." Hope thrust her fingers in Riley's face.

"How'd you do that? Splinter?"

"Yup." Hope took her hand back and stared at the small groove in her flesh. She used to whine and freak out over such injuries, but had since grown to find them fascinating, a mark of pride even. To her, small wounds were proof that she had been working hard or had been doing something fun.

"What about you, Peter? Any splinters over there?" Riley asked, trying not to think about what was to come.

Peter shook his head.

"He got a big bruise on his knee though," Hope crowed for him. "Show it to my mom."

"Legs stay under the table, please." Lauren directed her gaze at Hope as opposed to Peter, knowing the quiet kid had no intention of lifting his leg up to show Riley his bruise.

Dinner continued on in this manner, with Hope narrating her and Peter's entire day. Claire wasn't there tonight, eating with one of her friends, and none of the parents had anything to discuss, so Hope was allowed to ramble on, Riley frequently having to remind her to take a bite of her food.

Once the meal was over, the dishes cleaned and put away, Riley knew it was time.

"Hope, can I speak to you for a minute?"

Her daughter got this look like she had done something wrong but couldn't figure out what.

"You're not in trouble, sweetheart."

Abby was giving Riley a questioning look as she took Hope into the privacy of Claire's room, but Riley offered her no explanation.

"What's wrong?" Hope asked the moment the door was closed, her voice shaking a little. Maybe she was thinking like her mother, coming up with the worst-case scenario.

"We're going to have to stay here a few more days," Riley started with, sitting down on the edge of Claire's bed. "Is that all right?"

"Why? Did something happen back home? Is everyone okay?"

"Everyone back home is fine, you don't need to worry about them. Can you sit here with me?"

Hope hesitated, her body standing on nervous energy, but she managed to walk over and unlock her knees to plop down beside her mother.

"Do you know what cancer is?"

"It's a thing that kills people. Is it Mr. Bill? Does he have cancer?"

"It doesn't always kill people, some are lucky."

"Does Mr. Bill have cancer?"

"Yes, but he's not who I want to talk about." This conversation was getting away from Riley.

"Is he a lucky one?" Hope's voice was tight.

"I'm sorry, sweet pea, but he's not." Riley found herself comforting her daughter about Bill's cancer, when she was supposed to be talking about her own.

"How long? Can I go see him?"

"He still has quite a bit of time left, don't you worry, his case is a slow one. He'll be coming back to the container yard with us, and he'll have lots of time to tell you more stories."

Hope didn't cry, her eyes remained dry, but her face had this funny sort of tightness to it. Like she was upset and thought she shouldn't be, or she wasn't really upset and thought she should be.

"Hope, I have breast cancer." She said it like ripping off a Band-Aid.

Hope's face turned to her so fast, Riley feared she'd injured her neck.

"But I'm one of the lucky ones," she added quickly, before her daughter could have a meltdown. "The other doctors can actually help me."

"How?" This time tears did well up, Hope's eyes becoming glassy.

"I'm going to have what is called a double mastectomy. They're going to remove my breasts, and the cancer along with them."

Hope looked directly at Riley's chest. "You're not going to have boobs anymore?"

"I think it's a fair trade to get rid of the cancer, don't you?" Riley tried to make a joke, and could feel that the smile wasn't quite right on her face.

"Is it dangerous? The double-whatever?"

"It's surgery, and all surgery comes with risks, but I have the best doctors to do it, even one who's done this procedure before."

Hope suddenly buried herself in Riley's side, her arms wrapped tightly around her ribs, threatening to crush them. Riley took the skinny girl in her arms, lifting her up and placing her on her lap. She let her daughter cry it out, soaking her shirt.

"Your Aunt Cameron should be here sometime tomorrow. I'm going to be woozy after the surgery for a day or so, and so she'll look after you in the meantime."

"Will I be able to come see you?" Hope's voice was muffled by Riley's body.

"Of course, right after it's done. You can even wait outside the surgical suite, if you'd like."

Hope's head nodded, and Riley began stroking her hair.

"It'd make me very happy to see your face first thing when I wake up."

"Can I tell Peter?"

Riley bit her lower lip. Abby and Lauren would know once Riley went for the surgery, but if Hope told Peter, then Peter would tell them.

"Can you wait until tomorrow? They'll all know by then."

"Why can't they know now?"

Riley didn't know how to answer that. The first response that jumped to mind was that she was scared, but there was no way she would tell her ten-year-old kid that. She was supposed to be comforting her, not making her worry more.

"I'd just rather they know tomorrow," Riley eventually said, rather lamely. "Do you think you could keep it a secret? Just until the morning?"

"I guess," Hope sighed, her grip finally slackening. "Can Peter also wait outside the surgery place?"

"If he wants to. Abby and Lauren will probably plan to wait there with you once I tell them."

Hope pulled away, wiping at her face with her hands. Riley managed to find some other topic for them to discuss—an easy one Hope enjoyed—while her emotions settled down.

"Peter and I were going to play a board game tonight, can you play with us?"

"Of course."

When Riley finally left Claire's room, Abby was staring at her, waiting to know what was going on. Riley signed that they could talk about it tomorrow. As she followed her daughter and friend all the way downstairs to where the games were kept, Riley wondered how well she'd be able to sleep tonight.

***

Beyond the fence, Riley kept her feet planted, her hands gripped tightly around the machete, as the zombie came toward her. The smoke from the burning tree debris had lured several to the area. Riley had instantly volunteered to help take them out once she heard. It was a better way to pass the time than just sitting on the dock and watching the river. She had taken up a position in the long grass where she could still see the moment Freya returned with Cameron, but now she could take out some aggression at the same time.

Once the zombie was close enough, Riley's blade sank into its skull with a heavy *thunk*. Winchester stepped around her as she freed her blade, ready to take on the next one. As soon as Riley had her machete back in hand, two other volunteers grabbed the body and dragged it away from underfoot. Once the horse-drawn cart that was rattling around outside the fence came back around, they would throw it into the back, and the corpse would be brought to a designated area. Riley didn't know what they did with the fully dead once there, whether they burned them, used lye, or brought them far enough away to leave them out in the open where the animals could get to them. She didn't even know if they searched the corpses for useful items or blood-free clothes.

"Good one, Mom!" Hope called from the safe side of the fence. She hadn't left Riley's side since getting up that morning. Now, she stood watching her mom take out zombies, her fingers linked through the mesh. It was practically a sport, but Riley knew her daughter understood the dangers. She didn't mind Hope watching the procedure, as it was a good lesson. Later, she'd sit down with her and explain exactly what they were doing, how she and Winchester were working as a team, watching each other's backs, and keeping one another safe.

After Winchester had beaten down the next zombie with a long crowbar, it was Riley's turn again. A grey, naked, sexless being was stumbling toward her. It had been so chewed up, rotted, and withered that there was next to nothing left to distinguish it as a former human being. Whoever it once was, was long gone. Riley's blade sliced the top of its skull clean off, the bone having turned weak and brittle over the years. That zombie must have been wandering for a very long time.

Hope made a sound that was half-cheer, half-disgust as the top of the thing's head flew free.

As Riley stepped back from the body, she spotted a solitary canoe coming up the river. Her focus zeroed in on her sister, paddling in the front.

"Winchester, I'm out," she said, having explained earlier that this would happen.

He nodded as he prepared for the next dead. One of the body movers took Riley's place as she headed for the fence. It didn't take too long for her to scramble up and over the chain link. Hope's expression had become dour; she hadn't been looking forward to her aunt's arrival. Together, they made their way to the top of the rocks closest to the dock. The smaller dock still wasn't completely ready for service, but it should be soon. It didn't take long for Abby and Lauren to join them, as they had specifically been helping with the dock so that they would know when Cameron arrived.

"I'll go tell the doctors to get ready," Abby volunteered. She continued to stand beside Riley a moment longer anyway, her eyes begging her to say something, but Riley had no idea what. It had been a difficult conversation that morning.

"Peter's sorry he couldn't be with you this morning," Lauren spoke to Hope for something to say.

"If he were so sorry, he wouldn't hide in the computer lab," Hope responded with a huff and a crossing of her arms.

For some reason, Peter couldn't handle the news or the thought of standing by his friend while her mom waited for surgery. He had squirreled himself away in the computer lab to work on advanced math problems and ignore what was happening.

As the boat drew nearer, Riley noticed something odd: Freya wasn't aboard. In the middle of the boat, Dakota's cowboy hat distinguished her, while in the back sat Brunt paddling. As they neared the dock, Lauren called out and waved them to the rocks, carefully picking her way down them to help out.

Cameron scrambled up with ease, leaving Brunt and Dakota behind to struggle along with Lauren. She reached the top and immediately swept her twin into a bear hug, no words needing to pass between them. As Riley tried not to cry on her shoulder, she realized that soon it would be much easier for everyone to tell them apart, even if she cut her hair to look like Cameron's.

By the time the embrace ended, Dakota, Brunt, and Lauren had all joined them. Hope and Dakota passed a few whispered words, Hope's face trying to maintain a tough appearance. Riley caught only a few words as Dakota placed her hat on Hope's head, saying it was for luck. Looking at Brunt, he merely nodded in greeting, under strict orders no doubt from Cameron not to ask questions.

"So where's Freya?" Lauren asked.

"She was asked if she could help out with something back at the container yard," Brunt told her. When he saw Riley looking at him, he quickly added, "Nothing important, Boyle just wants some fresh eyes," in an attempt to keep her from worrying.

They walked back to the Black Box, Riley holding hands with Cameron and Hope, no one saying a word.

Down in the medical centre, the doctors were ready and the surgical suite was prepped.

"Give me a hug," Riley held out her arms to Hope.

Hope hesitated, and Riley knew what she was thinking, that if she hugged her mom now, it might be for the last time.

"I'm going to be sore afterward; it'll be a few days before I'll be able to hug anyone again," Riley told her, convincing herself that she didn't have the same thoughts.

Her ribs were nearly crushed by her daughter, but Riley relished the feeling. She stroked Hope's hair and back, then leaned beneath Dakota's hat to kiss her cheek.

"I love you, sweet pea."

"I love you, Mom."

Carrying those words with her, Riley entered the surgical suite, taking one last look at Hope, who was holding Dakota's hand. Cameron stood protectively behind them both, managing a smile that didn't look too worried. Abby was clearly the most concerned, her fingers fidgeting with the cross around her neck.

"You ready?" Robin asked as Riley entered. It was weird to think she'd be the one on the table this time.

Riley nodded, and began taking off her shirt and bra, overly conscious of Josh and Dr. Lewis's presence. They had no patient surgical gowns; after the surgery, Riley would only be covered by a blanket. Maybe they could have covered her with a sheet while she was still conscious, but Riley thought to hell with that, they were going to see her breasts anyway. They'd be the last ones to see them as they were.

"So the anaesthetic is going to hurt a bit going in," Haily explained as Riley lay on the table. She was quick to start the IV, her ability to find a vein swiftly and painlessly still top notch.

"How are you feeling?" Dr. Lewis asked, the only one of the day much to Riley's relief.

"Hungry," she replied, refusing to admit to her fear.

Dr. Lewis chuckled. "We'll make sure to have something good for you when you wake up."

Riley nodded.

"Count backward from one hundred," Haily instructed.

There was a burning in her arm as she counted, the anaesthetic flooding her system, mixing with her blood. Riley counted, knowing she wouldn't get far, having seen others pass out before reaching ninety.

As a darkness swept over her, she tried not to think about it being the last thing Mathias saw and thought of it anyway.

15
Evans Is Thinking

Although Evans walked at the head of the column, he no longer considered himself the leader of his party as they moved through the storm-soaked streets. He continued to play the figurehead, making sure his authority remained intact after whatever happened, but he wasn't making decisions like he once was. His party had become a kind of mob, an angry rabble. Evans still wasn't sure what had happened to Wycheck, but the discovery of his boots amongst the strangers' gear was more than enough to persuade the others. Now, they were following a map to a container yard that, based on the way the map was marked up, was their home base. Evans wasn't entirely sure what would happen when they got there and would rather not think about it. He thought the strangers were innocent, maybe not of killing Wycheck, but of the other murders pinned on them. A bullet was very different from a knife, and none of the other killed party members' gear was with their supply wagons. Of course, to everyone who was looking for someone to blame, this just meant that there was more than one group of people from the container yard who had attacked them.

Evans glanced over his shoulder at the party behind him. Even with the addition of the strangers' wagons, the line was shorter, more clumped together. The searchers who had been off scouring the surrounding area were now back with the party, tightly flanking its sides. At the very back, their prisoners were restrained. Evans wondered what would happen to them when they reached the container yard. He was glad that the others hadn't decided they were worthless, and that killing them was the best course of action. Unfortunately, that might not always remain true.

The party continued forward for several more minutes until a commotion brought them to a halt.

"What's going on?" Evans asked, as Ki-nam came riding up alongside him.

"It's one of the horses we managed to keep ahold of from the furniture store. It's acting up, being stubborn and nippy."

"Let's go see."

Evans followed Ki-nam and his horse to the middle of the party where the strangers' carts were being pulled. One of the horses pulling the second cart had stopped walking, refusing to move. When anyone came near it, it threw its head with its teeth snapping like a zombie's and attempted to rear. Their own horse, the one they had paired with the newcomer, had also stopped obeying orders, its head twisted away from its pulling mate in an attempt to avoid getting nipped.

Evans looked to Leo, who had been driving the cart. The man just shook his head. Nathan was also nearby, having climbed down from the seat of the other strange cart, the one whose horses were behaving, but even he wasn't approaching the horse. Everyone kept their distance, wondering how to handle the situation. Evans was concerned about the strange horse hurting their own and knew that soon someone would suggest shooting it. It wouldn't be the first night they ate horsemeat.

"Give me a moment," Evans told those within hearing. He headed for the back of the party where their captors were restrained. As he came into view, all three watched him warily; the one he thought was the youngest, Bryce, was stiffening. Although Evans hadn't personally beaten him, he hadn't done much to stop it either. He studied the three of them, while they studied him.

"That one," he pointed to Danny.

Arman, who had chosen to watch the prisoners personally, released Danny's restraints.

"Come with me," Evans told him. "Just remember that we still have your friends."

"I understand," Danny nodded as he climbed down off the back of the cart. A worried look passed between him and Bryce, while Lenny never took his eyes off Evans. Lenny had proven to be a talker, attempting to negotiate even during the assault, but now he remained quiet. Talking hadn't worked for him, so now he was studying.

Evans led Danny forward, toward the troublesome horse. Every time he glanced over his shoulder at the captive, Danny's eyes were darting here and there, glancing at all the glaring faces around him. His hands were tight at this sides, and shoulders hunched, ready to fight or flee should the situation arise.

"Your horse is causing some trouble. Do something about it," Evans instructed as they reached the front of the cart.

"That's Thumper," Danny commented, a small note of surprise in his voice. "He doesn't like to pull carts, not unless he's paired with Potato."

"We have only one other of your horses. That grey one with the next cart up." Evans pointed to where he could make out its head and ears.

Danny shifted around a bit until he could see for himself, but then shook his head. "That's Soot."

"So your horse is worthless to us."

"No, no! I can get him to walk. Just give me a chance."

Evans noticed that the slight panic in Danny's voice pleased those around them.

"I'll need someone to get Soot and bring him here."

"Nathan? Would you mind?"

Nathan shook his head and went to get the horse. Danny began approaching the annoyed beast, Thumper. He kept his eyes averted, moving toward the horse sideways, as Evans had seen Leo and Nathan do before with skittish horses. Thumper kept snorting loudly. He tossed his head less, seeming to focus on Danny's approach.

"It's okay, boy," Danny whispered as he inched closer. "It's okay, Thumper, I'm right here. You're okay."

Evans watched as Thumper's ears perked up at the sound of Danny's voice. When their captive got close enough, Thumper lowered his head, allowing his muzzle to be gently stroked while he snuffed up Danny's scent.

Between whispered soothings, Danny asked if someone could unharness the other horse, the one standing next to Thumper. Leo seemed eager to do it, but also moved in a slow, deliberate way. Thumper snorted at the newcomer, but Danny continued to pet him and whisper to him, attempting to guide his head to face the other way. It helped when Nathan returned with the grey horse, Soot. The wild horse seemed to recognize his companion and whickered at it; the grey horse replied with a soft whinny. Once the other horse was free of the harness, Nathan knew to walk the grey one over to take its place without being asked.

"I thought you said it would only pull carts next to some other horse?" Evans inquired.

"Yeah, Potato," Danny continued to speak as if still talking to the horse, "but he won't bite Soot. If you let me walk beside Thumper, he'll follow."

His words were greeted by a lot of uncomfortable murmuring. Several people didn't like the idea of Danny walking along, free of their makeshift 'prison' at the back. Some found the idea so unappealing, that they were back to demanding the horse be shot.

Evans mulled it over, weighing the pros and cons. It wasn't easy to find a well-trained horse, but there was more to it than that. By giving the prisoner a little bit of slack, he could better observe how he behaved. Evans didn't believe that Danny was the murderer he was being called, and perhaps letting him show that to the others might sway the other party members a little. Or it might turn them against Evans. He had to find a happy middle.

"Ki-nam, you got any rope with you?"

The former North Korean had been hovering around the periphery of the goings-on, his horse so perfectly obedient to him, that there was no risk of it walking into the gathered cluster of people and hurting one of them. Ki-nam took a climber's rope off the back of his saddle and tossed it over to Evans. People were still muttering their disapproval as he carried it over to Danny, the troublesome horse now relatively calm.

"Hold out your wrists together," Evans ordered.

Danny did so, obeying the command immediately. Maybe he realized that Evans was helping him in some small way.

After using one end of the rope to bind his wrists, Evans wrapped a few coils around Danny's waist, with enough slack between them so that the captive could move his arms around. The rest of the rope was then tied to Thumper's harness, effectively binding the two captives together. That was another reason Evans wanted to save the horse: it had become a prisoner just as the humans had, a potential bargaining chip depending on what happened when they reached the shipping container yard.

"Can you tell my friends I'm tied here?" Danny asked in a low whisper so that only Evans could hear him. Evans gave him no response, just tested his knots and stepped away.

"Show's over, everyone," he barked to those assembled. "Let's keep moving."

Instead of moving to the front of the line, Evans walked on the other side of the grey horse, keeping an eye on Danny. The young man was doing as instructed, keeping the irritated horse calm and moving forward. Although he could reach the knots that bound him to the horse, he didn't touch them or try to pull them loose in any way. Evans couldn't quite make out what Danny was looking at, not past the horseflesh and harnesses, but the young man seemed to focus mostly on Thumper. Evans guessed his eyes darted around to those near him from time to time, tracking their movements and the extent of their glares. Evans would've done the same.

Once he determined that Danny wasn't going to do something stupid, and that no one else was going to assault him, Evans dropped back to the rear of the line. The eyes of the remaining two captives, Bryce and Lenny, locked onto him the moment he was within sight.

"Your friend is fine, at least for now," Evans told them. "As long as he keeps doing his job, nothing will happen to him."

He got no response from the two still bound to their chairs. Deciding he wasn't going to get one, Evans began heading back to the front of the line.

"Wait," Lenny spoke up before he got very far.

Evans dropped back again, looking up at the black man.

"None of us have eaten in a long time, especially Danny. May we have some food, or at least water?"

"Shut up, prisoner!" Arman shouted, causing Bryce to flinch.

"It's alright, Arman, it's a reasonable request. How long has it been since Danny ate?"

"He missed dinner the night you took us, so whenever he ate lunch I suppose."

"I'll see what I can do."

Evans left the prisoners and slowly made his way forward along the line. He barely got past the cart holding them when Arman's horse trotted up alongside.

"Are you actually going to feed them?" he sneered.

"I'm not going to deny them water. Can you see to it that they get some? Preferably without spit in it."

Arman sneered. "I don't understand why you're being so accommodating."

"Do you know what we'll find at that container yard? Because I sure don't. Three of these people got away, so the odds are they'll know we're coming. I'd rather have as many bargaining chips as possible, and they're worth more if they're unhurt. Can you get them a bit of water? Maybe just give them a bottle each, and leave it up to them to decide how much they drink during the journey."

The wheels in Arman's mind were spinning behind his eyes. He was probably doing the math about how far they still had to go, and how a bottle wasn't much for that length of time. In the end, he seemed satisfied and consented to give the prisoners water.

Evans crossed in front of the rear cart so that he could come up behind Danny. Before reaching him, he swung his pack to his front and dug out a small container. Inside, was a literal trail mix of edibles Evans had picked up along the way: various nuts and seeds, along with dried berries and fruit that he had traded for at the last friendly settlement. Once his pack was settled again, Evans stepped up beside Danny, who startled slightly at his reappearance.

"Your friends tell me you haven't eaten in some time. Here." He held out the container to Danny.

Danny hesitated, eyeing the contents suspiciously. Evans pretended he wasn't watching the young man out of the corner of his eye as he reached into the container, plucked out some of the contents, and ate them himself. Danny still hesitated a moment longer, but his stomach won out, and he pinched some food between his fingers, then stuffed it in his mouth. Evans knew Danny couldn't hold the container and eat from it at the same time, not with his bound wrists, so he kept pace, monitoring just how much he ate. He also knew that if he left Danny alone with the food, someone would inevitably smack it out of his hands and that was just wasteful. No one would dare smack food out of Evans' hands.

***

After travelling all day, everyone was weary, no longer caring about Danny walking alongside the horse. Throughout their journey, Evans would drop from the front of the line to the back, checking on both party members and prisoners, and then walk back up along the opposite side, asking the people there if they were all right. As the sun began setting, casting the sky in a vivid orange, the black and white cat trotted alongside Evans again, only to disappear when Ki-nam came near on his horse.

"Elijah checked out that space marked on their map. It looks like somewhere we can spend the night; it's big enough."

"Good, everyone could use the rest."

From mouth to mouth, word was passed down the line that they would be stopping for the night soon. The news lifted the spirits of the party members, all of them eager to take a break. Having memorized the map, which Ki-nam carried, Evans led the party to the marked location. It was a recreational centre and Elijah stood outside, waiting by a pair of double doors that led into a gymnasium. The band of teenagers he had brought with him for the reconnaissance mission were already set up inside, their lanterns glowing in a corner they had claimed for themselves.

At first, Evans was unsure if the gym would fit everyone plus the horses and carts, not comfortably, but when he got inside, he saw that a pair of doors in one wall led to a second gymnasium.

"Have you searched the rest of the building?" he asked Elijah as people began streaming in behind them; some party members found spaces for themselves, while others didn't settle in yet, waiting for Evans to give the okay.

"No, but see these fold-up bleachers? With a bunch of us, we can easily move them to barricade the doors that lead into the rest of the facility. Unless you want to see what else is here? There might be more rooms we can spread out in."

"No," Evans shook his head. "We're only staying here the one night, so we're going to stay close together. Gather some volunteers to move those bleachers."

Elijah nodded and set to work.

Evans guided most of the people into the second gym, planning to keep the horses and carts near the door where they had entered. Although the prisoners' smaller carts fit through easily enough, it took more careful manoeuvring to get their own through. The horses were

167

unharnessed and, accompanied by a monitor each, they were taken to nibble on the grass in a nearby overgrown lot. Bryce and Lenny were still bound to their chairs, but now sat against one wall of the gym. They watched the procedures with Danny, who stood bound next to them, the end of the rope that had been tied to Thumper now tied to a bracket in the wall.

"Where are we going to keep them?" Arman asked in a low voice, his head flicking toward the prisoners as the final cart was squeezed in through the doors.

"There's an equipment room there. We can put them inside and put a guard at the door." Evans had opened every door in the gym before they could be blocked off, verifying what was on the other side. As soon as he saw the equipment room, he knew he was going to put Danny and his friends in it.

Eventually, the horses were brought into a section that was roped off for them by using the carts as posts. Evans untied Danny from the bracket. A couple of men joined him, ready to pick up the two who were bound to their chairs. Once Evans gave the nod, they brought the prisoners to the equipment room.

"Untie them; they won't be able to do anything in here," Evans ordered, taking off the rope that held Danny.

One of the men grunted in disagreement, but they all obeyed, freeing Bryce and Lenny from the chairs. It was pretty obvious the prisoners couldn't do much in this room. It was small, smelled of rubber, and was very dark once the metal doors were shut. All the equipment had been removed as a precaution, even the single dead light bulb. From the other gym, Evans could hear some of the kids giggling with delight, punctuated by the bouncing of a recently inflated basketball, and overlaid with the rumble of the spinning wheels of scooter boards. Evans thought they should take the air pump with them and maybe even the scooter boards; they might come in handy one day. He'd take a closer look at them later.

"I'll make sure you get some dinner provided you behave yourselves in here," Evans told the prisoners as he stood in the doorway. They were all rubbing the spots on their skin where the restraints had been tightest. Evans then shut the door, casting them into darkness.

In the second gym, almost everyone had already set up their tents and tarps; each one a glowing bubble from the lantern, flashlight, or candle inside, the canvas jiggling as people laid out their sleeping bags and mats within. In the aisles formed by the tents, kids were racing on the scooter boards, zooming along the dusty hardwood from one wall to the other, occasionally spinning out of control. Older teenagers were also finding joy in the small square boards with the four omnidirectional wheels.

Back in the first gym, most of the people had opted not to bother with the privacy of tents and tarps, merely laying their mats and bags down on the floor. Evans picked out a spot for himself near the equipment room, intending to make sure that the door remained shut; that no one opened it from either side. No sooner was his mat laid down, than the black and white cat reappeared, making himself comfortable on Evans' stuff. Evans sighed at the thought of car hair and possibly fleas transferring to his things, but at least his bedding would be warm when he decided to lie down.

Going back outside, Evans waited for the other party members who wanted to talk about what was going on. During their walk, it had been decided they would meet just outside wherever they stopped for the night. Evans stood under a long-dead light pole in a weedy parking lot, far enough away from the door to prevent accidental eavesdroppers, but close enough for his solar-powered lantern to be spotted. Eavesdroppers weren't really a problem; Evans let whoever wanted to, come to these things, but he understood that some people didn't want to know, and others didn't want their kids knowing.

Ki-nam and Arman showed up first, Elijah and Old Salt following not far behind them. Evans suspected he'd see the same group as when they decided to leave the townhouse, but then wasn't surprised when more arrived this time. The same mother as before was here; however, the father of a different family joined her. Two of the newcomers came to participate: an elderly man on wobbly legs, and a couple of members from Arman's team, most notably those who had found Wycheck. Even Leo came out, despite his dislike of groups and decision making. He lingered around the fringes of the meeting. He was probably there to make sure nothing happened to the horses.

"So by now you all know where we're going," Evans started off with.

"What's going to happen when we get there?" was the immediate response from the father.

"The majority of the party will hang back; only a few volunteers will continue forward to see about this container yard."

"What if they're hostile?" the elderly man asked. Several people jumped on his question in agreement while others answered him, saying they had already proven themselves to be hostile.

"That's something we'll have to figure out when it happens," Evans shrugged. "We don't know anything about that place yet."

"Get the prisoners ta tell us," Old Salt offered his opinion. "Get them ta talk about the defences there."

Several more cries of agreement.

"They're not going to tell us anything," Evans shook his head.

"How do you know if you don't ask?" Elijah wondered, his voice making it an actual question and not a judgement.

"If someone grabbed you in the middle of the night and was heading toward your camp, would you tell them anything?"

"Anyone would talk if you hit them hard enough," one of Arman's men grumbled.

"Yeah, they'd talk, but would they tell the truth? Probably not. Besides, do you really want to be the man that tortured someone? Because I gotta say, I wouldn't want to travel with you if you do."

Arman's man turned sheepish and looked down at his feet.

"And that goes for all of you. If this party turns sour, I'm out of here. I understand beating on that young man, Bryce, the first time. People were angry and upset, needing a release. I'm sorry it had to be on him, but that's not going to happen again."

A few exchanged looks, considering Evans' threat to leave. Evans knew it wouldn't happen. They would have to get the whole party on their side. If they didn't, and they made a move against him, they'd be cast out on their own. The reason people joined the party in the first place was so that they weren't alone anymore.

"Can't we just not go to this container yard place?" one of the newcomers asked timidly.

"These people are murderers!" Arman turned on her. "We know for a fact they killed Wycheck, and they probably killed the others as well."

"Others?" the father asked, as a ripple of similar concern waved through those who weren't in the know.

"Remember Carol? Lee? Moore? They didn't just disappear or have an accident. Someone cut their throats."

"And you didn't tell us?" the mother wheeled on Evans.

"There was never any danger to the group," Evans attempted to calm her. "Everyone who was killed was alone when it happened. There's a reason I always tell people to partner up, to never be by themselves."

A couple of people now looked at Arman, wondering why his searchers hadn't followed this basic instruction, one they virtually all knew before even joining the party. It was dangerous to be alone.

Arman didn't bother to give them a real response. "We can't let them get away with this."

"What if their place is unassailable?" the old man questioned. "If they're as dangerous as you say, maybe we should just leave them alone."

"We're going to at least investigate," Evans answered. "Knowing where people are and what kind of set up they have has always benefited us in the past. As I said, once we see the place, we'll make a decision as to what we'll do next. We'll be there tomorrow."

Evans sighed as the group went over the same ground, again and again. It was essentially a discussion of anger versus fear. They weren't going to come to an agreement, so he planned to do what he said he'd do, as it was the best middle ground he could find. Only volunteers would go near the container yard, the rest could stay safely back. Whatever happened after that would happen; Evans just intended on surviving it.

When the others realized that further talk with this group was pointless, punctuated by the arrival of a handful of zombies, the meeting was called to an end. In the darkness of night, they headed back inside the gyms leaving behind Arman, Ki-nam, and Elijah to take out the dead. Evans knew the group members would discuss things further with people who were likely to take their individual sides, who would see things from the same perspective. As he shifted the cat and lay down on his bedding, he was glad that they would be there by tomorrow. Any longer and his party might tear itself in two.

***

This time, the prisoners were with the first cart. Evans had ordered that all three of them be tied up as Danny had been the other day, bound to the team of captured horses pulling one of their own carts. There had been some disagreement about this; people worried that with all of them together, they might make some sort of break for it, but Evans managed to persuade them that that wouldn't happen. He personally walked beside the prisoners, Leo drove the cart, and Arman and several of his men surrounded them. They wouldn't get the chance to attempt an escape.

"Anything you want to tell me about the container yard before we get there?" Evans asked Danny without looking at him.

Unexpectedly, Danny actually spoke. "You're making a mistake."

"How so?"

This time Danny kept his silence. His words could be taken several ways, and Evans wondered which way he had meant. It could be that Danny was protesting his innocence again, or that the container yard was going to slaughter the party when they arrived. Either way, Evans knew he couldn't stop what was unfolding, only mentally prepare himself for it.

It was a very silent journey with the party members worried about what was to come. Those who could do so while on the move checked that their weapons were ready, while others held tightly to loved ones.

Some of them had been in a battle before, even a siege after some slavers had kidnapped a few of their people, but this was the first time they were so divided about the attack. Once someone died, and Evans felt sure that someone would, they would all swing one way or the other, retreat or push forward.

"There's the warehouse," Arman pointed.

It had been decided that the party members who weren't volunteering were going to stay with the horses, carts, supplies, and children in a warehouse on the outskirts of the container yard. Not knowing how much of the container yard was inhabited had made it a bit of a risk, but Evans didn't want too large a gap between them. As they approached, Evans was pleased to see that it was a stable-looking structure, clearly unused. Debris had built up along the edges, predominantly on one side, over the course of several storms. Some of it had to be cleared away to get the doors open. Once it was, a few holes were discovered in the roof at the far end that let in the light, but it would do. There was easily enough room for the entire party to fit inside while avoiding the holes.

"Volunteers, meet me outside when you're ready." Evans shrugged out of his pack, placing it on a cart. He then started untying the prisoners from their horses.

Evans, Ki-nam, and Arman were the first ones out, each of them holding the end of a prisoner's rope. Gags had been bound tightly around their mouths so that they couldn't scream and give away positions, but the blindfolds had been left off. They waited several minutes, and then Evans was surprised when a lot more volunteers than he had expected joined them. Either several people had been convinced during a late night talk, or a bunch would rather be where the action was than waiting for word. More likely it was a combination of both.

"Everyone ready?" Evans asked once it appeared that no one else would be joining them. He was answered by a lot of solemn nodding.

"Remember why we're here. These people killed our friends," Arman spoke, shaking Lenny's rope in the process. He got a few grunts and quiet, yet encouraging, vocalizations in response. No one would outright cheer or war cry, not without knowing exactly where the container yard camp was.

"Split into three groups, each of which will be following either myself, Arman, or Ki-nam," Evans ordered. As a shuffling of positions took place, he watched the worried faces peering out of the warehouse. Young Annabelle was one of them, the black and white cat dangling absurdly from her arms. She would probably get scratched up soon if she kept holding it like that.

Once the volunteers had formed their groups, Evans nodded to the other leaders. They weren't going to separate much, never more than a container aisle over from one another, but it was safer than being all clumped up.

"Just remember, the prisoners are our bargaining chips," Evans whispered to them, holding his gaze longer on Arman.

Arman grunted, but they both nodded. Now they were ready. Evans led his group into the nearest aisle.

The container yard was a maze, with several right angle turns, but thankfully no blind alleys. They quickly learned that the three groups would have to share a path from time to time, and so would have to take turns, keeping a safe distance between them. Evans' eyes darted everywhere: around corners, to the tops of containers, to exposed container doors. There were far too many places for someone to hide in this warren, and he kept his shotgun poised and ready to fire at any of them. They came across a single zombie, his ragged clothing and loose skin having somehow become caught on a container latch. Evans let the man behind him take it out, a quick and quiet knife through the eye socket. It was the only thing that moved in this place besides them. Beside him, Danny began to tense and Evans knew he was getting close.

They rounded a bend. Evans saw the large open space between the containers on either side of him, and the ones straight ahead. He had just enough time to realize that those containers were definitely a man-made wall, before the shot came. In a single moment, there was the whine of a bullet passing nearby, a muzzle flash from the wall, and a spray of blood from Danny's shoulder. The crack of the rifle came less than a second later.

"Get down!" Evans screamed as Danny fell to the pavement.

Grabbing his bound prisoner, Evans ducked into cover with him, ending up behind a different container from everyone else: a sort of island where he couldn't get back to the aisle that led away without first crossing within sight of the camp. Evans ignored his predicament, and inspected Danny's injury. He had been hit high in the shoulder, the bullet having torn a chunk out of his trapezius. It was so close to a head shot that Evans had to believe that had been the intention. Did they know it was their own man? Unlikely, but it still meant they were shooting to kill.

"I need a med kit!" Evans shouted, removing Danny's gag and pressing it to the wound.

One came clattering over on a scooter board. Evans looked over his shoulder and saw Elijah giving him a thumbs up from a place of safety. Apparently, he not only decided to bring the board from the gym, but had correctly assumed it might be useful during their raid. Evans nodded his thanks and set to work patching up Danny, who writhed in shocked pain beneath his hands.

Arman's group had begun to return fire. Lenny cowered on the ground beside them, tied to Arman's belt. As more and more shots rang out, Evans knew that Danny was right. It had been a mistake to come here, but it was too late to turn back now.

16
Misha's Awake

Misha was woken by a low whine next to him. It had been steadily increasing in frequency over the span of months: Rifle needing to go out in the middle of the night.

"Okay, *bratishka*," Misha mumbled as he sat up on the mattress. Rifle was wiggling next to him, trying to get up, while still whining deep in his throat. Without any light to see by, Misha was still able to get his arms around the dog and place him upright on the container floor. In the darkness, the other dogs shifted, some of them annoyed by the disturbance while others looked forward to a late-night trip outside the container.

Stepping carefully, Misha made his way past the dogs who had gotten up and were standing in the way to the container door. He slid the simple inner latch aside, not having bothered with the bigger, more secure one, and pushed open one of the doors. A stream of fur burst forth from his container as the dogs exited. Misha waited patiently for Rifle to make his way over, and then walked slowly out with him.

"Where are we walking tonight, old man?" Misha asked in a whisper.

The night was cloudy and dark with only a few reflective surfaces visible, and only those not in shadow. Misha walked slowly between the containers more from memory than from any sort of vision. Rifle chuffed beside him.

When he chuffed again, Misha looked down at him. It wasn't unusual for Rifle to give some sort of reply to his questions, but an unprompted sound usually meant something. The sound of dog nails on concrete came clicking up behind them, but Rifle was focused forward, his ears not even twitching backward to listen to who was coming behind them. Misha glanced over his shoulder and spotted Bullet, his patches of paler fur easier to make out than Rifle's in the darkness. Bullet caught up to them and started to keep pace just behind Misha, also focused forward. Whatever Rifle had caught the scent of, Bullet seemed to have noticed it too. Concerned about what it meant, Misha headed for the wall in the direction they were pointing, reluctantly leaving Rifle behind.

Even in the dark, he spotted movement on the wall, and once he got close enough, he made out whispered voices, but not their words. Misha's heart leapt into his throat. Freya had shown up the other day, claiming a need to check on their storm damage personally. They were fine, as they usually were; just a few things that hadn't been properly bolted down needed to be fished out of the river, while other items had sunk to the bottom. If they ever found another scuba tank, Misha and a few others were capable of retrieving that stuff. Something else had happened during Freya's visit, however. Boyle and Karsten had taken her aside for a private conversation, and her face was exceptionally stern afterward. Misha thought he knew what might be happening, as it had happened before with other people. Evidence had been found of a fairly severe crime, but there were no suspects. Anyone from the container yard could be the perpetrator, and so someone from the Black Box was brought over to help investigate. Misha was sure he would have heard something if someone had turned up murdered, so what sort of crime could it have been? Was this activity on the wall a part of it? Were vital supplies being stolen and handed off to someone on the other side?

"Hey, whoever's down there, can you help out?" a whispered voice called down from the wall. Apparently, Misha had been spotted. "We got a horse here."

A horse? In the middle of the night? Misha looked to Bullet at his side. The dog wasn't growling or whining, just curiously cocking his head at the wall. Looking back, Misha could just make out Rifle, still plodding toward them. He also did not appear alarmed.

A flashlight clicked on and shone in Misha's face. "Misha? You gonna help or what?"

"Yeah, yeah, just stop blinding me." Misha had raised his arms, attempting to shield his face and preserve his night vision, but it was already blown. After the light was removed, he had to hold his arms out like a blind man, searching for the nearest ladder. By the time he found it, he was able to see well enough to climb. When he reached the top, he heard Rifle huff and flop over, taking a break until it was time to go back asleep.

On top of the wall, Misha could make out a cluster of people gathered around an opening. It appeared to be most of the wall guard, which had Misha nervous. In this darkness, they needed to be especially aware. He nearly tripped over the feet of someone sitting in shadow, his or her back pressed up against the second level of the wall.

"Here, I made a torch," someone whispered. After a few sparks from a lighter, the torch went up bright and fiery and was slotted into a nearby bracket.

Misha immediately looked outward, hoping the light didn't draw the attention of something dangerous out there. He then looked down at the feet he nearly tripped over and saw that it was two people. Shaidi and Larson were side by side, panting slightly between drinking some guards' water and eating late night meals. Concerned, Misha went to the opening in the wall and looked over. Some of the wall guards were down there, giving food and water to a pair of exhausted and sweaty horses, but there was nothing and no one else.

"Where's Danny? Where are the others?" Misha asked the two who had returned alone.

"We're waiting for Karsten and Boyle, they should be on their way. Let them eat, its been over a day since they last had food," a guard answered for them. "Help us with the horses."

Misha agreed to help, but his mind was racing through all the worst-case scenarios, which got pretty terrible. The guards had already erected the crane that Harry built, his mechanical engineer knowledge invaluable, and now lowered the horse harness over the side. The first horse danced a bit, none of the horses being fond of the crane, but it was too tired to struggle for long. With the horse strapped up came the hard part and explained why so many guards had gathered. Although the pulley system built into the crane lessened the overall weight, it still took several men hauling to raise the horse. Misha waited at the top, the pullers having climbed down inside the wall. He worked the brake so that if people slipped, the horse wouldn't suffer a fall. Once the horse reached the height of the opening, Misha guided it through, whispering comforting words. The head of the crane swung until the horse was past the wall. They then worked in reverse, a more difficult job to control and required more focus from Misha with the brake, until the horse was on solid ground again. Releasing it from the harness, everyone prepared to do it again with the second horse.

When both horses were finally safe, they were led away to their pseudo-stables. It was then that Boyle and Karsten appeared. They were sweaty and tired, and it didn't take a detective to figure out that both had helped with the lifting of the horses. Shortly after they mounted the wall, Shaidi and Larson stood up on shaky legs and the torch was snuffed out. The guards, although desperate to know what was going on, were ordered back to their posts. Misha had the freedom to follow the others back down off the wall where they could talk more safely on the ground.

"Tell us," Karsten said, not bothering to ask the questions everyone wanted to ask. Misha hadn't been the only one roped in by the guards: two others who couldn't sleep for whatever reason also stood around.

"Bryce, Lenny, and Danny have been kidnapped," Shaidi said, her voice harsh with exhaustion.

Misha's blood turned to ice and his knees felt weak. When Bullet leaned against him, he was nearly pushed over.

"We were attacked last night," Larson picked up the story. "Don't really know by who. Me, Shaidi, and Jon managed to get out of there with two of the horses."

"Where's Jon now?" Boyle asked.

"There was no way all three of us could ride the horses back, not as fast as we wanted to move and not bareback," Shaidi said, shaking her head.

Misha hadn't noticed the horses' lack of saddles and reins until she mentioned it.

"Jon stayed to follow the group that grabbed the others. We stuck around, hiding, until we found out they had found our map and were heading here," Shaidi told them. "The moment we knew, Jon volunteered to stay behind and keep an eye on them while we got here as fast as we could to warn everyone."

"Are the others still alive?" Boyle asked the question that was trapped in Misha's throat.

"They were when we left." Larson looked down at his feet, clearly ashamed about abandoning his brother and the others. "We didn't see much of them; it was too dangerous to get close, but they were alive."

"How long until they get here? How many of them are there?" Karsten had gone cold and calculating, becoming the submarine captain he had once been.

"They should arrive sometime tomorrow. Or today. You know, after the sun's up," Larson fumbled. "I can't say I counted, but there seemed to be a lot of them."

"I'd put them at around four dozen, although that's a rough estimate, and they weren't all combatants," Shaidi added. "I saw some kids with them."

"Kids?" In the dark, Boyle's expression couldn't really be seen, but his voice conveyed his confusion. "I've never heard of a group with kids surprise attacking another group, especially one that would take hostages and then head to their main camp."

"They also had old folks," Larson mentioned.

"There's a first time for everything," Shaidi shrugged. "We certainly don't know their motives, just that it happened. *Is* happening. We need to prepare for them."

"Okay. You two should get some sleep for now; we'll get the rest of the details in the morning," Boyle excused them, although they continued to hang around. "Karsten? I think we better get planning."

Karsten grunted his agreement.

"Should we warn everyone?" Misha asked, the first opportunity he had to speak since learning of what happened.

"Not right now," Karsten shook his head. "I believe Larson when he says they won't get here until after sun up, and if they've stopped for the night, which is likely with kids and elderly, they might not even be here until the afternoon. Still, we'll be prepared by morning. We'll inform the morning guard before they start their shift, and then everyone else as they get up. We need to bolster the numbers of people we have up there. Cancel any jobs outside the wall and any unnecessary ones within."

"I agree. Let's go check our numbers," Boyle led Karsten away, the two putting their heads together to plan, their conversation falling into a whisper that got harder to hear the farther away they got.

Shaidi and Larson drifted off together, trudging back to their containers, while the other two who had been listening in disappeared into the shadows.

"Rifle?" Misha whispered, wondering where his dog had gone.

He heard a wheeze as Rifle got on his feet and plodded out from the shadow alongside the wall. Bullet was with him, looking up at Misha like he could explain what was going on.

"Come on, boys, we're going to need some sleep if we're going to deal with this tomorrow."

Together, they made their slow journey back to their container. Not all the other dogs had returned by the time they went inside, but that was okay. They would be fine outside, but Misha left one of the doors open anyway. He didn't think it was going to rain before morning, and he wanted the added sunlight to wake him. That is, if he could even fall back to sleep.

***

When the morning came, Misha found himself sitting on a stool in the opening at the front of his container. People glanced at him as they got up and headed for breakfast or the toilets; they weren't used to seeing him there, not at this time of day. Misha paid them no attention; they would learn soon enough what was going on as they were handed their half-rationed breakfasts. With an expected siege, food was being conserved more than ever as Boyle and Karsten prepared for everything, including being cut off from the Black Box. Misha waited for his assignment, glad that Karsten had picked up a fresh load of food just the other day.

The dogs had picked up on his stress and were confused about the break in routine. They wandered in circles in front of the container, clearly wondering why they hadn't gone on a run that morning. Even Rifle was up, standing on stiff legs beside Misha, his ears up and listening for danger. Misha didn't think he had slept much either. After going back to bed, his *bratishka* had made a lot more noise than usual, grunting and sighing and shifting positions on the mattress. Rifle always knew when something was up.

"Hey, Misha!"

Misha turned and spotted Brunt walking toward him. He raised his hand in a half wave to acknowledge him, and Brunt jogged the rest of the way over.

"You know about what happened?"

"Yeah. You here to give me an assignment?"

"Actually, I'm not. Cameron asked me to let you know we're going to the Black Box with Dakota."

Misha frowned. It wasn't like them to leave at a time like this.

"Apparently, they have an injured animal over there and want Cameron to consult. It's why Freya came over here, to get her." Brunt wasn't lying, but he seemed to be relaying information he didn't quite believe.

"Why are you and Dakota going, then?"

Brunt shrugged. "Cameron asked us to come. Dakota wants to see her friends, so that's fine. I wanted to stay, but she was really insistent."

That would explain why Brunt thought he had been lied to. Cameron wouldn't insist he come, not with an impending attack, unless she had a good reason. Her reason was apparently something she didn't want to reveal until they were away from anyone to whom Brunt could spill the beans. Misha briefly wondered if she was pregnant and going to the Black Box to confirm it. It was the best outcome he could come up with off the top of his head and decided to believe that was the reason, even if she was a bit old for a baby now.

"All right, I guess I'll see you guys when you get back then." At least he wouldn't have to worry about their safety during the impending attack.

"Yup."

Neither of them mentioned the fact that Misha could very well be killed before they got back depending on what happened. After a moment of standing there without being able to think of anything else to say, Brunt left. Misha checked the barrel of his rifle again, even though he had thoroughly cleaned it the moment there was enough light. Unable to wait any longer, Misha got up and headed to the community building, hoping they had an assignment for him this time. When he had gone to get his breakfast earlier, Boyle and Karsten were still hammering out the details, including where to put various people. All nine of Misha's dogs came with him.

The centre was crowded, and no one complained when the dogs came inside. All the tables and chairs had been pushed back and piled up around the walls, while extra cots and mattresses were found and laid out in the space. The centre was becoming a makeshift infirmary, preparing for the worst. Upon the largest, continuous blackboard surface, a diagram of the container yard had been drawn in several shades of chalk and carefully labelled. On a nearby whiteboard, the labels corresponded to people's names: those who would be in charge of each area. Misha was glad to see he wasn't one of them. He could take orders, but not give them.

Weaving through the crowd of people who awaited their assignments, a few holding their food without eating it, Misha spotted Larson. He knew him pretty well. The boy used to have a Golden Retriever that had passed away from old age a couple of years ago, as had many dogs from before the Day. The way he had treated his dog had caused Misha to like him, but he also got to know him through Bryce and Becky, the boy's cousins turned siblings. Misha had once saved Becky from drowning shortly before boarding the Diana, and had then checked on them fairly regularly when they had adopted old Shoes, the Basset Hound, from him.

"Misha, I'm so sorry about Danny," Larson spoke the moment he saw Misha was close enough to hear him.

"Don't worry about it. I know you would have done more if you could, even if your brother wasn't among the captured. Do you have an assignment yet?"

Larson shook his head, and so they waited together. The dogs threaded through the crowd, looking for scraps and head scratches, but they never went too far, always circling back to Misha. Rifle and Bullet never left his side, the old dog sitting and leaning against Misha's leg. A few times, someone came over to ask Larson what he knew about the people who were coming, and he answered as best he could despite being obviously uncomfortable.

"All right, everyone, settle down!" Boyle's voice called out over the heads of the crowd as he stood up on a table. "I'm assuming everyone here is aware of what's happening?"

No one said they didn't while a majority nodded solemnly.

"Good. Now, as you know, we didn't have time to reconnect the bridge to Animal Island after the storm. This means no one can go there for safety. This centre is the safest place, and I hope anyone too young or too old to fight on the walls will stay inside. As for the rest of you, form two orderly lines at either door, where you will be given an assignment."

The crowd shuffled as they obeyed. Larson and Misha stood in the same line together, the one that headed to the door where Boyle was.

"Do you see Freya anywhere?" Misha asked, scanning the crowd for her face.

"I didn't even know she was here," Larson admitted. "Why?"

"It's nothing, never mind."

The line shuffled along as the assignments were doled out. Parents who were given orders that didn't allow them to stay with their kids, stepped to one side just outside the door, giving their children last minute instructions and hugs. The older kids all had knives and slingshots, and were prepared to defend their younger siblings if it was called for. Misha suspected that with the size of the invading force, they'd be okay, but neither Larson nor Shaidi had gotten a good look at their supplies, and couldn't say whether or not they had any heavy artillery. One well-aimed RPG could easily blast a hole through their wall and kill dozens.

"Misha, will your dogs take orders from other people?" Boyle asked when he reached the front of the line.

"Not really," Misha shrugged. "Not all of them even listen to me that well."

"But they'll be following you out there?"

"Most likely. They know something's going on, so they'll stick close."

"I'm putting you on the wall."

Misha felt his muscles tighten, although the dangerous assignment wasn't unexpected. He was a really good shot after all.

"Would you mind leaving a dog or two in the centre? They might help keep the kids calm and can sniff over anyone who comes in injured, just in case."

"Yeah, I'll pick a few to stay." Misha understood the part about the kids, but a sniff check? They were people attacked by people, not zombies, so why would they need the dogs to sniff for possible infection? Did it have something to do with Freya being there?

There was no time for questions though, as Boyle gave him his specific location and Larson stepped up to receive his assignment next. As Misha located some nearby rope to tie up the dogs who were staying until the doors could be closed, he heard Larson complain. It was obvious that he hadn't slept despite his exhausting journey here. Boyle wanted him to find a place to lie down, to keep him in reserve for the nightshift if things lasted that long. Misha knew Larson stood no chance of winning the argument, that he would be left out of the battle's beginning.

Misha picked three of his dogs to stay at the centre. He chose the Retriever/Lab mix, Trigger, because she was pregnant, Barrel, the stumpy Doberman because the kids liked him, and Stock, the ugly Pit Bull-possibly-Bull Dog-possibly-Pug mixture. Stock was not a pretty dog, whatever he was, but he also looked fierce, which might bring some comfort to those inside the centre. Barrel looked up at Misha with dejected eyes as he was tied up to one of the centre's support posts.

"Don't you look at me like that," Misha told him. "I'd love to stay in here with you."

With the three dogs secure, he checked the diagram to see who would be in charge of his area. It was White, who usually worked as a lookout when outside the wall. Misha was a bit surprised that Boyle hadn't chosen one of the other team leaders, but then maybe they were needed to help out elsewhere. Anyone who'd be going up on the wall didn't need much instruction.

Jogging to the wall, Misha mentally prepared himself. It had been awhile since he had to shoot at living human beings, and he still dreamt about the other time. Often he dreamt about when the Diana was under siege, when he had to fire at invaders. The dream usually ended with sharks.

White was standing at the base of the main section of wall, out in the open where those assigned could easily find him.

"Misha, you're just up there, two left of center," he pointed while double checking a notebook he carried. "You'll be working with Carson."

Misha nodded and headed for the ladder. He was glad to be on the main section of wall and not assigned to the far end near the rocky shore, where they hadn't yet finished doubling the height, leaving anyone over there without as much protection. Carson, a wall guard who Misha saw regularly but didn't talk too much, was waiting for him. The upper container doors had already been moved to seal off the wall save a small gap.

"I hear you're a better shot than me," Carson said as they briefly shook hands. "I figure you lie down in the shooter's position and I'll back you up. Let me see what kind of rifle you have."

Misha handed the gun over, letting him inspect it. While he waited, he glanced over the side, down at his dogs. Rifle and Bullet were sitting nearby, looking anxiously up at him, while the remaining four wandered about, wondering what they should do.

"Yeah, we got a fair amount of ammo that'll work with this. I'll keep you in supply." Carson handed Misha back his gun. They had recently begun to make bullets, but there still wasn't that much ammo. Misha hoped he didn't have to fire a shot, and that if he did, only one.

Lying down on the warm, irregular metal surface, Misha lined his rifle up with the small opening, staring out at the somewhat distant containers they had yet to search.

The sun crawled across the sky behind some clouds. With every passing minute, Misha became more uncomfortable, but he refused to move beyond a subtle shifting. He knew that when that other group came, things would happen fast. He wasn't aware of it, but he was even blinking less frequently.

Something moved amongst the containers. A tiny reflection off something metal cast a pale beam of light onto the side surface of an upper container. Had Misha not being staring at the same thing for as long as he had, he would have missed it: an easily dismissed shimmer that he might still have written off if it weren't for the tiny bit of movement and barely vocalized murmurs of other nearby watchers who had also seen it. The light hadn't been far into the stacks. The wires that made up Misha's muscle system tightened, his body hardening in place, wrapped around the rifle. He regulated his breathing and waited, counting in his head, peering through the scope.

The first person to enter Misha's sights was Danny.

NO! the scream never made it out of his mind and past his lips. The next rifleman over pulled the trigger, too frightened, too tense to see properly. Misha watched the blood spray, saw Danny go down.

Then everyone was firing, the men amongst the containers diving for cover, shooting back. Several shots pinged off the metal around Misha, forcing him to roll into cover temporarily. The moment it was safe, he rolled back.

Where is Danny? Where is Danny? he kept thinking, scanning the spaces. There was his blood, but where was he?

"Why aren't you firing?" Carson was yelling at Misha from behind, not daring to shake him as he seemed to want to, worried about throwing off Misha's shot.

Misha completely ignored him, watching through his scope as a medical kit flashed through an opening, sitting on something with wheels. Were the supplies for Danny? He had to hope so.

A stranger poked around the corner where the meds had come from, a rifle in his hands. Misha had a perfect shot to take him out, clean through the head. Instead, he pulled to the right, firing at the container next to his face, the spark causing the stranger to quickly withdraw.

Misha couldn't shoot anyone, not until he knew Danny was all right.

17
Dean's In Motion

His sieve of a mind couldn't remember why they were heading in this direction. He shuffled along, the center of a comet made of rot, moving over the land as a diseased amoeba. Behind them, they left a trail of trampled everything; small, weak structures collapsed against their force, frail zombies fallen and unable to get back up beneath the feet of those behind, flesh, organs, and even limbs torn off, dropped to the ground, forgotten. A persistent, never-ending moan always announced their coming, scattering the animals, and a reeking, slippery mire always let one know where they had been.

A tiny puff of smoke, black and wispy had risen briefly in the distance. It's what Dean was heading for, even if he had no idea. Smoke frequently meant humans, and he was hungry. He was tired of eating the rotting flesh of his companions; he wanted something fresh. With such a large mob around him, it wouldn't be easy; he'd have to fight through his own kind to make sure he got a bite, but he could do it. He had done it before.

Saggy blue shirt bumped into him, the result of being bumped by another. Dean reacted by stumbling into the zombie on his other side, continuing the kinetic chain until it managed to ripple to the edge of the horde. This happened frequently while they were on the move, with the weakest of them getting knocked over, and never getting back up again. If Dean had a mind that wanted to look down, he would see his feet covered in the filth of those ahead of him. At the back of the comet horde, where the slowest zombies were thinned out, they wouldn't even be able to see their feet for the debris they were slogging through.

They were like a storm, a new natural disaster. Very few had stood against them, and none had survived. Only those who hid, who stayed quiet had weathered their coming and lived to tell the tale.

Dean walked on, unaware of his southerly course.

II
The Watchers

Mark Green pulled himself out of the river mud, fighting the suction threatening to keep him in place. He had just narrowly avoided being seen by one of the peripheral zombies, one of those that separated from the flood to wander off on their own. They were dangerous, for if one got excited and managed to alert the others, the entire comet could turn in its direction.

Free of the mud, the twenty-six year old sprinted off through the woods, leaping over fallen logs, ducking under branches, and barrelling through bushes. He knew he was far enough away not to worry about the noise he made, but he still instinctively avoided the louder, snappier branches on the ground. Mark had been running for a full five minutes, not an unusual length of time for him, when he reached the tiny camp. *Camp* was barely the word for it. There were no tents, and at the moment, no fire. Nestled against the root system of a large, fallen tree within a jumble of rocks, a tarp splattered with natural colours was easy to miss if you weren't looking for it. Not caring about the puddle that had gathered next to the tarp after the storm, Mark crawled underneath it. Gathered inside were his teammates, his family, all four of them crunched together within the hollow, only somewhat cleaner than Mark himself. There used to be more of them, but they had been lost along the way. Suzanne was the only person crazy enough to join them, the only one who hadn't known Dean when he was alive.

"They're definitely moving in the direction of that large settlement," Mark reported, accepting the water that Suzanne held out to him and taking a large swallow.

"Fuck," Boss sighed, running a thick hand across his flat features. "Can we get there in time?"

"If we move now, and we move fast, I think we can make it."

"Right, are you good to keep going?"

"Always."

"Then you, Suz, and Tommy haul ass. Betty and I will handle the gear."

"Can *you* get there in time to get behind the walls?" Tommy asked as he duck waddled his way out from under the tarp.

"What does that matter?" Boss grumbled. "We've been fine outside before, and we'll be fine again. Now run your young asses off."

Mark crawled out after Tommy, Suzanne right behind him. All three left behind their packs, taking only their running belts each of which held a pistol, an extra mag of ammunition, a knife, and a bottle of water. They also left behind their two oldest teammates, who weren't really that old. Boss was the only one starting to look it with the dash of grey in his hair, the increasing lines in his face, and the bad limp he had developed after breaking his leg just under a year ago. Betty would take care of him though; she was tough as nails and determined to keep everyone from dying.

Tommy led the way, setting the pace at a jog instead of Mark's earlier sprint. They had much farther to go this time. On Tommy's belt, he carried two additional items: a compass and a map. Although each of them had a well-trained sense of direction and a good memory for places, it would be foolish not to bring them along.

"So how was your mud bath?" Suzanne teased as she hurried along just ahead of Mark. Soon, they wouldn't be able to talk and run, but for now she wanted more details about Mark's investigation.

"I feel so pretty," he responded.

She laughed and glanced back at him with a flash of bright brown eyes. Her very short, golden hair still shone, even in this flat light. That hair was the first part of her that Mark had fallen in love with, back when it was long and worn in a pair of French braided pigtails. It had been kept short, like his own, for years now, but Mark still loved the way it caught the light and how it felt beneath his fingers.

"Any problems?" she asked next.

Mark reported the details he knew she wanted. He told her how close the wanderers got, where they went—under the river water for the most part in this instance—the animals he spotted, and other odd bits, like the license plate that was nowhere near a car or road. By the time he was done, he was out of words. Suz wasn't, and she recited the details back to him, a sort of memory game they played. When Tommy showed no interest in conversation, she sang for a bit, some old rock and roll song, until she couldn't anymore. They fell into a vocal silence, listening to the rhythmic pounding of their feet, and the steady exhalations of their lungs.

The three of them ran for a long time, moving through both woods and streets, a marathon that took them wide around the comet herd, around Dean's mob. Mark could still picture the bullet-headed man when he was alive, when they had first met. After Mark had gotten separated from the people he knew, he managed to get back to his apartment where the mercenaries found him. Dean had sat on his couch, one of his large boots propped up against the edge of the coffee table. Thinking of Dean inevitably led to remembering the school where the mercenary had been tricked by the scientists there into being infected. Mark had disliked the scientists, especially the one named Roy, the moment he had clapped eyes upon them. His first instinct had proven to be right.

Once the shit hit the fan and the school needed to be evacuated, the mercenaries who had been looking after Mark, brought him along, led by the black man, Boss. They separated from the rest of the group, who were heading to a prison, a place they thought would be no different from the school. Instead, they stole a canvas-backed truck planning to drive to Seattle, where Mark's mom lived. They never did make it that far, at least not then. Mark couldn't remember exactly how long they had been travelling before learning of Dean's continued existence as a zombie far smarter than the others. For a while they thought that he was somehow following them, but then he stopped. They decided to make it their duty to follow him, and to warn everyone they could of his coming. Ever since then, they had been tracking the ever-growing herd around him. When Suzanne became the sole survivor of a group after Dean's horde passed through them, she joined the team. It was the only time their numbers had increased, instead of decreased. The team was far too familiar with tragedy. None of them had ever been able to get close enough to Dean to put him down, despite numerous attempts. His wall of murderous flesh had so far proven to be impenetrable.

Mark had no idea how long they had been running. His mind wandered through the corridors of his memories, his body followed Tommy and Suzanne on autopilot, and he drank when he was thirsty. Sometimes he thought of things that happened before the zombie outbreak, like riding on the back of his friend's motorcycle, weaving through traffic. Other times, the memories came from after the outbreak: memories like spray painting messages for his dad, hoping the man was alive and would find him, and the first time he kissed Suzanne, shy and embarrassed as they sat side-by-side on a bridge, their fishing lines in the water.

The distant, echoing crack of gunfire brought Mark out of his reverie. Tommy slowed them to a stop, all three walking in tight cycles to keep their muscles from seizing, and popping open their water bottles to take a drink.

"That can't be good," Suzanne was the first one to comment.

"They must be under attack by someone," Mark agreed.

"Doesn't matter if there's two groups, they both need to get to shelter before Dean gets here," Tommy shook his head.

"How are we going to handle this?" Mark deferred to the older man's wisdom.

"Do we have something to use as a white flag? Something we can wave on the attacker's side, provided this isn't a civil war going on within the walls."

"There's my shirt," Suzanne instantly volunteered, stripping out of the sweaty thing. Everyone on their team had seen each other naked on more than one occasion, so there was nothing odd to them about Suzanne standing there in her sports bra.

"All right, I'll take that and try to find the attacking leader if that's what's happening," Tommy instructed. "Mark, go spy on the wall, and find the best way to approach them once we get any outsiders to understand the situation; but be careful, they may shoot anything that moves out here. Suz, you're going to watch our backs. Find somewhere up high and keep an eye out for Dean's approach."

Both Mark and Suzanne nodded their agreement to his plan. With the decision made, they split up, Mark and Suzanne kissing and placing their foreheads together briefly, as was their custom. They didn't need to say the words: they understood how the other felt completely.

Mark wasn't sure what the best way to spy on the wall would be; it had been a while since they had first discovered and made note of the settlement, and they had never before made contact. He decided that circling around the edges of the yard would be best. He chose a side at random, and crept along, using anything he could to hide himself.

Just as he was reaching the river that ran along one side of the container yard, a metallic sliding sound from behind froze him. It was the sound of a long blade being drawn: a deadly warning. Mark slowly raised his hands, keeping them far away from his gun and knife so that whoever was behind him wouldn't think he was a threat. In his mind, he prepared all the usual words to inform the person about Dean's comet herd, readying himself to field a lot of questions. When he turned to face the man who had managed to sneak up on him, the words died in his throat.

The sword slowly lowered. "Mark?"

"Jon?"

Section 3:
Antagonize

18
Evans Is Wrong

It was all messed up, just as Evans had feared it would be. Lead flew through the open space, through no-man's land, seeking out flesh. The gunfire was starting to die down some as Evans' party began to realize they weren't landing many shots, if any. This tactic wasn't working: all they were doing was wasting ammo. Evans himself hadn't yet fired a shot. He sat behind the container, alone with Danny, patching up his wound. Although no expert on such injuries, he thought the young man would live. Evans had laid his captive on the pavement, telling him to stay still and stay calm as he had removed his binds, gag included. Danny had so far done as he was told, more concerned with the pain radiating outward from where he had been shot than trying to fight Evans.

The gunfire finally petered out altogether, with the last volley from the container wall, making sure that the party stayed under cover.

"This isn't working," Arman lamented.

"No shit," Evans grumbled only loudly enough for Danny to hear him.

"We need to spread out more, get a better look at that wall," Arman continued.

"How? Every time we poke our noses out, they nearly get shot off," someone that Evans couldn't see spoke from beyond Arman. With his ears ringing with gunfire, Evans couldn't identify the speaker through his voice either.

"Some of us will head backward through the containers and circle around. Maybe other parts of the wall are less defended."

"No," Danny croaked from the ground.

"Tell me." Evans knew he needed Danny's help to get out of this, despite Arman's bravado.

"We outnumber you, out gun you. The whole wall is defended. Your best chance was surprise, but obviously you didn't have that. You don't have the power to get in there." Danny spoke through gritted teeth, trying to move his jaw as little as possible.

Evans looked up to where Arman was organizing his group, picking people to flank another part of the wall. He had no idea what Ki-nam was doing with the other group beyond Arman's. As he looked back over at Elijah, he knew the teen was waiting for orders, as was everyone else huddled up around him. Nicks and punctures marred the side of the container they were hiding against and peppered the container behind them where it was exposed by the gap.

For the first time in a long time, Evans didn't know what to do. Arman was riled up, all for the continued assault, especially now that they had been shot at. Evans knew the man well enough to know that he saw this as verification of the deaths the scavenger teams had suffered: these people were to blame. Perversely, the continued attack would only result in more being injured and killed.

"We should retreat," Evans finally spoke loudly enough for those clustered up by the containers on either side of him to hear.

There was a pause as Arman had to let the words sink in, his group now nervous, unsure who to listen to.

"No! We can't let up now!" Arman yelled, almost forcefully enough for those on the wall to hear him. Maybe he wanted them to, wanted them to think they were retreating when he was really just spreading his people out.

"We need to regroup, and replan. This isn't working, as you said. We should consider our options somewhere safer, make sure the injured are being taken care of, and then try again with a smarter plan. We know where the wall is now, what it looks like. We can take the time to think things over."

"I agree," Elijah immediately backed up Evans, spurring others to nod and mutter agreements as well.

Arman's face was red with anger. He saw the move as cowardice, not strategic thinking. Although he was great at organizing the scavenger teams, he did not have a mind for war.

"And what about you?" Arman retorted. "How are you going to back away? You have to cross through an opening first, exposing yourself, and you're not the only one of us. You're going to get shot trying to retreat."

He was right, of course. There was no way for Evans to fall back, even if he didn't have an injured man with him. As his mind raced to think of a way out of this, he became distracted by the people around Elijah. They had all turned and were looking down the path they had taken to get there. It didn't take long for Evans to figure out what was happening, as Julianne joined them, out of breath.

"Julianne? You shouldn't be here; get back to your kids," Elijah said what Evans was thinking.

Julianne panted, trying to gather enough wind to speak. Evans immediately feared the worst, that some people from the wall had waited outside and were now attacking them from behind.

"There's a man…he needs…to talk to you," she gasped, looking at Evans. She must have sprinted the entire way and gotten lucky that she had ended up in the same place where Evans was.

"What man? What about?" Evans asked her.

"You should really…hear it…from him." Her eyes were full of fear. Whatever this man had said really spooked her.

"I can't leave this spot, Julianne. Can he be brought here?"

She nodded.

"I'll go get him," Elijah volunteered. "Julianne, rest here a moment, and then someone else can accompany you back to the others."

"Just tell me first, is everyone else all right?" Evans asked.

"Yes," Julianne nodded again. "The man is not from here. He let us disarm him." She was getting her breath back, and someone else had finally found some water to give her.

"I'll be quick." Elijah took off through the containers, younger and more used to sprinting than Julianne was.

"What's going on?" Arman asked. He wasn't quite close enough to hear everything.

"We're staying put for the moment," Evans told him. "There's been a development. Hold off on anything until we know what's going on."

Arman fidgeted, not liking indecision and being out of the loop.

"Pass the word along to Ki-nam."

Although he still looked angry, Arman did as he was told. He wasn't a complete idiot; he knew if something was happening with the non-combatants they had left behind, it had to take first priority. Evans and anyone else trapped behind containers without a safe exit would be abandoned there if need be.

"Do you know what this is about?" Evans whispered to Danny.

Danny tried to shake his head, but it made his injury hurt too much. "When we know an attack is coming, everyone retreats behind the wall and stays there until the threat is gone."

The threat. That's what Evans and his party were right now: a threat to these people. The more he was around them, the more he concluded that there was no possible way they had had anything to do with the deaths of Carol, Hector, Lee, Moore, and Millia. Wycheck was a different story, but they couldn't know what really happened there. If Danny and his friends had told the truth, then it was an honest and easy mistake to make. Thinking of Wycheck's busted leg, Evans could easily picture him limping along, moving no differently from a zombie when viewed at a distance. How he had busted his leg was a different matter. They may have been involved, they may not have. Evans was thinking that Danny and his group were innocent, but convincing Arman and ceasing this needless battle would be difficult. It wasn't easy to explain a gut feeling, to convey to someone else the virtually baseless trust you felt for another. All too easily, Evans could be made to look like a naive fool.

The silence was oppressive. Nobody from his party spoke, and no one on the wall made a sound loud enough to carry to them. An occasional shuffle while changing positions, or a soft moan from one of the wounded was all that broke the stillness. Eventually, Evans' ears recovered from the ringing of the gunfire and he was able to hear water. He remembered the map, how the container yard was nestled in a ninety-degree corner where a river met a large bay.

It was easy to tell when Elijah was returning with the mysterious man. The slapping of their shoes on the concrete rose up out of the container maze, heading toward them. Evans could almost feel the tension building beyond the wall, as they no doubt heard the sound as well. He imagined himself in their position, the gunfire stopping, a possible argument being heard across the way, and now the running of feet heading toward them.

When Elijah appeared, he was breathing somewhat heavily, but was in much better condition than Julianne had been. The man, however, got his breathing under control rather rapidly despite being drenched in sweat. Everyone looked at him warily, eyeing his short red hair and freckles, his old, dirty clothes, and the white fabric that hung from a back pocket.

"That's Evans there," Elijah told him, pointing across the opening.

The man made to move across to him, but Evans held up a hand and stopped him.

"You might get shot; best stay where you are to say what you have to say."

"All right then." The man dropped to the pavement, crossing his legs so that he was eye to eye with Evans, who hadn't stood up after bandaging Danny. Behind him, Elijah picked someone to walk Julianne back to the others now that she had rested.

"My name's Tommy," the redhead spoke, "and you're going to want to stop this little skirmish you have going on with these people."

"Are you one of them?" Evans asked quickly, before Arman could chime in.

"One of the people behind that wall? No, never met them, although a friend of mine is currently attempting to talk to them to tell them the same thing I'm about to tell you."

"And what's that?"

"There's a zombie horde on the way. A big one, the biggest one you can possibly imagine. I could tell from your gear back at that warehouse that you're a travelling group, am I right?"

"You are."

"Ever come across what appears to be a gigantic slug trail? Bunch of slimy stuff, trampled earth, maybe some weak structures knocked over?"

Evans nodded curtly. He had seen such a thing some time ago, when his party had been a lot smaller and made up of different people. They had decided to head directly away from the place, not wanting to think about what had caused it.

"That was them, the mega herd that's on its way here. I was able to hear your gunfire from quite a distance back. I'm glad you've since stopped firing, but it may be too late. There's quite a number of smarter than average dead heads in that group, one really smart one in particular, and if they heard you, they're coming straight here."

"And what are you suggesting we do?"

"Well, it's too late to run." Tommy shook his head, seeming genuinely disappointed by that fact. "Your best option is to make nice with the people beyond that wall. Nice enough that they'll let you hide on the other side of it, staying dead quiet until the herd passes by."

Arman made a scoffing sound behind Evans.

Tommy leaned sideways to speak to him. "Hey, you can go back to shooting each other afterward for all I care, I'm just here to warn you about the zombies."

"And how do we know you're telling the truth?" Evans asked him.

"You don't," Tommy shrugged. "I can show you pictures of the horde so that you know it exists, but you'll have to take my word on it that it's coming this way."

"What's in it for you? Warning us?"

"Nothing, really. You know how I mentioned there's one really smart one? Well, he used to be a friend of mine. Ever since we learned that the mega horde has gathered around him, my remaining friends and I have taken it upon ourselves to track them and warn any groups who find themselves in its path. Of course, if you'd like to donate a few supplies to our cause afterward, we certainly wouldn't say no."

"Let me see the pictures." Evans wasn't sure what to think yet. Viewing the photos would give him some more time.

Tommy turned to the people at his back. "Your buddies back at the warehouse have already thoroughly checked me over; I'm not armed, just taking out the photos." He reached into a back pocket and took out a Ziploc baggie, which he then tossed over to Evans.

Evans opened it up and flipped through the Polaroids within, his guts twisting with every image. Tommy certainly wasn't lying about the mega horde, and, based on the way he was acting, he had obviously had experience with warning other groups.

On the ground next to him, Danny attempted to rise so that he could view the photos as well, only to groan in pain and lie flat again.

"You ever seen this?" Evans mumbled, turning one of the pictures so that he could see. It showed a gorge somewhere, completely packed with zombies, all of them funnelled into a wide, jagged line that stretched on until a bend took them out of sight.

"No," Danny replied, a hand travelling on its own to his stomach as if he might throw up. Evans couldn't blame him. Such a massive collection of dead was virtually unheard of; they usually broke apart into smaller herds before getting to that size.

Here was the opportunity Evans was looking for, an excuse to stop the fighting, provided those on the other side of the wall were willing.

"I hate to say it, but time is of the essence," Tommy spoke up. "If we're quick, we may be able to do something about your supply carts and horses."

"We have a way of getting them over the wall," Danny spoke up.

"Would they let us in?" Evans asked him.

"If you're willing to surrender your weapons, then yes, they'll let you in. Your group will probably be confined to a handful of containers during the ordeal, but you won't be treated badly as long as you co-operate. Afterward, they'll let you go, although probably with a minimum of ammunition so that you're not encouraged to start shooting us again."

"But they would give our weapons back?"

"We understand how easy it is to die out here without them. If it were just someone like you, then maybe not, but you have kids and what not with you. We would never put them in unnecessary danger."

"All right then." Evans returned the pictures to the Ziploc and tossed them back across to Tommy. "We're going to trust you."

Arman made a disgruntled noise, but he didn't argue. He wouldn't risk the non-combatants like that.

"So what do we do?" Evans asked Tommy.

"Well, considering how long this has taken, I'm guessing my friend got inside and has had the same conversation with their leaders. Hopefully, they also agree. I'm going to go out there and find out."

"You could get shot."

"You could always get shot," Tommy said rather cryptically, his eyes darting downward.

The lithe-bodied man stood up, pulling the white fabric out of his back pocket. Once it was in his hand, Evans could see it was actually a T-shirt. Tommy waved it across the opening several times, making sure it was seen. He then stepped out after it, continuing to wave his makeshift white flag. He wasn't shot. With both hands up, Tommy began walking toward the wall. Evans risked spying around the corner to watch.

"I'm looking for my friend, Mark," Tommy called out when he was halfway across the space.

There was no reaction from the wall for several seconds, until one of the container doors on the upper level swung open, revealing a young man. He waved to Tommy, and Tommy waved back. Once he reached the wall, Tommy stopped to speak with the young man, whom Evans assumed was Mark. He could also spy a couple of people behind Mark, probably the leaders of the camp listening to every word. Evans wished he could hear as well.

"I don't like this. A deal is being struck without us," Arman grumbled, speaking what Evans was thinking.

"I'm afraid we don't have much of a choice," Evans told him.

"But what if this is all some sort of trick?"

"Then we've been tricked. I'd rather that, than risk it being true and getting stuck out here."

Arman sighed. "Fair enough. I just don't like that we have to rely on these assholes for help."

Evans didn't like having to rely on anyone for help, but that's not the way the world worked.

Waiting for Tommy to return felt like some of the longest couple of minutes in Evans' life. The only time he looked away from the proceedings was when Danny shuffled a bit behind him. The young man was trying to get into a more comfortable position on the hard concrete. Mostly, Evans watched what he could of the people at the edges of the container doors. Mark held no interest for him, he was just like Tommy, but those spying back at Evans were the people he would have to deal with.

When Tommy finally turned around and jogged back to where Evans was waiting, Evans rose to his feet.

"We have a deal," Tommy smiled. "You might want to send someone to go get those others at that warehouse."

"What's the deal, first?" Arman demanded.

Evans glanced back at him, a silent request to keep his anger in check, although he had the same question.

"Your leaders will go first, bringing the prisoners you apparently have. When you approach the wall, hold your guns by their barrels, as far from the triggers as possible and out from your bodies. You'll be allowed to supervise everyone coming in, although you'll be disarmed and your hands will be bound. The children, wounded, and anyone else unable to properly defend themselves will go next. That's at my recommendation before you go jumping down their throats for it. It's just a precaution in case the zombies show up before everyone gets inside. Once everyone is in, you'll be shepherded to a holding area. Those of you doing the actual attacking out here will be put into some containers, but those not perceived as a threat will be let into some place they call the community centre. Apparently, it's where their own non-combatants have been sheltering during this whole kerfuffle. Sound good?"

"Good enough," Evans nodded. "Arman, pass the word to Ki-nam and everyone else; we should get this started. Untie Lenny and Bryce first. Let's not show up with them trussed and gagged. The fastest person who can hear me right now, go get the others." Evans turned to Danny. "Think you can walk?"

"With help."

After slinging his shotgun through the loop on his belt, Evans helped Danny to stand, keeping a firm hand under his arm to make sure he stayed upright. He then took his shotgun back out and flipped it over to hold its barrel like a club.

"Arman? You ready?" Evans looked over at him just as the man finished untying Lenny. He did not look pleased about it, but nodded.

"Let's do this then."

***

Danny could walk on his own more or less, the high placement of his injury not affecting his legs, but Evans kept a hand on him anyway. The last thing he needed was for Danny to collapse on his way to the wall.

Arman and Lenny fell in line with them, while Ki-nam drifted over with Bryce. He had been a lot farther down in the container maze than Evans had realized. The North Korean's face was devoid of expression, giving Evans no clue as to how he felt about this. Together, with Tommy, they headed to the opening where the redhead had spoken with Mark, the container doors now completely out of the way. Several other spots along the wall were opening as well, and a strange contraption of pulleys was being assembled near one.

"Danny, you all right?" A very pale man with black hair and ghostly eyes looked down on them.

"It wasn't you who shot me, was it, Misha?" Danny asked him.

The pale man, Misha, shook his head.

"Good, I didn't want to think your aim was off."

Evans wondered if that meant the shot at Danny would have killed him had this guy been the one pulling the trigger, or if the bullet had been intended for Evans.

A rope ladder clattered down the side of the container wall, and Misha was shifted out of the way by someone behind him.

"My name is Boyle," the new man stepping to the edge of the container told them. His eyes lingered on battered Bryce. "This is an unusual situation we find ourselves in. Hopefully we can all get along."

"I hope so too. My name is Evans, and that's Arman and Ki-nam."

"Good to meet you, I guess. Send our men up, and then you'll be next."

Evans helped Danny to the ladder. He struggled to climb it using only one arm, but a powerful pair of hands reached down and hauled him over the top once he was close enough. Looking from side to side, Evans was glad to see some metal A-frame ladders being set up before the wall openings, as they would be easier for the elderly. Bryce climbed the rope ladder next, followed by Lenny.

"You first," Boyle pointed to Evans. "Hand up that shotgun once you're close enough."

Evans did as he was commanded, wanting this to go as smoothly as possible. His gun was taken and disappeared as it was handed through a gathered crowd.

"You'll get it back when you leave," Boyle told him.

"Like a coat check," Evans attempted to inject a bit of humour into the situation, although it wasn't his strong suit.

"You got it," Boyle smiled, acknowledging his attempt. He then turned back to the opening. "Now you."

Evans was shuffled across the wall to a second ladder he had to climb down. At the bottom, his sword and knife were taken from him and laid on a large tarp where his shotgun already rested, and then he was patted down for more weaponry. Looking around the place, Evans could see they stood no chance. They were well armed here, with more rifles that were better for distance than the many handguns his party carried. There were also just more people. They had as many combatants as Evans had people in total. He couldn't help but wonder where their food came from. Once he was cleared for weapons, Evans' hands were bound together by a zip-tie, but they were careful not to make it too tight. Really, if Evans had to, he knew he could get out of it using his teeth, but for now he'd co-operate.

Allowed to stand to one side, Evans watched the proceedings, Arman and Ki-nam doing the same nearby. The wounded were assisted over and quickly divided into those who needed medical attention immediately and those who could wait. Evans was glad to see a surprising number of people who acted like doctors taking care of them. As the kids came over the wall, they looked frightened and unsure, their parents still below.

"It's all right," Evans called to them. The sound of his voice and spotting his face calmed several children.

"They're not going to take my doll, are they?" little Annabelle called back to him as she was moved to the ladder to get off the wall.

"No, they won't take your doll," Evans told her without really knowing. He looked to the man who had been assigned to guard him, a squat but powerful-looking fellow. He nodded, letting Evans know that he hadn't just lied.

The children were grouped together while they waited for their parents, but the elderly came over ahead of them.

Evans was momentarily distracted when the pulley system went into use. He was impressed by the way they were able to lift a horse up and over with everyone working together. It didn't shock Evans when he noticed that the first horse over was one of their own. Beyond that, a second pulley system was being set up.

The elderly joined the children, and then the parents came over. Despite all of them being non-combatants, the pile of weapons on the tarps was growing; even many of the children carried a blade. As soon as the parents were with them, the group was escorted deeper into the container yard, presumably heading for whatever the community centre was.

He spotted Tommy off to one side, talking to two young men. He guessed one of them was Mark. The other carried a katana on his back, a blade Evans thought he might have seen before. Both young men were soaking wet, leading Evans to think that they had gotten around the wall by swimming at some point.

A young woman Evans didn't recognize came over the wall. She was separated from the others and for some reason wasn't wearing a shirt.

"Mark! Tommy!" she called out, waving at the two.

Tommy immediately ran over and Evans could make out just enough words to hear him explain to the people surrounding her that she was part of his team. Some terse words were exchanged, and then she was let down. Tommy's white T-shirt flag was handed to her and she slipped it on. The one Evans guessed was Mark walked over and then quickly led her to meet whoever the other soaking wet man was: someone Evans was pretty sure had been with Danny's small group when his party members attacked them.

When Evans finally returned to supervising his own people, he noticed they were moving faster. His combatants were coming up the wall now, several forced to gather in clumps as they caused a backlog. It clicked in Evans' mind then. The woman had been watching for the zombies. She was here now because they were close.

Evans studied the wall itself. At two containers deep, it was certainly thick enough, but was it heavy enough? Did these people think to fill the containers with junk, rubble, or even fill them with cement when they became part of the wall? He had seen that the upper ones weren't. Although the two containers were easily good enough to keep out humans and most zombies, would they be able to withstand the pressure of thousands of corpses pressing against them? And there was always the height problem. If they managed to remain unseen, unheard, then the zombies would have no reason to start piling up, to start climbing over top of one another. They would simply bump into the wall and change direction. If they knew humans were beyond the containers, however...

Evans silently urged his people to hurry up, to climb faster, to ignore their reservations about these people. He didn't care if they were caught out there and devoured; he just didn't want them to give away their hiding spot.

Out of the corner of his eye, Evans spotted Arman taking a sliding step to his right. It drew Evans' attention, wondering what the scavenger was up to. The pale man, Misha, who might have been guarding him, had his back turned to Arman, who was sliding still closer. When Arman spread his fingers, Evans realized what he was about to do but it was too late to scream at him to stop.

Arman lunged, wrapping his fingers around Misha's skinny neck. The man thrashed, his body made of pure muscle, but Arman's was as well, and he clearly outweighed him. Evans knew what Arman was planning. He was going to use Misha as a hostage, to bargain that the party get to stay together and that it be the container yard people who got locked up until the zombies left. From a distance, it was impossible to tell if Arman was already cutting off Misha's oxygen supply. However, Arman had apparently chosen the wrong man to grab.

Before any human could react, a furry streak burst forth from alongside the nearest containers. Evans had just enough time to identify it as a grey muzzled German Shepherd before the dog leapt upon Arman, digging his teeth into the man's shoulder.

Arman screamed, the weight of the dog throwing him to the ground. He dragged Misha down with him, but quickly let go so that he could draw up his arms to defend himself. Misha rolled away, quickly scrambling back up onto his feet.

"Rifle, stop!" he commanded. The Shepherd released Arman and limped over to Misha, who dropped to his knees again to check over the obviously old dog.

Evans had run over during the confrontation, as had several other people, but he reached Arman first; he had to. Even with his hands bound together, he was able to deliver a solid punch to the side of Arman's face. The scavenger had sat up just in time to get knocked flat again.

"You fucking idiot," Evans hissed at him as a pair of arms looped under his to pull him away. "We need to get along with these people."

Arman lay on his back, stunned, his face rapidly swelling as his shoulder bled. Evans could only hope that his display kept the container people on his side, that they weren't going to change their minds about sheltering them just because of Arman's bone-headed manoeuvre.

As Evans was dragged away, he saw several other dogs in the area, all of them hunched low, their hackles up, their lips twitching in a snarl, and all of them pointed at Arman. He had really chosen the wrong person to mess with. The furry beasts made their way over to Misha, sniffing him in a familiar way as he scratched their ears.

With a large man on either side, Evans was ushered through the container yard. Despite being told that he could monitor the proceedings, they had decided that he had seen enough. He was manhandled toward a large warehouse structure that was in much better condition than the one in which his party had holed up. From inside, he could hear the muted sounds of people and guessed that it was the community centre. Evans was moved past it, toward a handful of containers alongside the building. These had clearly been storage units for these people, as evidenced by the piles of stuff heaped around the outside of them, and several people were hurriedly emptying the last one. The door of a container was opened, and Evans was shoved inside.

Even once the door closed behind him, there was light in the container. Some strange light bulb-like thing poked through the ceiling, too bright to get a good look at. The container was already partially filled with his party members, none of them bound like he was, but all of them nervous.

"Did everyone get over the wall?" Old Salt separated himself from the group to ask.

"I don't know," Evans answered honestly.

"Don't know?" Leo asked from where he was hunched alone in the corner, looking oddly frail. Nathan was nowhere to be seen; he must have been stashed in one of the other containers.

"Arman did something stupid. I had to punch him to save face, and they decided to put me in here."

"I heard that shirtless girl talking," Helen spoke up next. "She said the zombies are getting close."

"Everyone will get over, don't worry. It looked like just about everyone was in before I got dragged here."

People muttered and murmured but eventually fell silent. Not knowing how much sound would carry outside the container, they didn't want to risk making any noise loud enough to be heard beyond the wall. Evans moved through the crowd, seeing who was in there with him and scrutinizing the metal walls. He spotted what appeared to be an emergency hatch in the ceiling near the back. In the same vein as being able to chew through his restraints if he had to, he could also lift someone up to that hatch. Hopefully no one was as stupid as Arman in the other containers and decided to attempt some half-assed jailbreak.

At the back of the container, he leaned against the corner and slid down to a sitting position. A familiar black and white creature appeared between people's legs and rubbed against his shins. Someone had carried the cat in, and for some reason it had been locked up in the container with them. Evans found himself glad it wasn't out there with the dogs and actually gave it an uncharacteristic head scratch.

One by one, everyone else in the container sat down in whatever space they could find. It seemed that Evans was the one to bring them to capacity, because the doors weren't opened again to let in anyone else. By pressing his ear to the metal wall, he could hear the sounds of people moving about in the container next to theirs. They were calm sounds.

As the cat climbed onto Evans' lap and made itself comfortable, Evans wondered how long the wait would be before they were released. He also planned what he should do if the zombies didn't just pass by this place.

19
Doyle's Burnt

With every passing moment, the sun got lower in the sky and the shadows deepened. Doyle was grateful for that. The roof had been a searing inferno despite the cloud cover, driving him and the others to seek out whatever shade they could find. James had brought a tarp with him, which he had strung up from an air conditioning unit on the roof for the girls to lie beneath. He joined Doyle in the soft shadows cast by the ledge surrounding the roof. They had all been lying up there, unmoving so as to produce as little noise as possible. With the edge of the tarp pinned to the ground between them, Doyle couldn't see the women and wondered how they were fairing. At least he wasn't completely bored, what with the books they had taken. Doyle found the best way to pass the time was to read a chapter, then listen to the zombies below for ten minutes before starting the next one.

Based on the sounds of things, a lot of the zombies had moved off, but not enough yet for them to risk an escape. Several still bumped around in the bookstore below, crashing into shelves and each other. Shoes and bare feet dragging over the pavement let them track the ones moving outside, with a dozen or so getting stuck in a loop, following one another around the building. It was impossible to tell where all of the stationary ones were. A couple wheezed and moaned as they pawed at the walls, but there were always more who were silent. Doyle was content waiting for James to voice a plan.

When the sun had finally gone, making it impossible to keep reading, Doyle thought about sleep. It wasn't exactly comfortable on the roof, but he had slept in worse conditions. Between the Day and getting to the Diana, he had been on the move a lot, sleeping in whatever safe space he could find. He distinctly remembered the sixth night being the hardest: the first night he had spent alone, away from Gathers Moss and their tour bus. His intention had been to gather information, find a safer place to hide, and get some food in the process. None of that had worked out the way he planned. Instead, he spent the night crammed in a janitor's locker in some building, unable to lie down or completely stand up, his limbs crunched at awkward angles. A trio of zombies had shuffled about just outside, cutting him off from his fire axe that he had foolishly put down for a moment. He had spent hours in that locker, drifting in and out of consciousness, all of his limbs going numb and tingly. When at last some distant noise had drawn the zombies away, he almost hadn't been able to escape: his body no longer worked correctly. All his muscles and joints screamed when he finally found himself free, lying on the hard floor in a completely different pose. He hadn't been able to move without agony for several minutes. The next night was better, when he slept in an industrial-sized laundry hamper full of towels. It was the day after that when he met Canary and her group, and chose to stay with them. Eventually, Doyle convinced the group to go looking for the band, or what was left of it, but Gathers Moss were gone by the time he returned. It wasn't until later that he found Quin again by accident, along with Robin and April, the rest of the band dead or gone insane.

Moving very slowly so as to create the minimum amount of sound, Doyle rolled from his side onto his back. With nightfall, the clouds overhead were invisible, just an all-encompassing expanse of black. He hoped it wouldn't rain again while they were up here. Although the rain would give them some cover with the sound drowning out their movements, he and James would be forced to get under the tarp with the girls. They'd still get soaked, and it would be crowded under there. He hoped it rained somewhere nearby; a huge thunderstorm that distracted and lured the zombies away, but not here. Doyle didn't want any rain here.

Closing his eyes didn't seem to have any effect on the amount of darkness; Doyle was essentially blind either way. Casting his mind elsewhere, to some happy, warm, bright, and comfortable place, he attempted to sleep.

***

It had been a rough night for everyone. Doyle had woken up frequently, always worried that death was imminent. Once the sun had started to re-emerge, the clouds now broken up into large puffy amorphous shapes, it had helped, because he could see a bit into the grey when opening his eyes. As the sun continued to climb, however, it got to be unhelpful. The bright light made it more difficult to fall back asleep once awake, his circadian rhythm attached to the fire ball's position in the sky.

Glancing over at James, Doyle could see that he was awake, lying on his back, his eyes open and staring at nothing. All of Doyle's bones hurt from lying on the stiff surface of the roof all night. He wanted to get up and stretch, but wasn't about to attempt that without James' go ahead. As he continued lying there, the cobwebs of sleep completely leaving his mind, Doyle realized that today would be worse than yesterday. Without the constant cloud cover, the sun would be even hotter. Already, they were on the wrong side of the roof for shade, and if they were still there at noon, there would be no shade to speak of outside of whatever they could produce with the tarp.

Carefully stretching out an arm, Doyle tapped James on the shoulder, letting the other man know that he was awake.

What's today's plan? Doyle signed. His signing had always been slow and a little clunky, but this morning it was especially bad, with him having to remain lying down, and trying to angle certain gestures to make them easier for James to see.

James held up a finger; Doyle didn't need to know sign language to know he was asking for a minute. Very slowly, and with a considerable amount of muscle control and strength, James sat up. He peered over the edge of the roof, carefully leaning to look down the length of the wall. Doyle could still hear the zombies trapped in a shuffling circle, so he knew they hadn't all wandered off in the night. Focusing so much on James, Doyle nearly startled when a hand briefly gripped his ankle; only his intense desire to keep still and silent held him in place. Looking toward his feet, he saw that Canary had crawled over on her hands and bare feet. He gently tapped James to get his attention.

Can I help? Canary signed, sitting back on her haunches to free her hands.

I'm trying to figure out how many are out there, James signed back.

Canary nodded and then headed out across the roof. It was eerie how silent she was, making only the occasional sounds: skin lifting off tar paper, or a light ruffling of clothing, which was easily swallowed by the scuffling from below. She made her way around the roof, peering over all the edges, then worked her way to each skylight to look inside the bookstore. Satisfied that she had seen enough, Canary made her way back to them, moving a bit like a spider, which was kind of unnerving. When she got close, Doyle could see that she was sweating and trying not to pant: her method of silent motion was taxing her body. With a fluttering of her hands, she gave her report. James seemed satisfied with the numbers.

"All right, there's no need to be completely silent anymore," James whispered, his voice dry with disuse. "Let's go gather around Rose."

Under the tarp, Rose was sitting up and waiting for them.

"Here's what we're going to do. One of us will distract the zombies, lure them all to that corner of the building," James pointed. "Once they've gathered there, we sneak off the opposite corner and book it."

"I should lure them," Canary volunteered. "I'm the quietest and should be able to cross the roof without drawing them back around afterward."

After her recent display, no one argued. Besides, she had seen the zombies and might be able to tell if one hadn't yet shown up.

"Let's gather with the packs in the corner. Canary, give us a thumbs up when we're good to go. Remember, not too loud. We don't want to draw in the dead that have already wandered off."

Canary nodded and headed for the corner. While the others took down the tarp quietly and made sure all the packs were secure, she took out her screwdriver and began tapping the metal end on the edge of the roof. It didn't take long for the zombies to start getting riled up and making their way toward her, especially when she began whispering down at them, proving she was a living human and not just some wind-blown object.

Doyle peered over the edge, watching the last of the zombies make their way around the building. Despite the fact that the bookstore was only one storey high, the ground seemed very far below. It wasn't the height that bothered Doyle; it was knowing how easily he could land wrong and break his ankle.

When Canary gave a thumbs up, James didn't hesitate. He scrambled up onto the ledge, then hopped off the other side, hitting the ground and rolling with practised ease. Once he made sure that none of the zombies were coming to him, he waved for the packs to be passed down. One by one, Doyle dropped their bags over the side, where James caught each one and placed it out of the way. The weight of the books constantly threatened to knock him over with their impact. Then Rose was helped over the side. Doyle lowered her as much as he could with James half catching her to make sure she landed gently on her feet.

Turning back to Canary, Doyle waved her over. He wasn't going to leave the roof until he was sure everyone else had. Canary picked her way across the roof, not using the creepy yet silent method she had employed earlier. The zombies were groaning loudly enough now that they swallowed up most of the sound. Doyle lowered Canary over the side of the roof the same way as Rose, being careful with her bandaged hand. Although the stealthy blonde could probably get down easily on her own, she still wasn't wearing shoes, so it was better not to take the risk. Once she was down, Rose handed over her boots.

It was Doyle's turn next. With no one to lower him, he had to use the same method as James. As his feet hit the ground, he let his legs collapse beneath him. He didn't roll nearly as neatly as James had, he couldn't just spring back up onto his feet afterward, but when he came to a stop in an awkward sprawl he found his legs hadn't been busted up. Scrambling up onto his feet, he quickly joined the others who had just slung on their packs. Taking his from James, Doyle shrugged into it as they ran, not caring where they went for the moment, so long as it was away from the bookstore.

Doyle had to suppress the urge to laugh, his body sore yet delighted to be running. He was reminded of a time when he was a teenager. Some friends had convinced him to join them as they broke into the high school one summer night. They didn't really do anything, just walked around the dark halls and made a bit of a mess, but a security guard had shown up and nearly caught them. Using a clever trick not that dissimilar from the one used against the zombies, Doyle and his friends had managed to escape, all of them laughing like loons as they fled across the football field.

After they had run a few blocks, James had them slow down and then head into the nearest building: a former fast food joint. They hid inside for a while, sitting behind the counter and watching for any zombies that may have been following them. Satisfied that nothing was going to come staggering in behind the little group, they decided to have breakfast on the dusty floor.

"If we start heading back now, we should get home fairly early tomorrow," Doyle mentioned to make conversation.

"Good, 'cause we're runnin' low on food," Rose pointed out. They were all eating and drinking less, trying to stretch out what they had.

"This trip certainly went sideways," Canary commented.

Doyle tried to hide his embarrassment, his shame. It was his fault they were all out here, and it was for such a stupid reason, too. He wished he had never thought of coming out here, that they had all just stayed in the Black Box.

"I'm having fun," James grinned. "I nearly shit my pants a few times, but it's good to get the heart going and to remind ourselves why we need our fences."

Doyle wondered if James had noticed his reaction and was saying that to make him feel better, or whether he was being honest. It was impossible to tell with him.

"Anyone actually know where we are right now?" Rose asked. "Which way is home?"

"I know how to get home from the bookstore, so where are we in relation to that?" Doyle asked, looking at James. He figured James would know.

James shrugged. "I didn't pay attention to direction out there. I know we're about five blocks away."

Canary stood up and looked over the counter out the windows. "I can't say with complete accuracy from here, but based on the shadows I think we went north."

"That's pretty much the complete opposite direction we need to go," Doyle sighed.

"I suggest we swing east a bit to avoid the zombies at the bookstore, and then pick our way back south again. What do you think?" James turned to Doyle.

"West would actually be better."

"Then we'll swing west first."

"Fine with me," Rose shrugged.

Canary sat back down.

"How's your hand?" Doyle asked her, gesturing to the wound she had gotten scrambling up through the skylight.

"It stings a lot, but I think it's all right." She lifted her hand to look at the bandage wrapped around it. "It didn't take very long to stop bleeding, but when I checked earlier, it was still a very angry-looking red."

"You should get it checked out by a doctor when we get back," James recommended, "just to make sure it hasn't gotten infected or something."

Canary nodded. "That's the plan."

The four of them sat quietly with their thoughts as they finished their meal.

"Well, we should get going," James finally spoke about a minute after the last of them had stopped eating.

Doyle was still feeling stiff as he got up, his joints complaining. He wished for a heat wrap of some kind, or even a long hot bath he'd never get. Based on the way the others were moving, they hoped for the same thing.

James took the lead, guiding them along shop fronts until they reached a street that would take them west. Doyle brought up the rear, checking behind them at least every minute to make sure nothing was following them.

Their pace was slower than it had been previously. Not only were they sore, but they knew a pile of zombies had been in the area recently, and they may not have gotten far.

When they returned to a residential area, it was mutually agreed that they would travel through backyards, taking the time to climb over fences. No one felt particularly safe out in the openness of the streets.

"Did you hear that?" Canary whispered as they approached yet another fence.

James paused with his hands along the top, as he was just about to hoist himself up and peer over.

"I don't hear anything. Did it come from the other side of the fence?" Doyle asked.

Canary shook her head. "I'm not sure."

James let go of the next fence and walked along it until he spotted a hole in the wood. Pressing his eye to it, he looked into the next yard.

"I don't see anything," he pronounced after watching for half a minute.

"What did it sound like?" Rose asked Canary.

"I'm not sure. By the time I noticed it, it stopped."

"An unknown sound that could have come from anywhere? There's no point hanging out for that, let's keep moving." James grabbed the top of the fence again and pulled himself up. "Looks clear." He slipped over the top to the other side.

Doyle quickly tested for rotten or loose boards, and when none were found, he made a stirrup out of his hands to help Rose. With his help, she scrambled up and over into the next yard. Canary continued to hesitate.

"Canary? Come on. If we get out of here, we don't need to worry about what that sound was." Doyle hauled himself up the fence. His arms were going to be really tired when they were done.

Canary looked around one more time, and then followed after him.

The next yard was a weed-eaten mess. Something about it made Doyle think it wasn't taken care of even before the Day. There were no toys, no barbecue, the porch was small and slumped, and nothing suggested a garden had ever grown there. He was delighted to see a hole already made in the far fence, a board having come loose and sitting cockeyed.

A very loud groan filled the air.

Doyle spun around, pulling his axe off his back and holding it aloft. His eyes darted frantically about the yard, searching for the zombie. The others had the same reaction, but there was nothing. They were alone in the weeds.

"I think that came from the house," Canary commented.

"A zombie can't groan that loudly," James pointed out. "It had to be—"

He didn't get to finish whatever he had been going to say. A loud pop filled the air, reminding Doyle of his days as a firefighter. When it was immediately followed by a massive creak, he knew what was going to happen a split second before it did; not nearly enough time to warn anyone. The house whose backyard they were in must have suffered extensive water damage or rot, possibly even termites, and the earlier storm had been the final straw. With a lot of snapping, cracking, and a great whoosh, the back half of the house collapsed.

Debris flew through the air: splinters and nails and bits of plaster, amid a great cloud of dust billowing out across the lawn. Doyle quickly raised his arms over his head in the most basic attempt to protect himself as he dropped to the ground. It was over in seconds. Doyle coughed, choking on the dust as he attempted to clear it from his eyes.

"Is everyone okay?" he croaked, trying to spot the others.

"I'm all right," Rose responded first, somewhere to Doyle's left.

"Me too," James called out.

"I'm alive, but I think I need some help." Canary's voice was frightfully small sounding.

Doyle pushed himself up, getting to his feet so that he could survey the damage. More than half of the house had collapsed, becoming a pile of debris with a large chunk of the roof sitting on top. A couple of shingles, bits of drywall, insulation, and a few household items continued to fall, unable to hold onto the edge of the house that was still standing. Doyle suspected it wouldn't be standing for much longer. Already he could hear a few low groans and creaks.

"Where are you, Canary?" he asked, his eyes searching through the yard that had become coated with the grey-brown dusting.

"Here." Her hand raised up, not too far away. Doyle's first thought upon seeing it was relief, as she was too far back to have been crushed.

With his boots leaving prints behind him, Doyle made his way over. The moment his eyes figured out proper shapes and colours, he realized what was wrong. A piece of thin copper piping speared straight through the meat of Canary's calf.

"Don't try to move," were the only words able to escape Doyle's mouth.

"I'm not," Canary told him.

"What's wrong?" James staggered over, holding one of his arms, although it wasn't bleeding. "Oh, shit."

"Do we pull it out or leave it in?" Rose asked, joining them beside Canary.

"I think you're supposed to leave it in until a doctor can look at it, just in case it's plugging up an artery or something," Doyle answered.

"How am I supposed to get to a doctor like this?" Canary's voice broke a little. "Are you saying I have to have this thing in my leg for a whole day?"

"Calm down," James spoke gently, holding out his hands. They were covered in house dust like the rest of him. "Let me take a look before we go making any decisions." He knelt down beside Canary and began inspecting the wound. He had brushed the dust off the arm he had been holding while walking, and Doyle could see a dark bruise forming there.

"You're also bleedin'," Rose spoke to Doyle.

"Huh?"

Rose pointed to his upper arm. When Doyle turned his head to look, he saw that she was right. He wasn't bleeding much, but that may have only been because a nail was plugging up the hole.

"I sure hope we still got some tetanus shots back at the Box," Rose commented. "Want me to pull it out? I've got a claw hammer."

"Go for it."

Doyle couldn't watch as Rose gently hooked the claw end of her hammer around the nail. She didn't give him a countdown or anything, just yanked it out with a swift tug. Doyle's eyes rolled and he gritted his teeth, biting back the urge to cry out.

"All done," Rose deposited the nail in Doyle's hand. It was thankfully short, a roofing nail if Doyle wasn't mistaken.

"I think this is better than it looks," James pronounced of Canary's leg.

Doyle sat down nearby, taking some water and bandages out of his pack to patch up the hole in his arm.

"Are you sure? Because it looks pretty bad," Canary's voice wavered.

"It's actually fairly near the surface, not near any arteries. Should be safe to just pull it out."

"*Should* be?" Canary questioned him.

"Would you rather keep it in until we get home tomorrow?"

Canary thought it over. "No. Do it."

"And let's hurry up, there's no tellin' what'll be drawn here after that," Rose gestured to the half-collapsed house.

"The rest could go any minute as well," Doyle added.

James instructed everyone in what to do. They cleaned the wound site, the copper pipe, and prepared the medical supplies.

"I'm going to have to stitch you up," James told Canary. "Admittedly, I'm not great at it, but I'm all you've got right now. I'll do the best I can. We'll monitor it closely on the way back, and we'll take you straight to the doctors when we get home. Sound good?"

"Not really, but as you said, it's all I've got right now."

"Everyone else ready?" James looked at Doyle and Rose. They both nodded.

Doyle had the worst job, in his opinion. Putting on a pair of James' gloves so that the rubber palms would give him a better grip, Doyle wrapped his hands around the protruding pipe. The far end had been crumpled and twisted into a pointed spear tip that should retract smoothly.

"When it comes to Band-Aids, do you prefer they get ripped off fast or slow?" Doyle asked Canary.

Just as she was about to answer, he jerked on the copper pipe. The sliding squish revolted him. He had heard similar sounds and felt similar sensations when dealing with the dead, but it was different knowing that Canary was alive. Rose quickly slipped her something to bite down on as a scream attempted to bubble out of her. Thankfully, the pipe came out as smoothly as they had hoped, not causing any extra damage along the way. Once it was clear of Canary's leg, Doyle was left holding the bloody thing while James set to work. By the end, Rose was lying across Canary to pin her torso, while Doyle struggled to keep her legs still. Without any sort of topical anaesthetic, she felt every pinch and pull of James' needle. By the time it was all over, with Canary's leg wrapped in a clean white bandage, the plaster dust on her face had become gummy with sweat.

"You didn't throw it away, did you?" Canary panted, looking at Doyle. The bit of wood Rose had given her to bite down on had slipped out of her mouth, now marked with clear teeth impressions.

"The pipe? No, it's right here, why?" Doyle picked it up from beside him.

"I lost my screwdriver during the collapse. I think it would make a good replacement." She grinned, looking a little bit insane in the process.

A moan came from somewhere other than the remaining house.

"We gotta get going," James reminded them, stuffing the remaining medical supplies into his pack.

Doyle realized he had dropped his axe during the collapse and had been too concerned about Canary to pick it up. A flash of worry shot through him as he wondered if he had lost it like she had lost her screwdriver. Luckily, the fire axe was much bigger than a screwdriver and was easily located amongst the layering of dust.

"We'll go around that house." James gestured to the hole in the fence they had been heading for before all this happened as he helped Canary up onto her good leg.

Rose picked up Canary's backpack and strapped it to her front in the reverse position of her own. Doyle took Canary from James, slinging her arm over his shoulder and taking nearly all her weight upon himself. He wished they had time to make some sort of sling for her leg, to keep it held up so that she didn't risk putting any weight on it.

The group squeezed through the fence and then headed for the street around the far side of the next house. There was no way they could continue climbing over fences with the state Canary was in.

"Christ," James muttered as he stepped out onto the front lawn first.

As Doyle joined him, he saw what James was worried about. Although they were lucky that the direction they wanted to go was clear, behind them was a different story. A pack of slow zombies was shuffling toward them, originally drawn by the sounds of the house and now lured by the sight of living humans.

"Even walkin', we can outpace them. Come on." Rose turned and trudged on, looking small beneath her load of two bags.

Without any other choice, the other three followed. Doyle kept his axe in the hand that wasn't wrapped around Canary, while she held her bloody pipe on the other side. James soon took the lead again, rifle in hand and at the ready.

"Look, look, look!" Rose stopped, having glanced behind them.

At first Doyle didn't understand her excitement. The zombies were still coming, passing the half-collapsed house now. Then he noticed that the house was leaning farther forward than its neighbours. With another great crack and a whoosh, the front gave out, the remaining roof sliding down into the street and ploughing into the corpses.

It was impossible not to cheer at the sight. They had finally had a bit of luck.

***

When the sun started setting, they located another place to spend the night. After watching the house collapse, and not up to the task of clearing a whole building, they picked a large garden shed. Once they carried out the standing racks of sports gear, the larger, outdoor kids' toys, and the lawn mower, there was enough space for three of them to lie down comfortably while the fourth kept watch. With a flashlight and gentle fingers, James checked on Canary's wound, changing her bandages in the process. They would be out of clean dressing soon.

"Maybe we should make you some sort of leg sling so that you don't have to keep holding it up on your own," Doyle suggested, remembering his earlier thought.

It was Canary who rejected the idea. "I want to be able to try hobbling on my own if something happens, and I don't want some weird sling thing getting in the way."

Half of their remaining supplies were eaten, the other half held back for breakfast. After that, it was get home or find a food source. Rose volunteered to take first watch, while James would cover the middle of the night, and Doyle would take the end. Canary insisted she could keep watch with a bum leg. They were just sitting inside the shed and listening to whatever was outside after all, but no one sided with her. She needed rest.

Doyle wiggled around on his bedding until he found the most comfortable position, his arm throbbing where the nail had bitten into it.

Surrounded by the smell of earth, old oil, and what he took to be stagnant water from a pool in a nearby yard, he fell asleep.

***

By the time the others awoke and were ready to eat, Doyle was practically starving, but he had forced himself to wait. By eating at the same time, they were all likely to get hungry at the same time, making it easier to decide if and when they had to stop for food on the way. They were close though; it shouldn't take them too much longer to reach the bridge, and then the Black Box.

After checking Canary's wound again, they headed out, this time with James carrying the extra pack.

As they moved through the streets, they came across the occasional zombie. It was always solo, however, and slow so that Rose could easily trot up to it, bash its head in with her hammer, and then swiftly return to the little group.

"By the time we get back, you're going to be so used to having me on your side that you'll walk lopsided when I'm gone," Canary teased Doyle, her voice in the usual low whisper.

"I'm worried about that side of me getting cold, it's already used to being warmer than the right."

"Well, I'll still need a crutch to help me get around for a while even after the doctors see me, so maybe if you're nice I'll let you be the crutch."

Doyle chuckled.

They slipped through the same gap in the fence they had when first arriving at the suburb and headed for the railway bridge. It was harder going through the trees with Canary's injury, but it didn't slow them down too much. Once they reached the tracks where it was open, they moved at a decent pace again.

"I gotta say, after this, I don't think I'll need to go outside the fences again for a long time," Doyle commented as they walked. Canary agreed with him, but the other two gave non-committal responses. Doyle knew that Rose enjoyed the excitement, the danger, but he couldn't be so sure about James.

At the bridge, Rose checked for danger and gave the all clear. As they headed across, Doyle wondered what had become of the zombies who had been crossing the other bridge. They had likely found the Black Box and been killed, their packs then looted for stuff.

There were no zombies the entire time they followed the tracks. It seemed to Doyle that the closer they got to the Black Box, the more relieved he felt. He was looking forward to being back inside, back where there was running water and a comfortable bed. Although his plan to get books had gone disastrously awry, it had also been a successful mission. He held onto that thought as they drew closer and closer to home.

A bullet cracked into the pavement at their feet, causing all four of them to dive for the nearest cover behind the edge of a building. They were close enough for it to have come from the Black Box. Doyle was about to yell out, to identify themselves, when James clapped his hand over Doyle's mouth and shook his head.

What's going on? Canary signed, sitting on the ground against the wall, where Doyle had put her down.

James didn't answer. He took out his binoculars and peered around the corner with them, looking for only a second before pulling back into cover.

It's no one we know, he signed to the little group.

Someone's outside our fences and shooting at us? Doyle signed back, trying to wrap his head around the idea.

James shook his head. *They're on the inside of the fence.*

Doyle replayed James' motions through his head, making sure he had the translation right, as signing wasn't always exact. Someone they didn't know on the inside of the fences?

Maybe someone new joined us while we were gone, Rose suggested, but her eyes were filled with panic.

James shook his head again. *We wouldn't have someone that new guarding the fences.*

So what are you saying? Canary signed quickly, swatting James' leg to make sure he was looking right at her.

I don't think we have control of the Black Box anymore.

20
Misha's Panicking

Misha was glad to see the horses come over the wall, to see that they were safe and unharmed. He wanted to go check on Danny, to ask how he was, but the doctors were currently tending to him and Misha knew it was best he keep out of the way.

Someone walked past Misha, saying his name, but Misha didn't catch the whole thing; the man hadn't spoken loudly enough to be heard over the goings-on.

"What?" Misha asked for clarification, but it was too late; the man had kept walking and now couldn't hear Misha.

Assuming it must not have been important, Misha turned back to watch the wall. When the first two carts were lifted over, he knew that all the horses were inside, and redirected his attention to the people. They were climbing over the wall faster now than when Misha had last checked.

An alarm bell went off in Misha's head a split second before the hands wrapped around his neck. His own hands shot up in response trying to pry loose the fingers that were suddenly cutting off his air and blood supply. His body reacted on automatic, thrashing every which way, but his unknown assailant was stronger, able to keep his hold.

Machete! Grab your machete! Misha's mind finally started screaming.

Before he could follow through, something roared up behind them. With a scream, the man who had grabbed Misha fell to one side, dragging the pale Russian down with him. As soon as the hands slackened, Misha rolled away and scrambled back up onto his feet. He was surprised by what he saw.

The man who had attacked him was one of the people they were allowing over the wall, the one whose face was frequently twisted with anger and annoyance. Rifle was on top of him, his grey muzzle latched onto the man's shoulder.

"Rifle, stop!"

Rifle released his jaws and limped over to Misha with blood on his teeth. Misha dropped to his knees, consumed with worry that his brother had been hurt, wrapping his arms around the old dog and checking him over. Rifle hadn't done anything that physically intensive in a long time.

The first person to reach the confrontation was the other man from over the wall, the one who was apparently their leader and looked like he had Viking blood running through his veins. Just as Misha's assailant sat up, the blond man delivered a cracking punch to the side of his face. The blond's face was oddly expressionless as he did it.

"You fucking idiot," the blond leader hissed at Misha's assailant while Harry grabbed him, pulling him upright. "We need to get along with these people." Although emotion was present as he spoke, there was a still a strange sort of detachment, like it wasn't quite the right emotion.

As the opposing leader got dragged away, Misha noticed his other dogs coming over, all of them snarling in his attacker's direction. They would have done the same as Rifle had the old dog not reacted first. Misha scratched their heads calming them as they turned, whined, and sniffed worriedly at him and Rifle.

"What the fuck happened?" Karsten shouted as he arrived on the scene. "Who was guarding this *arschloch*?"

A ring had formed around Misha and his attacker, who was being held painfully against the ground by White. Misha wanted to leave, wanted to take Rifle to a vet. The German Shepherd was leaning into his embrace, allowing Misha to hold him upright.

"I asked Misha to watch him while I went to take a piss," someone from the ring spoke.

Misha's head shot up, his eyes quickly locating the culprit. It had been the man from earlier, someone whose name started with a J or a G that Misha had never learned.

"What?" Misha barked, his voice harsher than usual. He was so worried about Rifle he didn't even notice the swelling pain building around his throat. "I didn't fucking hear you! And I said as much!" Were he not holding Rifle, he would have gotten up and assaulted the man. All around him, his dogs bristled in response to his outburst.

Karsten stepped forward, his hands held out to either side in a separation gesture. "We still need to get the rest of these people over the wall. Someone drag this piece of shit to a doctor and a holding container. Better yet, find him a place where he can be alone; we'll deal with him later. And you," Karsten pointed at J or G, "we're going to talk later about this. You too, Misha, but tend to your dog for now."

White hauled the assailant up onto his feet, then frog-marched his bleeding prisoner away, a woman following with a gun ready. The ring dispersed, leaving Misha with Rifle and his dogs.

"Come on, *bratishka,* let's get you checked out." Misha stood, carefully lifting Rifle. The dog was still heavy, but he was lighter than when he was younger.

Misha carried the Shepherd between the containers; Bullet stayed right alongside, the other dogs circling like worried satellites. Misha wasn't even entirely sure where he was going. Normally, he trusted

Cameron with these sorts of things, but she wasn't here: she had gone to the Black Box for some unknown reason. He knew one of the other vets was on Animal Island, but the bridge was disconnected. Were other vets on the island as well? Were they all there, leaving him alone and half-panicked?

Misha then remembered what he had been doing just before being attacked: watching the horses. If there was a vet still in the container yard, he or she would be with the horses, checking them over. Misha redirected his course to head to the makeshift stables, located near to where the wall met the river.

By the time he got there, Rifle was making annoyed grunting sounds and wiggling somewhat, wanting to be put down; Misha was dripping with sweat. Thankfully, he was right about the veterinarians looking over the horses and settling them. There were two working with the large animals.

"Help," he called weakly to them, not only out of breath but suffering from a sore throat.

An oddly proportioned man named Nedry, whom Misha had seen working with Cameron many times, turned. Seeing that Misha was carrying a dog, he rushed over.

"Bring him here; there's a blanket you can lay him on. What happened?" Nedry briskly asked, guiding Misha to a small pile of horse blankets.

Misha gently lay Rifle, who grunted, down on the pile.

"He jumped on someone, and I think he hurt himself," Misha relayed rapidly in a scratchy voice. "He was favouring his right front leg a lot."

Nedry looked pointedly at the bruises blooming around Misha's neck, and then the droplets of blood around Rifle's grey muzzle, instantly figuring out why the old dog had been jumping on someone. The vet stroked Rifle's head, whispering soothing words to him, then began his examination.

"Bullet, stay back," Misha commanded when the younger dog tried to nose in on what was happening. All the dogs were curious, forcing Misha to give them sit-and-stay commands a few feet away. He then hovered over Nedry like a nervous mother.

"Well, he doesn't appear to have broken any bones or dislocated anything," Nerdy pronounced, "and I can't locate any bruising, or anything that would suggest internal damage."

Misha sighed with relief.

"Cameron mentioned once that he has some arthritis?"

Misha nodded.

"Without any scans or anything, I would guess Rifle either just aggravated his arthritis, or, more likely, pulled a muscle. Either way, he needs rest for that."

Misha closed his eyes and took a deep breath, so grateful that it wasn't anything worse. He didn't know what he would do if Rifle was badly injured while protecting him.

"Would you like to leave him here, or can you carry him some more?"

"I can carry him back to my container. He'll be more comfortable there."

"Sure, but maybe take a bit of a break first; you look like you could use it. Has anyone looked at your neck yet?"

"Not yet."

Nedry nodded, understanding that Misha was more worried about Rifle.

"Do you have a toothbrush for Rifle? It would be good for his teeth to clean off that blood."

"I will." Misha had toothbrushes for all the dogs. He didn't have any toothpaste for them, but even just using water made a difference. The dogs were always getting into things, killing mice and rats, and gobbling up whatever food anyone dropped. If Misha didn't brush their teeth, their breath became as bad as a zombie's, and when several of them began stinking up the container, it quickly became unbearable. He wished he could do something similar about their farting.

Taking Nedry's advice, Misha took a break before carrying Rifle back to his container. Sitting on the ground and gently probing his neck, he watched as the two veterinarians finished preparing the horses and their stalls. Their containers were already full of padding, wrapped around all walls and the ceiling to reduce noise, but it looked to Misha like more had been added. The floors had a lot more hay laid down than usual. The vets had placed blinders on the horse's faces, in all likelihood because there were more of them than usual in the containers, some of them strangers. All of them were tethered to loops bolted to the metal walls, and Misha watched Nedry give one of the horses an injection, likely a sedative of some kind. Misha wondered how many humans would accept a sedative if offered one.

***

The dogs began to get fidgety. They paced with heads low and ears high, constantly twisting their heads around to look toward the wall. Misha knew exactly what it meant.

"The zombies are almost here," he warned the vets, getting back on his feet.

The two of them nodded as Misha picked Rifle up again. The dog flattened his ears, not appreciating being manhandled, but he kept silent. He knew what was coming.

Misha hurried to his container as fast as he could, the other dogs threatening to trip him they were pressed so closely around his legs. All throughout the container yard, he saw closed doors. Most people were choosing to ride this out in their own homes, sealed off and hoping not to have any contact with what was coming. Misha would have bet that those who had headphones and functioning music players with charged batteries were currently selecting their play lists.

By the time he reached his own container, Misha could hear the moaning. He gently lay Rifle down on his bed, and quietly commanded the rest of the dogs to their mattresses. They were anxious and looking to Misha.

"Stay. You'll be safe here, just stay quiet." It was a pointless command, for he knew they wouldn't make a sound. Dogs these days knew to keep silent in the presence of the dead. They were also forced to stay, as Misha closed the container doors, hoping the dogs wouldn't think to push on them because they couldn't be latched from the outside. Rifle's bloody teeth would have to wait.

Running back to the wall, Misha thought he'd help out. It turned out to be unnecessary, as everyone had made it over and the ladders were now being drawn up.

"Misha," a half-whispered voice called out.

Misha turned and spotted Jon waving at him, standing with the two men who had warned them of the coming zombies and helped negotiate a deal between the two groups. There was also a young woman with them, whom Misha didn't recognize.

"You okay?" Jon asked in a low voice when Misha got near.

"Sore, but fine," Misha answered in a whisper, tempted to use sign.

"They're farther than you think," commented Mark, the guy who swam along the river with Jon. Misha hadn't seen them arrive, but heard about how they were scooped out when the negotiations began. The cloudy day meant they weren't completely dry yet.

"There's so many, you can hear them from farther away than other zombie herds," clarified the girl. Misha still didn't like how loudly they were speaking.

It seemed Jon didn't either, as he continued to whisper after giving them a mildly irritated look. "Misha, this is Suzanne, Tommy, and Mark. Mark and I were best friends in high school."

Misha couldn't hide his startled response. For many years, no one had run into someone they knew before the Day, not since they boarded the

Diana. It explained why Jon had helped Mark get in and why they listened to him so readily.

"I know, right?" Jon grinned at Misha's reaction. "We got separated on the Day." He then turned to Mark. "After this, we'll visit the Black Box. Abby lives there, and so does Claire."

"Seriously?"

"Wait, is that the Claire you told me about? The one who lived in your apartment building?" Suzanne wondered. She was whispering now, but it seemed to be out of courtesy rather than the fear Misha and Jon felt.

"That would be her; they did live in the same building," Jon said, nodding.

"Oh, then we *have* to go see them," Suzanne insisted. "Did you know he carried around a med kit for years because of her?" she spoke to Jon and Misha.

Mark's face turned a bright red.

"Same colour as that," Suzanne teased Mark before planting a kiss on his cheek.

"Where have your leaders gone? Boyle and Karsten?" Tommy asked, looking around the area.

The last of the attackers were being hustled away from the wall and taken to the containers where they would be held for the duration of their stay. All the carts that had been hoisted over were left sitting where they had been placed, able to wait until later to be dealt with. The last of the exterior ladders were being tucked away, and the openings in the upper level were being sealed off. Karsten and Boyle couldn't be seen anywhere.

"Maybe I can help," Jon offered.

"I want to be able to get somewhere high," Tommy turned to him. "Not anywhere near the wall, but somewhere where I can see above it."

"Why? Won't that risk the zombies being able to see you?" Jon frowned, disliking the idea as much as Misha did.

Tommy shook his head. "I probably won't need it, but just as a precaution. I need a spot where I can see beyond the zombie horde without seeing the horde itself."

"We'll wait until you need such a spot," Misha told the redhead.

Tommy shrugged. "Where can we go to sit this out? I'd rather not be outside if I don't have to be."

"We'll go to the community centre," Jon suggested. "Come on, it's this way."

"I'm going back to my container," Misha told him. "Tell Danny I'll come by and see him after this is over."

"Will do."

As Jon led the foreign trio away, Misha heard him telling Mark that Danny was the same Danny who had been his foster brother. The whole situation was strange to Misha, and he found himself hoping he never ended up in a similar one. He was a very different person than he had been before the Day and wouldn't know what to say to someone who knew the old him.

Checking the wall one last time, Misha found it virtually abandoned. A few guards were sitting against it, unafraid—or trying to look unafraid—of the approaching sound, but no one was on top. As he returned to his container, he found the alleyways around it even emptier than they had been earlier. People who had had their doors open previously, suddenly decided they didn't want to hear quite that well and had closed them.

As Misha ducked into his own container, the dogs all stood up, and then lay back down when he closed the doors behind him. He not only latched his doors shut, but he placed the several wooden beams he had in their brackets. Once that was done, he moved to the back of his container and proceeded to check the ladder that let him reach the emergency hatch. The dogs looked on curiously as he climbed up and popped it open. Misha didn't care about the growing noise of the zombies: he wanted to make sure he had a way out ready to go.

Sitting on his bed beside Rifle, Misha let the other dogs pile around him. He wished that they were all there, that he had had time to go and retrieve the ones who had been left at the community centre. They would be safe there, with lots of company to keep them calm, but Misha wished he could physically see them, to know for himself that they were okay.

As the minutes ticked by, the monotonous moan got ever louder. As it built up and built up, Misha wondered if they had needed to take so many precautions to keep quiet. He would never suggest otherwise, but at the same time, it seemed that the zombies wouldn't be able to hear anything over the sounds they were making. It reached a peak point and Misha imagined all the rotting flesh pressed up against the wall and wedged within the container maze. They would break upon it like a tide, forced to the sides where they would either fall into the river, the bay, or manage to loop around upon themselves. It shouldn't take too long, especially once the splashing of the first few drew the others.

Once they were gone, there was going to be a massive cleanup to do. There were bound to be stragglers to deal with, but also undead debris. With a group that size, there would be bits of skin, hair, bowels, clothing, and who knows what else falling off them, not to mention what would have gotten scraped off as they passed between containers. It would be a gross job, but Misha would rather do that than just sit there like he was. Maybe another big storm would come along and wash all the gunk away.

Several minutes had dragged by and the sound hadn't abated. Misha hadn't heard any splashing, but that was understandable, as the zombies were making so much noise he was unlikely to hear it. Still, a dread inched its way up his spine. Based on the rate in which the sound grew, he had a rough estimate of how fast the zombies had been moving. By now, a fair number of them should have dropped off, decreasing the overall noise.

Misha kissed each of his dogs on their heads before standing up. He made a stay gesture with his hands, and then turned away from their watchful eyes. Moving slowly so as not to make any noise, Misha climbed up the ladder to the open emergency hatch, and slithered out on his belly. Even standing on the top of his container, there was no way he could be seen by anything over the wall, but he persisted in lying on his belly just in case. The volume of sound only got louder outside his box.

Crawling along the container, he looked around the area. A few people were poking their noses out of either their doors or hatches, their expressions worried. Misha hadn't been the only one to expect the zombies to be leaving by now. Wiggling over to the front of his container, he lowered himself over the edge and dropped to his feet. It wouldn't be easy to get back inside, but he figured he could borrow a ladder from somewhere.

Walking as fast as he could while remaining silent, Misha made his way toward the community centre. He wanted to check in with Boyle, ask him his thoughts on the matter. He'd probably also see a doctor while he was there; the stress was tightening his already-pained throat.

When he reached the centre, he spotted movement off to one side. Over near the toilets, Mark was pacing nervously back and forth. The sight made Misha feel worse than he already did, and he beelined for Jon's apparently old friend. Mark stopped pacing once he noticed Misha and stood still. He seemed to be hoping that Misha was just going to one of the toilets, but his shoulders slumped as he realized that this was not the case.

"You're worried." Misha didn't ask, he accused in a low whisper.

Mark didn't respond and Misha began to wonder if he had even heard him, but the man would have seen his lips move, would've made some sort of gesture for him to repeat himself.

"What's wrong? What's going on?" Misha demanded to know.

Mark glanced around the area. Making sure no one could possibly overhear them? Or looking for a way out of this confrontation? Either way, there was nothing.

"I don't know," Mark finally admitted.

"What do you mean, you don't know?"

"Exactly that. I don't know what's going on out there. They should be leaving by now. I've never seen the comet horde act this way before."

Misha thought about how long this man and his group had been following the zombies outside the wall. He realized how dire that meant their situation was.

"Do you need that high spot you mentioned earlier?" Misha asked.

"It could help, yeah."

"All right. We're going to tell my leaders first, then I'll find you that spot." Misha led him back to the community centre, his eyes drifting toward the wall standing in the distance. On the other side, death seemed to be waiting for them.

21
Dean's Stopped

The dead all moved at the same pace, forced together by the narrow aisles between the containers. If Dean could think about it, he'd realize he was barely moving on his own, but being pushed along by those behind him. He was holding onto a memory as he inched through the metal maze. He remembered hearing gunfire. It had been faint, distant, but he had heard it. Gunfire meant humans, meant hosts to pass on the infection. Dean had succeeded in personally infecting a few humans, but none of them turned out like him. They were smarter than the average shuffler, able to be taught tasks and usually in more control of their bodies, but he had never found anything as intelligent as him. He wasn't exactly lonely—he could no longer feel such emotions—but on occasion he desired something more than the rot around him. Another being like him would make hunting easier, would make controlling the others easier. But there was nothing else in the world like Dean.

When the maze ended, Dean was no longer being pushed along as the zombies spread out through the open area. Across the way was a barrier of shipping containers, without any gaps between them. There were no humans. There was no sign of anything living.

Dean continued to move toward the barrier, the other zombies still packed fairly tightly around him. They always wanted to be close to the most living thing in the area, which almost always was him.

There was something about the containers ahead. Dean couldn't get very close before the zombies ahead of him formed a clump he couldn't press into. He stopped against their backs, his dead, goggled eyes scanning over top of them.

These weren't just containers, this was a *wall*.

A wall, why was a wall important? Dean couldn't remember. There was something about this being a wall that he should be able to figure out.

As he stood and stared, the other zombies filled the area, stopping with him. They were waiting for him to move, their collective wheezing groans never changing. The horde was eerily still, zombies who'd normally be tempted to roam unable to do so as they were penned in by the others.

Dean studied the wall, trying to remember what it meant.

22
Abby's Anxious

Abby sat in the waiting room with Cameron, Brunt, Dakota, Peter, and Hope. Lauren wanted to stay as well, but it had been decided that at least one of them should be working.

"I'm thirsty; where's the nearest tap?" Cameron asked, getting to her feet.

"There should be one in the room across the hall," Abby told her. There were others in some examination and recovery rooms, but Abby didn't know if those rooms were in use

"Want to show me?" Cameron glanced at Hope and Dakota. It was clear to Abby that she wanted to say something, but not in front of the girls.

"Sure, I could probably use a drink myself." Abby stood and the two of them went into the medical lab across the way. Abby could count the number of times she had been in there on one hand with fingers to spare, because every time it made her shudder. Any sort of laboratory equipment had that effect on her now, knowing it was a place like this that had made the contagion.

"I didn't want to worry Riley by telling her, but I think you should know. I'm sure everyone here will learn soon enough."

Cameron's words rang ominously in Abby's ears. Whatever she was about to say, couldn't be good.

"There are some people heading to the container yard, supposedly to attack it."

"What?"

"Shaidi and Larson returned last night. Apparently, they were attacked while out scavenging, and Danny, Bryce, and Lenny were all captured. The group is now heading to the yard, and it shouldn't be too much longer before they get there."

"What about Jon? Is he all right?" Abby knew that Jon had been out scavenging; he always made sure to send word over the radio about when he'd be out.

"Apparently, he stayed behind to track the group's movements, to keep an eye on things in case they change."

Abby located the nearest stool and sat down, her mind digesting everything. "We should go. We should round up some volunteers and go help them."

Cameron shook her head. "They have things under control. If they need us, they'll radio for us."

Abby finally registered the tension in Cameron's body. Seeing it in Riley over the past few days had made her think of it as the default setting, but Cameron was quite different from her sister.

"Come here," Abby stood up again, opening her arms.

In a very un-Riley way, Cameron stepped forward and allowed herself to be hugged, embracing Abby in return. The woman's home was being attacked, and here she was, unable to help because she had to make sure her sister was okay. It couldn't have been an easy decision to make.

"It'll all work out," Abby attempted to soothe her, stroking Cameron's short hair.

After a minute, Cameron let go and stepped back. Her eyes were moist, but with a quick swipe of the back of her hand, they were dry again.

"I suppose I should get tested," Cameron commented, looking around the space they were in.

"That can wait until later, once this is all over and done with."

Cameron nodded in agreement. "Well, we should get back. The operation isn't supposed to take very long, and the others will wonder where we are."

"Does Dakota know? About the impending attack?"

"To be honest, I'm not sure," Cameron shrugged. "I didn't tell her, but it was pretty obvious that something was going on by the time we left, and she may have overheard someone talking."

Together, the two women returned to the medical centre's waiting room. Abby looked over at the three kids, who were huddled together against the wall away from the adults, whispering conspiratorially to each other. Hope kept glancing at the door to the operating room, waiting for it to open. Dakota didn't seem too concerned, trying to keep a conversation going, while Peter, who took some coaxing to sit here with his friends, sat quietly listening as he usually did. All they needed was for Becky and Adam to join them and the set would be complete. Again, Abby wondered if she should move to the container yard so that Peter could be with his friends.

The door finally opened as Josh exited the operating room. As he walked toward Cameron, Abby, and Brunt, Hope shot to her feet and hurried over, eager to get the news first hand.

"The operation went well," Josh told them, getting a collective sigh of relief in response. "She's not awake yet, but you can go see her in a minute. I should warn you, though, you might see some tubes sticking out of her."

"Tubes?" Abby's brows pinched together.

"After an operation like this, excess fluids can build up, so there are tubes to drain it. It might look gross, but don't worry about it."

"Can I go see her now?" Hope asked, tugging on Josh's hand.

"Just give doctors Robin, Haily, and Lewis a bit more time to clean up."

Abby imagined the bloody rags and tools being gathered in a bucket to be washed and disinfected later. She wondered what would happen to Riley's tissues. They had a sort of graveyard in remembrance of people who had died since arriving at the Black Box, but there were no bodies in it. Everyone was buried under a crop field to help fertilize soil, their decay drawing in needed worms and other such insects. Would the tissues they had removed from Riley end up the same way? Or would it be decided to do something less respectful with them, like use them as fish bait or mix them into the pig feed as protein? Abby decided she really didn't want to know. She missed the wastefulness of the world before the Day.

Josh disappeared back into the operating room, saying he'd come get them the moment they were allowed in. Abby sat back down with Cameron, but Hope didn't move. She waited impatiently near the door, her fingers fidgeting with one another. Watching her, Abby realized she had been fidgeting with the cross hanging from the fine chain around her neck. It had become a habit whenever she was worried or relieved, as if it somehow communicated her thoughts to God, both the prayers and the thanks. Glancing over at Cameron, Abby saw that she still looked nervous despite the news that everything had gone well and guessed it was because of what they had talked about.

When Josh finally did return, Hope didn't wait for him to say anything; she simply pushed past him to get into the room, nearly bowling over Robin who had been behind him.

"You can go in, although she's still asleep," Josh told the others.

There was a bit of bumping as Abby, Cameron, Brunt, Peter, and Dakota tried to enter the room, while Robin, Haily, and Lewis attempted to exit. Josh stayed put, ready to answer any questions Riley's visitors might have.

By the time Abby got to Riley's bedside, Hope had already situated herself on a metal stool next to her mom, her body stiff, not knowing what to do.

"You can take her hand," Josh told her, the girl immediately reacting to his words.

Abby found it difficult to look directly at her friend. Riley was mostly covered by a blanket, but the bandages still showed and the tubes poking out from between them were mildly disturbing.

"She looks so much smaller," Cameron whispered, as if her voice might wake up her sister. Brunt wrapped a comforting arm around her shoulders.

Abby mentally agreed with her. Sure, Riley was physically smaller, her breasts having been removed, but it wasn't just that. Still hooked up to IVs and unconscious, she appeared frail, a lot more delicate than Abby ever imagined she could look.

"Will she be staying in this room, or will she be moved?" Brunt asked Josh, his arm slowly sliding away from Cameron as she found another stool to perch upon across from her niece.

"We're going to keep her in here for a few hours, provided we don't need it for an emergency surgery, but we'll eventually move her to the more comfortable recovery room. Hopefully, she won't have to stay there long before she can start walking around and sleeping where she wants."

Although Hope and Cameron settled in to wait for Riley to wake up, Abby couldn't stand around that long. Now that she knew her friend had made it through the worst, she found she was eager to get back to work on something.

"Do you guys have a place to stay overnight?" Abby directed her question to Brunt.

"Not yet."

"I'd offer, but Riley and Hope have already claimed our spaces." Not that Riley needed one anymore, not at the moment at least.

"I didn't expect anyone to have enough room for all three of us, so we brought sleeping bags and mats."

"Well, if you don't find any better accommodations, then my floor is open."

"Can I sleep on the floor in Peter's room?" Dakota immediately asked.

"Sure," both Brunt and Abby replied, unclear as to which one of them the question was directed.

"Hear that, Hope? You, me, and Peter are gonna have a slumber party."

Hope tried to look excited for her friend, but couldn't quite manage it. She would likely be out of sorts until her mom woke up.

"I should get going," Abby eventually said, not knowing of another way to put it. "Lauren will want to hear the news, and I should be working."

"Thanks for sitting with us, Abby," Cameron told her with an honest smile.

"Peter? Are you going to stay here with your friends?"

"Do I have to?" Peter hadn't approached the bed at all, only glancing at Riley from across the room. He was clearly uncomfortable.

"Of course not."

"Come on, Peter. Why don't you show me what there is to do around here?" Dakota walked over to the younger boy and hooked her arm around his. "Hope, do you want to come?"

Hope shook her head. "I'm going to wait for my mom to wake up."

"Fair enough. We'll come back later when she's done being Sleeping Beauty. Take care of my hat for me." And with that, Dakota virtually dragged Peter out of the room until his legs managed to find her pace.

"Is there anything I can get you guys while I'm gone? Food, drink?" Abby offered.

"We're fine," Cameron told her.

"I can get them something later," Josh added.

"Maybe carry our bags to your place?" Brunt asked hesitantly. "Whether we end up sleeping there or not, it's probably best to get them out of the waiting room."

"Sure thing." Abby slipped out of the surgery room, glad to be away from its smell of disinfectant and blood. It was easy to locate the three packs belonging to Cameron, Brunt, and Dakota, as they filled the space beneath several waiting chairs. The heaviest, most likely Brunt's containing the mats and sleeping bags, she slung on her back, while the lighter two that probably held clean clothes she could carry in each hand. Weighed down, she stepped out into the hall.

As she made her way toward her apartment space, Abby wondered where Lauren would be. She might have gone to the computer lab, typing up what she knew, or she could've gone back outside to help with any tasks out there. It was even possible she was assisting someone somewhere else inside the Black Box.

Her thoughts about where to look first were interrupted as she neared an elevator on her floor. Jo was standing there, looking at the elevator doors as if waiting for them to open, but none of the buttons had been pressed and the indicator window above the doors revealed that the cab wasn't moving.

"You have to press a button," Abby spoke as she moved toward him. She hadn't explained how elevators worked during their initial tour, and only now realized he might not know. Depending on the group he had been with, he may have spent the majority of his life without electricity, and when it was available, it probably wasn't used to power anything like an elevator.

At the sound of her voice, Jo startled and spun to face her, his eyes wide and frightened.

"I'm sorry," Abby stopped advancing toward him. "I didn't mean to scare you. Do you remember me? Abby? I showed you around the other day."

Jo nodded, his posture relaxing but only slightly.

"If you want the elevator to come, you have to press either the up button or the down button, depending on which way you want to go." Abby nodded toward the panel, her hands too full to point. "Do you want me to help you? Where are you trying to go?"

Jo shook his head, then turned and ran away toward a staircase. Abby felt badly for frightening the boy. The Black Box must be such a strange place to him, one in which he knew no one. She decided to try to get Peter, Dakota, and Hope to play with him next time she came across the boy. She wondered who he was currently staying with. Should he even be allowed to be alone so soon?

The weight of the bags pulled at her arms and shoulders, urging her to continue on back to her apartment.

Entering her home, Abby quickly located a place to put the bags and piled them up. She called out for Lauren and peeked into the various rooms, but her partner wasn't there, meaning she'd have to search. Abby headed down to the computer lab first. Lauren wasn't there either, so she changed direction and went all the way back up, heading outside. Her legs had gotten quite the workout by the time she found Lauren. She was in the new field with Winchester, inspecting it for any last rocks that may have been missed. They didn't have many ploughs and weren't going to take any chances damaging one.

Lauren was happy the moment she spotted Abby, knowing the surgery had gone well simply by reading her expression. After passing on the pertinent information, Abby helped search the field, glad to turn her mind to something else.

That night, the dinner table was crowded. Claire had offered her bed to Brunt and Cameron, volunteering to sleep on the couch. She and Dakota did most of the talking throughout the meal, neither of them having seen the other in quite some time. Hope was there, looking brighter than earlier, but remaining quieter than normal. Her mom had woken up and spoken with those present, but she was very tired. She drifted in and out, making it hard to hold a dialog with her. Hope had wanted to stay with her mom, but both Cameron and Riley double-teamed her, insisting that spending the night here was better. Josh had promised to remain in the medical centre and watch over Riley, who had been moved out of the operating room and into a proper recovery room. Hopefully, she'd be able to leave the medical centre tomorrow or maybe the day after, provided there weren't any post-op problems.

"Are you sure you're okay on the floor?" Cameron spoke at the door where Peter, Hope, and Dakota were all spending the night. "You can share with me and Brunt can take the floor."

"No, I'm fine," Dakota responded, a slight whine and huff in her voice conveying her annoyance with the question.

"Hope, are you all right?" Cameron asked next.

Abby wasn't close enough to hear the quiet reply, but assumed it was in the affirmative as Cameron backed out of the room and closed the door. Abby and Lauren had both already said their goodnights to Peter. They were lucky with him. He wasn't like other boys, and didn't get embarrassed kissing his mom's on the cheek at night, or getting kisses in return. Abby was just waiting for him to reach his teenage years and become a hellish nightmare, expecting puberty to change everything.

"You all settled?" Abby asked Claire as the young woman shifted around on the couch, getting her pillows exactly how she wanted them.

"I'm cool. Goodnight."

"Goodnight, Claire. Goodnight, Cameron."

"See you in the morning." Cameron disappeared into Claire's room while Abby shut the door to her own.

"I am wiped," Lauren sighed as Abby changed into her pyjamas.

"Tomorrow we should get back to typing," Abby suggested. She then kneeled down beside the bed to say her nightly prayers. Along with a few specifics, mostly for Riley on this night, Abby always prayed for luck. It was the most important thing to have these days.

After she crawled into bed, Lauren snuggled up beside her. "Your hands are cold," she whispered in the dark.

Abby deliberately tucked them under the hem of Lauren's shirt, pressing them against her soft skin. Lauren squeaked and swatted at her.

"I'll remember this next time my feet are freezing," she teased.

Nestled together in the warmth of their bed, the two women fell asleep. It wasn't long before they were woken again by the ugly blaring of sirens.

***

Abby's body reacted before her mind was even awake and aware. In a tangling of limbs, she flailed against Lauren, who was equally confused, finally falling out of the side of the bed and onto the floor. Everything was red, a small yet bright emergency light above the door having flickered to life. The repeating, high-pitched chirp of the alarm was like having ice picks periodically thrust into her ear canals. Abby scrambled around on the carpet for a moment before finally getting her legs under her and standing.

"Are you all right?" Lauren asked, already up and jamming on a pair of shoes.

Abby nodded as she located her boots first, not bothering to tie them on as she followed Lauren out into the living room. The alarm was slightly quieter here in the larger space, but more lights made the room equally red.

"Is it a fire?" Claire asked loudly over the sound. She was ready to go, wearing her boots and jacket, weapons in hand.

Abby and Lauren both shook their heads. Without an announcement, they had no idea what was happening. Lauren moved to the cupboards where go-bags were kept, while Abby went to the kids' room. Within, the kids were already getting their shoes on, their faces frightened but determined. The last time an alarm like this had gone off around them, they ended up trapped in a room by fire. Mathias had rescued them, but lost his life in the end. Abby always felt a degree of responsibility as she remembered the incident. She had been guiding Hope, Peter, and Claire to the evacuation point, when Claire's hand slipped free of Peter's and they became separated. In the mob, Abby hadn't been able to spot the kids, the press of bodies eventually forcing her forward, and prayed that they would have to follow as well. Somehow, Dakota had found them, and the kids ended up back in the room in which they had spent the night. They were lucky to have survived.

"Is it a fire?" Hope mirrored Claire's words, her voice far more shaky.

"I don't think so," Abby told her in hopes it would calm her. "Are you ready to go?"

"In a minute." Dakota was sitting on the floor, pulling on a pair of pants beneath her nightgown, the task made more difficult because she had put on her shoes first. As she got up, she grabbed her hat and jammed it onto her head. "Okay, let's go."

Back out in the living room, Brunt and Cameron were fully dressed, their packs on their backs. Brunt held a rifle in his hands.

"We have to get my mom," Hope spoke to Cameron.

"She's in the medical centre, too far for us, but others will help her. Remember, Uncle Josh is down there with her. He won't let anything happen to your mom. Grab your bag."

Lauren passed packs to Abby, Claire, and Peter, all of them quickly sliding into the straps. Abby dashed back into her bedroom, quickly returning with a pair of belts, each of them holding a holstered pistol and a knife, which she and Lauren strapped on over their PJs.

"Peter, take this." Lauren handed the boy a cleaver from the kitchen. He had been taught all about guns and knives, including how to use them, but hadn't yet started carrying a blade around.

Dakota had donned a belt similar to Lauren and Abby's except the gun was a slingshot. She put on the pack Cameron handed her, as Hope filled her arms lifting Riley's bag.

"Hand that here, sweetheart," Brunt told her, taking the pack from Hope. He slipped his arms through the straps in a reverse fashion so that he wore it against his belly. "You have a weapon?"

Hope nodded, briefly taking off her pack to pull out a rather large hunting knife. She also jammed a slingshot into the waistband of her pyjama pants, not owning a belt like Dakota's.

"Let's go." Cameron moved toward the door.

Everyone buddied up, knowing all too well how easy it was to get separated from a larger group. They also kept one hand free for their weapons. Lauren clasped hands with Claire, Brunt with Dakota, Cameron with Hope, and Abby with Peter. Lauren and Claire volunteered to bring up the rear, which meant Abby had to lead the way, knowing the Black Box layout better than anyone. With her hand clamped firmly over Peter's—the boy not complaining even though it was probably hard enough to hurt—Abby stepped out into the hallway.

All along the length of the corridor, doors were opening as sleepy-eyed residents emerged. Nearly all of them had weapons, go-bags, and nervous postures. Abby followed those who had already begun to move, keeping Peter close by her side. The red lights of the hallway weren't as ominous, diffused by the regular ceiling lights that were still on. The strength of the siren waxed and waned as Abby headed for the stairs, passing the speakers that were screaming the high-pitched sound at them.

"Stop! Stop!" someone started shouting as Abby approached the stairwell.

She was jostled as a man pushed through the crowd. He reached the door to the stairwell and threw himself across it, not letting anyone else pass. A ripple of concern and confusion moved through the evacuees.

"Don't go outside!" the man yelled to be heard over the siren.

It took a moment for Abby to recognize him given the odd lighting and stressed expression. She didn't know much about him other than that his name was Thomas and he worked helping Crichton organize things.

It seemed Cameron knew him, however, as she wormed her way next to Abby, Hope in tow, and called to him. "Thomas, what's going on?"

"We're under attack!" he informed them.

"Is it the people who were attacking the container yard?"

"The yard is being attacked?" Abby was just able to hear Hope's worried question over the din. It seemed that if Dakota knew, she hadn't told her friend.

"We don't know who it is, but they're attacking from both sides! Everyone needs to get back to their room and wait for instructions!"

"What do you mean 'both sides'?" a member of the gathering called out.

"They got into the basement somehow! Now hurry up and get back to your apartments before they show up here and find us all standing around with our thumbs up our asses!"

The crowd was slow to turn, word having to be passed back, but they did turn. When a gunshot rang out from the stairwell, it spurred them on much faster. People began pushing and Abby found herself both grateful and terrified to be near the rear of the mob.

The stairwell door opened with a squall. Abby glanced over her shoulder just in time to see Thomas take a gun butt to the face by a foul-looking man, but then Abby rounded a corner and they disappeared from sight.

"Peter, run!" Abby shouted to him, releasing his hand. The boy would be able to slip through the crowd faster on his own, to get away from the rear. He hesitated briefly, so Abby pushed him forward, shoving him between two adults ahead of them. She didn't know where the others were in the crowd.

Heavy footsteps came pounding down the hall behind Abby. Had the siren not cut out at that moment, she might not have heard them. Turning on her heel, she raised her knife and attempted to draw her pistol at the same time. The man was too close, too fast. His rifle butt lashed out, striking Abby's hand and knocking the gun free. She stepped closer to him, slashing with the knife, but he backed up just enough so that she caught nothing but T-shirt. Abby pressed forward, her blade flashing in the air, forcing the strange man to keep retreating. She cut him a few times, but nothing serious, just a few grazes that weren't much more than scratches. He smelled repulsive, like one of the rotting corpses outside, but Abby wouldn't back away. She was giving the others, the kids, more time to escape, to get behind secure doors.

From the corner of her vision, Jo appeared, watching as she fought with the man.

"Jo! Get out of here!" Abby yelled, never taking her eyes off the man she was assailing.

A blunt object connected with the back of her knee, causing Abby to stagger. The man took the opportunity to back away several steps, giving him a chance to gather himself. As Abby bumped into the wall, she turned to see what had happened. Jo was standing there, his small muscles rigid. He looked ready to attack Abby. To attack Abby again, as he had already kicked the back of her knee.

The reeking assailant came for Abby again, swinging his rifle butt at her like a baseball bat. She ducked just in time, but now it was his turn to press in on her. Abby found herself scrambling backward, dodging the swinging rifle. A blow crunched into her shoulder and she cried out, but continued backward, glad that the other end of the gun wasn't being used for whatever reason.

With a lucky shot, Abby managed to throw her foot up between the man's legs. It wasn't a solid connection, but it was enough for him to stumble back in pain. The kick also threw Abby off balance, causing her to spin in an attempt to catch herself. She saw her pistol lying against a floorboard nearby. She was going to dive for it, when a hand grabbed her pack and yanked her backward. The force was enough to lift her off her feet, but she kept them under her, even as she was swung and thrown into the wall.

"You bitch!" the stinking man screamed as he hurled a punch toward Abby's face.

Abby got her knife up and managed to give him a fairly good gash near his elbow, weakening the blow before it struck her. Pain flared out from her cheekbone, spreading across her face. She ignored it, realizing that the man who had attacked her had backed away in his own pain. Abby fled down the hall, understanding that if the fight continued, she would lose. She almost made it back to the stairwell when a heavy weight struck her back, knocking her down, her head bouncing painfully off the floor as her knife skittered away. She flailed as she attempted to right herself, the weight fighting back. Eventually, after wriggling out of her pack and rolling to her back, she was able to make out that it was Jo who had tackled her. The boy kept trying to pin her limbs, but Abby was stronger. She managed to get her knee up against Jo's chest, then extend her leg, kicking him up and over her head. She rolled back onto her stomach, prepared to push up onto her feet, when a much heavier weight flattened her, a familiar smell letting her know who it was.

"Goddamn, cunt," the man's breath huffed in her ear.

"Don't kill her," a calm, unfamiliar voice spoke from the direction of the stairwell door.

"She didn't cut you and kick you in the balls!" the man on top of Abby shouted, finally managing to grab her arms and secure them against her back with his weight.

"You would have done the same in her position," the calm voice told him.

Abby twisted to see who was talking, but the man was deceptively ordinary, possessing a face devoid of readable expressions.

"Put her with the others we managed to grab," the mystery man continued.

As Abby felt herself get roughly bound, she hoped that the kids had made it back to the apartment, that they would be all right.

23
Danny's Hurt

Danny was leaving impressions on the tough scrap of leather between his teeth. First there was the stinging of the antiseptic, and now it was being followed by the bite of a needle and thread. Knowing others may be injured worse than him, he had refused any sort of painkiller or numbing agent. He was determined to tough it out, although he was beginning to think that was a terrible decision. Just as he was about to give in, the doctor finished up, securing a bandage over the wound.

"Thanks," Danny spit out the leather, sweat rolling down his forehead and cheeks.

Looking around the community centre, he spotted Bryce being administered to. Getting up from the plastic chair, he made his way over.

"How're you doing?" Danny asked as he gingerly sat down beside him.

"Great," Bryce said sarcastically, having to peer at Danny through swollen, wincing eyes. All of his cuts were being dabbed with antiseptic. "You?"

"Getting shot is no picnic either. Have you seen Riley around?" Danny was surprised it wasn't his sister-in-law who patched him up.

"I'm not seeing much, but she wasn't one of them, sorry."

"Where are Becky and Larson?" He thought they'd be by Bryce's side.

"I think Larson is currently helping to monitor that other group coming in. Becky is sitting with one of Misha's dogs somewhere. She's not keen on watching this." Bryce gestured to the careful application of a bandage to his head.

Danny noticed that someone had retrieved a chunk of ice from the freezer container they kept running with a crowded array of solar panels placed on top. "Shouldn't you be holding this to your eye or something?" he commented.

"Not until I'm done," the woman tending to Bryce glowered at Danny.

"All right, sorry." He attempted to raise his hands in a calming gesture, but succeeded only with one hand. His injured muscle didn't like any movement from either his shoulder or neck, the pain quickly interceding.

"Riley went to the Black Box with some patients a few days ago and they're not back yet," the woman told Danny, her voice taking on a more sympathetic tone. She probably hadn't meant to come across so snappish; the stress of the situation was weighing on her.

Danny looked around the community centre again, twisting his body but not his neck to do so. Strangers were entering the centre, predominantly little kids and elderly folk, along with a few adults who looked like parents. They had all been stripped of gear and weapons and were being herded along one wall. The people from Evans' party clumped fearfully together, their eyes constantly darting about, studying the people of the container yard while also trying to avoid eye contact. Danny felt sympathetic towards them, having been a captive to strangers so recently himself.

"I'm going to go see who else is around. I'll come back and check on you later, okay?" Danny spoke to Bryce as he rose from his seat.

"Sure, whatever," Bryce mumbled, his words imprecise as the woman gently cleaned his split lip.

Danny walked through the crowd of the container yard's non-combatants, saying hi to those he knew. He found Becky with one of Misha's dogs where Bryce said she'd be, her friend Adam perched on a stack of chairs against the wall. His friendship with Bryce and Larson, as well as being Hope's uncle, ensured that he knew this entire group of young friends.

"Hope go with Riley to the Black Box?" he asked as he approached the duo. The dog that lay on the floor was Trigger, the one Danny mentally thought of as the happy breed.

"Yeah," Becky nodded, running her fingers through the dog's shiny fur. Was Trigger fatter than last time Danny had seen her? "Dakota's there too. Cameron and Brunt took her this morning. You don't think they were running away, do you?" The look in Becky's eyes as they met Danny's suggested this idea had been worrying her.

"I sincerely doubt that," Danny told her, although it was strange. Why would Cameron and Brunt leave? From his understanding, they had known Evans' party was coming since the middle of the night, and neither of them was the kind of person who shied away from any sort of fight. There must have been something else going on that no one had bothered to inform him as yet.

"Got a good view from up there?" Danny redirected his attention to Adam.

"Yeah, I can see all the bastards as they come in," the boy answered.

"They're not bastards, not all of them."

Adam gave him a serious and confused look.

"They're not that much different than us; they just made a mistake is all."

"You guys were kidnapped, beat up, got shot, and now a mega zombie horde is coming after they shot at us. I'd call that something more than a mistake." Adam could be an angry little thing at times.

"Even so, most of them weren't involved in any of that. Certainly none of the people that have been led in here. As for the zombies, that might have happened anyway. Hell, me and the others out scavenging could've ended up bringing them here."

Adam's lips pinched together in a tight line. He was still angry, probably still angry with Evans' people, but had decided that Danny wasn't an ally in this and couldn't be converted.

"Just keep your distance and everything will be fine," Danny said as he left. He meant that both for the kids' safety, and for the safety of Evans' party. If Adam went over there, he'd surely find a way to start a fight with another kid his size, with Becky probably more than willing to back him up after what had happened to her brother.

Wandering through the community centre, he spotted Lenny against one wall, his eyes half-closed. Danny recognized the posture as one Lenny used when he was tired, but too nervous to completely fall asleep. His body was resting while his mind was not. Danny couldn't say for certain, but he thought the older man hadn't slept at all when they were locked in that gym storage cupboard. He hadn't slept much himself, but was younger and continued to keep alert with a combination of pain and adrenaline. At no point did Danny spot Larson, Shaidi, or Jon, so he figured they were outside somewhere. Danny had heard through the grapevine that the man who warned them of the mega horde had known Jon from before. Danny wondered if he knew the person as well, since he and Jon were foster brothers way back when.

Eventually, Danny found himself over by Evans' people. There was a clear gap separating them from the container residents, no one daring to cross the self-imposed, no-man's land. Only a few of the container residents were among the others: medical volunteers checking for injuries or running infection tests, plus a handful of guards. Two more of Misha's dogs threaded around legs, checking out all the new people. As Danny stepped out into the empty space, he was aware of several people on both sides watching him. Evans' people were especially wary, recognizing that he was their former captive and could be holding a dangerous grudge.

Danny looked at the group, his eyes finally settling on a woman close to him who wouldn't look away. She had the fierce gaze of a protective mother, ready to fight against overwhelming odds for her brood.

"Is everyone treating you all right?" Danny asked, trying to sound as friendly as possible without overdoing it.

The woman was wary about answering, carefully thinking through what she should say. She simply nodded in the end.

"Good, I hope we can get past everything that's happened. I don't know if our two groups could ever become friends, but we'll get through this and go our separate ways, no hard feelings." Danny hoped the container residents behind were listening, as his words were meant for them as well. He found he felt partly responsible for Evans' people. Had their paths never crossed, they would never have found themselves in this situation, relying on the kindness of people they had shot at.

A ripple ran through the community centre. Apparently, the zombies had been spotted at last; everyone fell completely silent. Without the constant surrounding chatter, it was possible to hear the moaning, despite the community centre's thick shell, its fair distance from the wall, and the sound having to compete with the nearby water slapping against the container yard's concrete sides. The noise continued to grow as the mob neared the wall, the groaning of corpses constantly escalating. People were tight with fear on both sides of no-man's land. Danny did his best to appear calm, while his heart was actually galloping in his chest. Several others were attempting the same, hoping their calm exterior would soothe others. As Danny watched, some of these people began sitting down, either on nearby chairs, cots, or the floor itself. Danny did the same, right in the middle of no-man's land, an attempt at being a bridge between the two communities. It was working; other people started sitting down as well. Their postures remained rigid, ready to spring back up at a moment's notice, but it was less nerve wracking than having everyone stand around as if about to bolt. Tiny children were clutched on their parents' laps, being taught the heavy importance of silence, while slightly bigger tots bunched at their sides. Older kids, like Adam and Becky, huddled together with their friends, trying to show they were brave enough not to need their parents. A few gave up quickly, hurriedly seeking the safety of trusted adults. Roughly a dozen teenagers, those not quite old enough or trained enough to have been helping outside, had a perversely eager look in their eyes, as though they wanted everything to turn to Hell. They weren't so stupid as to do anything no one else was doing, but they were feeding off the fear and turning it into their own energy, many of them skulking about the centre, unable to keep in one place.

Danny began counting people he could see. It wasn't a practical exercise. He lost count a few times, and probably counted people moving about more than once, but it was a distraction. It was something to do that wasn't thinking about what would happen should the zombies get over the walls.

***

Minute after minute ticked by, and the sounds of rotting corpses hadn't slackened in the slightest. A new kind of nervousness started to spread through the community centre. The longer this went on, the more edgy people became. Even the teenagers' attitudes changed; no longer excited, they became more fearful by the second. People who had been standing sat down to clasp their knees, preventing themselves from overreacting. Others who had been sitting, Danny included, found they could no longer keep still and got to their feet to pace and wander. Danny walked up and down no-man's land, the space giving him a significant amount of room. His shoulder ached, and he held his sore arm with his good one, thinking he should've gotten a sling for it.

After a couple of laps back and forth, Danny discovered all three of Misha's dogs hanging out around the door.

"Go on, shoo," he patted their rumps with a quiet word, gesturing for them to go elsewhere in the centre. The dogs clumping by the doors would only make people more jittery, thinking that they knew something the humans didn't. The dogs should be among them, helping keep the people settled.

When they didn't move, Danny cracked open the door and peered out, using his body to keep the pooches from worming free of the centre. Through the slit he created, he spotted Misha talking to someone who had his back to the building. Their quiet voices weren't nearly loud enough to cover the distance, but Danny bet Misha's dogs could smell him and that that's what they were reacting to.

"They know Misha's outside," Danny told the nearest container resident, knowing that she could inform anyone else who was concerned about the dogs. "I'll go see what's going on."

Inching the door open just a little more, Danny squeezed out and shut it behind him.

"Get back inside," a guard outside the centre hissed at him.

"It's fine," Danny told him.

"You're injured," the man pointed to his shoulder, "you need to stay inside."

"It's not that bad. Look, I'm just going to go talk to Misha over there. Some of his dogs are inside and have become aware he's out here. The way they're bunched up by the door is making people more nervous than they need to be. I'm going to ask Misha to either go somewhere else, or come inside."

The guard hesitated. Clearly, he was under orders to let no one leave the centre, at least no one who needed to be in there, such as the injured, the young, and the very old.

"Your name's Lee, right?" Danny had seen him around, as he had seen everyone around the container yard, but had never had an opportunity to interact with him directly.

"That's right," he nodded.

"I'm Danny, one of the scavengers who got kidnapped."

"I know who you are."

"Then you should know I've gotten first dibs on a lot of good stuff. I'd be willing to trade you something if you let me break the rules just this one time. Just so I can help calm down the people inside."

Lee glanced warily around the yard. They couldn't have everyone just running around, as that would certainly draw the attention of the zombies, but letting out just one more man? One who was a scavenger, used to dealing with this kind of thing?

"All right, we'll trade," Lee finally acquiesced. "After all this is over, I'm coming to look at what you have."

"Deal." Danny shook the guard's hand, glad that his bribe had worked instead of getting him into more trouble. There were advantages to being a scavenger.

Danny didn't get far before he watched Misha and the other man head toward him and the community centre. The man Misha had been talking to was a stranger, although there was something vaguely familiar about him, even at a distance, which made Danny guess he was visiting from the Black Box. Not wanting to waste his bribe, Danny continued to walk out to meet them.

What's going on? he signed to Misha once they were close enough. He knew sign language was going to cause pain in his shoulder, but he vastly preferred it over speaking with the zombies so close.

Where's Boyle? Or Karsten? Misha replied instead, emphasizing his mouth movements around the names. *They inside?*

No, I didn't see either of them in there. Danny kept glancing over at the stranger who was openly staring at him. *What?* he finally asked the young man.

"You're Danny," the stranger stated in a whispered voice.

Danny nodded, resisting the urge to add a *what of it?*

"Do you remember me? Mark Green?"

It finally clicked why this man looked so familiar. Mark and Jon had been best friends before the Day, and Danny could recall memories of the two of them sitting on the couch in the living room, or hanging out in the garage with the radio turned up. He must have been the one who showed up to warn them of the mega horde.

Danny clasped his hand in a shake. "Of course I remember you," he whispered, realizing he must not know sign language. He had to be careful to control his enthusiasm and keep his voice down, although the constant droning moan that filled the air helped. "I'm surprised you're alive." Over time, Danny had learned what had happened to everyone in his tightly knit group during the Day, including Mark's disappearance. "You knew Abby too. She's living in our other camp, with Claire."

"Yeah, Jon told me."

Danny nodded, because of course Jon would tell him that. He then returned to Misha, remembering that more important things were happening despite having a million questions for Mark.

What do you need Boyle or Karsten for?

I'm not going to repeat myself. Help us find them and you can figure it out then.

Danny nodded and pointed toward the wall, figuring they were somewhere near it. If a breach was going to happen, the former military lieutenant and former submarine captain would want to know about it right away, first hand, before it got worse.

As they headed toward the wall, all the tiny hairs across Danny's body began to stand on end. He found himself moving slower, his limbs not wanting to carry him along their present course. Turning his eyes toward Misha, he saw that he seemed to be reacting the same. Mark appeared more relaxed than either of them, perhaps more accustomed to the sound after following the mega horde for so long, but he had matched his step to the others. All of them tread lightly, not daring to let their shoes make even the slightest scuffle, despite the fact that there was no way they could be heard over the wall amongst the racket the zombies were making.

Danny had been partly right. Karsten was standing near the wall with two others, one a stranger and the one named Tommy who had spoken with Evans, while a few other brave souls were scattered along its length, weapons in hand. Boyle was nowhere to be seen, but it was possible he was at the other end of the wall, around the corner, keeping an eye on the shorter section near the bay.

The female stranger spotted them first and raised a hand in greeting. Mark waved back, and the other group of three came toward them. The girl kept patting the top of a fist into the palm of her other hand as she walked, seemingly following a pattern that made no sense. Danny wondered if it was a nervous tic, or if she was listening to music within her mind to help cope with the unnerving soundtrack with which the container yard was being bombarded. Karsten held a notebook and pencil, the pages covered in lettering from more than one hand. Apparently, not even whispering was allowed this close to the wall.

Misha signed something that Danny hadn't been able to fully catch out of the side of his vision. Whatever it was, Karsten agreed and pointed in a new direction for all of them. Maybe he was taking them to Boyle.

They moved between the containers of residents until arriving at Karsten's. He opened the door and gestured for everyone to enter. Once a kerosene lamp was lit, Karsten not having a bottle light, the doors were then sealed behind them, blessedly dampening the horrid noise.

Danny took a quick look around Karsten's container, never having had an opportunity to do so before. It was very neat and tidy, not filled with clutter like his own. Karsten also had more personal items than anyone else, having moved everything from his captain's quarters on the German sub before a storm had forced it to sink permanently.

"So you have some sort of plan?" Karsten looked from Misha to Mark, keeping his voice quiet enough to be heard only within the container.

"What do you need the high point for?" Misha asked Mark.

"If I could get high enough to see over the comet horde, I can communicate with the rest of our team," Mark informed them.

"No, you'll be spotted," Karsten immediately negated the plan.

"We've done it before," Tommy was quick to add. "We stay out of sight of the zombies. We keep to a spot where we can see over their heads, but not see them, which means they can't see us. The others on our team will have followed the comet horde and found a high spot behind them where they'll be looking out for us."

"How do you communicate over such a distance?" Danny wondered.

"Mirrors and Morse code," the girl replied. It was then that Danny realized her hand patting hadn't been as random as he thought. She had been telling Mark something as they approached. Had Karsten caught it? He would know Morse and would know what she had said.

"What would be the point?" Karsten challenged the outsiders. "What would communicating with your team gain us?"

"If the zombies are facing us, the others can safely observe them. They can find out what's going on, why they aren't moving away," Tommy spoke calmly. "Some information is better than none. It'll give us something to work with. Depending on what's going on, the others may even get the zombies to leave using fireworks or something."

"It's not hard to get onto the community centre roof," Misha spoke up. "I believe you can see across the whole yard from up there, except for where the stacks are too tall. The slope of the roof would also provide something to hide behind."

"Where's Boyle? Shouldn't he be involved in this conversation?" Danny asked, not particularly liking that only one of their leaders was present.

"He's busy investigating potential escape routes," Karsten told him.

That seemed odd to Danny. Everyone knew the escape routes: the weak would take whatever boats might be at the dock, the rest would cross Bitch Bridge to Animal Island, and if the bridge was out, they would swim. There were no other routes.

"I think we should do it," Misha spoke again. "Like he said, even a little bit of information is better than none. I want to know why they're not leaving like they should."

"I agree," Danny decided. "I don't think any of us were at the prison, but remember the stories? Remember what we were told about Roy, and how he figured out a way to breach the walls there?"

"Roy?" both Mark and Tommy said at once, their spines becoming stiff.

Karsten looked at Misha and Danny, clearly deciding whether or not he wanted to say something in front of them.

"Danny probably heard me telling Evans," Tommy offered as a way of getting him to speak.

"There's a super smart zombie in the horde outside," Karsten grudgingly spoke. "Roy kind of smart."

Danny *had* heard something along those lines being mentioned, but he hadn't thought of *that* level of intelligence. He had only heard stories, but they were enough to chill his blood. Beside him, Misha seemed to have the same reaction.

"So that's why you guys believed me so quickly," Mark sighed. "I had a feeling it wasn't just because I used to know Jon."

"Tell me about Roy." The calmness had left Tommy.

"You seem to know already." Karsten faced the younger man, always willing to stand up to anyone.

"The intelli-zombie was created by Roy," Mark told them.

"By bite?" Danny couldn't keep the fear from squeaking his voice somewhat.

"No. No, thank God," Mark quickly soothed the swiftly agitated container trio. "Your Roy, was he a scientist? Could you tell?"

"He wore a white lab coat with a name tag, which is why he was called Roy," Karsten told them.

"Sounds like the same Roy then; we never did learn what happened to him," Mark said, looking at Tommy, who nodded. The girl was staying quiet during this part of the conversation.

"After the evacuation of Leighton, we ended up in the same place as Roy. He and some others were conducting experiments on the zombies, but we never learned the specifics. He ended up turning our friend Dean into an intelligent zombie, or intelli-zombie as we started saying. When the place became overrun, we fled, not following the rest of the evacuees. We know they took Dean with them, but not what happened to him after that. All we know is that he eventually escaped and came across us, and we've been keeping an eye on him ever since. We never learned what happened to Roy; I lost track of him during that second evacuation." Tommy relayed his information in as quick a manner as he could.

"There were rumours he injected himself with something. If he created this intelli-zombie, as you call it, then he could have injected himself with the same thing. Some of us always wondered if there might be another, a first subject, maybe more, but we always hoped that they were destroyed," Karsten sighed.

"What happened to Roy? Did you manage to kill him?" the girl wondered, finally speaking up. There was a note of hope in her voice.

"From what I've heard, people just fled the prison, leaving him behind. I don't think anyone knows." Danny looked to Misha and Karsten who nodded their agreement. "Could he also still be wandering around?"

"Maybe." Tommy shrugged. "He'd likely have the same mega horde gathered around him though, and I feel my team would have noticed another one if they started in roughly the same place. We've never come across a comet horde slime trail that wasn't caused by Dean's group; we kept track. Either Roy is dead, or he wandered off into the ocean, which is basically the same thing. We were always hoping that one day Dean would walk into the ocean and get sucked down by the undertow. Once he got dragged out to sea, he might not think to come back, or get stuck in a chasm or on a coral reef until the forces of the sea tore him apart. Unfortunately, he's never stepped foot in a large body of water. It's as if he knows."

"Maybe that's why he stopped outside," Danny suggested. "Maybe he knows that going sideways will lead him into water, and he can't turn around because of the body mass." He really hoped that was all that was happening.

"We can't know for sure without some eyes on them," Tommy said, pushing their idea.

"All right. All right, Misha, get one of them up on the community centre. I want you up there with them, as well," Karsten finally relented.

"Maybe someone who knows Morse should be up there with them, just in case," Misha suggested slowly, his eyes sliding over to Mark, Tommy, and the girl, knowing his distrust could be taken offensively.

"Right," Karsten agreed. "While we get set up, Danny, can you find Jans? He was my radio operator and knows Morse better than anyone."

"I know him, and sure thing." Danny was grateful to be given a task, something to focus on.

The outsiders had no complaints with the plan and so it was agreed upon. Karsten opened the container and blew out the lantern while everyone began to disperse.

After the dim interior of the container, Danny found himself blinking repeatedly in the bright, outdoor light, and wanting to cover his ears against the sudden increase in sound. As soon as he managed to orient himself, he headed off in the direction of Jans' container. Whenever Danny wasn't out scavenging, he helped unload containers beyond the wall, a job that frequently had him working with people like Jans. He had gotten to know most of them fairly well, conversation being the best way to pass the time while hauling.

Reaching the correct container, Danny found it locked and so he knocked. He was careful not to knock too loudly, not wanting to startle anyone inside. A woman opened one of the doors and peered out at him, blinking in the light the same way he had.

Can I help you? she signed, a bit clumsy as those who didn't use it often usually were. She was probably on kitchen staff, or some other duty that kept her within the wall.

I'm looking for Jans, Danny signed back, wincing at the pain in his shoulder again.

By the wall, she pointed where she thought he might be.

Danny thanked her and trotted off, not getting far before the jostling of his shoulder and the louder sound of his feet forced him to slow. As he walked as fast as his injured arm could tolerate, he held it with his good arm. At least the pain was keeping him awake and rather alert.

Near the wall's corner, he spotted Jans. The man had the short and bony stature of a boy who hadn't yet hit puberty, but with his grey hair, craggy face, and multiple scars from fighting off boarders during the Diana raid, it was impossible to mistake him for a youth.

Getting his attention, Danny rapidly relayed where he was needed, using as few gestures as possible. When Jans started to ask a question, Danny just shook his head and pointed back toward the community centre with his good arm. Karsten could explain everything to him once he was there.

As Jans ran off, Danny found himself wondering what he should do next. He thought about heading back to the community centre, but also wanted to find Boyle and let him know what was going on. Looking down the length of the wall in both directions, Danny could see no one who matched Boyle's description, so he wasn't there. Could he be looking into an escape route like Karsten claimed? That just didn't sit well with Danny.

As he started walking, determined to locate Boyle, he felt a bead of sweat run down his torso beneath his shirt. As he continued to search, looking down rows of containers for anyone that might be him, he felt another bead. This one gave him pause, as it was in the same spot as the first one. In Danny's experience, he didn't sweat like that. Looking down, he saw a red stain blooming across his shirt. It wasn't beads of sweat he was feeling, but blood. He had torn open at least one of his stitches.

Cursing to himself, Danny redirected back toward the centre. After this, there was no way he'd be allowed back out. He was going to be confined in there with the others, only able to wonder what was going on outside.

He got back just in time to see Misha setting up a ladder against a container holding some of Evans people. One of the doors was open, and it looked like Tommy was quietly explaining what was going on so that the noises wouldn't freak them out. The guard outside the centre glowered at Danny as he approached, his eyes focused on his injury. Danny didn't give him the satisfaction of an acknowledgement, just squeezed back in, careful of Misha's dogs who were right there again, since he was outside.

As Danny looked for the person who had patched him up the first time, he continued to wonder where the hell Boyle was.

24
Nessie's Frustrated

Nessie stood outside the community centre, her hands wrapped firmly around the head of her cane. She had spent too much time in the centre, bunched in with everyone else ever since before that other group came and shot at them. She was only allowed to go to the toilets in a group and accompanied by a guard. She needed some air and so had slipped out the side door. The main door had dogs clustered around it, and there was no way to just simply step out of the roll up at the other end, so she had picked the little side door between the heavy containers filled with supplies. A guard stood right next to her, making sure she didn't wander off like she wanted to. Nessie wanted to go back to her container and check on Dragon, who was locked in his cage in the dark. It was the only way to make sure he kept quiet, but Nessie worried about the bird. She also worried about that zombie the kids had found before the storm hit. Once it had blown over, Nessie, with the kids in tow, had immediately made their way to where Boyle and Karsten were organizing the cleanup. Pulling them both aside, with the kids huddled together behind her, Nessie explained what had happened. Together, they all went to check it out only to find the zombie was gone. Evidence of it still remained: gross smears on the walls and floor, the U-bolt that had held its chain, but the thing itself had vanished. Whoever had imprisoned it in there must have seen Nessie and the kids discover it and then risked going out in the storm to move the thing.

Nessie shifted her weight back and forth, knowing that Boyle was even now searching for evidence and discreetly asking questions. The moment that other group had been dealt with, he got right back to work. When that mute woman, Freya, had arrived from the Black Box, she was quickly wrangled into service as well. It had been a long time since she had visited from the Box, and therefore she couldn't have been involved in this, which was why Boyle and Karsten convinced her to help. It didn't take much convincing. Nessie wanted to help too, but was confined to the centre. She also understood she wasn't completely off the suspect list. Although the kids had been with her when she first looked at the thing, and had stayed with her until she had reported to Boyle and Karsten, their alibis weren't completely trusted. They were kids, after all, and she had many things with which to bribe them.

A sound, barely discernible above the moaning beyond the wall, drew her attention. She turned around and looked up at the building, hoping it wasn't a creaking that indicated a new weakness in the structure.

"It's all right, ma'am, someone's just climbing onto the roof. Some sort of plan of Karsten's," the guard whispered to her.

"Ma'am?" Nessie turned to the guard, her whispering combined with a scolding tone. "You know my name, Cohen, use it."

"Sorry, Nessie," the young man mumbled so quietly it was nearly inaudible.

Nessie let a moment pass before whispering in a much kinder voice, "What sort of plan?"

"I don't know; they didn't give me all the details. They just told me someone was going up on the roof and not to worry about it."

"Well, I'm worried. Want to go find out what's happening?"

Cohen shook his head. "I'm not leaving my post. And you're not walking off either."

Nessie sighed. She was just so *bored*. There wasn't much to do in the centre but sit around yakking, and now that the zombies had shown up, people weren't even doing that. There was only so much she could write in her notebook when nothing was changing. She wondered what Bill was up to over in the Black Box, how his health checkup was going. She wondered if this situation would get bad enough that the people here would need to call the people over there for help.

The roof couldn't be seen from where Nessie stood, the angle far too sharp and the distance too great. She stared up at it anyway, attempting to divine Karsten's purpose for sending someone up there. Perhaps she should go back inside and slip out the other door that was closer to where they'd be climbing up. She wouldn't be able to see the roof from there either, but maybe there'd be someone she could ask questions of.

Cohen was also staring up at the roof and when Nessie turned around to look out into the container yard, she spotted someone moving from one container aisle to the next. This was a common occurrence, not even that unusual during siege times, but it was the way the individual was moving that bothered Nessie. Whoever it was—she was guessing male, based on her brief look, but it could have been female—had been hunched over and scurrying. Like he didn't want to be seen.

"Did you see that?" Nessie whispered to Cohen, knowing that he hadn't.

"See what?" he asked, turning to face the same direction.

"Someone just moved over there," Nessie pointed. "They looked like they were up to something."

"They looked like they were up to something?" Cohen repeated in a disbelieving voice.

"They were moving like this." Nessie pulled her shoulders forward and bent at the waist, walking back and forth a short distance. "Only they were moving much faster, almost a jog."

"So? Someone probably decided to wait this out in a different container and they're afraid of being out here."

It was a perfectly reasonable explanation, but Nessie wasn't so sure. She had information that Cohen didn't.

"Can I trust you, Cohen?"

"Of course you can," he replied, confused by the question.

"No, I mean, can I really trust you? Are you a good man?"

Cohen paused a second before answering, his eyebrows becoming conjoined in their confusion. "I'd like to think I am."

"Okay, I'm going to tell you something that only me, Karsten, Boyle, and a small handful of others know. We've been keeping it quiet so as not to alarm anyone. You understand?"

Cohen slowly nodded.

"You know those containers we keep near the short section of the wall? The ones over in the corner that are supposed to be converted into new living spaces eventually? Well, a zombie was discovered chained up in one."

Cohen visibly flinched and paled at the news.

"The zombie has since disappeared. We think the culprit knew that his secret had been discovered and used the cover of the storm to move it. Boyle's been investigating and has personally searched the rest of the containers over there, but there's no sign of where the zombie's been taken. Hopefully it's been destroyed."

"What if it's not?" Cohen asked the question Nessie had been hoping he would ask.

"Imagine what would happen if that person lost control of the zombie right now? Or worse, deliberately let the thing loose? It would cause chaos, havoc. People would think that the zombies outside had gotten in. They would start screaming and running, which would definitely alert the other corpses, and then they really would start coming over the walls."

It was almost possible to see the gears turning in Cohen's mind.

"It's our duty to go after that person and find out what they were really up to," Nessie prodded.

Cohen shifted in place, torn between the orders he had been given, and the information Nessie was feeding him.

"The longer we wait, the farther away from us that person gets."

"All right, fine," Cohen gave in. "I'll go check out what's happening, but you have to stay here. Do you promise?"

"Sure."

Cohen gave her a look like he didn't quite believe her, but could no longer hang around. He was soon moving away as quickly as sound restrictions would let him.

Nessie watched him disappear from sight, trying to decide what she would like to do. Did she want to go after this person as well? Find Boyle and tell him about it? Or check out what was happening on the roof? Although she had half-heartedly promised Cohen she wouldn't move, she intended to break that promise. She even thought up a way to keep Cohen out of trouble should that arise. There was an advantage to being one of the elderly, in that Nessie could simply forget she had made such a promise and people would believe her. Strangely, the thing holding her back was leaving the door without anyone outside of it. Most people weren't like her, weren't going to risk leaving the safest building in the yard, but it wasn't them Nessie worried about. She worried about the little kids who might wander off, disappearing out the door the second eyes weren't on them.

Standing outside the door, Nessie resisted the urge to tap her cane on the concrete, a habit she developed when nervous. Coming up with a possible solution, she turned to the door and poked her head through it. Scanning faces and postures, she searched for someone who could help her with her predicament. When she spotted a gangly teenage boy, she thought she was in luck. Unfortunately, he wasn't facing her way, and Nessie didn't want to leave the door. Staring hard at the side of his head, Nessie hoped that the kid would feel her eyes boring into him.

Eventually he turned, although it took nearly three minutes and Nessie had almost given up. The moment Nessie knew he could see her, she waved him over. The kid looked around, thinking that she was gesturing to someone else. Nessie pointed at him and gestured him over again. When he pointed at himself for clarification, Nessie nodded with an exasperated sigh. Continuing to look around him as if this were some sort of mistake or trick, he made his way over to where Nessie stood half-in and half-out of the building. As soon as he was close enough, Nessie clasped his arm and pulled him outside. He clearly became agitated about the sudden increase in zombie noises.

"How old are you, kid?" Nessie whispered to him. Whatever his age was, he had already hit puberty and had sprouted up taller than her.

"Fifteen," he puffed out his chest, looking like he was about to debate the 'kid' comment, but then decided against it. "Shouldn't we be using sign?" he said instead with a complex wiggling of his fingers and arms that probably meant an approximation of the same thing.

"Look at me, you think I'm young enough to be learning that shit?" The truth was, Nessie had tried to learn. She really had, but every time she finally got down one word, another slipped out of her mind. She continued to practice letters and numbers once a week, in case of emergency, but trying to learn more than that was beyond her capability. "You got a gun?"

The teen turned and showed her the small revolver holstered just behind his hip.

"Good, leave it there. But you're going to do something for me, and for everyone else inside that building, understand?"

"What?" he asked warily.

"You're going to stand here, and make sure no one slips out, especially the little ones."

"Like a guard?"

"Exactly like a guard."

"Where's the guy who's supposed to be here?"

"That's what I'm going to go find out, but I can't leave this door until I know it's being properly watched. Can you do that? Can I trust you to do that?"

The teenager nodded immediately, his eyes lighting up with the responsibility. Nessie was relieved that she seemed to have chosen well, that she had picked a boy who *wanted* a job like this, an opportunity to prove he could handle himself and follow orders.

"If you have any questions, go to one of the building's corners and flag down one of the other guards, but don't step around the corner. Make sure that this door is always within your sight when you're not in front of it. Got it?"

"I got it," he nodded again, causing his hair, which needed trimming, to flop about on his head.

Nessie nodded back and patted him on the shoulder. She then turned and headed off toward the container that had held the zombie. She knew there was no way she could catch up to Cohen and whoever it was that had gone sneaking by, but she could look for Boyle. Figuring out what was happening on the roof still had her mighty curious, but potential danger within the walls was a greater priority. Technically, neither was her business, not since she had told Karsten and Boyle about what the kids had found. It was up to them now, and usually Nessie was fine leaving it at that, but with everything that was going on all at once, she was no longer content to sit on her heels. She bet if more people knew, more of them would be trying to get involved as well. Nessie wondered if that was part of the reason why Boyle and Karsten weren't telling people, and not just because they didn't want to tip off whoever it was keeping the zombie.

As Nessie made her way between the containers, cane clasped firmly in hand, she thought about how secrets had started this whole debacle. Everyone knew it was Marble Keystone's secret science that had created the virus thing in the first place, and that they had released it upon the unsuspecting population of Leighton. Had someone decided not to keep either of these secrets before it was too late, something may have been done to prevent them. But many tongues were held, including several who were now living in the container yard. Nessie was willing to bet everything she owned that the zombie-holding culprit was someone who used to work in the White Box in some capacity. She wondered if they were attempting to develop a cure. A noble cause, sure, but when it put everyone in danger by allowing a zombie in their midst, it resulted in immediate banishment, no exceptions. No one knew for sure, but it was generally considered that a search for a cure had resulted in that Roy monster outside the prison. Nessie had hated living in that prison, and as she walked along, she was reminded of why. Although she almost never went outside the wall here, she at least had the option, unlike living at the prison. Now, with the zombies gathered outside, it was the same.

It was unsettling how empty the yard was. Nessie knew that people were hiding behind most of the container doors she walked past, but there was no sign of them, no indication that they were there. She was used to most of the doors sitting open, inviting guests to pop in. People were always moving about outside, going from one task to another, the sound of their footsteps and light conversations drifting on the air. Now, all was barren and silent save for the groaning of the dead. Nessie found herself regretting leaving the community centre. Even though uncomfortable and boring, at least there were people everywhere.

***

It took Nessie longer than she expected to find Boyle, and when she finally did, she didn't know what to say. He was inside the container in which the zombie had been confined. Nessie had walked past it several times because the door was closed. When she finally pulled it open, she was blinded by a flashlight pointed directly at her face. As it lowered, she made out Boyle and Freya in the dimness of the container. They were huddled around the U-bolt that had held the zombie chain, a toolbox beside them. Their eyes bored into Nessie. She realized how suspicious she must look, showing up here. Beyond the wall, the sound of the zombies was louder than ever, the single stack of containers less effective at blocking the sound.

Freya said something in sign to Nessie, but she had no idea what. Nessie twisted her hands around her cane, unsure what to do. There was no way she was going to speak aloud this close to the zombies, something she hadn't thought about earlier.

Boyle gently tapped Freya's wrist, and then signed something to her when she looked at him. It drew a nod from Freya, who looked back at Nessie and gestured for her to come over to them.

Nessie resisted shuffling her feet like a guilty child as she entered the container and made her way over.

Reaching behind her, Freya took out a small chalkboard from a pouch and then a piece of chalk from a pendant she wore. She quickly scribbled some words down and handed both items to Nessie without getting to her feet. She was asking what Nessie was doing there.

Nessie wrote back in a careful script, not wanting any of it to be illegible. She didn't tell them everything, just that she had seen someone suspicious-looking who Cohen had gone after, and that Karsten was up to something that Boyle should probably know about. She left out the part about being bored and wanting to help. Now that she was here, she had no idea what kind of help she could possibly offer.

It took several iterations to get this message across on the small chalkboard. Each time, Freya read the response, then passed the chalkboard to Boyle so that he could read it. The two then held a conversation in sign which Nessie had no hope of following. Finally, Boyle stood upright as he handed the chalkboard back to Freya. He made two gestures while looking at Nessie: an open palm directed at her chest, and then a finger pointed at Freya. Nessie didn't need to know sign to understand that he was telling her to stay put and that Freya was in charge. Nessie nodded.

Boyle left the container, leaving Nessie alone with the intense-looking woman. Nessie knew that it was because of her that the Diana had been attacked, although she wasn't to be blamed. She had just been trying to escape those monsters, and Nessie couldn't fault her for that. Still, she wondered if other people did and how she handled it. Was her being mute a hindrance, or did people see that as punishment enough and leave her alone?

Whatever it was Boyle and Freya had been doing before Nessie showed up, Freya returned to it. She plucked a wrench out of the toolbox and compared it to the bolt that held the bracket down. It was slightly too big, so Freya returned to the toolbox to search for a smaller size. Nessie wondered if the bracket was being removed simply for removal's sake, or if there was some way to use it as evidence. The lighting in the container was dim, her eyes not sharp enough to tell if it had been dusted for prints. If they *had* found prints, did this mean they were going to take the fingerprints of everyone in the container yard and manually compare them? That seemed like a long and arduous process that not everyone would agree to. Even before, when computers could make far more accurate matches, people didn't want their fingerprints taken. Maybe they'd be less reluctant since they couldn't be stored in a database? It's not like their prints could be compared to any previous files or records. Hell, their prints probably wouldn't be kept here very long, not without taking up space that could be used for more important things.

Nessie wondered what the next step in the investigation would be. Searching all of the containers one by one? Her first reaction to that thought was that she wouldn't mind, she had nothing to hide, but then she remembered that she did. There was a box under her bed right now with grenades nestled inside. She certainly couldn't claim those as a personal weapon. Of course, it was unlikely Boyle would perform a container by container search, even to find someone who had brought a zombie over the wall; the people wouldn't stand for it. Too many were hiding various forms of contraband, from extra weapons, to drugs, to foods that should be shared at the centre. No, Boyle wouldn't perform such a search. Unless he found a way to do it in secret. Nessie's hands tightened around her cane again as she realized that Boyle and Karsten were absolutely clever enough to come up with something.

A shadow appeared in the doorway, prompting Nessie to spin around. One of her hands moved to the silver bear on her cane, ready to draw out the sword hidden within. It was only Jon, one of the recently returned scavengers. He glanced at Nessie, and then held a conversation with Freya in sign. After a few minutes, he left again.

Was Jon part of the investigative team? He had been away from the yard when all this was discovered, so it was possible he wasn't on the suspect list. Maybe he had just come by looking for Boyle as Nessie had. But then why would he know to look here?

The sound of the groaning zombies was beginning to get to Nessie. She found herself becoming increasingly agitated as the monotonous moan dragged on and on. She wanted to go back to the centre.

When Freya finally succeeded in freeing the bracket from the floor, she put it and the bolts that had held it into a large Ziploc bag, taking precautions not to touch them. Did that mean they had found prints, or that they hadn't looked for them yet? Or did it mean nothing, and Freya was just making sure that if anyone else wanted to check for prints later, they wouldn't find hers.

As Freya moved for the doors, Nessie pantomimed writing. Freya understood and handed her the chalkboard and chalk. Nessie wrote down that she'd like to go back to the community centre. She was both uncomfortable and afraid spending this much time near the wall. Freya nodded, but instead of letting Nessie return on her own, she walked with the much older woman. Had Nessie been by herself, she probably would have returned to her own container to check on Dragon, but wasn't going to try that now. As she walked, relieved to be heading away from the noise, she came to the conclusion that checking on her bird would have been a bad idea anyway. He might have been tempted to make some noise given how long she had left him alone.

As she thought about her bird, a flutter of feathers startled both Nessie and Freya. For a brief second, Nessie thought that somehow Dragon had escaped both his cage and the container, that maybe the suspicious looking individual had released him. The thought was quickly dispelled, however, as the bird was both larger than Dragon, and white in colour. It was a seagull that had landed between the containers to peck at a stain on the pavement.

Nessie looked at Freya wondering if she was thinking the same thing. It was highly unusual that this bird had decided to land here so close to so many zombies. Would it continue to be irregular and start squawking? It seemed to be getting irritated as it figured out that the stain held no food for it. Gripping the bear on the end of her cane, Nessie prepared to shoo it off, but Freya held her back with a hand to the shoulder.

Stepping in front of Nessie and putting down the toolbox, Freya then loosened the strip of leather she always wore around her waist. Plucking a smooth stone from a small pouch on the side of her belt, she deposited it into the thickest part of the leather, in the middle of its length. Having stepped a safe distance from Nessie, she began to swing the sling in tight, fast circles.

The seagull looked up, its eye drawn to the fast motion. Nessie watched as its wings began to expand, its body tighten, readying for lift off, but it never got the chance. The stone whizzed free of Freya's sling, striking the bird square in the eye and snapping its head back. The bird collapsed into a heap of feathers, with blood leaking out of its crushed skull, dead.

Nessie relaxed the tension that had built up in her, both surprised and impressed by Freya's skill. If others knew she could do that, then she probably had no trouble with people blaming her for what happened to the Diana.

Just as Freya bent over the seagull, Nessie caught up to her, after scooping up the toolbox en route. The younger woman took a rag out of her pocket and wiped off the stone before returning it to her pouch. She then picked up the bird by its legs—why waste potential meat?—and held out her other hand for the toolbox. Nessie was happy to hand it back, as it was kind of heavy, and risked clattering if not held level. With the dead bird in one hand, the toolbox in the other, Freya fell in step with Nessie heading back to the community centre.

Upon reaching the centre, they were able to spy Boyle standing alongside Karsten, both men looking up toward the roof. A short distance beyond them were two strangers. They must be the people who had warned them given that they weren't locked up. Freya walked straight over to the leaders, handing Boyle both the toolbox and the drawstring bag into which she had put the Ziploc.

"Thanks, Freya," Boyle whispered, placing the items on the ground beside him.

With Nessie's courage returning in the presence of more people, and the slight reduction of sound that distance created, she sidled up alongside the container yard's leaders. They were both looking up at the tops of the containers that had been hastily emptied in order to incarcerate the group that had attacked them. On one of them, a ladder had been erected and leaned against the edge of the community centre's roof. Misha stood on the ladder, looking toward the peak that those on the ground couldn't quite see. He was gesturing in sign language, likely relaying for whoever was on the roof. After a moment, Nessie realized he was simply signing letters. She could have translated on her own, but decided against it, knowing she'd probably end up in the middle of a sentence and get lost. Looking at the leaders again, she saw that Karsten had a notebook in his hands and was jotting down each letter.

"What's going on?" Nessie whispered to Boyle. Anyone who came out and spotted Misha could decipher on their own, so it probably wasn't a secret.

"The three people who warned us about the zombies? There are others in their group on the far side of the horde," Boyle whispered back. "They found a tall tree or something, and are using a mirror and Morse code to communicate with their guy on the roof, completely out of sight of the zombies. Jans is up there monitoring the situation and translating the Morse for us."

Nessie wasn't entirely sure who Jans was. She knew he was one of the German submariners, but a couple of faces popped into her mind and she couldn't narrow it down from there.

"They know where the really smart one is," Karsten whispered louder than anyone else as he briefly read the page. "It's just standing there, staring at the wall."

"Can we take him out somehow?" Boyle asked.

Karsten shook his head. "Apparently, he's wearing a lot of body armour, helmet included. We don't have anything powerful enough for that distance."

"Shit," Boyle whispered to himself.

The two strangers who were watching wandered over.

"We could try setting off fireworks to draw them away, but I don't think they'll work on Dean," one of them offered. "We haven't seen him become fixated on things very often, but it's nearly impossible to redirect him once he has. It might peel away a few of the dumb ones clustered around the edges, but they're likely to return here once the fireworks stop. They're drawn to Dean."

"So what do you suggest we do?" Karsten glowered at him.

"Evacuate," the man shrugged. "Do you have some other place you can go to across the water? Eventually, they're going to figure out a way to get over that wall. If you're gone when they do, they'll eventually leave."

Karsten's expression darkened further, but he said nothing. No other ideas were offered.

Nessie imagined what it would be like to move back into the Black Box. She didn't like it there, being underground. And with everyone returning, it would swiftly become overcrowded again. There wasn't enough space for all of them. She thought about her go-bag and what else she might be able to carry. There was no way to bring everything. Sure, they could return when the zombies left, but the man had used the word 'eventually' twice. He had no idea when the zombies were going to climb the walls, nor when they'd leave.

"I might have an idea," Nessie spoke up, a little louder than she meant to.

The others all turned to look at her.

"Come with me." Nessie turned and began walking toward the containers. Boyle, Freya, and one of the strangers followed after her, while the other stayed behind with Karsten.

Nessie led the small group of people down an aisle of containers. The sun was late in the sky; they were going to begin losing the light in an hour or so. As Nessie walked, she wondered whether that would be better or worse. The sound would become more terrifying for sure, but then most zombies had even poorer night vision than the living and so they'd have a lower chance of being spotted if something *did* happen.

Upon reaching her container, Nessie opened it slowly so as not to make much sound. Not so much because of the dead, but because she didn't want to wake Dragon, who was probably asleep in his cage.

"*Mama?*" came the bird's whispered voice from the other side of the blanket. He wasn't sleeping after all. Nessie pursed her lips to keep from answering. He was probably frightened. She couldn't say a word to comfort him, however, because it might encourage him to be even noisier. Instead, she ignored his large cage and moved toward the back of the container, waving the others to come in after her. She lit a candle to provide light when the door was shut since the bottle bulb was growing dim. She moved to her bed. The other three gathered around as she knelt down and reached beneath the place where she slept.

As her fingers found the box, she hesitated. She would get into trouble for this, there was no doubt about it. There was a possibility that nothing good would come of it, but thinking about moving back into the Black Box, and how Dragon always looked so sad seeing so little of the sky, spurred her on. She gripped the box of grenades and pulled them out.

"Would we be able to do something with these?" she asked as she opened the lid and revealed the contents.

25
Riley's Out Of It

All day Riley had been drifting in and out of consciousness. She had never taken an anesthetic before and apparently it hit her system hard. Plus, her body was using all her energy just to heal. She had woken up in long enough bursts to comfort her daughter and to thank her sister again for coming. She asked a few questions of Josh, but left the majority of them until after her visitors had gone. She wanted to know if the cancer could still be present, if there were complications he didn't want to say in front of the others, what all the technical details were.

"Riley, you've asked that already," Josh told her from where he sat on the next bed over, the only other person still in the room. She had finally been moved out of the surgery room and into a proper recovery room. There were no other patients in the rest of the beds; they must have been in the other recovery room. Had Riley requested the privacy, or did Josh just understand on his own?

"I'm sorry, I'm having trouble remembering everything you say."

"That's because you're exhausted. Your body needs sleep, so let it."

Whenever Riley had the energy to keep her eyes open, she always directed them to her vitals monitor. Since she struggled to remember the numbers they emitted, constantly looking at them soothed her.

"You're sure the memory thing isn't an issue?" Riley worried. "It's not some sort of side effect? It's not permanent?" She thought of Nicky and the memory problems the woman suffered from.

"Trust me, you're fine. I was put under anesthetic when they fixed my leg, remember? Everything was pretty loopy for me then too. I just had a generous helping of adrenaline to help balance it out. Not a good combination for teaching two scared women how to cast your leg, though, I must say."

"Which is why you're going to break that leg again someday." Riley rolled her head across her pillow to see the leg in question. "It's not straight."

"So you keep telling me," Josh grinned. "Now go back to sleep, it's getting on night anyway."

"Don't you have to be somewhere? Like dinner? With Anne? Won't she worry?" Riley had already been fed, taking much longer to eat than normal.

"She knows exactly where I am, and I have dinner here with me," he said, gesturing to an area of the room that Riley couldn't see from her current position. "Knowing you, you probably shouldn't be by yourself right now. You'll only end up trying to get out of bed and making a mess of things. No, I'm staying here all night." He swung his legs up onto the bed he was sitting on, stretching out along its length.

He was right, of course. Riley had already tried to get out of bed once, but was briskly stopped. She wasn't being an easy patient.

"I'm sorry." It seemed to her she was apologizing a lot.

"Don't worry about it, you'd do the same for me."

Riley remembered the way she had let him get out of the ambulance on the Day, after she had explained what she believed was happening—what *was* happening as it turned out—and how he had decided to return to the hospital to warn the others. She wouldn't go back herself, wouldn't help him, wouldn't help anyone, thinking only of her own safety. But things were different now. Her family had become a weird mix of unrelated people for whom she would sacrifice almost anything. Only Hope was held above them, the number one priority in her life.

Riley's eyes closed again while she was thinking, the medical machines a surprisingly soothing sound for her. It didn't take long before she was unconscious again.

***

When the sirens went off, Riley's mind was as exhausted as her body, not ready to leave the soft folds of sleep. Still, she pried her eyes open, dragging her head around to look at her monitors. She had to know what was wrong with her. Blinking several times, she couldn't believe her eyes had focused correctly and were accurately reading the numbers. According to the monitors, everything was fine except for an elevated heart rate, easily explained by her fear.

It finally hit her that the siren wasn't coming from her monitors, but from the ceiling, along with a red light. Rolling her head across her pillow, she looked to the door. Josh was there, dragging empty beds across it, barricading them in, pausing only briefly to turn on the main overhead lights—he must have put them on a dimmer setting when he had decided to sleep.

"What's going on?" Riley asked, but her voice was too soft to compete with the noise.

With nothing left to push in front of the door, Josh finally turned and looked at Riley. Seeing her open eyes staring back at him, he quickly made his way to her side. Just as he reached her, the siren cut out, causing them both to glance briefly at the ceiling.

"What's happening? Is it zombies?" Riley asked.

"No, humans. At least that's what I heard." Josh started looking over all the equipment hooked up to her, probably debating whether or not it was safe to free her.

"What you heard? Was there an announcement I missed?"

"No. I was still awake when the siren first went off so I went out into the waiting room. Robin came running in from the hallway, claiming there were armed strangers heading up the stairs."

"*Up* the stairs?"

"Yeah, they must have gotten into the vehicle elevator shaft somehow."

Josh left her side and went to the cupboards at the back of the room where some medical supplies were kept. He returned with a scalpel and handed it to Riley.

"Biggest blade I could find." His own knife was larger, secured in a sheath at the small of his back.

"It'll do." Riley carefully held the blade beneath her blankets, just as a heavy pounding began at the door.

"Open up!" a gruff voice shouted from the other side.

"Where's Robin now?" Riley whispered.

"In the other recovery ward. She'll be fine; a few of them have guns in there, including her."

The beds in front of the door trembled rhythmically with the heavy pounding, accompanied by the sound of splintering wood.

"Don't try to fight them," Riley warned Josh as he reached for his knife.

"Why not?"

"One knife against whatever is smashing through that door? Wait for an opportunity."

There was no time for Josh to reply, as the door was finally forced open enough to allow someone to enter. Riley closed her eyes, pretending to be asleep, her adrenaline making it impossible to actually do so. Still, she peered through her eyelashes. A large man entered the room carrying a small battering ram, the kind police forces used to use. He dropped the ram with a loud clang to the floor, quickly spotting Josh and levelling a revolver at him.

"Turn around," the man told him.

Josh was holding up his hands and did as he had been commanded.

"That knife. Drop it on the floor." There was a lack of anger or madness in the man's voice that worried Riley. He was completely aware of what was going on. He spoke with the detached coldness of someone who had done this before. It wasn't personal, their reason for being here, which was far worse.

Josh removed his knife and dropped it.

"Kick it away," the man commanded, and Josh obeyed. "I've got this room covered," he then called over his shoulder. "Just some skinny doctor and an unconscious woman."

Riley couldn't hear the reply from the waiting room. The big man started moving toward her, but no one came through the opening behind him. She closed her eyes completely, making sure not to tense up. A hand grabbed the top of her blanket and began to pull it down. She refused to react, praying he didn't see the scalpel in her hand. The blanket never got that far, however, as it stopped after exposing her bandages.

"Jesus Christ, you people here are butchers?"

Riley gambled that the man had turned to look at Josh as he spoke and risked opening her eyes. The gamble paid off, and her quick reflexes zeroed in on his turned neck. Mustering all the speed and strength that she could, she sat up and lashed out with the scalpel. The blade cut through the man's soft tissue like butter, the muscles providing more resistance. Pain screamed through Riley's chest at the exertion; at least one of her stitches popped open. As the man stumbled away, with a hand clamped around his neck, she fell back, flat on the bed once more, trying not to scream. She didn't want to alert whoever was in the waiting room.

Josh was at the big guy's side in a moment. As soon as Riley had made her move, he had dived for his knife, scooping it up off the tile. Although bleeding, the man wasn't bleeding enough. Josh corrected that issue, plunging his knife into the man's side, over and over, aiming for all his organs and the abdominal aorta. As the large man collapsed to the floor, a booming gunshot rang out from the waiting room, closely followed by two more. Josh wheeled around to the opening, no longer concerned about the big guy; he was already dead, lying prone in a large circle of his own blood.

Robin popped into the room, a shotgun held ready before her. Her eyes quickly scanned over the blood covering Josh, and the heap on the floor.

"You good?" she asked.

Josh nodded.

Robin left the room once more, her voice giving out orders about how best to secure the medical centre.

"I'm going to wash off my hands and then I'll be right with you," Josh told Riley as he headed for the sink at the back of the room, doubling back once to pierce the attacker's skull.

Gritting her teeth as the pain slowly subsided, Riley nodded. She hoped her daughter was safe.

III
The Sneak

Jo shyly peered in through the doorway of the security centre. Several men and women milled about, acquainting themselves with the systems. A few cameras displayed views from around the place and outside, but most of them were dead. Jo wondered if they had always been dead, or if the people who hadn't been captured were breaking them.

"Journey, come in," spoke a voice from the centre of the room.

Jo shuffled through the doorway. He was nervous, having been spotted by Logan with her expression in its usual unreadable rock of decision making. The woman stood in the middle of everyone, supervising their progress with the systems. A man squeezed past Jo, heading straight for Logan. She turned her steely gaze to this newcomer who was there to give a report. Jo looked away, his eyes trailing along the inner wall. There were drops of blood by one of the baseboards.

"Come here, Jo," Logan returned her attention to him. She stood with open arms and a small smile on her face. The man who had given his report was leaving again in a hurry.

Logan was smiling. It lit Jo's heart, making him unafraid. He went straight into her arms and received a brief, but comforting hug. It had been a long time since he had felt her warmth and revelled in it.

"You did great, Journey. Really well. I told you, you could do it."

Praise from Logan was all Jo ever wanted. He smiled brightly up at her, ready to do anything.

"Tell me, what was the hardest part?" she asked.

Jo's smile fell as he didn't want to admit that any of it was hard, but he knew better than to lie. "They were really nice to me."

Logan nodded. "I know, it's hard when they're not bad people. Do I need to remind you why we do this?"

"No, ma'am," Jo shook his head. He was well aware of the 'whys', just as all the other children were.

"Good. Now, I need your help one more time."

Jo felt light again. To be needed was the greatest joy of all.

"You and I are going to go to where the prisoners are being kept. I would like you to pick out which ones I should talk to first."

"I can do that!" Jo nodded enthusiastically.

"I'm sure you can. Barton?" she turned to a man at a computer next to her. "Keep an eye on things here. I'm going to go have a chat with our new friends."

"Yes, ma'am." Barton's scarred head jolted in some version of a nod. Jo wondered if he'd ever be relied upon like that by Logan.

"Come on, Journey," Logan's hand briefly alighted upon his shoulder as she stepped past him.

Jo quickly fell in step behind her. He felt proud to be walking along with Logan, prouder of himself than he had ever felt before. He wondered what the other children would think when he told them. If he even got a chance to; Logan might keep him by her side as her assistant! Wouldn't that be great!

Section 4:
Ultimatum

26
Misha's Curious

Misha moved through the recently fallen darkness, wondering what the summons had been about. Once the sun was down, it became too difficult to communicate with those outside the walls. The flashlights weren't as easy to spot as mirror-reflected sunlight—although the darkness did help with that—and nobody wanted to burn through batteries unless it was really important. Misha thought that since they were done talking to them, he was done for the night and could go to bed. It was while he was deciding whether to find himself a space in the community centre or find a way to climb back up onto his container in order to get inside, that Boyle had approached him and told him to meet at the end of the dock in an hour.

The night was clear; the large U-shaped concrete dock stood out as a pale patch within the dark, faintly glittering water. He could see a few people already moving about at the end. There appeared to be at least ten of them, more than Misha had expected. As he approached, another group of five drifted from between some containers ahead, also moving toward the dock. That put the count at sixteen including him.

When Misha reached the concrete, he glanced behind him. There were three more people moving through the darkness, coming toward the dock as well. Why were so many meeting out here? Were even more coming? He thought about his dogs, concerned for their safety. If some sort of plan to quietly abandon the yard was taking place, he'd fight whoever he needed to in order to go back for them.

As soon as he got close enough to make out features, Misha started putting names to people, hoping that would give him some sort of explanation. There was the old woman who was always sewing things sitting on a fairly large metal box of some sort. Flanking her like a pair of guards were Boyle and Karsten. Grouped next to them were the three outsiders: Tommy, Suzanne, and Mark. Jon was moving from them to a cluster made up of Danny, Bryce, Larson, Lenny, and Shaidi, who were most likely the group of five who had arrived just before Misha. Scattered about on their own, Harry shifted from foot to foot, Jans paced in tight circles, and Freya stood perfectly still, looking over the group. Attaching himself to the fringes of the gathering, Misha looked back again, spotting the same three as before but no others. As they arrived, he identified them as White with two sharp shooters from the wall, Katrina and Yasmin. Outside of Nessie, everyone here was extremely capable of handling themselves in a rough situation, and the majority knew about what was really on the other side of the wall: Dean, the overly smart zombie.

"We're all here. Gather in please, I don't want to have to speak too loudly," Boyle gestured for the group to pack in around him, Karsten, and Nessie. Nessie continued to sit where she was, her hands busily cutting up strips of leather.

Misha manoeuvred himself so that he was shoulder to shoulder with Jon and Danny, who had gotten a sling since Misha had last seen him, that secured the arm attached to his injured shoulder against his belly.

"I'm going to make this as quick as I can," Boyle said to the group, the lapping water helping to cover his words. "For those of you who don't know, there is a super smart zombie beyond our wall. I'm talking about Roy kind of smart."

Those who hadn't known revealed themselves by shifting uncomfortably.

"We've only been able to come up with one plan in order to deal with him. We can't just shoot him; he's too far and covered in armour. Instead, we're going with these." Boyle patted Nessie on the shoulder, who then stood up.

The older woman moved over to Freya's side, handing her the strips of leather. Karsten bent over and unsnapped the latches on the metal box, then lifted the lid to reveal its contents. Just in case it was too dark for some, Boyle clicked on a flashlight and illuminated the grenades for a minute, making sure everyone knew what they were.

"We have thirty-six in here, two for each of us."

Misha guessed that Nessie wasn't being included in that count.

"Now, based on the coordinates we were given, Dean, the smart zombie, is a bit too far from the wall to throw these at him. At least, too far if we wish to remain hidden. Freya here, is going to teach us all, Karsten and myself included, how to use a sling."

Most of the gathering looked warily at one another.

"What about the rest of the zombies?" Harry asked, ever the thinker. Leave it to the man who guided their construction of the wall to immediately think ahead.

"The three who warned us of their coming have people out there, the ones who gave us Dean's co-ordinates, who are able to spy on the horde from behind. When we're ready, they're going to set off fireworks immediately after our first volley of grenades, and continue to do so for a while after our second. The dumb zombies are drawn to this Dean thing which is why we can't use them now, but if he's dead, the fireworks should draw them off."

"*Should*," Lenny emphasised, poking a hole in the plan. "And what about the ones that aren't dumb? The regularly smart ones?"

"According to our new friends here," Boyle nodded at Tommy, Suzanne, and Mark, "the smart ones are usually the closest to Dean. They're likely to be taken out by the grenades as well. Still, there will be some who'll assault the wall, both dumb and smart. We'll have to be ready for them. We've sent some others to reconnect the bridge to Animal Island. Those who can't fight will be moved over there tonight, and then we'll disconnect the bridge again. They'll be safe even if things don't work out the way we planned."

Misha rolled his shoulders, attempting to loosen the tension that was building up in them. This plan was crazy, but it wasn't like he could think of a better one. He was worried about his dogs, who wouldn't be sent to Animal Island.

"I don't think I need to learn to use a sling," Harry spoke again. "Just attach two grenades to two of my arrows. I should be able to make the shots that way."

Boyle nodded, not objecting to the idea. It was unfortunate that they didn't have bows and arrows for everyone as they had been hard to find, and most were at the Black Box.

"I'd like to gather a team to move a few containers inside the yard," Harry continued. "If we grab some of the empty ones, we can bridge a few gaps between the housing containers to make an extended walkway on top of them."

"Can you do it silently?" Karsten asked him.

"Maybe, if we go really slow, and we're really careful. If not, I'll work out a method to use spare ladders to cross the gaps, although they won't be as safe to cross."

"Whatever you can come up with."

Harry removed two of the arrows from the quiver he always wore upon his back and handed them to Boyle, who then passed them over to Nessie.

"Do you mind figuring out how to attach a pair of grenades to these?"

"I'll need to get some things from my container, but I can do it. Just leave them with the grenades for now and I'll bring my stuff here."

"I'll be heading toward your container to get some of my men around there. I'll walk you." Harry stuck out his elbow.

Nessie made a comment too quiet for Misha to catch as she looped her arm through his elbow, then the two of them headed back toward land in the darkness.

"Right, we should get started then. Freya?"

Freya went around the group and handed each person one of the strips of leather. There were at least a dozen more than they needed, but Freya seemed to have picked out which ones she thought were the best, and even appeared to have selected a few specifically for some of them.

"Um, will I be able to do this with my injured shoulder?" Danny asked as he was handed a strip.

Do you have full movement with this arm? Freya signed and then gripped his uninjured shoulder.

Danny rotated it, showing that he could. Freya gave him a curt nod, and turned to Misha.

Misha accepted his strip of leather, running it through his hands to get used to the feel. He had never used anything like a sling before. He knew the younger kids had taken to carrying around slingshots, but unlike some of the adults, he had never borrowed one to take a few test shots. He had never even used a bow and arrow before; a spear gun was the only non-bullet-throwing projectile weapon he had experience with.

"We don't speak sign," Mark confessed to the group as Freya gestured something before handing him his sling.

"Freya is mute," Boyle informed the outsiders. "If she says something you need to know, we'll translate for you." Considering that he didn't translate right then, whatever Freya had said was deemed unimportant.

"When this is all over, think you can teach us sign language?" Mark whispered to Jon in such a low voice that Misha almost didn't make it out.

"So long as you teach me Morse code," Jon whispered back.

"Everyone has a sling now?" Boyle looked about the group and confirmed that they all did.

"Could you all please pick up a grenade?" Karsten ordered next. "Take care not to let the pin come out; I don't think I need to tell you why. I want you all to get used to the size and weight of the grenade."

A sort of circular line formed, and everyone walked past the box, plucking a grenade from its protective padding. Misha very carefully removed his, treating it like a delicate egg. He had seen enough war movies and played enough video games before the Day to respect the power of the small explosive. He looked to Danny, who was holding his just as carefully.

"Don't be afraid," Karsten said as he bent down and picked one up for himself. "The pins are more secure than you think." He started tossing his grenade from hand to hand, causing several people to hold their breath. "You need to get comfortable with them. See the pin?" He pointed it out on his grenade in case anyone was confused. "When you pull that, it'll allow this spring loaded lever here to fly free. Hold the lever in place, and nothing will happen. Let it fly off, and you have three seconds before it explodes. This means you'll have three seconds to drop it into your sling and fire it over the wall."

"Only three?" Lenny's voice wavered slightly.

"That's why we have to train with the slings most of the night," Boyle told them all. "With the large number we're letting loose, I doubt accuracy will be all that important, but speed will be."

Misha wondered if the grenades really had a three-second fuse, or if Boyle and Karsten were just saying that as a safety precaution. If the fuses were really four or five seconds, telling them they had to be good enough for a three-second fuse reduced the risk of an accident. It wasn't like the zombies were going to throw the grenades back. Still, make one mistake with the small explosives and several people could end up suffering.

"By the time your training is done, if you feel you're not capable of loading and firing within those three seconds, we'll give your grenades to someone else," Karsten continued. "Now, we're going to head to the rocky shoreline near the bridge to Animal Island and search for stones roughly the same shape and weight as the grenades you're holding. Bring the grenades with you for comparison, and so that you can adjust to having them with you."

"Unfortunately, due to the proximity to the wall, we won't be able to use flashlights or anything," Boyle added quickly, "so be extra careful with your footing. Let's go."

Boyle, Karsten, and Freya all turned to lead the way up the dock and back to shore, where they would follow the edge of the concrete wall until it became the rocky shoreline. Misha fell in step beside Danny, trailing along behind Bryce and Larson. He cradled his grenade in both hands, feeling its bumps and ridges. Despite what Karsten had advised, Misha didn't think he'd ever be able to get used to it.

***

"*Oomph.*"

Misha had seen Danny slip on the slick rocks, a rush of air unintentionally leaving his lungs. Misha quickly scrambled over to his friend, who had already pushed himself back upright.

You okay? Misha asked, using the simplest and most visible gestures in the darkness.

Danny nodded. Thankfully, he had fallen on his good arm, sparing his wound from further pain. Misha held up his grenade, silently asking Danny where his was. Danny showed it to him still firmly clasped in the hand held by his arm sling.

Turning away, Misha resumed moving around the rocks, searching more with his hands than his eyes for good stones. Danny hadn't been the first to fall over, and he wouldn't be the last. Several people had already taken a tumble on the wet, slippery rocks, but so far they had all been lucky. With the rocks and stones occasionally shifting beneath their feet, it would be too easy to break something.

Glancing outward, Misha spotted the dark shapes in the water. A group of people were performing the arduous task of reconnecting Bitch Bridge. They had swum over earlier and were now using the remaining kayaks and canoes to haul the bridge around. A few people still bobbed in the water, making sure nothing separated and attempting to silently organize the whole endeavour. At least the water wasn't very cold. After getting someone to hold his grenade for him, Misha had gone in a few times himself. By diving down near the shore, he had been able to locate several good rocks with his hands. Thinking he should do this again, he scanned his surroundings for someone to hold his grenade, someone who wasn't injured like Danny. This first person he came across was Freya.

After signing to her his plan, she nodded curtly and held out her hand for his grenade. She appeared to be as comfortable with them as Karsten was. Misha wondered if she'd ever used a grenade before. He knew nothing about her life before the Day, and very little of the years before she showed up at the Diana. From what he did know, he had no interest in learning more. He liked Freya and had no wish to know more about the pain she must have suffered.

Slipping into the water, his clothes still soggy from his last dip, he felt the usual moment of tension grip his chest. He had always loved the water, always loved swimming, but ever since a shark had dragged Mathias away from him, things had been different. Now, he was constantly on the alert for the silent creatures beneath, never entering the water if he bore any injury that might bleed. It was even more dangerous in the dark, although no one had ever encountered a shark this close to shore. They rarely encountered sharks at all, except for the occasional fisherman who might catch a small one. Still, Misha thought of the sharks as he waded in deeper.

Off to his right, the end of the wall let him know where the shore suddenly dropped off into deeper water. The last pair of containers rested at the edge of the lip, kept from sliding off by several metal bars that an underwater scuba team had driven into the rocks. At its deepest, the water reached two-thirds of the way up the containers. A small chunk of netting hung down so that a swimmer could climb up. The drop off was a fortunate feature of the rocky shore. Any zombies who wandered in over there were likely to sink off the edge and never be seen again. Animal

Island was surrounded by the same steep drop, meaning they didn't have to worry much about a corpse wandering up out of the water. There was nothing they could do about swimmers though. A zombie with enough sense to swim could easily get around the wall, although normally they'd be put down by a wall guard before getting that far. Tonight, there were no wall guards and a seemingly endless number of the dead were out there. When he had approached the wall earlier, Misha could hear a few of the zombies stumbling in the shallows, but none had gone deep. Something, apparently this Dean thing, was keeping them from wandering too far. All it would take was one swimmer striking out on his own, rounding the end of the last containers, and spotting the humans on the other side. Unless by some miracle the thing's throat had been ripped out, it would alert all the others and a flood of flesh would be upon them.

As he moved through the shallows, testing the rocks with his feet, Misha kept a close eye on the edge of the containers and kept an ear cocked toward the wall. When he slid under, he did so as smoothly and silently as he could, slipping straight down until he was completely under. Only then would he flip over, taking care not to break the surface, and grab at the rocks below. Whenever he felt what might be a good one, he stuffed it in his pockets, where he'd carry it until he left the water. On the rocky shore stood several baskets on some large, flat slabs where everyone deposited their stones after finding as many as they could carry.

Closer to the wall than he had dared to search before, Misha found a good cache of stones. Submerging several times in order to gather them all, he filled the pockets of his pants, including the back ones. Were it not shallow enough at that point for him to stand, he would have had difficulty treading water by the time he was done. Weighed down, he began slogging his way to shore, moving at an angle away from the wall and being careful not to splash much. Unfortunately, someone else wasn't so careful.

Misha couldn't tell who it was due to the darkness and distance, but someone else had entered the water. Maybe this person had seen how many stones Misha had been able to find and thought to do the same. Whatever the reason, the individual burst out of the water farther down the shore, and scrambled toward the dryer rocks in great splashes. Based on the compact frame, Misha guessed it was Karsten who met this person at the water's edge, quickly pinning the flailing limbs to cease any further disturbance.

All went still as no one dared to move. Even the kayakers and canoeists had stopped paddling, having witnessed what happened at the shoreline. Slowly, they began to lose what ground they had made as the floating bridge dragged them backward. Misha stood stock-still, frozen in place, partly in and partly out of the water. The stones in his pockets seemed to become heavier, trying to drag him back down beneath the surface. Although some small piece of him seemed to think this might be a good idea, to go where everything was silent and dark, he couldn't bring himself to move even if the rest of his mind agreed. His body was locked.

Had the cadence of the groaning beyond the wall changed? Had they heard the splashing and learned that living things were nearly within their reach? Or was Misha's accelerated mind just making that up? Had they mistaken the sound for a fish, or maybe not even heard it over their own cacophony? It almost seemed reasonable to Misha that they could hear his heartbeat. The vital organ within his chest was struggling against its confines, the blood rushing through the veins in his ears audible despite the dead, a sound like ocean waves.

Freya was the first to move. She took one careful step toward Misha and the wall, then paused. After a few seconds, she took another, and then another, bending over to place the two grenades she carried in a nook between two rocks. The mute woman moved with perfect stealth all the way to the container wall and stood beside it, her ear cocked up toward the upper edge. She waited another several seconds, Misha's eyes locked upon her, ignoring what anyone else might be doing behind him. Not satisfied with what she heard, Freya followed the container wall into the water, slowly passing the gaps created by the tilted containers, gaps that had been filled with rocks, concrete, and any other heavy debris the humans could get their hands on. Once she got deep enough, Freya started to swim, her body gliding smoothly through the water. Misha had to resist literally biting his tongue when she reached the netting and started climbing up. He didn't know what she expected to see as she disappeared over the upper edge; he could only hope that the zombies wouldn't see her.

A tense minute slid by, during which Misha couldn't bring himself to breathe. His heart was hammering harder than ever, adrenaline pouring through his limbs to the point where he had to resist shaking. A quiet portion of his mind wondered if he was going to pass out. Twice before in his life he had: the first when a 747 he was in attempted a water landing, and the second when he had learned the city of Moscow—capital of his first country and home to some of his relatives—had been nuked in an attempt to stem the zombie virus's flood through Russia. If he passed out now, the stones in his pockets would surely drag him under and there was a chance that he would drown. It was this thought that got him to take in a fresh breath, although it was a manual operation and he couldn't take in a second.

Finally, Freya appeared once more. Lying flat on top of the container, she shot her arm into the air, her hand silhouetted against the star-filled sky in the position of a thumbs up. Misha immediately shot his own arm up, repeating the gesture for anyone who couldn't see Freya as well as he could. His lungs began working on their own again, as the muscles in his body loosened. He sank low in the water, exerting just enough effort to keep his head above the surface. Glancing over at the others, he saw they were equally relieved, several continuing to pass along the thumbs up while they all slumped over. Karsten was the first to move, dragging whoever it was that started this whole thing out of the ocean. The people in the kayaks and canoes moved next, hoping to regain the ground they had lost.

Having stopped watching Freya, Misha startled slightly when he heard movement in the water near him. She had quietly swum over to his bobbing head, an exaggerated expression of concern on her face asking if he was okay. Stiffening his legs, he stood back up to his full height, moving slowly so as to reduce splashing, and gave her a nod. She nodded back, then smoothly slipped beneath the surface, probably having felt a good stone with her foot.

Misha slogged back to shore, partly crawling across the rocks. He headed straight to the big flat rock holding the baskets where he emptied his pockets, relieved to be significantly lighter. It seemed everyone was gathering at the baskets, so he chose to stay there as well, letting the adrenaline work its way out of his body by repeatedly wringing his soaked clothing and putting back on the boots he had left beside the baskets.

When Lenny arrived, even in the low light it was easy to see that his dark skin was deeply flushed. Add to that his wet clothes, and it was obvious who had caused the commotion.

It's okay, Shaidi was signing to him. *After the Diana, most people would panic if something large brushed their leg.*

So that's why he had gone splashing toward shore. Misha wondered if he would have done the same. More accustomed to the ocean than others, he was used to the occasional brush with seaweed, fish, or various bits of detritus, but if he felt something he thought was a shark? He didn't know how he would react. Maybe he would have fled to shore in the same way, and as such, found he couldn't be angry with Lenny. Besides, it seemed he was beating himself up enough about it, Shaidi's words having zero effect on his shame-filled face.

Freya was the last to arrive, depositing the stones she had gathered into one of the baskets. Boyle signed to her, asking if it looked like they had enough to train with. She nodded, then handed Misha his grenade, which he had completely forgotten about. Gripping it in one hand, he grabbed the handle of the nearest basket with the other. Katrina gripped the opposite handle, and together they hauled the heavy basket up off the rock and began shuffling awkwardly with it back toward the dock. There were more people than basket handles, so halfway there, everyone carrying switched with those who weren't.

Upon reaching the dock's end, they found Nessie sitting on the box of remaining grenades, working out the best way to attach one to an arrow. Freya told everyone to take a short break while she went through the stones, picking out the ones that wouldn't work. Misha chose to sit on the end of the dock, his legs dangling over the water. The moment he was down, exhaustion swept over him, dragging his chin down to his chest and his eyelashes together. He hadn't slept well the night before, what with the impending attack, and the day had been full of high-energy tasks. The adrenaline was over half of what was keeping him upright, and its departure left more exhaustion in its wake.

A slight tug on the back of his shirt caused Misha's eyes to fly open, and his head to twist around. Danny was standing there.

"You looked like you were about to fall in," he whispered, moving around to sit down beside Misha. "You all right?"

"Just tired," Misha admitted. He was also scared, but there was no point in admitting that as well. Everyone was scared.

"Yeah, me too," Danny nodded.

"You think you're going to be okay to do this with that arm of yours?" Misha asked, mostly to keep talking. It was something to focus on, something to keep his eyes open.

"Don't know. Swinging should be fine, like Freya said, but it's loading I'm worried about. I'll need to use my bad arm to help with that, and I'm not sure I trust it to hold out in the situation we'll be in." Danny shuddered as though cold, despite the warm night.

"How's Bryce doing?" Misha changed topics. "I'm assuming not bad considering he's part of this ridiculous endeavour."

Danny turned to look at his scavenging teammate. "He seems stiff, but I'm sure he'll be fine slinging. I'm more worried about his swollen eyes affecting his aim. If his perception of distance is off, he might end up damaging the wall, or worse, the grenade could bounce back toward us."

"Bryce is smart. If he doesn't think he can do it, he'll give his grenades to someone else."

"This plan is insane."

"I know, but then sometimes the best plans are." Misha was thinking about the Day, when he had first met Danny and the others. They had formed an insane plan in order to escape a prison, one that had Misha throwing a firebomb and running for his life. He had been running with Mathias and Tobias then, while Alec provided sniper cover. All of them were dead now, none having survived the Diana.

While Misha sank ever deeper into his memories of that time, Freya finished her sorting. Danny once again startled him back into the present, but this time it was by simply moving to get up.

The stones had been organized into several piles, clearly depending on how similar they were to the grenades. Nessie had moved off of the grenades' box, so the potential slingers could return the ones they had been carrying. Misha was amazed he had forgotten he was holding his while sitting at the water's edge; however, the indentations in his palm suggested he had been holding on very tightly.

Freya delayed returning hers to the box. Holding up her sling and grenade, she showed everyone the best way to load it. By hooking the lever so that it was on the outside of the leather strip, they could pull the pin after loading and save some time. Considering they had only seconds, Misha was relieved none of them would have to be wasted getting the grenade into position in the sling. Freya mimed pulling the pin to make sure everyone understood.

Lining them up at the edge of the dock, Freya handed out a stone to everyone. She was starting with the pile that was least like the grenades, presumably teaching them how to sling properly before teaching them how to sling the small explosives. After a few demonstrations—her stones arcing as high as they would need to in order to clear the wall and plopping so far out into the water that they could barely be heard—she moved down the line and got each person to sling their first stone. No one was anywhere nearly as good as Freya, but some weren't bad considering it was their first time. Misha's first attempt had no height to it, the stone whizzing low out of the sling, managing to skip twice on the wide river's surface before breaking the water tension and disappearing below.

Once everyone had fired their first shot, Freya gathered up the next round of stones and handed them out. This time, before someone fired, she gave them advice and instruction on how to improve their shot. Those standing beside the outsiders who had warned them, quietly translated her signs, even when the advice was not directed at them so that they could learn from the mistakes of others. Misha over-compensated with his second shot, the stone going virtually straight up, barely getting enough distance to clear the edge of the dock and land in the water.

One stone and one person at a time, Freya taught them to sling. They spent hours at it, working their way up to the stones most like the grenades. They focused on only one target, one way to aim, allowing muscle memory to sink in. If anyone wanted to learn to sling properly, to get as good at it as Freya, they were to learn on their own time afterward. Misha was pleased to see his progress and the progress of others. They were getting good, hitting the height and distance that Freya wanted of them. Only White and the stranger, Tommy, couldn't seem to get the hang of it. In the end, they bowed out, giving up their grenades to more competent slingers. It was quickly decided that Freya, Boyle, Yasmin, and Bryce would get the extra grenades, having proven themselves the best of the bunch. It seemed Bryce's injuries had no effect on his capabilities to swing a sling.

After the last stone had been thrown, Boyle and Karsten dismissed them all with orders to sleep until sunrise. That wasn't a lot of time, but Misha was grateful for even a single hour. But first, he headed to the community centre to pick up his dogs.

In small batches, groups were leaving the centre. Bitch Bridge had been connected and everyone not staying to fight was being moved there. It seemed a lot of people that were usually in the non-combatant category were staying to fight. The only people without a choice in the matter were children under thirteen, clearly pregnant women, the badly injured or sick, and elderly who were too frail or too blind to wield a gun. Misha didn't stay at the centre long; the moment he picked up his dogs, he headed for his container.

Ladders had already been set up to reach the top of the containers, making it easy for Misha. One by one, he got his dogs up. They had learned to climb ladders, but it was awkward for them. Misha had to keep behind each dog, offering whispered encouragement, pushing on their butts, and half catching them when they slipped. Other ladders, some lashed together, bridged the gaps between the container rows. It seemed Harry was still trying to quietly move containers to bridge other gaps, but it was slow going. Nessie must have offered him all the good, large scraps of leather and thick wool she had, as they had wrapped them around the long logs they used for rolling the containers. This slowed the process down considerably, as each time they had to move a log from the back to the front, they had to rewrap the wool and leather, which tended to loosen and fall off. Still, it quieted the process considerably. Too bad the same couldn't be said for the clicking of the dogs' toenails on the container tops.

Upon reaching his container, Misha wasn't terribly surprised to find Bullet snoozing next to the opening in the roof. The dog was very clever and had no difficulty with ladders. Leaving the other three with him, Misha climbed down into his container, prepared for the scent of dog piss. He was pleased to discover none of them had peed during his absence, the container smelling only of their fur and breath.

Curling up on the mattress beside Rifle, Misha hoped to follow orders and sleep until sunrise. Or maybe until a bit before sunrise; he wanted to make sure all of his dogs were up on top of the container before anything happened. Up there would be the safest place for them.

Rifle huffed next to Misha as if hearing his thoughts and not liking the idea of having to climb a ladder. Misha had to admit he didn't like tomorrow's ideas either.

27
Abby's Captured

Her face throbbed in time with her heartbeat, her cheek swollen and bruised. Abby didn't want to think about how bad it would have been if she had not cut the stinking man's arm, if he had managed to hit her with all his force. Other parts of her body pained her as well, from the various bruises blooming about her, to the friction burns stinging her skin. She refused to cry out or complain, sitting still with the others who had been captured. At least three dozen of them were being held in the cafeteria, sitting shoulder to shoulder on the bench seats that lined the tables, their arms tied painfully behind their backs, ankles lashed to those beside them. Many of the other captives bore injuries similar to Abby's, the ones who had fought back but ultimately lost. A few, mostly guards from outside, had worse injuries, but whoever these attackers were, they patched up the bullet holes they had put into people. Not all the fence guards were in the cafeteria, however, which said to Abby that they had probably been killed. None of them would have simply run away. Of course, not everyone was hurt. There were those who had been quickly cornered and knew their odds were better with surrender. In one corner of the room, at a table sat several children along a bench, their parents bound and worrying at a separate table. Abby kept silently thanking Thomas who was secured across the table from her, the entire left side of his face turned unnatural colours. If his warning had come any later, she and her family would have been in the stairwell, and then all of them would have been sitting in here.

The only sound in the room was crying. A few adults, mostly parents, wept silently but the main concentration of sobs came from the children. The kids were largely ignored by their captors, but if any adult tried to talk, one of the large men posted around the room would stride over and swat the back of the individual's head with a curt "shut up." Everyone learned quickly not to speak.

The guards seemed to have no problem with people looking around, so Abby did just that. She put a name to every captive she could see, which was nearly all of them. A lot of people she knew only slightly, but her nearly eidetic memory put names to the faces. Every time someone new was brought in, she added them to her unfortunately growing list. It was especially heartbreaking when she spotted Crichton and Bronislav at separate tables, with bruises, black eyes, and cuts to match everyone else. She had hoped at least one of them would have escaped capture.

She wondered if the invaders knew that the two of them were the Black Box's leaders.

Abby took the time to study the guards. She came up with mental names for them based on their features, such as Scar-twin and Clean-twin on either side of the door, Bruiser for the one who did most of the head smacking, Fidget for the guard who patrolled most often, and so on and so forth. She deliberately committed even the smallest details of these men to her memory, so that if they ever got out of there, Abby would be able to recognize them again.

The door opened and another captive was dragged in. Winchester was hog tied and carried by three men and a woman, his eyes darting wildly about the room. They paused briefly when they met Abby's and again as they fell upon on the children. He said nothing as he was borne to an empty space along a bench, apparently having already learned the no-talking rule. The woman cut his legs free, then held the blade to his throat as he was manhandled onto the bench between a fence guard and a farmer. Once seated, one of the men crawled under the bench to lash their legs together. A thin trickle of blood ran out from Winchester's hair, sliding past his ear and down to his chin. The woman with the knife to his throat noticed. She checked out the injury on his head that had produced the blood, and deemed that it didn't need bandaging. Only then did she withdraw her blade. The moment it was safely away, Winchester jerked back, attempting to strike her with his skull. The woman was fast, however, and nimbly dodged away.

"I wouldn't try that again if I were you," she threatened, taking her knife back out and placing the tip against the back his neck.

"But you know I had to try at least once," Winchester calmly replied.

"Fair enough," the woman said with a grin, her teeth an unexpected mixture of black, grey, and yellow compared to how nicely the rest of her looked.

The four who had dragged Winchester in then departed the cafeteria, leaving the captives alone with the guards once more.

Winchester sought out Abby's eyes from his place two tables over. He stared hard into Abby's eyes, then glanced at those next to her. He did the same motion three more times before Abby figured out what he was trying to communicate; or at least what she thought he was trying to communicate. She shook her head to let him know that no one else with her had been taken, that Lauren wasn't there. Winchester nodded, then proceeded to take stock of their surroundings as Abby had, seeing who *was* there that he could identify and had the angle to spot. Most people had done this once seated; definitely those who had fought the hardest. Abby didn't like that some people seemed to have given up, that they stared at their laps or laid their faces flat on the table. She wondered if some of those people were just faking their hopelessness, making themselves appear docile, but Abby had no way of knowing. For now, she kept vigilant, taking in all the details she could, silently deciding who would be the most useful in various situations. Unfortunately, her imagination wasn't nearly as good as her memory, and so she could only think of a limited number of situations that might occur.

One such thing she couldn't foresee did happen. The next time the door opened, it wasn't another captive being brought in; a woman walked into the space, with Jo tagging along behind her, eating what looked like porridge or perhaps oatmeal out of a small plastic container. Abby hadn't imagined seeing Jo again, and the well of anger that opened up toward him shocked her. It was because of him that all this had happened. They had taken him in, malnourished and exhausted, conditions he couldn't fake, and in return, he opened the way for the wolves. He was just a boy; this couldn't have been his idea, but seeing him standing there, wearing the clothes they had given him, a smile on his face while he ate… Abby never thought she'd be capable of hurting a child until that moment. In that moment, she would have throttled him if she weren't tied up.

"Who here is your leader? Did we capture him or her?" the woman asked, her eyes scanning the faces of the prisoners. "Who in this room is highest on the food chain?"

Although a few eyes looked to Crichton or Bronislav, enough of the residents looked at others to make it go unnoticed.

"No? Not going to step forward? All right, that's fine." The woman carried herself with an air of authority, with complete confidence. She looked down beside her at Jo. "See anyone here you think we should talk to?"

Jo's eyes absolutely lit up. He carried his food with him as he walked around the room, looking at everyone seated there, his hand occasionally dipping inside the container to pull out a glob and shove it into his mouth.

"This one," Jo pointed to Crichton.

All the hairs stood up on the back of Abby's neck. Had anyone told Jo that he was one of their leaders? Or had he just picked him because Crichton was the one who was there when he woke up? The one who asked him questions?

A couple of guards stepped forward to separate Crichton from his tablemates, as Jo continued to move around the room. When he neared Abby, she poured all the hate she could muster into her eyes. When he noticed, the boy paused.

"And this one," he said raising a finger to point at her, glancing over his shoulder at the other woman. The moment he turned back to face Abby, she spat on the boy. The shock on his face was rather satisfying.

Wiping the saliva off on his shirt, Jo continued his walk around the room, his shoulders taking on a hunch they hadn't had previously. Guards began releasing Abby from those next to her, taking more precautions than they had with Crichton but otherwise not reprimanding her for the spitting episode.

"No one else," Jo finally said, walking shamefaced back to the woman's side.

She paid him no attention as her cold eyes continued to sweep over the group. Abby watched her as she was brought over to where Crichton stood against one wall. Their legs were then lashed together.

"Which one in here tried to talk the most?" the woman eventually asked the scarred twin.

"That woman there. Kept trying to talk to the little ones," he immediately replied, not having to think about it.

Abby noted he had pointed to Ellen whose three boys were all bound at the table with the other children.

The woman shook her head. "Which one tried to talk to other adults the most?"

"Her," Scar-twin pointed at Brittany, who had been doing her best to keep people calm and unafraid despite the blows she had taken for it.

"Bring her too, then," the woman decreed.

"It's all right," Brittany immediately told those around her as the guards made for her position. "Everything's going to be fine."

"Quiet," Bruiser grumbled, smacking her upside the head, as he had already done many times before.

Brittany kept quiet as she was untied from her neighbours and hauled over to Abby and Crichton.

The woman turned to the other twin, the clean one, to ask her next question. "Not including the children or the adults brought in with them, who here has been the most docile? Who's been co-operative?"

"I'd say him," Clean-twin rasped. He had no obvious external injuries like his brother, but it seemed he had taken some internal damage at some point, his voice hoarse from it.

"And who seems to be the most afraid?" the woman asked next as the guards grabbed Seth, the supposedly co-operative one.

"Him."

Abby hadn't been able to see the face of the man that Clean-twin pointed to, because its owner had never raised his head since she had arrived. As the guards removed him from the table, a whine escaped the man's throat. The sound was like that of a pitiful dog, but there was a familiarity to it for Abby. Her memory of the sound was validated when she saw Clive's face. It was actually a relief to see he was the most fearful, as his fear wasn't directed at the attackers, not entirely. Clive had various mental problems and neuroses that he had suffered from since before the Day. He didn't like being near a lot of people, he hated being touched, he wasn't fond of the outside, and change was a nightmare for him. Sitting in the truck that constituted the entrance in their fence was the perfect job for him, as he virtually never left the cab and was completely okay with rarely interacting with other humans. He had been in the motel where Lauren had been taken, never leaving the bathroom he had crawled into. On the Diana, he spent all his time locked up in his room, which was down the hall from Abby's. Josh had been taking care of him as best he could while aboard the ship, and Abby had heard that pathetic whine of his a dozen times as the doctor entered Clive's room after chatting with her. Abby would rather have him as part of this little group than someone completely sane and afraid of the invaders. She suspected she knew what was going to happen, even with her limited imagination.

Tied together at the legs and waist, their arms still bound behind their backs, the five people removed from their seats created a sort of chain gang.

"All right, I think that's enough. I'll take them from here, thank you." The woman smiled and nodded to the guards. "I believe you know how to get to the basement from here," she spoke to Crichton who formed the head of the line. "Please lead the way."

Crichton scanned the room, looking into the faces of everyone remaining behind. He then turned without a word or gesture and walked awkwardly through the door, forcing Abby and the others to follow. The woman tailed Clive, who shuffled along awkwardly, with his head down and shoulders hunched, occasionally letting that somewhat eerie whine escape his throat.

"Journey, why don't you go above ground and find the rest of the children? I'm sure they'd love to see you," the woman spoke as they reached the stairwell. "I hear they're gathered around a train of some sort."

"I'd rather stay with you," Jo said in a quiet, sheepish voice.

"And I'd rather you didn't. Go on now."

Jo trudged up the stairs as they headed down, turning and casting a forlorn look at the woman.

As they moved downward, they passed either a man or woman posted at the doorway to each level. Every one of them greeted or acknowledged the woman trailing them so that Abby was able to learn her name was Logan. They stopped only once on their descent, at the water treatment facility.

"Have you gotten in yet?" Logan asked the man in the stairwell.

"Not yet," he replied with a shake of his head. "Jo told us that he saw what looked like important equipment near that door there, so we don't want to go blasting through it. We'll have to wait for the torch. It's unfortunate that some of these rats managed to get in there and barricade it before we could reach the place." He sneered at Abby and her group as he said this.

"Keep trying," Logan told him. "Continue on," she then said to Crichton.

As they reached the parking level, Abby glanced over the railing, down the stairwell to where the door led into the power generation facility. A bright light and sparks filled the lowest level. She quickly determined that they were trying to cut their way in using a blowtorch, which was what the man on the water treatment level was waiting for. Abby grinned to herself, knowing there was no way they were getting in like that, not without a hell of a lot of time and a whole ton of fuel. That door was thicker and more secure than anything else in the entire Black Box.

Within the concrete structure of the parking level, several of the invaders were busying themselves around the large elevator shaft. It wasn't easy to see from a distance, but it appeared to Abby that they were lowering supplies down. They clearly planned on staying.

Logan directed the line of prisoners to a corner of the space, where a ring of folding chairs had been set up. The calm man who had told the stinking man not to kill Abby was there. He counted how many people had arrived tied up and removed two chairs from the ring, readjusting the others to form an even circle. Abby didn't like seeing that man here. Something about him creeped her out, and knowing what this was likely to end up being, made his presence worse.

"Stand along the wall, please," Logan ordered the line.

They did as commanded. The calm man started with Clive, untying him from the group and bringing him over to a chair. Clive kept squirming in his seat, threatening to slide off or tip it over while the man attempted to tie him to it.

With the speed of a striking viper, the calm man slapped Clive's face; not as hard as he could, but hard enough to no doubt sting. Clive's whine took on a higher-pitched note, but his body locked up, allowing the man to finish securing him. He continued along the line, tying one person to a chair at a time, so that Abby was second to last, and Crichton was put in the final seat. Abby noticed with ill-ease that she could clearly see each member of the group that had been brought down.

"This is going to be simple," Logan spoke, circling around the outside of the ring like a shark. "I'm going to ask questions, and you're going to answer. Easy, right?"

No one acknowledged her. Abby focused on Seth, worrying about him the most since he had been labelled the most co-operative.

"I'll start with something simple. Who's in charge of this place?"

No one moved, everyone continuing to ignore her.

"I'll try again. When there's a problem, such as me and my people breaking and entering, who do you all turn to?"

Silence and grim faces.

The man stepped into the ring, seemingly picking Brittany at random, and slapped her across the face. This time he slapped hard, the sound of flesh striking flesh loud within the concrete corner. A tear escaped Brittany's eye, but she pressed her lips firmly together as the side of her face began to bloom red.

"No? No one is going to tell me?" Logan continued to circle, her voice never changing in tone. "Let's try something else then. Who has a key to that door downstairs?"

No response.

Smack! This time it was Crichton who was struck. His face remained unchanged beyond the handprint that formed.

"Who has a key?"

This time Abby felt the sting of the blow. There was a horrible bite to the way the man slapped, but Abby merely sat up straighter. She had been slapped before, when she was younger and by someone whose strike had a deeper emotional impact. This man meant nothing to her.

"Who has a key?"

Smack! Clive this time, with his sad whimper.

"I want a key."

Smack! Abby again, this time on the same side of her face that was already swollen and bruised. She bore down on the pain, refusing to say a word. She thought of the time her mother had slapped her, not nearly as hard but even more painfully because of who she was. It was one of Abby's last memories of her family. They didn't want her to go to a school in Toronto; they wanted her to stay close where they could continue to drive God into her, hoping to cure her of her lesbian ways. Abby had always been quiet during those years, simply taking the emotional abuse, but once she had her escape, she let all her anger out. She told her mother all the things she thought about her and God at the time, a vile stream of words kept inside finally released. Abby hadn't even been able to get it all out before her mother's hand struck her face. They hadn't spoken directly to one another since, and Abby felt fine knowing that she was most likely dead.

Logan asked about a key to the generator room until everyone had been slapped at least three times, some of them more. No one said a word, not even Seth who had locked eyes with Crichton's cool, calm gaze.

"How do I get your people out of those other rooms?" Logan abruptly changed her question.

When still no one spoke, the calm man drove his fist into Clive's belly. Clive couldn't even whine, as his breath explosively escaped his lungs. Instead, the sound he made was an awful gasping, as his lungs attempted to suck air back into them.

"I'd rather not have to kill them all, so how do I get them out peacefully?"

Clive was struck again, this time the toe of the man's boot striking the soft spot beside his kneecap. When Logan asked again, the top of Clive's thigh was hit, and then his upper chest, and finally he was punched full on in the face. Blood trickled down the fence guard's chin from a split lip. Before Logan could ask again, the man pulled out a pistol, although he held it by the barrel, ready to swing the thing as a club.

"Stop! Leave him alone!" Brittany finally cried out.

Thinking of her family, Abby glowered at her. Claire, and Peter, and Lauren were in those rooms, along with Hope, Cameron, Dakota, and Brunt. Brittany had no real family, and Abby wasn't sure she had friends who had become like family. At least Seth had those, which might have been why he managed to keep quiet.

Logan stopped her circling behind Brittany and leaned down to speak in her ear. "He'll stop hurting you and your friends when you answer the question."

"I can get them out," Brittany spoke, licking her dry lips briefly as she thought up what to say. "I'm their grief councillor, they'll listen to me."

"No they won't," Abby quickly spat out. "Sure, they come to you for comfort, but they're not going to leave their safe zones because you ask them to. Maybe one or two, but the rest will stay put."

"I helped evacuate the Diana," Brittany retorted.

"Yeah, but you didn't start the evacuation; no one would have moved if you had tried."

"Will you tell me who your leaders are? Who *can* get them out?" Logan asked Brittany.

"No," Brittany said sheepishly to the floor.

"And what can you tell me?" Logan turned her gaze to Abby.

"I'm not telling you anything."

Logan drifted over to stand behind her and speak in her ear as she had with Brittany. "So you want the pain to continue?"

"Bring it on, bitch."

The man who had been inflicting pain nodded, having seen some signal from Logan. He quickly flipped his gun around, pointed it at Brittany, and pulled the trigger. The gunshot pounded into Abby's ears, her natural reflexes causing her to flinch and nearly knocking over her chair. She was shocked as she looked over at Brittany, a hole in her shirt expanding with red. The woman had been shot in the heart, not the head.

"And she was the one most likely to give me information based on her being the first to crack," Logan said to the group. "The fact is, I still have a whole room of people up there. I'll kill you all and bring down another group, let them see your corpses. Maybe then one of them will talk."

The gun swung to point at Abby. Tears escaped her, unbidden, but she kept her teeth clamped firmly together. She would die for her family if that's what was needed of her. She sent out only one silent prayer while she sat there, staring down the infinite blackness of the barrel. She prayed for a headshot, to not be turned into a zombie after her soul had departed.

"Stop," Crichton spoke quietly before the trigger could be pulled.

"I didn't expect you to crack," Logan said to him.

"I'm not cracking. I'm not going to give you answers to your questions, not all of them, but I will negotiate."

"And who are you to negotiate?"

"I'm one of the leaders you're looking for."

"Crichton—" Seth seemed ready to argue against him, but he was silenced by Crichton's sharp gaze.

"Before we discuss anything, however, you have to do something for me."

"Really?" Logan sounded intrigued. "And what might that be?"

"Keep that poor woman from turning. No one deserves that, and even you must see the danger in it. Never trust that you have control when a zombie's in the mix."

Logan walked around to look Crichton in the eyes, entering the circle for the first time.

"How do I know you really are one of the leaders?" She leaned down so that they were eye to eye.

"Abby, I want you to tell them what you know about me." He spoke without looking at her, keeping his eyes on the woman before him.

"Crichton—"

"Just do it, Abby."

Abby sighed. She didn't want to talk, but it seemed that this was the way it was going to go. Crichton must have some sort of plan if he was willing to talk.

"Commander Crichton was a high-ranking mercenary for Marble Keystone," Abby started, watching the reaction that always occurred when Keystone was mentioned. "During the evacuation of Leighton, he was put in charge of a prison outside the city that evacuees were brought to. Once it was obvious that Keystone had fallen, he loaded all the survivors into a convoy and headed for Toronto, where a pair of planes were waiting. These planes took us all to the ocean where a ship was being prepared for us. That ship was the Diana you heard Brittany mention. Crichton was in charge there, keeping us all safe for five years, until pirates finally managed to sink us. Crichton's been protecting people from the start."

"That's a nice story, one in which a name could easily be replaced with another." The entire time that Abby spoke, Logan hadn't even glanced at her, keeping her attention on Crichton. "Who are the other leaders?"

"I won't tell you that."

"Do you even *have* other leaders?"

"I won't tell you that."

Logan sighed and stood up straight. She turned to the man with the gun. "What do you think, Aster?"

The calm man, Aster, shrugged. "Couldn't hurt to talk to him."

"Keep her from turning first," Crichton insisted with a nod in Brittany's direction.

Aster aimed and fired so quickly that Abby was startled again, having to bite back a cry, alert to the fact that the gun had been pointed at her up until that moment. Another hole appeared in Brittany, this time along the hairline of her hanging head. Bone and brain matter erupted out of the other side, splattering along the back of the chair and floor. Abby turned her head away.

"All right, *Commander* Crichton. Let's talk."

***

Abby found herself in yet another seat, but this time her hands were bound in front of her. She thought for sure that when Logan decided to talk with Crichton in a more comfortable room, Abby and the others would have been left behind with Aster, or brought back to the cafeteria. Instead, they were invited to come along; probably as a security measure, to make sure Crichton always knew who was really in charge of the

Black Box now. It had been very surprising when a new pair of guards untied her arms from behind her back, and retied them in a way that allowed her to hold some ice chunks chipped out of the Black Box's freezers and wrapped in rags. She wanted to refuse any help or act of kindness from these people, especially after what had just happened to Brittany, but she knew that if both of her eyes swelled badly, it would be a hindrance she couldn't afford.

"There, this is better, isn't it?" Logan commented, pulling over a chair to sit facing Crichton. Abby, Clive, and Seth were all kept to one side, separate from them.

"Thank you for the ice," Crichton began politely as if his legs and waist weren't bound to the chair he sat upon.

"You're welcome. So, tell me, who has a key for that door downstairs?"

Crichton shook his head. "That's not where we start."

"It isn't?" Logan wondered, a hint of laughter in her voice.

"No, we start with what your plans are for the people if they leave their apartments."

"That depends on you."

"In what way?"

"Co-operate, and they'll be fine. Make things difficult, and they won't be."

"So you're willing to let us all go? Or are you thinking of taking everyone prisoner?"

"It would be very tedious to hold you all prisoner, not to mention a drain on our supplies."

"It would be, but that doesn't mean you wouldn't do it." Crichton was clearly trying to get her to say the words.

Logan seemed to pick up on this and decided to stop dancing around it. "I would let your people go."

"All of them?"

"Yes, all of them."

"Crichton, too?" Abby spoke up.

"Yes, yes, Crichton, too, so long as you give me what I want."

"Good, then we're clear on what I want. I'm assuming what you want is complete control of the Black Box, which includes being able to get into every room."

"I also want your supplies. Make no mistake, I'll let you leave, but you'll be taking nothing but the clothes on your backs."

"We'll die out there without supplies!" Seth cried out, to Abby's confusion. "You have to let us take something."

"That's your problem, not mine. I'm sure you'll find a way. Here, I'll let you take this advice: break into smaller groups."

It suddenly dawned on Abby that Seth was very clever. Based on the way Logan spoke, she had no idea about the colony at the container yard. It was unlikely that Logan would give them boats, so travelling around the large bay and crossing the rivers would take days and be dangerous, but at least they had a place to go. It would be crowded and supplies would be tight, but they had a safe place. At least, it was safe if they had dealt with their own problem better than the Black Box had. Were the two incidents related? Based on what Abby had heard from Cameron, she didn't think so.

Crichton gave himself time to think, as if debating what Logan had said about not taking supplies. "How do I know you're not lying?"

"You don't," Logan shrugged. "Now, how do I get into that room downstairs?"

"There's already someone in there," Crichton told her. "If I give the evacuation order, he'll be the last to leave. Once he's out, all you have to do is prevent the door from closing behind him."

"And how do I know you're not lying to me? That that room isn't empty?"

"Take me to the control centre; I can talk to my man from there. I'll get him to bang on the door as many times as you want, to prove to your men down there that I'm telling the truth."

Logan leaned back in her seat, considering his words. "Very well. Let's go prove the existence of this man of yours."

With a gesture of her hand, a pair of guards flanked Crichton. Both he and Logan got to their feet and made their way to the door. Abby was left behind with Seth, Clive, and the two remaining guards. She didn't dare speak a word to the others, not wanting to say the wrong thing and somehow give up the container yard. Instead, she watched Clive, who had calmed down considerably. Now that no one was touching him and his face was hidden behind his ice-filled rag, he had managed to relax. Evacuating, if it did indeed happen, was going to be hard on him. It always was.

Abby had trouble keeping track of time in the silence. She was exhausted. The night had been long and hard, and she wasn't as young as she used to be. With the fear-induced adrenaline wearing away, she found it harder to keep her eyes open and her head up, but she managed until the overhead speakers crackled to life.

"Attention Black Box residents, this is Commander Crichton speaking."

Abby hadn't heard him use the commander title for himself in a very long time. Certainly not since the Diana sank. She found it odd that he used it now.

"This is an orange evacuation. I repeat, this is an orange evacuation."

"What's that mean? Orange?" one of the guards asked, stepping up to Abby and prodding her with the end of a rifle.

"It means we lost and to leave our stuff behind for you guys," Abby had to bite back an insult. "Blue means we have time to pack, such as if there's a slow rising flood. Red, which is usually issued via lights and sirens as you may have heard, means grab what you can and go. Black is get the fuck out as fast as possible, we're all about to die."

"I feel a bit insulted we weren't a black," one of the guards joked with the other.

"Mind untying us now?" Seth asked slowly. "So we can join the evacuation?"

The one who had prodded Abby untied her, and took away the ice. Apparently, they were very literal about giving them nothing, not even the rags. Abby rubbed her sore wrists and waited for Seth and Clive to be freed so that they could go together. She'd have to find her family once they were outside.

Clive whined and curled up in his chair.

"What's his problem?" one of the guards sneered. "Come on, get up." He pushed Clive, which only made him curl up tighter.

"Don't touch him; it'll only make it worse. Step back," Seth told the guards, who hesitated, but then did as he had directed. "It's okay, Clive. We're evacuating. We're going outside, won't that be nice? We'll be going back to your truck. Come on, I'll make sure no one touches you," Seth coaxed.

Slowly, Clive got to his feet.

"There you go. Come on, just follow Abby and we'll be back at your truck in no time."

Abby moved for the door, looking over her shoulder to make sure Clive was shuffling after her. Seth tailed behind him, making sure the guards kept their distance.

As Abby led the way toward the nearest exit stairs, she wondered how many more times in her life she'd be forced to move.

28
Danny's Unsure

Danny slept fitfully. The side he was used to sleeping on was the one with his injured shoulder, which meant he either had to lie on his other side or his back, neither of which was working well. He was in that strange zone where he was too tired to sleep. Even when he did manage to make it into the land of dreams, he couldn't stay there long, constantly thinking it was time to get up when it wasn't. Then there was the fact that his container was near the community centre. The people were silent as they were gathered in groups and moved to either Animal Island or to a place from which they'd be defending, yet Danny could somehow sense them moving around out there. Maybe that was just a psychological thing, but the occasional soft footsteps of someone walking over his container, and the sounds made as his solar panels were removed for safe keeping, certainly weren't. Neither was the constant drone of the dead. He wondered if Jon was sleeping all right on the bunk bed beneath his. Jon had always been a bit of a roller, so his movements didn't tell Danny anything, and he didn't want to risk asking only to end up waking him with his words. Mostly Danny lay still on his back, his eyes closed, listening to the sounds of his own breathing and the heartbeat in his ears.

At the opposite end of the container, one of the doors was opened a crack, letting in the faint light of the night sky and an even fainter breeze. When a stronger puff of air rippled across his skin, Danny opened his eyes and rolled onto his good shoulder to look at the door. It had been opened further by someone, the silhouette not quite identifiable. Whoever it was stepped inside and carefully closed the door behind him.

"Danny?" Even when whispering, Danny could identify the German accent as belonging to Karsten.

"Sir?" Danny whispered back.

"I'm sorry to bother you, but I'd like to request your help with something."

"Do you need my help?" Jon whispered from the lower bunk sounding like he hadn't been asleep at all either.

"It's all right, Jon, you go back to sleep, I just need Danny."

Wondering what was happening now, Danny slid off his bunk and carefully climbed down the completely vertical metal ladder that he and Jon had bolted on to replace the angled one the bed had come with. Once on the floor, he followed Karsten outside, glancing back to see Jon watching them from the darkness. What would they need Danny's help with that Jon couldn't do? He had two working arms after all, whereas Danny was temporarily crippled. Clearly it couldn't be a physical task.

Outside, the eastern sky had become a dull grey. The sun would be rising in maybe an hour or so. Danny tried not to think about the chaos and death that was likely to come with it. Karsten led him to the community centre and then past it. Through the open doors, Danny was able to see that only Evans' people were left inside, huddled around a couple of gas lamps, many trying unsuccessfully to sleep. When they stopped at the containers beside the community centre, Danny figured out why he had been called over. If they were going to risk having a massive horde of zombies come over their walls, it would be cruel to keep Evans and his party locked up.

"I've been told that despite what happened to you, you seem to get along with these people to some degree."

"I don't think Evans is all that bad." Danny hadn't really realized he thought this until he said it. "I just think he made a bad call letting an angry mob decide what his group should do."

"I can understand that," Karsten nodded. "It's easier to go with a mob, than try to change their minds. Do you think they will help us? If we give them their weapons back, will we regret it?"

Danny chewed on his lip as he thought, but he didn't have to think for long. "I don't think so. I mean, they wouldn't have much of a choice would they? No one is just going to stand there and do nothing when a horde of zombies is coming at them unless they want to die, and I don't think these people want to die."

"I'm more concerned about afterwards, once the zombies are gone."

There was no way Danny could know what would happen then.

"Of course, their children will be on Animal Island," Karsten continued, talking more to himself now. "I would rather not have to use them as hostages, but I could."

"I think we should talk to Evans. I mean, that's why you brought me out here, right? So he has a familiar face present while you deal?"

Such a small smirk crossed Karsten's face, it was almost impossible to see in the dark.

When Karsten approached the containers, the guards didn't even bother to ask questions, they just merely stood more alert when he grabbed one of the door handles. Danny wished he had a rock for his new sling, a silent weapon to use in case he was wrong and someone charged out. When the container door opened, no one moved inside. Several sleepy eyes peered out of the darkness, while those closest to the door blinked rapidly, attempting to focus on Karsten from their seated positions on the floor.

"I'm looking for the one named Evans," Karsten whispered to the half-asleep people. "There's something important we need to talk about."

The large form of Evans moved forward from the back, his blond hair and beard catching the meagre light before the rest of this face. He stopped at the threshold of the container, looking down on Karsten. Karsten was only slightly below average height, but beside Evans, he was downright short.

"May we speak in private?" Karsten gestured away from the container.

Evans looked out into the space, spotting Danny. "This door stays open and we stay within sight of my party members." It wasn't a request.

Karsten nodded and led the man out of the container. Danny tailed behind the two men, glancing once over his shoulder. Evans' party members were clustering at the door, being careful not to step outside. The men guarding the containers had grown more tense, but they kept their hands off their guns. Instead, they tightly gripped their clubs and knives, under orders not to risk a gunshot. Karsten stopped within sight of the container, but out of hearing range of both the people within it and those guarding it. Bearing in mind that they were whispering and the zombies were still moaning, they didn't have to go very far.

"As you can hear, the zombie horde hasn't gone away like we had hoped," Karsten waved an arm toward the wall. "We have a plan, but it's dangerous."

"You're not using my people as cannon fodder." Evans' voice was flat as he whispered, the lack of emotion making it hard for Danny to figure out what he was thinking.

"Of course not, we would never do something like that. But there is a risk of zombies coming over the wall. I want to ask you to stand with us, to help us fight them off should that happen."

Evans considered the thought, his eyes roaming around the container yard and taking in the activity.

"We'd move the kids and the infirm somewhere safe," Danny added. "Ours have already been moved to an island, and we're going to disconnect the bridge before anything happens."

"Will we get our own weapons?" Evans asked.

"Yes," Karsten nodded.

Evans looked back at the community centre and the containers where his people were being held. "Can I trust there won't be any friendly fire from your people?"

"No one here would dare risk that. We're not that angry with you. Can I trust the same from yours?"

"Not all of them," Evans spoke honestly. "There are a few that I would keep locked up for now."

"Then keep them locked up; that'll be your call."

Danny shifted nervously from foot to foot. It seemed to him that maybe Karsten was putting too much trust in Evans, and he hoped that wasn't because of what he had said.

"Tell me what the plan is." Again, it wasn't a request.

Karsten explained about the slings and the grenades, how people outside the wall were going to set off fireworks to hopefully draw a bunch away.

"You know how to use a sling?" Evans looked at Danny when it was mentioned he'd be one of the slingers.

Danny nodded, not wanting to admit that he and Karsten had only just learned that night. Evans' eyes then focused on Danny's injury.

"It doesn't affect my ability to sling," Danny whispered, showing Evans the motion he got out of his other arm.

"That's not what I was thinking." Evans said it so quietly that Danny almost didn't hear him. "We will help you," Evans whispered, redirecting his attention to Karsten.

"Good. Great," Karsten nodded again. "I'm leaving it to you to tell your people, and to decide who's going to the island and who's staying to fight, as well as who you think should stay locked up. Be aware that those going to the island won't be allowed to bring weapons with them. We have a few guards there in case a zombie manages to cross the water, but also our pregnant women can handle themselves and all our teenagers know how to use the weapons they carry. It'll be safe there, but anyone who demands a weapon has to stay here."

"I understand. Will my party be stationed together, or are you going to spread us out among your people?"

"Not knowing your people's skills, I would like to spread them out, but I can understand why they would want to fight beside people they know."

"We'll compromise then. Those I know who will be all right beside your people will be spread out, while the rest stay together."

Karsten agreed. "When your people are ready, head toward the wall. A man there will return your weapons to you. After that, come back here and find me; I'll tell you where to set up. Those not fighting can head straight to the bridge." He pointed in its direction. "Someone is already waiting there to help people across."

Danny didn't know what to do with himself. He felt like he had contributed nothing to this conversation, that Karsten had already known how it was going to go.

"You're coming with me," Evans told him unexpectedly.

The request startled Danny to the point where he didn't know how to respond; he just followed Evans back to the community centre. As the man stepped inside the building, he was recognized right away by those who were awake, who then had everyone else woken up by the time Evans and Danny reached the corner in which they were clustered. Evans explained the plan to his non-combatants, asking if any of them would like to volunteer to fight. Only a small handful did, the rest more than willing to cross the bridge they had never seen. With that done, Evans got them up and moving outside, wanting to make sure they had ample time to get to safety. As they left the community centre, a few glanced at Danny. They looked confused and afraid. Danny tried to smile for them, hoping he looked friendly as opposed to creepy.

Letting his fighters cool their heels awhile longer, Evans personally led the others to the bridge. Danny figured he wanted to see it for himself, to know where it was and how far the island lay. In the darkness, Bitch Bridge looked more dangerous than ever. Its long hodgepodge length of floats, barrels, and boats bobbed on the gentle waves, bending wherever the ends of two of the overlaid boards met. They were lucky the water was as calm as it was.

"I'll see you all across in groups of five," a man waiting on the shore told them. Danny recognized him as one of the veterinarians, all of whom had plenty of experience crossing the bridge. "Those two kayaks there will be pacing alongside us, so if you fall in, don't struggle even if you can't swim. They'll save you, even if they have to dive in to do it, just don't make any noise. Also, I recommend crawling if you can."

Evans looked at the light still slowly growing on the horizon. Danny knew he was worried about the sun rising before his people could cross.

"It's okay," Danny told him. "We won't put the plan into action until the bridge is disconnected, and we won't do that until everyone waiting here has made it across."

Evans scratched his cheek beneath his short beard, and slowly nodded. "All right. Let's go get the others then."

When they turned to head back to the holding containers, they had gained two more volunteers who would rather risk the zombies than that bridge.

***

Back at the holding containers, Evans first went to the one that had held him, which was still open. As he explained what was going on, the guards left to go take up positions elsewhere, adding weight to the truth of what Evans was telling his people. Danny watched as Evans studied the faces of every man and woman who exited the container. Two of them he stopped and turned back inside. The pair looked pissed and ready to argue, but the constant zombie groaning and a severe expression on Evans' face kept their mouths shut. Opening up each container, Evans repeated the process of explaining and picking out people he was worried about. Those denied the chance to fight, he moved into the same container and locked the doors. Once that was done, Evans found a ladder leaning against the side of the holding containers.

"Danny," he whispered, waving him over.

Danny had been standing apart from everyone, simply observing. He walked over to Evans to see what he wanted.

"Is this ladder going to be used to get people on top of these?" he asked, gesturing at the containers that had held his party.

"Most likely, yeah," Danny replied.

"What happens to the ladder afterward? Is it dragged up there?"

"Yes, to keep any zombies from using it."

"I want it put into the container I put the aggressors in. They may pose a threat to your people if armed, but I don't want them trapped in that box with no way out if something goes wrong."

"I'm sure we can arrange that."

"If my own people can be stationed up there, then we can put the ladder next to that opening I saw in the roof. That way, they can decide if and when the ladder needs to be lowered."

Danny thought that sounded like a good idea and said as much. He still didn't know why Evans was keeping him nearby; it wasn't like Danny could make any actual decisions. Maybe he was just being used as a source of information and happened to be the closest person free at the time to follow him around.

Once the aggressors were secure inside the container, Evans led the party members to where Karsten had indicated. As promised, their weapons were waiting for them. Danny stood to the side once more, watching as they silently went through the gear, picking out what belonged to whom. The weapons that had been taken from the aggressors and the non-combatants were divided equally amongst the fighters, and they dug through the contents of their carts for more ammo. Danny noticed several people hastily putting together packs of food. It was a good idea in theory, but he thought they would just weigh the people down. If a zombie came over the wall, that would mean it could climb in some way, so getting trapped on top of a container was unlikely. Danny guessed that maybe the packs of food would be useful if they found themselves hiding on the inside of a container, but if there was no way to draw those dead away, the food would only prolong the inevitable. Danny wondered where the carts were going to be put afterward.

Once everyone had collected what they wanted, some carrying all that they could, Evans led the party back to where Karsten was waiting. Everywhere he looked, Danny could see people moving about. On top of containers, people settled into their assigned positions, winces rippling through nearby folk whenever a particularly loud footstep fell upon the metal boxes. Everyone was being extra cautious not to drop anything. At one point, Danny spotted one of Misha's dogs staring down at him, but couldn't see his owner anywhere. On the ground, people scurried to and fro, delivering messages in sign, checking that all the containers were secure, putting loose solar panels away, and collecting more ammo. The horse containers were currently open, the veterinarians settling in with food and water; they would need to wait out whatever was going to happen, administering the remaining sedatives as needed. The stables were the only structures Danny didn't spy someone on top of. As they approached Karsten, Danny could make out the toilets; there were even people gathering on top of them, including an old man, who probably hadn't seen combat since the Diana sank, carefully climbing a ladder to join a young teen who must have just recently finished her gun training.

"Thank you for helping us, and in turn yourselves," Karsten whispered, allowing those near the front of the group to quietly pass his words to those in the back. "Once this is all over, you'll be free to leave with all of your equipment. We're also prepared to discuss your joining us here if some of you would like that, but for now, we have to get through this together." Karsten looked directly at Evans. "Did you share the plan with them?"

Evans nodded. "I have a request for placement of my people."

"Let's hear it."

"I want to have only my people on top of the containers we were held in, as well as that building next to it. If something goes wrong, I want them to be able to decide when my people locked in that container should be let out."

"All right, but make sure everyone knows to stay on this side of the roof peak so that they're not spotted. Some of my people are already climbing up there, but I can reassign them. It doesn't sound like you want to be up there yourself?"

Evans shook his head and offered no explanation.

"Danny, can you go clear the people off the community centre, and send them to me for a new placement?"

Danny nodded curtly and hurried over to the building. Just inside, Jon and some of the other slingers were making sure the food supplies kept in there were secure in tight containers being strapped to the wall to prevent any from tipping over. If the zombies were going to come over the outer wall, they didn't want the creatures finding their way into the community centre and contaminating their food. Danny wondered how the other slingers were doing. He guessed the same as him: nervous, but focusing on a task they had been given in order to get through the wait.

At the side of the holding containers, Danny attracted the attention of someone who had just climbed up on top. The sun was now adding some colour to the sky, making it easy for the woman to see and understand his signing. She was confused and annoyed by what Danny said, but passed on the message to the others who had already climbed up there, carefully moving between the solar panels. One by one, they made their way back down and headed toward Karsten. Danny followed after them once he was sure that the community centre roof had been cleared.

When Danny returned, Karsten held a notebook that he and Evans were huddled over, quietly talking to one another. Occasionally, Evans would speak to one of his men standing on his other side, who then left to deliver orders to another of their party. Alone or in small groups, members of Evans' party peeled away from the collective to set up at their assigned locations. The last group of people, the largest, was finally sent to the community centre.

"I'm going to check on my people crossing your bridge," Evans told Karsten.

"That's fine. We'll start the assault when you tell us that they're across and the bridge is disconnected."

Danny could see the respect the two men had for each other as Evans nodded, then turned to run off. It was weird to think that they had been shooting at each other less than twenty-four hours ago.

Time to find the others, Karsten signed to Danny.

Danny didn't need to ask who he was referring to; he simply replied that he had seen some in the community centre.

It didn't take long to round up all the slingers. None of them had slept heavily, and all had gotten up the moment the sky began to lighten. Most of them had found jobs near their meeting spot, keeping their minds occupied and hands busy. Once they were all together, they moved toward the wall, urging people still on the ground to get up on the containers and haul up the ladders.

When the box of grenades came into view, Danny felt his throat dry up and his bladder loosen. He had to excuse himself to go pee on the side of the wall, and he wasn't the only one. When he returned, he saw the women signing to each other, grateful that they had thought to go earlier and trying to joke to each other about the unpreparedness of men. All the smiles were forced, however.

White and Tommy had joined them, even though they wouldn't be slinging. Tommy didn't want to separate from his friends; White explained to Danny that he was going to help him load his sling. Danny was grateful that he wouldn't have to worry about his injured shoulder screwing him up at a critical moment.

The metal box had been waiting for them. Tommy opened it and handed out the grenades, while Freya positioned everyone, spreading out the best slingers who had the extra explosives. Danny was situated between Bryce and Katrina; White worked with him briefly to find the best place to stand that was out of the way, but close enough to load the second grenade quickly.

Karsten stood with his back to the wall, looking at the nearest container. Danny knew he was waiting for a signal from someone telling him that everyone was off the ground and all but one of the ladders were up. After that, they'd just be waiting on Evans. Danny again ran the path through his mind, reminding himself that he had to head around the nearest container row to get to the ladder. Not having been part of the discussion, he didn't know why the ladder wasn't situated as close as possible, but he couldn't distract himself with thoughts of that now. After getting up the ladder, he was to fall back to the second row, his injury forcing him to use a pistol instead of a more accurate rifle.

Danny watched as White loaded the first grenade, making sure the handle was outside the leather as Freya had shown him. The former police officer was going to pull the pin and duck out of the way, giving Danny seconds to let it loose over the wall. The wall looked so much higher than usual. Under normal circumstances, that would be comforting, but these weren't normal circumstances.

Trying to swallow the lump in his throat, he looked over at Bryce's battered features. Bryce noticed, and nodded in his direction, trying to appear brave but the wideness of his eyes, even the swollen one, gave him away. Katrina didn't look back as Danny turned his face to her. Her jaw was set tight, the muscles in her neck standing out. Her entire body was perfectly still, save the hand that held the sling. That, she swung gently back and forth, the grenade moving in a small arc.

Danny had to remind himself to breathe.

29
Evans Is Relieved

As Evans watched, the last of Karsten's men unhooked the bridge from the shore, walking out into the water with it to make sure it drifted away. All of Evans' party members who had needed to cross, were now safely on the island. He would never tell a soul, but Evans was glad the gigantic horde of zombies had come. It had been stupid and foolish to allow Arman's anger to whip up the others, to let them seek vengeance over a mistake and a misunderstanding. That had been the easiest route at the time; Evans had never been very good at persuading people to change their minds, especially ones so steeped in anger. Having met Karsten, and having seen how he organized his people, Evans knew that they never stood a chance in the assault. Sure, they would have managed to kill a few, but that would only have justified the container people's potential slaughter of his party. He was glad that they were now working together, that a future friendship could be established. This would make a good camp at which to resupply during his travels, a safe place to rest. That is, if everyone survived this plan of theirs.

Once the dock man was satisfied that it was floating away, he slogged back out of the salt water and headed toward Evans. As he neared, Evans picked up the man's bundle of weapons that had been left beside him to keep dry and handed them over. Together, they made their way to the ladder that had been left down for the two of them.

Evans climbed up first, not because he distrusted them to haul it up before he could climb up, but because he had farther to go once on top. He walked across the neat rows of containers, having to take long steps to reach the ones that had been placed sideways between them. Yesterday, when Evans was escorted to the holding container, he had seen that these were living quarters and knew that some of these containers had been recently moved to make travelling between them easier. They hadn't been able to move enough, however, so occasionally Evans had to traverse ladders and boards that had been laid across the gaps. He crossed these slowly, unsure of his balance and the way they sagged in the middle.

There was at least one person, sometimes more, on every container and they were all armed. Evans wondered if some of them had more ammo than others, or if the bullets were evenly distributed. Considering he didn't spot any ammo caches anywhere on the containers, he guessed that they had few enough bullets for everyone to be carrying them in their pockets. Here and there dogs wandered about: big dogs, little dogs, and the dogs that had surrounded Arman were standing and sitting amongst the legs of the people. All of their fur stuck out, many ears were flattened, and several curled their lips in silent snarls, not liking the zombie sounds and smells permeating the air. Several times, Evans spotted cats. They were huddled and bunched near the edges of the containers, some looking like they were trying to determine if they could jump down from that height. There were a couple of odd animals around as well. One man had a ferret wrapped around his shoulders; another woman stood beside a harnessed badger. Where the badger might have come from, Evans had no idea, but he kept his distance as most people seemed to be doing. He wondered how many more animals, how many more pets, were entrusted to the security of the containers. They would die slowly if the humans were killed. Evans briefly wondered where the horses were being kept, and whether that black and white cat was around somewhere as he hadn't seen it since being released.

As he approached the container nearest the slingers—balancing across a ladder to reach it—he noticed a drop in the number of people. Spaces had been left for those still on the ground, but there also weren't a lot of volunteers for the front line. Evans had volunteered; he wanted to see how the grenade throwing went with his own eyes. He also wanted to know the moment the zombies came over, if that was going to happen. Only two dogs were on this shorter row of containers: one of the dogs was the old, grey muzzled German Shepherd that had attacked Arman, while the other was younger, some sort of splotchy-coloured breed he didn't know. They stood in his spot, as close to the slingers as possible. Looking at the line of grenade throwers, Evans spotted the man who had been defended by the dogs and understood why they were there. Not wanting to risk being snapped at, he placed himself next to the furry beasts instead of trying to move them.

Meeting eyes with Karsten, Evans nodded. As far as he was concerned, they were ready. Over his shoulder, his large sword hung sharp and ready, while in his hands rested his shotgun, extra ammo weighing down his pockets. The sun had finally made its way above the horizon, turning the eastern sky pink as Karsten touched the shoulders of those on either side of him. Evans noted that one of the other slingers was Boyle, the container yard's second leader; Evans hadn't seen him since being led into holding. Other slingers included the small group who had warned them of the zombies, and all three people who had been captured by Evans' party. He guessed that because they were trusted and trained to go over the wall and deal with the zombies and people out there, they were trusted to handle this vital operation. The rest he didn't recognize, although one man on the end stood out as he held a bow and arrow as opposed to a strip of leather. The line looked to Karsten, who held up his hand that wasn't holding the sling. Tension filled the air, as everyone who could see it, knew what it meant. Then Karsten's arm dropped.

Pins were pulled and slings whirred. The bowman drew back, pulling the pin out of his grenade with his teeth by tugging on a string that had been tied to it. They loosed almost as one, the grenades arching up and over the wall. The moment they were visible to the zombies beyond it, their sounds became more agitated. Evans wouldn't have noticed if he hadn't been listening for it. They couldn't be heard for long because the grenades all exploded with sharp cracks and rumbles. A gout of gore was flung into the air so high, Evans could make out body parts, one leg landing on top of the highest container and then bouncing and flopping over to the lower one like a dead fish.

The sound of the zombies was like nothing Evans had ever heard. He had almost gotten used to the constant noise they had been making out there, but that was only some of them groaning for the hell of it. Now, every dead thing outside that wall was creating a racket, screaming, groaning, moaning, and gasping, their instincts telling them to alert others that life had been found.

The second round of grenades was less organized, more staggered as they reloaded at different rates. A lithe black woman was ready far sooner than the others, her second grenade going up and over all alone. It was soon followed by the bowman's second shot, and then a couple of the others. As they blew up, tearing the dead to pieces, the first of the distant fireworks screamed up into the air. Evans could barely hear it, and its fiery flower of light was diminished by the ever-increasing sunlight. *It's too far*, he thought.

One grenade went awry. Evans didn't know who had thrown it, but it hadn't been freed of the sling fast enough, and didn't have the same amount of power behind it as the others had. It cleared the top of the wall, but just barely, before it exploded. Instead of tearing zombies to shreds, the explosive force hammered into the containers right where two of them joined. The doors that had been barred between them were blasted open, making the wall suddenly shorter in that location, allowing Evans to see out toward the containers he had snuck through with his party. Any patch of ground he might have otherwise spied between there and the wall was covered with the dead, and all of them were surging toward him.

When the slingers were out of grenades, they ran for the edge of the row Evans stood upon. Only the bowman stopped at the corner, drawing a regular arrow to protect those coming after him if need be. A couple of people had three grenades and loosed them when ready; all but the black woman. She stood staring at the opening, her grenade resting in her sling with the pin still in place.

"Freya, come on!" Boyle shouted at her. He had started to retreat with the others when he saw she hadn't moved.

The woman, Freya, waved him away, her eyes never leaving the opening. Frustrated, angry, and hating that he was doing it, Boyle turned and ran, knowing he'd be of more use on top of the containers than on the ground. Evans was so focused on what was happening in front of him, he didn't notice when the dog man, Misha, lay down beside him with a rifle in his hands, or when a woman took up a similar position on his other side. He watched only the lone woman on the ground and the opening.

A zombie appeared, clawing its way up onto the container wall.

"Now!" Evans shouted, knowing he had a better view than Freya did.

She didn't know him, but she trusted his outburst. Pulling the pin, Freya's sling became an immediate blur. During the seconds that passed, the zombie struggled up onto its feet, with more quickly rising behind him as the dead learned to climb and piled up on top of one another. When she finally loosed the grenade, Freya's aim was perfect. The small explosive zipped up to the opening, then perfectly arched down to bounce between the first zombie's feet. It exploded right over the pile, shrapnel destroying the muscles of those who had managed to learn how to climb. The doors of the containers, already weakened from the first blast they took, dented and cracked, one of them shearing off to fall and crush even more of the dead. The force blew the standing zombie inward, its body tearing apart and scattering all over the ground below. Freya wasn't there anymore, she hadn't even watched where her shot had landed. The moment the grenade was away from her, she had bolted for the corner where the bowman stood.

Evans finally noticed the people who had stationed themselves around him. Without a rifle, he wasn't expected to shoot the things as they came over the wall, but he took a kneeling stance to shoot anything that made it to the base of their container perch.

There were so many. Already, more zombies were finding their way up, scrambling over the bodies of their fallen. The first shot came from Evans' left, from Misha, closely followed by a second shot from his right. Two zombies fell beneath the bullets, but they were quickly replaced by two more.

The fireworks are too far, Evans thought again. Maybe, if they were lucky, a few at the back would be drawn off, but with gunfire so much closer, that wasn't likely.

Shot by shot, the two flanking Evans took down the dead. At least the things were funnelled for the time being, but that wouldn't last, and every shot that missed a skull meant one less bullet to take out the ones behind.

"Reloading!" the woman on Evans' right shouted.

"I got them, Katrina," another woman, who was farther right, told her, easily falling into the back and forth pattern with Misha. When Misha shouted that he was reloading, the young man on his left, the one with the katana, took over. This was something that had been planned.

A bullet struck a zombie's torso, knocking it over but not killing it.

"Let it come," Evans shouted to the shooters. "Don't waste a second rifle shot on it, I'll take care of that one."

The thing flopped over the edge of the container wall, nearly killing itself by landing on its head. Sadly, the corpses of other slain zombies had fallen before it, cushioning the blow. Evans tracked it with the muzzle of his shotgun, waiting until it was close enough that he could be certain he'd take it down.

The roar of the shotgun was loud but effective as the zombie's head was taken off. Evans pumped out the old cartridge, instinctively grabbing it and stuffing it into a rear pocket. He had no idea if he'd ever get to make it useful again. Not knowing how often he'd get to reload, Evans pulled out a fresh shell and slotted it into the shotgun. He intended to keep the weapon fully loaded whenever he could.

The five closest to the opening adopted a rhythm. Whenever one had to reload, the person next to him or her would take up firing. If a shot was missed, a second shot wasn't taken: the zombie was allowed to stagger close enough for Evans to deal with it. Through their brief bits of chatter, Evans learned the other woman was named Yasmin, and the young man was Jon. All of them had been slingers, but were proving themselves better with rifles.

"Left side!" Boyle shouted farther down the container line, the call quickly repeated by Karsten and others.

Evans glanced left to see another pile of zombies had mounded up and over the top of the wall. More riflemen and women began to take care of them, the crack of their weapons adding to the cacophony of chaos.

More and more of the dead had to be left to Evans. They were surging over the wall now, being pushed by those behind, falling like a grotesque river. The opening was nearly entirely blocked by slain corpses, but more continued to crawl over them, heaved over the top by the masses below. The fully dead had formed a sort of ramp from the top of the wall to the ground inside. Rotting faces slid through blood and guts, occasionally hanging up on shattered bones, tearing themselves further in the pursuit of warm flesh. They were the slow creatures, the fast ones either trapped at the back or killed by the blasts, but the slick slide down gave them speed. It wasn't always easy to tell which head belonged to which moving corpse; a few shots were wasted on those that had already been taken down. Evans found the amount of time he got to spend reloading was growing shorter and shorter each time, as the number of cartridges he expended grew and grew.

"I'm out!" Misha was the first to shout, sliding out of his shooter's position, slinging his rifle over his shoulder, and drawing a saw-backed machete. The other three continued to make do without him, each one getting less time to rest and reload before having to take up shooting again. It didn't last long before Katrina shouted that she was out, followed by Jon and eventually Yasmin.

A dog barked sharply beyond Yasmin. The younger animal was looking down at a zombie Evans had missed that had made it to the containers, its half-missing hands pawing at the metal sides. An arrow swiftly appeared in its skull, the bowman quickly moving down the line to search for more. Evans immediately had to turn and fire at another corpse getting close. As more and more riflemen ran out of bullets, more and more of the dead reached the containers. Pistols, shotguns, arrows, and even Freya's viciously slung stones, tore through the nearby skulls, only to be replaced by more. Every time a corpse fell, another took its place, climbing through and over the bodies and getting just that much closer to the living people.

"They're coming up!" Misha shouted, having moved along the container without Evans noticing. He hacked at a head as it was dragged upward, the thing's arms sprawled across the top of the container. The sharp machete bit into the rot-weakened skull, taking out the brain within, the corpse sliding back to increase the pile's height as soon as the blade was freed.

Evans fired upon another zombie, and another, and another, but the fourth time he tried, his shotgun was empty. Reaching for another shell, his fingers found none. He was out.

Flipping the shotgun over, Evans swung the butt around and smashed the face off the zombie climbing up to him, its jaw separating to disappear amongst the rest of the miscellaneous body parts strewn about. Rising up off his knees, Evans hung his shotgun back in its hip holster with one hand, while drawing his broadsword with the other. He lopped off the head of a zombie coming up to him, already unsure if it was the one he had struck with the shotgun. Somewhere deep down, Evans' brain continued to separate the zombies, to identify the features that had made them individual humans, but he had learned to ignore it long ago. It was easier to see only the major anatomy points, the head, torso, and limbs. To go beyond that was to see the gore, the decay, the rot, the horror that had befallen the people these once were. For Evans, only the smell remained, threatening to choke him and bring up his last meal, the one he and the others had received in the holding containers. He did his best to breathe through his mouth, but then it became a taste. He hadn't thought to grab his scarf from the carts, but even it would do little against this sensory assault. The air was thick and heavy with it.

"Fall back!" someone shouted, Evans too focused on swinging his sword to identify who. "Fall back!"

Evans turned and saw that most of the people on the front line of containers had retreated back across the ladders and boards that connected to those behind them. Zombies had come over multiple points of the wall now and were crashing into the lower containers like ocean waves, some flowing up onto them, while others started flooding around the sides.

"Rifle!" Misha was bellowing from half way across the ladder, the younger of the two dogs Evans had seen earlier clutched tightly to one shoulder while his other hand still held the machete now dripping with blackened blood. "Rifle!"

Evans realized he was one of the last on the container, or at least one of the last who was still alive. He saw one man get dragged down, engulfed in dead flesh, while a few others had sustained bites. Those who had been bitten were continuing to fight, knowing they were taking their last breaths and using them to protect their friends and families from a similar fate.

Evans was about to be cut off from the ladder by the dead. On the container row behind him, people were shouting, afraid of shooting him and encouraging him to get out of the way. Some shots were taken anyway, brains blowing out of heads around him. Misha had retreated to the other container, putting his dog down and looking like he was about to run back across the ladder, when Evans felt something against his leg. Raising his sword, he prepared to hack down at it, assuming it was a small or legless zombie. At the last moment he recognized fur, and redirected his blow back up to the nearest dead thing, striking its crotch and shattering its pelvis. Evans lashed out with his boot, knocking it back into the others coming at him, causing many to lose their balance.

A reeking hand fell on his shoulder from behind, but it was gone before Evans could even finish turning around. The German Shepherd had grabbed the zombie's arm and dragged the whole thing down, where the dog shook its head, tearing the limb from the torso. Evans drove the point of his sword through the dead brain and the dog instantly released the corpse.

"I'm guessing you're the rifle," Evans grunted as he grabbed the old dog and slung it over his wide shoulder in the manner he had seen Misha use to carry the other dog.

Charging for the ladder, Evans swung his sword before him with one hand, using the flat sides more than the sharp ones. He didn't care about taking down zombies right now; he just needed to bat them out of his way and didn't want to risk the blade getting stuck.

Upon reaching the ladder, he couldn't slow, no longer being cautious as he had been when first crossing it. As the other side neared, his foot missed a rung, his leg sliding down through the opening. Evans hurled the dog from him, the old mutt yelping like a pup as it went airborne. Misha was watching and waiting, however. He caught Rifle, leaning out over the ladder to do so. Jon was right behind him, and yanked the back of Misha's shirt before both he and the dog could go over the side.

Evans barely made note of all of this as he twisted around, swinging his sword. Some part of him had registered the vibrations coming through the ladder as those created by a pursuer. This particular follower was dead, but still of reasonable intelligence, a smart one crawling over the rungs with alarming speed. It seemed not all of them had been taken out by the grenade blasts, but this one certainly died for good when Evans' sword bit into it.

Yanking his blade free, Evans scrambled upright, pulling his leg out from between the ladder rungs. He scrambled the rest of the way across using his hands, then flipped over into a seated position the moment he was on the container. At the other end of the ladder, someone Evans hadn't noticed earlier was about to come across. Everyone around was shouting encouragement to the man, urging him to come faster, but he was scared and picked his way along one rung at a time.

Evans, with his lower vantage point, spotted the bloody tear along the man's calf. Was it just a cut, a gash from an accident involving one of the two-bladed weapons hanging from the man's belt, or was it a bite? Was the man already dead? Right or wrong, Evans decided that he was. He'd be dead soon with the sluggish pace he was using to cross the ladder. Most of the zombies were too uncoordinated, missing the rungs and falling from the container and bridge, but each one got a little farther having watched those before it, or by walking over those that had fallen along the ladder's length. Evans started kicking the ladder.

"What are you doing?" Jon shouted at him, his voice barely heard over the crackle of gunfire.

"His leg!" Evans shouted back, still kicking, the ladder sliding sideways an inch at a time. It wasn't until a zombie grabbed the back of the man's shirt and pulled him down that Jon started helping. Evans had moved the ladder a fair way, but it was weighed down by the bodies on top of it. With Jon's help, they swiftly got it over the edge and clattering to the ground, spilling off both the man and the zombies who were swarming him.

Back on his feet, Evans quickly scanned back and forth, checking that all other temporary bridges gapping the distance between the first and second rows of containers were down.

"Come on, Karsten ordered everyone without ammo to the back of the containers." Jon took Evans' arm and guided him past the shooters, with Misha and his dogs accompanying them.

"I just need some shells and I can keep firing," Evans insisted, preferring the front where he could see what was happening.

"Not without a shotgun you can't." Jon gestured to his waist.

Looking down, Evans saw that he had lost his shotgun at some point, probably when he had fallen on the ladder. Cursing, he allowed Jon to continue leading him. The second row of containers was connected to the third via a recently moved one. The gaps were just large enough that they had to jump a short way to cross them, meaning that the first zombies to try would certainly fall.

Although Jon had been the one to tell Evans that they were to head to the back, it seemed that he felt the same and stopped when only halfway there. Misha hadn't kept up with them, stopping to gather up all the dogs they passed and bringing them away from the front. Evans wondered if they were all his dogs, or if some people were trusting him to take care of theirs. Evans headed along the containers, attempting to get as close to the community centre as he could, so that he could see how his party members over there were fairing. All around, the sharp crack of gunfire filled the air, and the smell of gunpowder mixed with the scent of rot. Even back from the firing line, tense postures and nervous brows were everywhere Evans looked. Guns were in every hand as eyes carefully scanned for targets. At the edge of the container rows, a few shots began firing as some zombies found their way around. Looking to the community centre roof, Evans spotted a muzzle flash at the farthest end, the one with a view around the edges of the container rows on that end. Evans bet it was Ki-nam, the one he had put in charge of everyone up there, and who had a high-powered rifle with a scope that would allow him to fire at those coming over the wall. The party members, all perched around the solar panels, were probably giving him their ammo if it was compatible.

When a few members of his party who were on the containers spotted Evans, they smiled and waved enthusiastically, glad to see he was still alive and presumably unhurt. For the first time, Evans looked down at himself to see the new streaks of blood that stained his clothes. There was even a chunk of something trapped beneath his bootlaces, but he'd deal with that later. He wondered how much splattering had landed on his face and reminded himself not to lick his lips no matter how dry they might feel. He wished again for his scarf even though it made breathing somewhat more difficult, but it was locked away in a container somewhere, and he had no idea which one.

Evans stalked to the end of the container row, pacing back and forth behind the line of shooters with his sword gripped tightly in one hand. The adrenaline wouldn't let him keep still. Every time someone near him fired their weapon, he hurried over to the edge to see if the zombies were flooding around it, but so far, it had only been random wanderers.

A great amount of shouting drew Evans' attention to the far end of the container row. It didn't take long for the words to be passed down.

"They're coming over the shorter section of the wall!"

Evans ran down the length of the containers, his boots thudding heavily against the metal surface, nimbly avoiding escape hatches and the ends of plastic bottles sticking up. He saw what was causing the commotion even before he reached it. A group of zombies had finally learned to scale a section of the wall that was only one container high. Because of the lower height, the zombies could get up and over more quickly, faster than the shooters could take them out. Once the dead hit the ground, they moved toward the container rows, some heading for the nearest one, others moving into the spaces between them. A lot of the zombies still remembered their short climb as they reached the next barrier of containers and immediately began trying to climb the new obstacle.

There was a strange shift in positioning happening. Most of the best shooters had been situated at the front of the container rows, with the weaker warriors defending the back rows. Although a couple of good shooters were over at the side, they clearly hadn't expected this many zombies to come over. Now, some combatants were moving away from the danger, frightened and fleeing, while the more bold hurried to take their places. Evans got on his knees, out of the firing lines, and squirmed between the legs of two shooters who were busy picking off zombies as they came over. Neither had noticed the danger looming below their feet until Evans thrust the point of his sword over the edge, impaling a zombie's face. Over the screams and shouts, he thought he heard a thank you before the shooters began firing at the wall again.

Wiggling into a better position, Evans knelt in front of the shooters, stabbing and slashing at anything that tried to rise above the container's edge. He got into another kind of rhythm, paying no attention to what the shooters were doing behind him. At one point, he thought he heard the call for the second line to retreat, but couldn't be sure. Everything had become chaotic as ammo was depleted, lines reformed, and people died. Evans was sure he was half-deaf from all the gunfire that had been thumping near his head. His focus remained on the dead before him, those trying to climb up, and the flashing of his blade that grew duller with every strike. He changed positions, his arms tired and his knees sore. He started kicking out at the zombies, knocking them off the pile that had grown higher than the container.

"Come on!" someone shouted, grabbing the back of his shirt and pulling.

Evans stumbled backward, his boots slipping in the blood. He refused to turn, to expose his back to the dead, but as he stepped away, he realized that that was what he was doing anyway. Zombies had been piling up on the sides he wasn't watching, and while other people had been taking them out, something must have made them stop. If Evans had stayed put, he would have been surrounded.

Once far enough back, someone else shoved Evans behind him and began firing at the zombies who were giving pursuit. It allowed Evans to finally take another breather and look around.

His people and the container yard people were hard to distinguish from one another. There were combatants everywhere covered in sweat, grime, and gore, all of them exhausted, frightened, and determined—at least the ones he could see. A lot more melee weapons had been drawn as ammo ran out, less-skilled shooters handing over their guns to those with a better eye.

"Evans! You're still alive!" Old Salt suddenly appeared before him, gap-toothed and filthy. It took Evans a moment to remember who he was. His past had been burned away in the heat of combat; there was nothing left but where the next thing he had to kill was.

Evans grunted some sort of response, his eyes quickly pulling away to look toward their feet, to search for the next zombie trying to climb up. He pushed past Old Salt to move to the edge, looking down into the gutter between containers. There were corpses scattered everywhere, but all of them appeared fully dead. Most of the climbers were farther along, back where he had come from. Evans made his way toward them.

"Evans, wait!" Old Salt was shouting behind him.

Evans had no time to talk to the man, not while the dead were still threatening them.

"Evans!" Old Salt screamed, just as someone bumped into Evans' side while running past.

The slick blood covering Evans' boots offered no traction. He slipped over the side of the container and fell.

30
Riley's Groggy

"Attention Black Box residents, this is Commander Crichton speaking. This is an orange evacuation. I repeat, this is an orange evacuation."

Riley had been resting with her eyes closed and thought that maybe she had fallen asleep. She pried her weary lids open to look for someone who could confirm what she heard.

"Josh?" she said weakly.

It was Robin who appeared above her first, the crowd of other people taking shelter in the medical centre buzzing around behind her.

"Did you hear?" Robin queried Riley as she took note of all her vital signs.

"Orange evacuation?" Riley hoped it was something else she might have heard but was doubtful.

"Yeah." Robin pulled out a penlight and shone it in Riley's eyes.

Riley squinted, resisting the urge to turn away. "I should be strong enough to walk, but I'll need help."

"No, no, stay put," Robin insisted. "Josh is grabbing a stretcher."

"I don't need one."

"Yeah, but to those guys out there, it'll look like you do. Anything we can get out, we're taking."

Riley saw the sense in her words and nodded. "Can you make it look like you've hooked an IV bag to me, but not actually have it dripping?"

"I could, but you may still need those fluids."

"No, I'll be alright. I can drink if you find me water. We'll save the bag for someone more desperate."

Robin nodded, then disappeared into the shifting blur of people. They had all moved into the operating room, the only room large enough that didn't have someone who had been killed in it, but they were now preparing to leave. Focusing, Riley saw people out in the waiting room, slowly removing their barricade, while everyone else scurried about, finding ways to hide what they could on their persons. Groping with her hand, Riley located the scalpel she had used to kill the man who had invaded their space earlier. Very gently, she tucked it beneath the bandages wrapped around her chest. When Josh showed up or Robin came back, she'd ask one of them to find more instruments she could hide.

Watching the people, Riley was happy to see the creative ways they were finding to smuggle out supplies. Injuries were faked, with bandages and gauze thoroughly wrapped around limbs so as to be reusable later. They were careful not to overdo it, but even a few gave them something they wouldn't have had otherwise. Those who were already ill and looked it, were receiving fake IVs; Robin was instructing them how to do it. Medical tape was peeled off rolls and used to hold small pieces of equipment and medicine to places like people's inner thighs, armpits, or the small of their backs, anywhere their clothes hung loose enough to hide them. Women carefully tucked things into their bras or even their hair if it was long enough, while others put what they could inside their shoes.

"Your chariot," Josh joked, appearing at Riley's side with an old, military canvas stretcher.

"Not something newer?" Riley wondered as he placed it on the floor beside her.

"We may want the canvas later. Also," Josh picked up Robin's shotgun, which was sitting nearby and placed it in the middle of the stretcher.

"The canvas will make it less obvious that I'm lying on something." Riley nodded in understanding.

"It's going to be really uncomfortable," Josh warned her.

"I'm uncomfortable anyway." The more time passed, the less effective the pain medication was, and the more she felt a dull, aching throb from her chest, not to mention the drainage tubes sticking out of her. Just knowing about them made her mentally uncomfortable, and she kept trying to convince herself that they weren't there.

"Can I get a hand over here?" Josh turned to the room.

A woman Riley didn't really know came over with a pillow in one hand and another pillowcase in the other.

"I made this; I thought we could tuck it under your head, claim we have to keep it elevated if they ask." The woman showed Josh and Riley the inside of the pillow. It was stuffed with gauze to give it a pillow shape, but there were also medicines carefully tucked into it as well, and maybe some other items Riley couldn't quite make out. The woman took the second pillow case and slid the first one into it in a reverse fashion so that nothing could slide out. "I'm also going to make one for Max."

"Make one for his head, and one with nothing hard in it for his hips. The ride is going to be really hard on him," Josh told the woman, who nodded and trotted off, leaving the false pillow behind. Max was the only one injured who definitely couldn't walk: his hip was broken in a fall when he slipped from the top of a train car a few days ago.

"You said you needed a hand?" Robin had come up beside them when the lady showed them her trick.

"Yes, we're moving Riley to the stretcher."

Josh helped Riley sit up, which took more energy than she thought it should and made her head swim all over again. Maybe she couldn't walk with support like she thought she could. While Josh gently lifted her upper body, Robin took hold of Riley's legs, and together they slid her over the side of the bed and carefully laid her down on the stretcher. The shotgun pressed annoyingly into Riley's spine, but she was glad for it. She liked having a gun so close. Josh tucked the false pillow under her head, poking at it to make it look natural, while Robin quickly hung the fake IV. The real one stayed attached to Riley's arm for now, but would be unhooked soon when they left. Josh pulled her blanket off the hospital bed and draped it over her before hurrying off to help someone else.

From the floor, Riley watched all the feet scurrying about and thought of Rose. She wondered if this was what it had been like for her when the Diana sank and the medical centre there had to be evacuated. Probably not, as smoke was coming in during that time, raiders threatened to board and shoot them, and Rose herself was delirious from both pain and the medication they had given her in the process of closing the wound that was where her hand had once been. Thinking back to how she had huddled next to Rose, waiting for the stretcher to come back, refusing to leave until her last patient was out, Riley thought that this wasn't so bad. Other than being forced to leave, the worst part was the way everyone avoided looking at her, even though her bandages were covered.

"Okay, time to go," someone by the door said morosely. The last piece of their barricade was slowly pushed away.

Josh returned to Riley's side with another man, unhooked her dripping IV and put the non-dripping one in its place, the bag hanging from a short pole attached to the stretcher.

"On three," Josh spoke to the man Riley thought she recognized but wasn't sure. "One, two, three."

Riley was hoisted into the air by Josh and the other man, the canvas folding partially around her. She did her best to lie in a position that looked natural, to make it appear that nothing was under her, even though the blanket hid the majority of her body. The stranger was near her head, while Josh was by her feet where she could see him. Riley couldn't see much of where they were going as she was being carried head first, so she mostly watched Josh and his expressions, her eyes darting to either side whenever something passed by.

As they exited the medical centre, they walked past an angry brute of a man wearing tactical armour and a scowl. In his hands he held an AK-47, not the most practical weapon against the dead, but it was certainly effective on the living.

"No way, this stays," a woman declared, approaching Riley's stretcher. Josh and the other man nervously stopped as she reached forward and yanked off Riley's blanket. Riley watched her face fall into a disgusted look as she saw Riley's chest. One of her tubes must have drained a bit of fluid at that point, because the woman's face instantly turned into one of utter revulsion as she half-dropped, half-tossed the blanket away from her. "Go, go," she waved them on, her eyes diverting to anywhere else.

As they moved down the hallway, Riley could hear random people being stopped for searches, and even witnessed a few as they passed by. Some items were going to be found, but they weren't stopping everyone and the searches didn't appear to be all that thorough.

Into the stairwell, they passed another guard, this one with an Uzi. A constant stream of people was making its slow way up the stairs as they stepped to one side.

"Hey, keep moving!" the guard barked.

"Give us a second; stretchers aren't easy to carry up stairs," Josh retorted.

"You should be grateful we're giving you that, or the clothes on your backs for that matter."

"Do you want to take care of her?" Josh gestured with his head to Riley.

The guard took a look and then sneered, turning away. "Just hurry up."

Josh gave Riley a wink. The fact that no one wanted to look at her for long was helping them out, but it certainly wasn't doing Riley's self-image any favours.

While Josh and the other man manoeuvred onto the stairs—Josh switching his grip to hold it up near his shoulders and keep the thing as level as possible—Riley searched the crowd for her daughter. Hope would be part of this slow moving train; she just didn't know which part. Riley was aware some of their own would have died during the assault, but she felt in her bones that Hope wasn't one of them. Cameron, Brunt, Abby, and Lauren would protect her just as fiercely as they would their own.

The stretcher moved up the stairs at the same pace as everyone else, so Riley didn't have to worry about people constantly passing by and getting that look on their face. Andrew, a patient of Riley's, joined them after a flight of steps, offering to help Josh with his end. Josh was grateful for the assistance, as the stretcher was wider than his shoulders and it was awkward for him to carry it the way he was. Riley wouldn't mind not being level, but then the shotgun might slide out from underneath her. Andrew didn't seem to mind her bandages or anything, treating her the same way Josh and Robin did. Riley wondered if his stomach was still full of foreign objects due to his compulsive-eating problem, or if he was going through all of this post surgery like she was.

Around and around the staircase they went. Riley spent most of the time looking up the middle, hoping to spy someone she knew. She could tell by the way Josh's head kept swivelling around that he was looking for Anne. Lots of people appeared to be searching for specific others, but no one called out or disrupted the flow of human traffic. At each level, they passed another guard, and more people slowly entered the stream, but none of them was Hope, at least not as Riley went by. Each landing was awkward for the stretcher-bearers as they attempted to keep it level, but after a few they got into a sort of rhythm that worked. Now when Riley looked up the stairwell, she could see the top.

Outside, the train of people continued, heading toward some section of the fence that Riley couldn't see. Two more of the invaders harassed parts of the line, searching for smuggled goods, but none of them approached the stretcher.

Another pair of people showed up and offered to carry the stretcher for a while. Josh and the others agreed, their arms exhausted from all the stairs. For a brief moment, Riley thought she was going to be left alone with people she barely knew so that Josh could go look for Anne, but she was mistaken: Josh merely stepped away to ask another patient how he was doing, then returned to Riley's side.

In a moment of weakness that she disliked herself for, Riley reached out and squeezed his hand. "Don't leave me alone, okay?"

"I don't intend to go anywhere," Josh assured her. "Even if you weren't here, I have other patients in the immediate area who might need me."

Riley wondered if that was true, or if Josh was just saying that to make her feel better, to make her feel less like a burden.

The sun had risen above the horizon as they approached the fence. A rumble like very distant thunder caused the procession to pause. Riley turned her head in the direction of the container yard, sure that the sound had come from there. She also thought she heard an even lighter, less consistent rumbling from, presumably, the same direction, but as others had started moving again, clearly not everyone had heard it. Was it coming from the yard? Or might the river be carrying the sound from somewhere else?

"Keep moving!" one of the invaders barked at her stretcher-bearers

Did the invaders know about the container yard? It was unlikely. Crichton would never have consented to leave so easily without having a refuge. Then what was happening over there?

"Josh?" Riley looked up at him, but he only shook his head in response. Was that because he didn't know, or because he didn't want to risk talking about the container yard with hostiles so close?

They passed through the fence by moving through the cab of a large truck that was imbedded in it. It was difficult to manoeuvre the stretcher through, but Riley bore the jostling in silence, wondering how Max was doing on the other stretcher. Was he ahead of her, or behind? Riley had failed to notice.

Outside the fences there were no assailants, but the flow of people kept moving.

"We're heading the wrong way," Riley whispered, noticing immediately. Although it was quickest and safest to take the boats between the container yard and the Black Box, Riley knew what the overland route was, and this wasn't it.

Josh just shook his head again, but this time his expression was one of confusion.

"It's all right," a voice ahead drifted toward them. "Just keep following the people in front of you, it's okay."

Riley couldn't see who it was until they were next to him.

"Winchester!" she called out.

Winchester startled, stared at her for a moment as he fell behind, then finally recognized her and ran up beside her stretcher.

"Don't worry, we know where we're going," he spoke in a rush, speaking more to Josh than to Riley. "Just follow the others; there's a plan. I don't know what it is, but Bronislav is leading us somewhere. I saw Lauren, Claire, Peter, and Dakota pass by a while ago. They were with your sister and daughter," Winchester briefly looked down at Riley before looking back at Josh. "I haven't seen Abby or Anne yet, but I'm sure they're all right; they're probably just behind you somewhere. Don't stop, just keep walking."

Before any questions could be asked, Winchester disappeared, heading back to where he had been before, urging people to keep moving and telling them that everything would be all right.

Riley wanted to tell her carriers to go faster, to catch up to her daughter wherever she was, but managed to keep her mouth shut. They were all going to the same place; they'd be together in the end.

As soon as the Black Box fences were out of sight, the column left the industrial roads and buildings to head into the woods. Robin came over and retrieved her shotgun from beneath Riley, bringing a relief that

Riley hadn't realized how badly she needed. Looking to one side, she spotted a fairly large and freshly dug hole. As she was pondering it, they passed another: this one with a man squatting down beside it. An unfolded tarp lined the bottom of this second hole, and the man was handing out baseball bats, crowbars, and bladed weapons evenly along the line.

Weapons cache, Riley realized as the hole disappeared behind them. She didn't see any guns though. Ammo was probably too precious to waste by having it buried out here. Still, some weapons were better than no weapons, and the tarp would come in handy. She hoped the first hole had been filled with the same, or maybe with food, and that it wasn't just a hole they dug in the wrong spot as they looked for the cache.

In a clearing, a fairly large group of people had stopped to rest. Without much sleep the night before, the long walk was wearing on them. A few sat around in their pyjamas, captives who hadn't had a chance to dress properly, but more were stripping off extra layers they had put on in order to get more clothing out. Riley's stretcher was briefly put down again, as another set of volunteers took over.

"Riley!"

She twisted her head around to find the source of the familiar voice, and spotted Brunt jogging toward her just as the new volunteers begin pressing onward. Riley didn't even need to reach out, as Brunt quickly scooped up her hand as soon as he had fallen in beside her. She was pretty sure he was checking her pulse.

"Good to see you got out okay," he said, grinning.

"Hope?"

"She's up ahead with Cameron and the others. I've been searching the line for you. Want me to go get her?"

"Yes." Riley felt confined on the stretcher. She wanted to get up and find Hope herself, but the moment she tried to rise, her head began to swim again and Josh gently pushed her back down.

"All right, I'll be back." Brunt took off running up the line, dodging around people and plants alike.

"What's wrong?" Riley frowned up at Josh whose concerned look put a damper on her good mood. "Is it something about the container yard?"

"I'm thinking about what Winchester said and wondering why Abby isn't with Lauren."

Riley hadn't realized how odd that was until he said it. Abby *should* have been with Lauren and the others, so why wasn't she? Was she okay?

"And yes, I'm thinking about the container yard as well. We didn't want to tell you before your surgery, but there was word that a group was heading there to attack them as well. The yard was forewarned and prepared, unlike us, but we have no idea if the two groups are somehow related. And that rumble... I have no idea what caused that, but it could have been from that direction, and if it was, that means there's still a battle going on."

"Is that why we're heading the wrong way?" Riley wanted to get angry for not being told, but she knew she would have done the same thing if she and her sister had changed places.

"I don't know. I don't know where we're going. I don't know if anyone has heard from the container yard since the attack over there was supposed to happen. I don't know anything, it seems."

Riley fidgeted and picked at her nails as she absorbed the information.

"Mom!"

Riley did her best to look around, raising her head as high as she could and turning it to look forward, both Josh and pain preventing her from twisting her torso.

"Mom?" Hope called, moving down the line alone, running ahead of the others, searching through faces.

"Hope! I'm here, sweet pea!" Riley called back, doing her best to wave her arm, but she couldn't rotate at the shoulder very much.

"Hope, over here," Josh added.

The girl came dashing up to them, a large smile of relief on her face. Riley wanted nothing more than to hug her daughter, but her limited range of motion, and the bandages and drainage tubes around her chest prevented it. Instead, she merely squeezed Hope's shoulders with her hands, grateful that her stretcher-bearers had stopped for the moment. Hope clasped her smaller hands around one of Riley's elbows and squeezed back as hard as she could.

"Look, I got my slingshot out," Hope proudly told Riley, pulling it out of the pocket of her pants once they started moving again. "Me, Peter, and Dakota have been finding rocks and things we can use in it. Dakota has hers too."

"That's good. That's very good."

As the rest of the group showed up, Riley was told the story of how they had started to leave, but got stopped before reaching the stairwell. Abby was separated from them at that point, and no one knew what happened to her. Once they had reached the suite of rooms, they barricaded the door behind them. Cameron, Brunt, and Lauren stayed out in the living room, while Claire took Hope, Peter, and Dakota into Peter's room, where they moved his bunk bed to block that door. The kids were given orders not to open the door unless one of the adults gave a special knock.

"I'm going to go look for Abby," Brunt said as soon as the group had settled into the pace of the stretcher-bearers.

"Can you search for Anne as well?" Josh asked him.

"Of course."

Riley didn't know if Brunt had ever met Anne, but he must have at least known what she looked like because he didn't ask.

"Thank you," Riley told Cameron and Lauren for what they had done for Hope. The two women brushed her thanks aside, as a lot of people in the march would have done the same thing. Riley thanked them again anyway.

A little farther along, Riley spotted a corpse among some tree roots. Its head was caved in, but the impact had happened long ago based on the dryness of the blood and brains. Riley wondered who had been the one to kill it, whether it was someone from the Black Box or not, and again wondered where they were going.

***

Brunt returned with both Abby and Anne, eliciting a happy response at the reunion. Neither of them knew where they were going either, and both told the group what had happened to them. Anne had been barricaded in one of the hydroponics labs, having gotten outside and witnessed the fire fight the sentries were in before being turned around. The hydroponics lab she ended up in had several tools she and others were able to use to secure the door. Other labs hadn't been so lucky, as the invaders were able to break their way in. Several people around Anne had been able to smuggle out seeds and a few clippings, but she had been searched, her pockets turned out and emptied, a woman even checking her bra. Unlike the medical centre, there was nothing like tape or bandages to secure the supplies in unusual places.

Abby told her story about being captured and the interrogation. Before the Day, she might have glossed over some of those details with the kids present, but now they needed to know that stuff like that happened. Josh checked over her wounds as best he could and decided that there was nothing serious.

A little while later, Brunt and Josh relieved Riley's stretcher-bearers. Cameron and Lauren offered to assist them, badgering the men by saying that having four people carrying would be easier than just two until they relented. Hope stayed by Riley's side, holding her hand the whole time.

"I think we're heading toward the ocean," Anne declared after many footfalls of silence.

"My sense of direction is terrible, but I think she's right," Abby agreed. "I believe we're angling toward it."

"But we're on the wrong side of the Black Box," Josh commented.

"Maybe we're circling around," Claire offered. "You know, so they can't follow us to the container yard?"

"Then why head toward the sea? Why not head straight east before hooking north?" Cameron wondered.

"Maybe it's easier to walk along the coast." Brunt shrugged with the arm not carrying Riley. "Or maybe there's another cache of gear and supplies out there."

They had passed a small group of people digging another hole. The majority of the unburied weapons went to the front of the column where they might stumble into a horde, while a large chunk of the remainder was held onto for the back, because a gathering was likely to come from behind them, drawn by the sounds of the march. Still, their little group had been given a baseball bat, which Anne was carrying, and Robin wasn't far away with her shotgun. If a big group of the dead showed up, their best option was to run, but a handful they could probably deal with.

"People are clumping up ahead of us," Dakota called out from where she was picking her own trail through the trees to their right, scrambling up and over some large rocks. "I think they're stopping past the trees. Maybe it's the ocean?"

"We'll see when we get there," Cameron told her, the nervousness in her voice obvious to Riley even if it wasn't to the others.

Riley wanted to twist around, to try to peer through the trees herself and see what was ahead, but she couldn't. She had only enough energy to keep awake, listen to the nearby conversations, and on the rare occasion add to them.

It was still a couple of minutes before they were in direct sunlight, the trees falling away behind them. Dakota had been right: people were clumping up and stopping, while the ocean crashed close by.

"Oh wow," Lauren was the first to say something.

"What? What is it?" Riley wanted to know, able to see only people's backsides.

Instead of answering, Lauren and Brunt guided their little group around and through the gathering of people, making for the water. Once they were in the clear, Riley saw it. Although everyone had been told that it was destroyed, the German submarine was floating in the water, secured to the docks of what might have been a factory at one time. People were making their way down the shore toward the docks, where they were being loaded onto it one at a time.

"They didn't scuttle it," Abby breathed, as amazed to see it as Riley was.

"That's one hell of a secret to keep," Josh barked, half-annoyed and half-excited.

"I'm sure they had their reasons," Anne insisted.

"I'm guessing she still runs if they're loading us aboard," Brunt commented. "We'll be able to get to the yard much faster now. Come on, we should get Riley there before all the bunks get filled up. We don't want to have to balance her on the hull outside."

With the stretcher between them, people were willing to part for the little group, although some grudgingly. For once, people were looking directly at Riley, either trying to decide if her wounds were bad enough to need the stretcher, or enviously wondering if they should wish the same injury upon themselves in order to get ahead of the line.

Bronislav himself stood at the end of the dock, keeping everyone orderly as they boarded the submarine. A few people stood around, delaying boarding as they looked for certain people, but most formed a ragged line and got on when they were told.

"You son of a bitch," Josh called to Bronislav with a huge grin on his face.

Bronislav merely shrugged in response and continued to move the line slowly forward and onto the sub.

"Are we going to go under the sea?" Hope whispered to Riley, the girl's grip tightening around her mother's hand.

"No, sweet pea," Riley assured her. "We won't be diving under; there are too many people to fit inside. Some are going to be sitting on top."

"Good."

Riley wondered what she was thinking about, but there was no time to ask. She and her daughter had to be split up while they hoisted Riley aboard. As she was raised above the heads of the crowd, she spotted Max's stretcher not far behind them and was oddly glad for it. She also saw a group of people with bladed weapons holding back a large but spaced-out horde of zombies that was staggering out of the nearby cluster of buildings. Hopefully, it never got worse than it currently looked.

After strapping her to the stretcher via her waist, arms, and legs, Riley was finally made vertical so that she could be lowered through the opening at the top of the conning tower. There were still so many people waiting to get aboard, she worried that they wouldn't all be able to fit, even when clustering up on the hull. She quickly put that out of her mind though. Hope was right behind her while the rest of the small group she cared for was making their way on board. As Riley sank into the belly of the sub, she hoped she'd be able to get some more sleep before arriving at the container yard. If there was to be another battle, she wanted to be on her feet for it.

31
Nessie's Wired

On the container farthest from the battle, Nessie switched her thin sword from her right hand to the other. Her hands were sweaty, her fingers slick on the handle. She wiped them off on her shirt and then returned the blade back to her dominant hand, plucking her sheath of a cane from where it stuck out of the side of her rubber boot. She liked to hold the body of the cane in her other hand as it would make a good bludgeoning tool should she need it.

"I don't like how close they're getting," old Willard grumbled beside her, just loudly enough to be heard over the gunfire, screams, shouts, and moans.

"I can't see them," Nessie admitted, the containers and people on them blocking her view of the zombies once they were over the high wall.

Willard shifted his grip on the big revolver he held. "Neither can I, but you can see the people easily enough. I don't like how much they've backed toward us, how many of them have been forced to crowd together over there."

Nessie immediately understood what he meant. She hadn't noticed it herself, but now that Willard pointed it out, it was easy to tell how far the zombies had pressed into their ranks by looking at where the greatest number of people were gathered. She turned and looked at the community centre, where the strangers and former enemies picked off anything that came around that side. Again, Nessie stuck her sheath into her boot so that she could hold her sword with her off-hand while wiping the sweat from the other.

"So, why'd you stay?" Nessie asked Willard to have something else to think about. He was definitely old enough and frail enough to have been allowed to cross the bridge with the others. The hand holding the revolver shook half the time, and Nessie often wondered if he'd be able to lift and fire it.

"Because I'm old," Willard answered. "They should have put me at the front. Let me die instead of the young kids. You?"

"I'm still too fit to send away," Nessie told him, although she would have stayed even if she weren't. There was a lot of grey hair and many teens not yet fully grown along the back line. She hoped they weren't going to be needed, especially the young ones. She felt ashamed to have been put in the farthest corner, but that's where she had been assigned, so that's where she stayed. The only people farther from the action were those put on top of the outhouses, as least as far as she could tell. If any zombies got past the far side of the community centre, however, then Nessie would be the farthest.

A wordless cry went up from somewhere near the middle of the pack, but whether it was a good cry or not, Nessie couldn't tell. Taking her whetstone out of her pocket, she sharpened her blade again, although it certainly didn't need it. She wished she had her knitting needles to keep her hands occupied. Maybe if she had taken the metal ones, she could have sharpened them into deadly points, so that way they were also useful as weapons. If they survived this encounter, sharpening them might not be a terrible idea.

A louder cry went up, and this one was definitely cheerful.

"What's going on?" Nessie asked Willard while squinting at the backs of the front lines.

"I can't tell," Willard answered, his worse eyes squinting even more.

Thankfully it didn't take long for word to travel to them. Apparently, one of the zombie piles had stopped sending new corpses over the wall. Now there were only two or three, one of which they thought might be petering off. Nessie hooted when she heard the news and couldn't help but dance a little in her boots. Finally, some news other than the front line being pushed back. Maybe they could do it; maybe they could hold off this horde.

Nessie looked around to see all the other hopeful faces. As her eyes swept past the shoreline, she spotted something that stopped her cold. A tiny figure was crawling around on the rocks. The size and co-ordination were definitely that of a toddler. Had he or she been forgotten somehow, or fallen in the water off Animal Island and gotten lucky with the current? Either way, the tot was not in a safe place.

"Help me with the ladder," Nessie turned to Willard.

"What? Why? Did someone fall off the container?" He grabbed hold of the metal with her and helped swing it over the side.

"There's a kid," she pointed with her sword.

"You sure that's a living kid?" Willard squinted again as he helped lever the ladder upright.

"No, but I'm not going to do nothing, because there's a chance it is."

"Be careful."

Nessie sheathed her sword to climb down. "You're welcome to come."

Willard shook his head. "I'll guard the ladder for your return."

The moment Nessie's boots hit the pavement, she questioned her decision. From down there, she couldn't see the toddler who had been down the slope of rocks near the water. Remembering when her niece had been that age, and then how Nessie hadn't been able to protect her on the Day, she stepped away from the ladder. Drawing her sword, Nessie moved toward the rocks.

When she reached the top of the jumble of stones, the boy—for that's what the haircut suggested—had nearly crawled his way high enough to meet her.

"Child, are you all right?" Nessie asked, remaining on the pavement as she never trusted her footing among the boulders and pebbles.

The boy looked up with an unfamiliar face, his skin pale and his eyes yellow. Nessie sighed.

"I'm sorry for what happened to you," she told the small thing as it rose to its feet and stumbled toward her with outstretched hands and a yawning mouth. The moment the zombie child came close enough, Nessie thrust the tip of her sword between its eyes, being as gentle as she could while still penetrating the skull. When she withdrew the blade, the boy fell backward onto the rocks.

Shouting from behind drew Nessie's attention. Several of her too old and too young companions had gathered along the backs of the containers and were pointing, while Willard was making gestures for her to hurry back. Nessie looked toward the water and saw that the zombie boy was not alone. A dozen or more sopping wet corpses were staggering out of the water, tripping and crawling up the rocks.

For the first time in a long while, Nessie ran. Her boots slapped against the pavement, as a stitch formed in her side. Reaching the ladder, she nearly collapsed, out of breath, and narrowly avoided cutting herself with her sword as she sheathed it again.

"Hurry up," Willard encouraged her as she grabbed the sides of the ladder. As soon as her cane was high enough, he plucked it from her fingers, letting her get a better grip to climb the last few rungs. Gunfire rattled from much closer by as people fired upon the water-logged dead. As she pulled herself up onto the container's top, she rolled to watch them coming. The aim of those firing was terrible, mostly planting useless body shots the times they didn't miss. Together, she and Willard pulled the ladder back up.

"How many shots do you have for that thing?" Nessie asked through gulps of air. All her joints ached in a way she had forgotten they could.

"Only the six currently loaded," Willard admitted. He hadn't fired a shot yet, waiting until the things were closer so that he wouldn't miss and waste a bullet.

Nessie swallowed a hard lump, trying to catch her breath before she needed to use her blade again. Finally, a headshot landed, and then a second close behind it. One after another the zombies fell, the shots no longer missing. Nessie looked along the containers and saw Misha and his dogs standing among a group of youths, most of whom didn't look old enough to be there. The young were loading and handing him their single-shot rifles so that Misha could fire one bullet after another. His aim was a lot better, missing as infrequently as the others hit their target. When one of the teens called that he was out of bullets, an elder took his place. The zombies were coming out of the water so slowly that Misha was doing most of the shooting. Only a couple of people at the far end needed to take care of the ones down there. By the time Nessie was feeling better, albeit still a little woozy, the water walkers and swimmers had stopped coming. If there were more in there, they hadn't found their way to the rocky shore, most likely sinking into the gorge. Hopefully, the current would prevent any other potential swimmers from making it to Animal Island.

Actually using her cane for its intended purpose, Nessie made her way to the other side of the container row. She scanned the backs of the congestion of people, trying to determine if they had been pushed closer, moved farther away, or were in the same place. She wasn't able to tell, so she assumed they hadn't moved. Looking along the ground between her container row and the next, she saw no corpses, moving or otherwise. Toward the far end, a container had been placed to bridge the gap, although there was still room for zombies to get by on either side.

The sun beat down unrelentingly. Nessie's run had dislodged the headscarf she had donned before the battle, so she took the time to readjust it. Not everyone was properly attired to be spending this much time in the sun; a lot were going to end up with some pretty bad sunburns. Nessie could already see patches of angry red forming in the exposed sections of skin of those nearest to her. She wondered if her own light coverings were enough, or if some part of her was burning as well.

Gunfire from the community centre had been relatively infrequent, so when it picked up in tempo, Nessie turned her attention toward the structure. What she saw dashed any hopes she had begun to hold onto. A sudden swarm of the dead must have come staggering around the containers between it and the wall, for they were surrounding the building rather quickly. Those on the containers nearest the community centre were firing at the corpses, but this particular group of dead seemed only interested in the people on the roof. Their recently formed allies were raining bullets down upon the rotting heads below, but it took surprisingly little time for them to become an island in a sea of dead flesh. Beyond them, the defenders on the toilets huddled fearfully at the back, nearly falling into the river. As Nessie watched, the emergency hatch to a repurposed storage container was pulled open and a ladder shoved through the hole. Those who had remained prisoners hastily scrabbled out, spurred on by the hands slamming into the walls of the container, afraid one might get the outer latch to open. Once up the ladder, the people continued to clamber upward, making for the higher safety of the roof.

A furry brush against her leg drew Nessie's gaze downward. One of the dogs had come over and was watching the community centre alongside her. When she looked up again, she saw that Misha, sweaty and panting beneath his hood, was perched on the container's edge only a couple of feet away.

"Can you shoot that distance?" Willard asked him.

"Easily, it's no farther than the rocks."

Willard held his revolver out to the man, his hand trembling.

Misha glanced at the gun but didn't take it. "You might need that. I'm going to move to the closer containers."

And just like that, Misha was gone again, crossing a ladder bridge to the next row. Two of his dogs were smart enough to run around to the container bridge in order to follow him, while the others whined and danced at the ladder's edge. One dog hadn't made to follow at all. The German Shepherd with the grey muzzle gently lowered himself to the metal with a loud groan, and then began panting heavily.

"You too, huh?" Nessie remarked to the dog. "Age sucks."

The nearby youths all left their posts to gather around Nessie and watch the community centre. She would have attempted to order them back, but unless zombies came out of the bay again, it didn't matter where they stood. Besides, the elderly all remained in place, watching both the water and the alley between the container rows. They would bellow if something showed up, and the young teens definitely had enough energy to swiftly spring back into place.

Nessie returned her gaze to the community centre. She had begun to notice a lessening of gunfire from all around the yard. Were there fewer zombies to kill? Were they in less danger so people took more time to aim? Or were they running out of ammo? She watched as the last of the prisoners hauled himself up onto the roof, the gentle metal slopes now crowded with breathing bodies, some forced to sit gently on the solar panels to make enough room. As two people hauled up the ladder that connected the roof to the holding containers, a third man picked up the rifle one of them had put down. Nessie didn't know why her attention had been drawn specifically to him, but it had been. While she watched, he checked that there was ammo in the magazine, and a bullet in the chamber. He then levelled the gun toward Nessie and the kids.

That couldn't be right, surely he was just pressing the gun to his shoulder and would aim down at the zombies in a second. Only he didn't. The man rested his cheek up close to the rifle, peering down the sights.

"No! Get back!" Nessie screamed, turning and shoving whatever kid she could lay her hands on, knocking over several of them.

There was no way to tell which *crack* came from the man's rifle, but Nessie felt the bullet punch into her hip. A hot slug of metal burned into her, the pain twisting her body so that when she fell, she landed on her back. Adrenaline kept her focused long enough to watch as the man's own people turned on him, trying to grab him and wrestle the gun away. In the struggle, he fell off the roof, and not on a side where there were containers.

As a pain-filled darkness closed in over Nessie, she hoped he survived the fall long enough to feel himself get torn apart by the dead. As the young ones gathered around her, fearfully shouting at each other, not knowing what to do with their extremely limited medical knowledge, she thought of Dragon. *Would he miss me?*

32
Doyle's Not In Charge

With Canary still hugged up to his side, Doyle continued to follow James in an arc around the Black Box fences. They rested a few times while James scurried off to get a look at the place, but each time he came back with bad news. Unfamiliar men and women were patrolling the fences, and a little while ago, black smoke began to rise from a body burn site. James couldn't get close enough to see who was dead, but he confirmed that there weren't many.

"Where are we goin'?" Rose finally asked in a whisper that Doyle thought sounded harsher than she meant.

"We need to check something," James told them, continuing to lead them in a direction that Doyle had never been.

"Check what?" Rose was agitated. A couple of times a zombie appeared, and although James was closer, she insisted on being the one to crush its skull with her hammer.

"If our people are inside or out."

"How will you be able to tell that?" Doyle asked this time.

"You'll see, we're almost there."

James was right; it hadn't been much longer. They reached the woods where clearly a bunch of people had been through recently, the foliage trampled flat.

"They evacuated," James spoke through a sigh of relief.

"Why come this way?" Canary wondered. Her breathing had become harder as the day went on despite the frequent rest stops. Her leg pained her; she was supposed to be with doctors by now.

"Because the submarine is docked this way," James told them.

Doyle, Canary, and Rose literally paused for a moment, letting James get an extra two steps ahead.

"What do you mean, the submarine?" Rose spoke louder than she should, a bit of anger now mixing with the irritation.

"We never scuttled the German U-boat. Not many know, only the crew and enough trusted others to send someone to check on it every couple of days and after storms. You probably didn't see any of it, but there were a lot of arguments surrounding the sub. Should it stay at the Black Box, or go with the others to the container yard? Should they search for torpedoes and missiles to rearm it? Should it always be crewed and ready to go? Crichton got worried that someone was going to steal it; that's how bad it got. So, he made a plan with Bronislav to make everyone think it sank. They went on a mission up the coast, as they had before, only this time they went when a storm was expected; the weather guys actually got it right. And when the crew came back on foot, no one suspected their story was a lie."

"That's insane," Rose huffed.

"You wouldn't think so if you heard how vehemently some people wanted to turn the thing into a weapons platform. Those houses we were exploring? They would probably be ash by now if they had gotten their way. And let's not forget about the nuclear core. Could you imagine if someone snapped and then got into the sub? Think of how much damage they could do, even just by creating a leak in the casing."

Rose responded with silence. Doyle didn't know what she was thinking, but he was remembering the bomb on the Diana. No one had been able to prove beyond a doubt that the woman named Hanna had set it off, but even if she had, no one knew why. James was talking about someone like her when he talked about someone snapping. If it really was Hanna, and she had really been working alone as it seemed, that meant a single person had brought about the Diana's eventual destruction. Crichton would certainly not risk a similar incident happening at the Black Box, which was why the power generator in the basement was always on lock down; only those who needed to get in there to monitor it were allowed through the heavy, metal door.

Deep in thought, Doyle didn't notice the hole until he stumbled into it, Canary drawing in a sharp hiss as she was pulled along.

"Sorry," Doyle whispered, and then repeated himself several times until Canary told him to stop.

"Looks like they dug up the cache. There's probably going to be more of these holes along the way, so watch your step." James continued to lead them deeper into the forest.

Doyle was tired and his shoulders hurt from helping Canary along. He could only imagine how she felt, hobbling through the woods. They were both sweating, but her skin had taken on a sickly look and texture that he didn't like.

"How far is the sub?" Doyle asked.

"Still a ways off, why?" James glanced over his shoulder, his eyes falling on Canary and then he knew why.

Doyle answered anyway. "We should probably take another rest then."

"No." Canary shook her head, her yellow hair falling lankly about her face. "This trail isn't all that old; I don't think it's been very long since they came through here. If we hurry, we'll catch them."

Both Doyle and James frowned at this.

"Why don't James and I go ahead while you two take a break?" Rose suggested.

Canary shook her head again. "We should stick together; we don't know what kind of dangers might be in these woods. I'm okay, we need to keep going."

Even though no one but Canary seemed to like the idea, they pressed on.

It was shady and slightly breezy beneath the trees, which was nice compared to the direct sun, but the bugs were bad. Between Canary and his fire axe, Doyle didn't have a hand with which to defend himself.

"I'm sorry," Canary mumbled.

"For what?" Doyle wondered as he slowly batted another mosquito away with the head of his axe.

"Mosquitoes have always loved me. You wouldn't be bothered by them so much if you weren't helping me along."

"Nonsense, we're in the woods, there are always mosquitoes." Although Doyle had to admit that there were more than when he had walked alone at the start of their outing. He blamed it on the storm awhile back; the bugs always got worse after the rain. They loved the damp ground.

"Zombie," Rose whispered, trotting off ahead of them to take it down.

"When—" Canary didn't get to finish whatever she was going to say.

"Jesus Christ!" Rose gave a startled cry.

James put on a burst of speed and leapt through the brush. Doyle wanted to run to Rose as well, but he and Canary couldn't move any faster than they were already. Doyle hefted his axe up into a ready position, while Canary raised the copper pipe that had wounded her so badly.

It didn't take long to discover what had startled Rose. There wasn't just one zombie, but at least a dozen, hidden from their sight by a large rock and a couple of thick tree trunks. Rose and James were busily hacking away at them by the time Doyle and Canary got there. They stood back and watched, ready in case one got past or came from another direction. There was no need to worry, however, as James and Rose massacred the whole lot.

"Are you bit?" James asked Rose when the final corpse fell.

"No, they just startled the shit outta me is all."

Still, James scanned her extremities and gave her the all clear. That didn't mean she hadn't gotten something in her mouth or eyes, and James as well for that matter, but there was no way to be certain if they said nothing. Wiping his blade off on some low bushes as he walked past, James moved them forward.

***

The walk was long, hot, buggy, and, mostly in Canary's case, painful, but when they noticed the sounds of the sea growing louder, their spirits lifted. Even Canary managed to pick up the pace a little. They had taken only one break since entering the forest. In a clearing, they had found a good log over which the women could empty their bladders; James and Doyle used the bushes on the opposite side. Based on the smell, it was obvious that those who had left the Black Box used the log for the same purpose.

When the ocean finally came into view, they headed straight for it, stepping off the well-trodden path. Although no one said it, they all knew they had missed the group and likely the boat as well. Rose forged ahead, reaching the shore first to see if the submarine was still in view. They may have decided to wait awhile in case Doyle and his small group returned.

As Doyle and Canary cleared the trees, they could tell by Rose's posture that the submarine was gone.

"It might be that speck way out there, but it's far enough that I can't tell."

James used his binoculars and agreed with Rose's assessment. It very likely was the U-boat, but there was no way they could let it know they were there, let alone get to it.

"Put me down. Put me down." Canary sank to the pebble beach, sliding off Doyle's shoulders.

"You might want to stand back up; there's some dead over toward those buildings," James told her, his eyes still hidden behind the binoculars but now he was scanning the shoreline. Doyle could make out the buildings, but not the dead.

"I need a rest. They're far away and won't notice us over here," Canary panted.

"Might be good to wash that leg o'yours in the salt water," Rose suggested.

"I know *I* could certainly use a soak." Doyle was used to feeling gross when on the move and dealing with the dead, but he preferred being clean.

"Why don't the three of you take a quick bath? I'm going to head toward the dock there, see if a note or something has been left for us." James stripped out of his pack, keeping only his weapons with him.

"I should come with you," Rose volunteered.

"I think it's best you stay with Doyle and Canary in case something wanders over here. Besides, you stink," he said, grinning. He then got up and disappeared back between the trees.

"Well I'm going in," Canary said, breaking the brief silence, and started to peel off her shirt.

Doyle's face turned red and Rose laughed at him.

"Look, he's all embarrassed," Rose teased. "Settle down, boy, underwear is no different than a bikini."

"I find most underwear to be more modest than most bikinis," Canary added, although she was simply stating it, not teasing Doyle. "Rose, mind helping me get these pants off?"

"It's gonna hurt, you sure you don't wanna leave them on?"

"No, they need to come off."

"All right."

Rose gently helped Canary while Doyle stripped down to his boxers. He waded into the shallows first, scanning for underwater threats, his axe in hand. The rocks were slippery, but easily gripped with his toes. After Rose had stripped down, she helped Canary into the water, their weapons sitting as close as possible without getting soaked. Outside of a hostile human with a gun, they had good enough sight lines to reach the items before a danger could reach them. Canary sat on the rocks where the water was just deep enough to slosh over her hips. She drew in a sharp hiss as her wound submerged.

"Watch out for sharks," Doyle warned Rose as she went deeper. "Canary's blood might draw them."

"Yeah, yeah," she said back, waving her stump at him.

It was nice to be able to talk above a whisper, the slapping waves covering them.

"The sea's calm today," Canary commented as Doyle waded shallower and sat down nearby, holding his axe draped across his shoulders, away from the water.

"That's good for the submarine." Doyle used one hand to scoop up water and rinse off his upper body, focusing mostly on his shoulder where he had been punctured by the nail.

Out where it was deeper, Rose dove beneath the surface.

"She should be careful of the undertow," Canary commented when the other woman's head popped back up.

"Try telling her that," Doyle chuckled.

Rose didn't stay in the deep for long, soon swimming over to them. She kept low in the water, using her hand and stump to pull herself along the rocks and looking like a strange, red-haired crocodile.

"Think there might be alligators around here?" Rose asked as she found a spot she liked, thinking along the same lines Doyle was.

"I doubt it." Canary shook her head as she inspected the wrappings around her wound. "Alligators tend to stick to fresh water from my understanding. Now salt water crocodiles I'm less sure of; I can't remember if there are any in the Americas or not."

"Salt water crocodiles?" Doyle hadn't heard of them.

"I liked watching the Discovery channel growing up. They're the really big ones."

"There might be alligators," Rose continued. "They get weird when they get infected."

"True," Canary nodded this time. "I still don't think there will be any here though. Don't they usually crawl out on land and start walking around when they get infected? I've never heard of one being found in the salt water."

"Sharks are what we have to worry about," Doyle told Rose again.

"And zombies," she added.

"Always zombies, and always people."

Doyle got out of the water first, letting the sun dry him off before getting dressed again. He kept his eyes roving along the shore and tree lines, watching for both threats and James. He was relieved when James showed up first, but surprised that he wasn't alone. The man with him carried a large pack and had a familiar face, definitely someone from around the Black Box, but Doyle didn't personally know him.

"Doyle, I think you know Jamal?" James introduced them once they were close enough to talk comfortably.

"I've seen you around but I can't say we ever really spoke. Hey," Doyle held out his hand and shook the one offered back in return.

"Right, you weren't at the prison," James suddenly remembered. "Jamal was one of our ward heads, so most people would know him from there."

"Were you one of the people at the...what was it? A hotel?"

"I think it was a motel," James corrected.

"No, Canary and I," Doyle gestured to Canary so the man would know who he was talking about, "are from a third party. We're from Leighton though. We managed to overhear your guys' transmissions and learned about the plane, so we made our own way there."

"I didn't know that," James said, surprised.

"Were you with Robin?" Jamal asked.

"Yeah, she was with us."

"Wonderful, I thought I recognized the story. I sometimes help out in the medical centre so I know her."

"So that must mean you have some medical training. Canary got hurt; a piece of copper pipe went through her leg yesterday. Can you take a look?"

"Sure, although I'm not a doctor; I just have field medic training. I was left with some medical supplies in case you guys showed up wounded, although I didn't think it would be so soon. Had you been maybe two hours earlier, you could've caught the sub."

By then Rose had helped Canary out of the water. She was lowered gently to the rocks where Jamal could inspect her leg.

"So it's as I guessed," James told Doyle, loud enough for Rose and Canary to listen in if they wanted. "Some group showed up and managed to storm the Black Box. They somehow got into the vehicle elevator shaft and were able to attack from both ends. Crichton was captured, and after a while ordered an orange level evacuation to prevent anyone else from getting killed. Not many died, but some have. They were led here, where Bronislav and Crichton knew the sub would be waiting. Jamal was left behind to look for us and watch for anyone from the attacking force who might be following their trail."

"Does he have a safe place for us to hide out while we make plans?" Doyle asked.

James shook his head. "He was up a tree. If he hadn't started throwing small sticks at me, I never would have spotted him. With Canary's leg, hiding up trees isn't really an option for us."

"So we should go look for a place."

"I'll come," Rose immediately volunteered.

"You're not even dressed yet," James pointed out.

"I will be soon," she retorted as she buttoned up her pants.

"I may end up needing an extra set of hands here," Jamal told them.

"Hands, emphasis on the plural," Rose immediately pointed out before James could use it as an argument against her, waving her stump for added effect. Doyle wondered why James seemed to be keeping Rose back more lately.

"Rose and I can find a place," Doyle offered. "James, you already know the area somewhat, so it's probably best you stay with Canary and Jamal in case you end up needing to run."

"All right." James sat down on the rocks without a word of argument. Doyle never could predict him.

"Grab some food first," Jamal advised them. "In the front pocket of my bag there should be some dried fruit and grains. Not great, but it's all they were able to leave me with."

While Rose strapped on her homemade prosthetic, Doyle got the food. The stuff in the front pocket was neatly organized into little cloth and leather bags, as well as a few surviving Ziplocs. He grabbed a Ziploc for himself and a leather bag for Rose. He knew she could use the fasteners to tie the bag open on her hip and eat one handed.

"We'll head away from the building, unless you think you might know a good area?" Doyle asked James.

"We didn't explore much to either side, so I have no advice for you. Sorry."

Leaving their gear behind and taking only their weapons, Doyle and Rose headed down the shore. The closer they could find a place to the water the better, just in case the sub came back for some reason.

"Well, this trip has certainly been a lot more than I bargained for," Doyle commented to Rose as they walked.

"If you're blamin' yourself, stop it," Rose told him unexpectedly. "No one coulda predicted half the stuff we ran into out here, let alone all of it together."

"Yeah, but for books?"

"So? People like books, why not get a supply of them? Besides, both you and I know this was not entirely about the books. You just needed to get out beyond the fences again, like I did."

Doyle had no argument for her.

"If it was your fault, then my arm is my own fault. No one blames me for that, not even myself anymore, so you gotta suck it up. Shit just happens, and sometimes it all happens at once. Stop the pity parties."

"Are you deliberately trying to sound like a sergeant from some movie?" Doyle was smiling despite himself.

"Little bit, yeah," Rose grinned at him. "Is it workin'?"

"Surprisingly so."

They had walked on a little farther when Rose thought she spotted something through the trees. Doyle followed her into the brush, where they came across a long-dead tree lying across the forest floor. Following it to its crown of brittle branches, they discovered another tree that had partly fallen. This second tree hadn't quite made it to the ground, as it had fallen against a hill at its backside. The torn-up root ball of the second tree tangled with the branches of the first. Doyle spotted bare rock beneath them both and thought there might be a sort of cave.

"Looks dry in there as far as I can tell," Doyle commented. He couldn't see much beneath the second tree, but it was on the start of the slope, so any water should run out down the rock. It must have been a very strong wind to knock the tree over in the direction it had.

"I'm goin' in." Rose crawled a little awkwardly with her prosthetic, and some of the old branches snapped loudly around her, but she got inside. "This is great." Her voice was faint.

"Yeah? I can't see you."

"Then it's perfect. We should be safe inside while we figure out what to do." Rose scrambled out, snapping fewer branches this time. Those she had broken, she brought with her and piled up on top of the others. "It's even bigger than it looks out here."

"Let's go get the others then."

By the time they returned to where their friends were sitting, Jamal had done all he could for Canary's leg, as well as looked at her hand. According to him, she should be all right if allowed to rest and keep off it, provided an infection didn't set in; he had given her the mere antibiotics he had but washing it regularly with seawater should help. After gathering up all their gear, the five of them went back to the deadfall and crawled inside. Rose was right: it was bigger once inside, a hollow in the rocks forming a natural cave in the hillside beyond the roots. Jamal had been given one of the large tarps that formerly protected a cache from the elements, so they took it out in case they needed to protect themselves from the same thing.

"You look nervous," Doyle told James.

"I don't like having only one way out is all, and we probably won't be able to hear if anything is moving around outside."

"Do you want to look for someplace else?"

"No, I doubt we'll find anything better than this."

"So what's our plan?" Canary asked from the darkest corner, where Rose was helping her get comfortable.

James turned to Jamal. "Were you expected to walk back, or is the U-boat supposed to return for you?"

"The sub is supposed to come back in a week."

"A *week*?" That sounded like a very long time to Doyle.

"There's enough food provided we ration. Other than the tarp and what few medical supplies I have, that bag is stuffed with as much food from the caches as we could fit."

"It would probably take us a week to walk to the container yard anyway, what with having to circle around the Black Box," James sighed.

"Will Canary be okay for that long?" Doyle asked.

"She should be fine, as long as we keep her hydrated."

"Is there a clean water source nearby?" Doyle wondered next.

"Not far from that tree where James found me is a fresh water stream. It should be all right if we boil it, and if you don't want to risk the fire, I don't think small sips will kill us."

"No, it'll just kill us with dysentery," Rose commented.

"We'll make a small fire for boiling," James decided, "but we'll build it beside the sea, away from our camp here. We should also keep our eyes open for anyone from that hostile group following the trail. It's really easy to tell which way we've gone; they'll be able to follow it even after a few days."

"That's partly why I was to wait here a week," Jamal nodded.

"We should send someone to spy on the Black Box, see what they're up to," Rose suggested.

"Maybe, but not today; it's too late for that. We should make sure this area is as secure as we thought, find the easiest route to the stream, pick a spot for our fire, and settle in for the rest of today." Orders came easily to James.

"So we're going to live in this cave for a week?" Doyle groaned.

"Looks like it. Best get comfortable."

IV
The Bird

Dragon squatted at the bottom of his large cage, huddled in a corner full of his own waste. The bird was hungry, but he didn't dare move. It was night-dark, too dark to see by, and there were sounds: horrible clanging and banging sounds coming from all around. He heard gunshots, a sound he was able to imitate, but they were slowly receding, fading. He knew what the groaning sounds were from: the things that should be dead. Queer creatures that ought not to be. He had never tried to imitate them and never would. He had no interest in trying to speak with such things. In the dark he roared, a mighty sound he had seen other living things retreat from. He roared and roared, until his little throat was sore and he was thirsty as well as hungry.

Section 5:
Obliterate

33
Misha's Lost

The bullets had dried up. At times a gunshot would ring out above the din, but for the most part they were all gone. The only ammo that remained were the rounds people had decided to hold onto in case of the most dire of emergencies. Misha didn't know what that would be, but he wouldn't begrudge them. He might have held onto one bullet himself had he thought of it.

Misha, along with almost everyone else, had finally come down off the containers. They formed ranks in the alleys between the metal boxes, bladed weapons at the ready. One row of humans would meet the zombies, hacking and slashing, destroying skulls, while the others held back. When that first row felt overwhelmed, they drew back from the dead mob, retreating behind the rest of the people, while the second row waited for the zombies to come a bit closer, so that the slain wouldn't be under their feet. Misha stood in the second row, awaiting his turn. He had no idea where his dogs were. Some might still be up on the containers, but others were let down. He knew that at least Powder, his tallest dog, was somewhere between this column and the one facing the other direction, sniffing humans for infection. The rest of his pack was scattered.

"Fall back!" someone in the battling front row cried out.

There was some bumping and jostling as Misha and his row pressed forward through the retreating row.

"Evans?" Suddenly, the big man with the sword was on Misha's left where he hadn't been before. He had been part of the first row.

"I'm not done yet," he growled, perhaps recognizing Misha, perhaps not.

It was because of Evans that they were doing this. Several people had watched the mad man fall from the containers and thought him dead. The bullet-riddled corpses below had broken his fall, miraculously saving him from injury. As people watched, Evans had gotten his feet under him and started swinging that sword of his. At any moment, people were sure he was going to be overrun, but he kept attacking, kept surviving, until eventually someone jumped down to help him. People began to realize that hand-to-hand was effective between the containers, where the number of zombies was limited to how many could fit between them. It didn't take long before everyone was down between the containers with blades in their hands.

Evans was soaked in blood from head to foot, only a few patches clear of gore. Someone else had managed to stop him long enough to upend a bottle of water over his face and wipe clear his eyes and mouth, but it could easily have been too late: Evans might be infected. Misha figured he knew this as they took their positions; it would certainly explain how he managed to keep going.

As his blade thunked into the first skull, Misha forgot about his hunger. With the second, he forgot about his thirst. The third skull allowed him to forget about how he needed to sleep, while the fourth seemed to make the weariness of his limbs disperse. He stopped counting after that. For every zombie he took down, another stumbled forward into its place, often tripping on the corpses of its fallen kind. Their lack of co-ordination slowed them down considerably as they stepped over the full dead, struggling to keep their balance. When he had time to think, Misha wondered how many zombies had been trampled by their own, or were still moving, trapped beneath the other corpses. There was no time to have such thoughts, however. All that mattered was where his blade landed and keeping track of the men to his left and right.

"Fall back!"

It seemed like the call came too soon, but as Misha retreated, all of his ailments returned, worse than ever, and he saw a lot more dead bodies ahead of him than he had before. As he threaded back through the waiting lines, he saw the nervous expressions on those who hadn't yet been at the front line. At the back of the column, where people had taken their turn, they wore different expressions: they were hard and tired. Several looked asleep on their feet, but stepped forward when the lines moved. Behind Misha there was a bit of an argument about getting Evans away from the front line.

"Here, water." Misha didn't see who had thrust the large cup into his hands; he just mumbled a thanks. He wanted to swallow the water in one gulp, but resisted. Instead, he made his way to the small, magnet-backed mirror someone had hung up in the space between the backs of the human columns and waited his turn to check his face for blood. There wasn't much; most of the zombies' blood was too thick to spray, splattering instead lower down on his clothes. Still, he took a clean rag from his back pocket and wiped off the dabs that concerned him. It would have come off better if he used some of the water, but he wanted to drink it, not wash with it. As soon as he knew it was safe to do so, that no blood would mix in, he downed his cup in one go.

As Misha turned to form the next line, someone on the container above him got his attention.

"Here, a bit of food."

Misha didn't bother to identify the offering; he just accepted it and ate as he walked. Powder pushed her way through some men and women, and bumped her nose between Misha's shoulder blades. The Great Dane was a gangly and very tall dog, and she gave Misha's entire body a thorough sniffing.

"I'm all right, girl," he told the dog, pushing her big nose away. "Go check the others. Go. Sniff check."

The dog stared at him a moment longer, then went back to threading between people, sniffing them all over. How the dogs could tell the difference between an infected human and the zombie remains that soaked into their clothes, Misha had no idea. What he knew was that no one wanted one of the dogs to start growling at him or her.

Misha joined the back line, between two different people than before. As the front line changed out, Evans was forced back along with them. Misha watched as the big man accepted his water, took some offered food, then consumed them both as he pushed his way back to a line closer to the front. Misha wasn't so eager, content to wait at the back.

Bit by bit, his line moved forward; the first line always ending up a little farther back, the zombies moving ever closer. He was barely aware of who was around him. He'd catch sight of a familiar face, maybe recall their name and what he knew about them, but then forget again shortly after they were out of sight. He wondered how many faces he would never see again, how many people had died today. He had seen the man on the community centre get tossed off the roof by his fellow travellers but not why. Others had slipped from the containers and, unlike Evans, were injured in the fall or couldn't get their legs back under them before the zombies piled on top. It seemed there was always someone screaming as their limbs were torn from their sockets. Or was that just in Misha's head? He thought he sometimes screamed while hacking and slashing, but he couldn't tell. He could no longer tell the difference between his voice and someone else's. The ringing tinnitus in his ears from all the gunfire certainly didn't help, but at least that seemed to be slowly fading as the ammo depleted, suggesting it wasn't permanent. Others might not be so lucky.

The next time Misha's line moved, they were once more the second line. Everyone had their turn at least once and were now on their second pass. When the call was shouted, Misha dutifully stepped forward with the rest of them, lifting his bloody machete for the first strike.

"Kill me when we're called back," a voice spoke to Misha from the left.

He glanced over between kills and the man beside him showed Misha a bloody bite on his arm. Misha hadn't even seen him get bitten, but the evidence was plain.

"Will you?"

"Will I what?" Misha caved another skull in.

"Kill me when we're called back. I'll take down as many as I can right now, but I'm not going to risk that I might be a quick turner. I won't put the back of the columns in danger like that. So will you do it? Drive that blade into my head when we're called back?" Several more zombies were taken down as the man spoke.

"You could just stay at the front," Misha suggested offhandedly as he kicked a corpse off his blade.

"I'm tired, man. I just want it over with."

"All right."

No more words were spoken between them. When the call to change lines was sounded, Misha didn't hesitate. The man who was vaguely familiar to him barely had time to nod at Misha before the bloody blade slammed into the side of his head. Although his skull was harder than that of a long-dead zombie, the blade sank deep enough to drive the light out of his eyes. There was a strangely peaceful look on his face as the man dropped to the ground, where Misha attempted to free his machete from his cranium. He yanked it out just before a zombie reached him and used the momentum to slice off the dead thing's head. As he made his way back to the waiting lines, the former second line having already taken position, people were shouting at him. It wasn't until he reached them and they started grabbing at his arms that he realized what they were saying.

"What the fuck is wrong with you? Traitor! How could you do that?" The words jumbled together, spilling out in several voices.

"He was bit!" Misha shouted back. "Look at his arm, he was bit! He asked me to do it! Ask the man on his other side, he must have heard! He was bit! He asked me! *He asked me*!"

The first few lines jostled Misha as he tried to get through, pushing and sometimes even spitting on him. Then he was shoved to the ground, and just like that, he was forgotten. As he crawled between legs, someone grabbed his arm and helped him back onto his feet. Misha looked up to find it was once again Evans. This time he wasn't bullying his way forward, but waiting in a line with a group of others. Misha thanked him, but Evans didn't seem to hear, his eyes locked forward. Misha made his way to the space between the columns to see if he could get another drink. He didn't find one this time, but someone offered him a whetstone so that he could sharpen his blade again after wiping off some of the gore.

Everyone lost track of how many times they had been on the front line, the back of their column slowly moving toward the back of the other column. At least that column, the one on the community centre side, seemed to stay in place due to the fewer number of zombies over there. Misha continued to line up, continued to wait his turn, continued to slay the dead coming toward him.

***

"Fall back!"

Misha moved forward with his line once again. He raised his arms and started swinging at dead flesh. By then, he couldn't really feel anything anymore. Beneath his clothes, he was slimed with sweat and his muscles ached, but the swimming in his head was all that seemed to exist. His body had become so used to the routine, Misha had to focus more on keeping from fainting, than he did on his blade. The next dead face, and the next dead face, finding them kept him upright. When suddenly there was no next dead face, Misha swung his machete anyway, assuming something had happened to his vision.

When the cheering finally got through to him, Misha snapped awake. There was no next dead face, because there weren't any zombies moving toward him, at least not any that were close to him. In fact, there seemed to be only four zombies that were both on their legs and stumbling through the other corpses between the front line and the end of the container row. The cheering was because they had reached the back of the horde and no more zombies were seen coming over the walls.

Misha couldn't believe it. He stood there, stunned, his eyes wide and barely seeing the thick carpet of dead before his feet. Had it really happened? Had they survived the onslaught? He looked to those on either side of him. Some were like him, staring in dazed confusion, while others were smiling, cheering, and laughing. Looking behind him, he saw more of the same, even a couple who were sobbing tears.

"We did it?" Misha turned to the man on his right only to realize that it was Dr. Richards.

"It seems we did." His face was equally stunned, but slowly he turned back into himself. "There's going to be wounded." And like that Dr. Richards was gone, disappearing through the column. Where he thought he was going Misha had no idea; no one had set up a triage for the wounded.

"What do we do now?" Misha wondered aloud.

He wasn't the only one thinking that, as a couple of others started to voice the same question. Soon, the joy simmered down as everyone wondered what to do next. Was there a plan? Were their leaders still alive?

"I need a few volunteers to come with me." Evans held his sword up above the column as he waded forward through it. "We're going to take care of the stragglers. Some of you others should get back up onto the containers and see what's happening elsewhere. The rest of you stay here, rest, and continue to hold this position. Wait for orders."

Everyone was so tired it didn't look like anyone was going to volunteer.

"I'll help," Misha spoke before he even knew what he was saying.

His voice got a few others to volunteer, and soon some people were climbing up the ladders back onto the containers.

"Powder!" Misha called for his dog. She happily bullied her way through the humans to reach his side. "Sniff check," he commanded while pointing out over the alley of corpses. Powder whined, but after some encouragement, she headed out over the dead.

"What's that about?" Evans asked Misha as he handed him a canister of water.

Misha gulped down the warm, nearly hot liquid before answering. "Dogs can't get infected. She'll find anything still moving underneath that, and she's heavy enough to cave in any chest cavities that we would. It should keep us safe from most bone shards if we follow her."

"Will she get hurt?"

"I certainly hope not, but I can clean and bandage any cuts she might get." Misha didn't like the thought of any of his dogs getting hurt for him, but right now he couldn't think like that. Right now they still had a job to do.

Evans and his small group of volunteers began to follow Powder out onto the bodies. He led the way, but Misha stuck closely behind him, watching the big dog. Powder wouldn't get close to any corpses still standing upright, their legs firmly wedged between the bodies of others, so as they approached the first one, she hung back, her tail tucked tightly between her legs. Evans found his own way to the standing zombie, being careful to step on what looked solid. Still, his foot often sank into the mire of organs, bones, and flesh.

Behind him, Misha heard one of the other volunteers retch.

"You okay?" he asked, glancing back only briefly.

"Yup," came the weak reply, "it's just the stench is so much worse when you're on top of them."

Misha wished the man hadn't pointed out the reek because he had managed not to focus on it until then.

"Just pretend it's a bog; that's what I did when I had to cross a mess like this once before," a different volunteer suggested. Misha decided it was best not to ask when the man had done this before.

Once Evans had thrust his blade through the face of the zombie, Powder moved forward again and they followed. A few times she stopped and growled at the ground before backing away. No one had to ask if that meant she found something still moving. Misha quickly learned he didn't care if Powder growled at the ground or not, and found himself stabbing every head he passed, just in case. Other than to pick out the round lumps of skulls, he didn't identify the mess. He didn't dare start to pick out what was limb, what was torso. If he had begun to see the slop for what it really was, he might have thrown up, and he couldn't afford that with the meagre amount of food currently in his belly.

They went as far as they could between the containers until they reached the corpse pile at the end, the one the zombies had been climbing to get on top of the containers. It was too high for them to continue.

"Should we climb it?" the man behind Misha asked, the one who said they should pretend it was a bog.

Evans looked ready to try.

"No," Misha answered before he could move. "It's too risky. Part of that might cave in, or landslide." *Body slide*. "It would be too easy to get trapped underneath."

The thought of having dozens of corpses on top of them while they suffocated in their rot put even Evans off the idea. Instead, the small group turned around and headed back to the column. Now bringing up the rear, Misha got to see he wasn't the only one stabbing at every visible head.

When the man right in front of him tripped, Misha grabbed the back of his shirt and kept him upright.

"Thanks, man."

Farther along, someone else wasn't so lucky. His foot must have caught on a long bone and he went down. Instead of trying to break his fall with his hands, he was able to overcome the instinct and use his arms as a splatter shield for his face while attempting to twist over onto his back. He landed on his side among the dead with a solid squish and a pop. The man behind him swiftly moved forward to help him back up.

"Are you all right? Did anything cut you?" he asked.

"No. No, I think I'm okay."

Still, the man who helped him stand checked his clothes for any tears or freshly flowing blood. Even a small cut in this mess would kill him.

Powder was happy to be back on concrete, her tail swinging from side to side, heedless of anyone around her. Misha had to say he was glad for the same as he stepped alongside her. Although she hadn't whined and wasn't favouring any legs, Misha checked her over for cuts anyway. Just because she couldn't get infected by the zombie virus, didn't mean she couldn't get other infections.

No one was doing much. People had found places to sit on the concrete, their backs against the container walls. More had climbed up on top of the containers and sat along the edges, their feet dangling over the sides. Ever since that one idiot mentioned the smell, it had been invading Misha's senses more and more. He felt repulsed by it, and soon started feeling sick. Maybe the air would be slightly fresher up above where there was the chance of a breeze, so he headed for the nearest ladder.

Powder whined as Misha left her. He promised he'd be back and scratched behind her ears, someone else taking over the job once he started climbing. Still, she whined until he was out of sight over the edge.

The stench still found Misha up above, but it didn't seem to be as sharp so he thought he might be able to tolerate it. Of course the stink was in his clothes, so there was no way to completely escape it. The dampness of his feet wasn't from water, and his pants were a completely different colour than they used to be below his knees. He wanted to take his sweater off but wasn't going to risk that just yet. Most of it was stiff with blood, and he wasn't sure he'd be able to get it back on once removed.

"Any orders come over yet?" Misha asked the woman nearest to him.

"Only that the injured are to be taken to the last couple of containers," she said, pointing. "The only ones not completely surrounded by a corpse carpet."

"I don't know why they're bothering," another woman added, and Misha was surprised to see it was Yasmin. She definitely wasn't part of his column, so she had either stayed up above, or had been in the next alley over. "Any injuries in this mess are sure to be infected."

"Some might be okay," the other woman told her hopefully. "And depending on how recent the infection is, amputation might save them."

"Pretty sure the amputation would kill them. It's not like we can get at our medical supplies."

Misha left the women to their argument. His body was tired, but still flooded with adrenaline and he found he had to keep moving for a little longer. At least he was able to stick his machete back into the sheath on his hip and give his arms a break. They felt like big, wet, useless noodles.

As he shuffled along on top of the metal, a couple of people eyed him suspiciously. Misha couldn't blame them: he knew what he looked like, and would have also warily eyed someone moving with the same shambling gait. There was no way to tell who had become infected, and those that had might prove to be quick turns. Someone didn't have to be very far from Misha to wonder if he could be a zombie. Fortunately, he wasn't the only human staggering around, and no one was going to risk killing survivors. Not after all the losses they had just taken.

At the opposite end of the container, Misha was able to see the community centre and what Yasmin had been talking about. Another carpet of corpses covered the concrete between the containers and the structure. Along the building's sides, they were stacked several bodies deep, completely blocking the doors. If the medical supplies were in there, there was no way to get to them until those corpses were cleared away.

The same goes for our food, Misha thought as his stomach burbled.

Men and women carefully tread across the body field, making sure everything was fully dead. Two of Misha's dogs were out there, big bulky Guard, and stumpy Barrel. The badger named Root was also terrorising the grounds. Misha spotted his gore-streaked body popping in and out of gaps between limbs and torso cavities, actively hunting down and killing any zombies that might still be moving. Root was very good at taking down lone zombies with his fierce claws and teeth, but he was a scary little devil when at it. Misha looked around for his owner, the former zookeeper who had found him as a lone cub and raised him. She was the only one who could properly tame him, especially when he was on a rampage like this, but she was nowhere to be seen. Misha prayed she wasn't dead, as it would most likely mean death for Root.

Turning his gaze to the water beyond the rocky shore, Misha thought he saw splashing. Remembering the dead who had staggered out of there, he headed toward it, thinking the worst. Although the number of corpses between the containers lessened as he headed in that direction, the breeze was coming from behind, pushing at Misha's back and bringing the stink with it. At least zombies didn't carry flies, but now that they were fully dead, the buzzing hordes would start to show up. As with the dogs, Misha didn't know how the insects could tell the difference between a zombie and a dead zombie, but it seemed they could.

As he crossed the ladder to the last row, he was met by Rifle on the other side. There were wounded humans and doctors scattered all about.

There were even some non-doctors assisting, either holding patients down, or acting as executioner for those who were infected and desired a quick death. It was chaotic. Misha had thought the screaming was in his head, a leftover ringing, but here was the source. People were crying out either in pain or horror or grief. There were more than Misha expected. A couple of people had taken friendly fire from badly aimed shots, some had been cut by blades during the crowding of the columns, at least one man that Misha could see was suffering from a gun that had exploded in his hands near his face. As he stood next to Rifle, the old dog leaning against his leg, Misha watched as a man started trying to amputate his own arm. It didn't look like he had been bitten, and based on the reaction of others they didn't think he had been either, but the man was sure. Misha felt weak, his legs trembling beneath him.

Rifle whined and looked up at Misha, his old brown eyes full of concern.

"I'm all right, *bratishka*," he patted the dog's head with his blood-soaked gloves. "I'm all right," he repeated over and over again as he crossed the containers. On the other side, the splashing was revealed to be people who were wading around in the salt water, which was good.

A long, gently angled ladder leaned against the containers so that the rungs were more like stairs. Lifting Rifle up into his arms, still muttering into his fur, Misha was able to make his way down. At the bottom, he didn't put Rifle down but continued to the water past the rocks. Without bothering to remove any of his clothes, he kept walking, straight into the shallows.

When finally he put Rifle down, the dog groaned, but it sounded like a happy groan to Misha. Even through his gloves, he could feel how hot the German Shepherd's fur was. Rifle stumbled around a bit on the rocks, half-walking, half-swimming, until he found a good place to stand. Misha continued deeper into the cool water, a dark cloud trailing behind him as it did from most of the others who had gone in before him. Misha didn't bother to draw his machete as others had, not caring at the moment about the swimming dead or even sharks. He just walked until he was chest deep and then sank beneath the gentle waves, his eyes squeezed shut. Under the water there was no smell, no screaming, no pain, no nothing. Misha stayed under until his lungs started to burn. As he stood back up, he felt cleaner, and not just in a physical sense. Turning to shore, he saw Rifle watching him, his head low to the water, his ears sideways. When Misha forced a smile for the dog, both head and ears perked up, even his tail lifted from where it had been floating on the surface. Apparently, Rifle had known Misha was full of shit when he said he was okay, but the smile comforted the dog.

As he headed back to shore, Misha stripped off his gloves, took the sheath off his hip, and pulled his shirt up over his head. Once he reached Rifle, the dog accompanied him to shallower water, to a spot where he could sit down and take off his boots. A few people in the water had lost all sense of shame and were obviously naked, but Misha had righted his head enough that he needed to keep his boxers and pants on. With one hand, he kept his gear beside him, the blood slowly seeping out of it as he shifted it back and forth over the rocks. Sharks would definitely be coming soon, but for now he wrapped his free arm around his brother's shoulder and let the old dog rest his big head against his chest.

He could still hear the screaming from the wounded, but with his attention focused on the lapping waves and Rifle's breathing, he could put the sound aside. He also focused on the smell of salt water, a much cleaner scent than the one that was coming at his back.

"We're going to be all right, Rifle," Misha promised, while his body trembled.

34
Abby's Confined

It was extremely cramped inside the submarine as Abby knew it would be. She was standing, pressed up against the metal leg of a bunk. On the lower berth, Riley managed to snooze after commenting about how she was surrounded by asses and crotches. On the upper bunk, Dakota, Peter, Hope, and Claire had all squeezed together, knees to chests, while next to them stood Lauren, Brunt, Cameron, Josh, Anne, and several others who weren't part of their group but had boarded the sub around the same time. Abby had never been inside the sub before. She had heard about what it was like from those who had crossed the Atlantic, but didn't understand until now just how horrible the journey must have been. Those people had had a little more space than this, but when they dived to avoid storms, it was no different. No one had told her just how long it had taken; perhaps no one knew having lost track of the days during their voyage, but it had been long and arduous. Abby hoped this journey would be drastically shorter.

"He's singing again," Lauren groaned beside her.

Somewhere else amongst the bunks was Quincy Beharry, lead singer and only known survivor of what was once the massively popular rock band, Gathers Moss. As they had waited for the U-boat to finish loading, he had started singing one of his songs. Lauren had never been much of a fan of the band to begin with, and the lone voice echoing through the metal tube was eerie. To say nothing of the fact that those old songs dredged up old memories that most preferred to forget.

"Let him sing," Josh said. "Every year his mind slips a little further. His music helps him."

Heavy drinking, drugs, and age had all taken their toll at rotting away Quin's mind. Abby would never say it to anyone other than Lauren, especially not Robin, but she was surprised the guy was still alive. To look at him was to wonder how he had survived the walk from the Black Box to the sub with his frail, shaking limbs and pale, thin skin. Eleven years ago, okay, he was still fairly spry to survive the Day, even only five years ago when the Diana sank. But since the sinking, the man had aged rapidly, getting worse every year as Josh had stated.

Abby's legs and feet hurt; she wanted to sit down but there was nowhere. She debated with herself about perching on the edge of Riley's bunk, but the gentle rocking of the waves prevented her. She was worried about a larger swell rocking the sub harder and knocking her over onto her friend, especially while she was sleeping.

The inside of the U-boat smelled of metal and sweat. Every time Abby closed her eyes, she remembered the inside of a locker she had once hidden inside on the Day. The smell was similar, as were the confined quarters. At least in here she could stand at her full height instead of being crammed into an awkward hunch, and her friends were around her as opposed to a zombie seeking her out.

Abby had a wealth of memories to retreat into, and she did so now. She recalled happy times with Lauren, like when they laid beside each other in bed, whispering secrets to one another like schoolgirls. Her mind tried to wander to racier memories, but Abby wouldn't let it as this definitely wasn't the place for them.

Outside of her memories, Lauren threaded her fingers through Abby's, bringing a smile to Abby's face.

***

Docking had taken some time, unloading even more. Abby was impatient by then, more than ready to escape the confining tube. Either her friends had registered that she was more anxious than they were, or Lauren had quietly said something, because she was chosen to exit first out of their group. She had tried to insist that Cameron go first, since she was the one who suffered from claustrophobia, but Brunt said he had to lead her out as she was keeping her eyes shut to the confining sights. There was much jostling and bumping as everyone formed a line when able, all of them exiting the U-boat one at a time. When Abby finally laid her hands upon the ladder, she silently cursed the person above her for climbing so slowly, but then quickly took it back. People were moving as fast as they could.

Abby was looking forward to the fresh air, so when the powerful stench hit her, she nearly collapsed back down the ladder in addition to almost retching.

What happened to the air? she wondered as she had to continue upward into it.

"Oh! Ugh! Gross!" Claire called out from beneath her as she registered the same. "What is that?"

No one had an answer for her, at least no one in the submarine. As Abby neared the sunlight and the source of the smell, she began to identify individual elements: fire, smoke, cooking meat, gunpowder, blood, sweat, and above all, rotten, decayed flesh. Only the salt water had a friendly smell; everything else suggested something horrible had happened.

Exiting through the conning tower, Abby kept moving as she quickly took in the sights. The people who had come over from the Black Box were huddling together on the dock, unsure about what to do, while those with weapons were clutching them securely. Beyond the squared-off-U-shaped dock was what had once been a space for washing tubs or sports during down time, but was now a pyre of burning corpses. An even larger pile of bodies was growing beside it. The people from the container yard were carefully monitoring the fire so as to use as little accelerant as possible. Everyone she saw who hadn't come over on the sub was moving like someone from a dream. Before she could make out anything else, Abby was down from the conning tower and onto the dock, where a slope blocked her view of the rest of the place. Still, she could see the flames and the thick, black smoke rising from the burning corpses.

Abby found a space on the dock for her little group to gather. They were joined by others they knew, like Robin, Quin, and Winchester. None of them knew what was going on. From what they could see, no one from the container yard had even come down to greet them.

On her stretcher, Riley was fully awake and alert, holding her daughter's hand.

"Come on, we need to find out what's going on." Brunt led the way, directing their group along the dock. Being a resident of the container yard made him bolder than those from the Black Box, but it wasn't much longer before everyone was making their way off the dock.

The heat of the fire was intense, felt from a good distance away. Those working to keep it going, feeding the bodies to the flames, looked up at the arrivals through their goggles and masks, then returned to their task. Not one of them wore clothes that weren't soaked in blood and other bodily fluids. Beyond the fire, more people wandered about, carrying corpses to add to the pile of those to be burned. All zombies, Abby hoped, although she wouldn't be able to tell if one had been alive this morning. She could barely tell that the people carrying the things were living.

"Let's get to the community centre; Robin and I may be needed," Josh recommended.

Following behind Brunt and Cameron, Abby saw that the bodies were being carried from everywhere. Down every container alley, pairs of people emerged with something dead between them, while others disappeared down them to get more. Some were even toting shovels and wheelbarrows, scraping up the remains that weren't solid enough to be lifted. Around the community centre were more corpses piled high around the walls of the building like snowdrifts, although a path had been cleared to one of the doors.

Inside, cots were scattered about, used wherever they had been tossed. Doctors hurried around them trying to take care of the patients as they screamed and writhed. Most of them were amputees, but some seemed to have sustained other injuries, such as gunshots or broken bones. Josh and Robin immediately integrated themselves into the hectic gathering, getting themselves filled in and joining the chaos. Along one wall, a small line of people were getting their blood checked for infection; a single doctor sat at a table with a microscope. A young-looking boy was with him, writing down the names of everyone who had been cleared in tiny print on a set of chalkboards and whiteboards that hung on the wall behind them.

"Bring me over there," Riley ordered from her stretcher that was currently being carried by Winchester and Brunt.

They obeyed, moving with the group as they brought Riley to where a stash of medical supplies were kept.

"Help me sit in this chair." Riley struggled to rise on her own, but with help was soon seated in a chair beside the supplies. "I may not be able to administer aid, but I can help organize this crap. Hope, I'm going to need your help."

Hope nodded, already knowing what to do as she opened the nearest container and checked what was inside.

"I'll help too," Dakota volunteered, while Peter also stepped forward.

"Should I stay here, or check on the horses?" Cameron wondered aloud as she spied other vets running about.

"Check on the horses," Riley recommended. "If they've already been seen to, return here. If not, get them ready to help move those bodies outside."

In a flash, Cameron was gone.

"Come on, Winchester, we'll get some gloves from my place and help move that mess out there." Brunt whacked him on the shoulder and they left as well.

"What can I do?" Quin asked as his large eyes swept the room.

"Stay with me," Riley suggested. "Find a clipboard or something and some paper. The kids will check the boxes, I'll identify the contents, and you can write it down. We'll keep track of what we have and what the doctors use. Think you can do that?"

Quin nodded, happy to take the seat beside her.

"Come on, we should see if we're needed outside somewhere; we'll only be in the way here," Lauren spoke to those remaining. Abby agreed and followed her back out into the sunlight with Anne and Claire.

"I'm going back to the sub," Anne said, unable to tear her eyes away from the devastation around them. "I'll make sure the medical supplies we smuggled out are moved to the community centre."

During their ride in the U-boat, all food and medical supplies had been passed from hand to hand, moved to one space for categorisation and safekeeping. Now they would need to unload it all.

"Maybe we should help move bodies as well?" Abby suggested hesitantly.

"No gloves," Lauren reminded her.

"I'm going to find Crichton, or Bronislav, or someone," Claire told them. "They'll have need for message runners, and I can do that."

"Okay, but be careful." Lauren kissed Claire on the forehead before letting her dash off.

"What can we do?" Abby was disoriented by the mess, the stench threatening to knock her over.

Lauren stood still and thought for a moment before answering. "People will need feeding, right? I noticed there's less of this mess over by the water. We'll grab some others to help start a smaller fire and cook up a hot meal over there. Nothing much, just soup or something."

Abby agreed, so the two women made their way to the shoreline to stake out a space. It wasn't hard to find volunteers over there. Both people from the container yard and the Black Box who hadn't been able to find tasks had gathered there, away from the disgusting sights. With their volunteers, they set to work finding tables, pots, bowls, firewood, and food.

"Where do you think Jon is?" Abby finally asked the question that had been eating away at her since she first identified the various odours.

"He'll be wherever help is needed most," Lauren assured her, but Abby knew her well enough to pick up the worry behind her voice.

Once people began to realize that hot food was being made, they started to flock to the tables. It seemed no one had had a proper meal since the night before, and it didn't take long for a weary line to form. A group of teens had taken it upon themselves to wash the bowls and utensils in the salt water when people were done with them, scrabbling back and forth across the rocks. Abby found herself moving from fire to fire, keeping the flames at a good height. She didn't stop until a barking drew her attention.

"Rifle? What is it boy?" Abby's throat tightened, wondering if Misha was still alive.

The old dog looked up at her, and then turned toward the water. He took a few steps toward it, then looked back at Abby over his shoulder.

"Here, can you take care of the fires?" Abby asked the nearest volunteer, thrusting her poking stick into her hands before the girl could answer.

Abby followed Rifle to the edge of the rocky shore. She knew a crowd of people had been wading around in the shallows, cleaning the gunk off their clothes, but she hadn't realized that one of them was Misha. The former Russian sat in the shallow water, his torso bare, his dogs wandering about. Two sat sopping wet on either side of him, while the rest picked their way around the rocks.

"Okay, Rifle."

Abby returned to the food tables and snaked a bowl of soup. She carried it back to the rocky shore and took off her shoes and socks before making her way down to Misha. He didn't move when she waded into the water beside him, soaking the bottoms of her pyjama pants. The round dog moved away, but the larger one wearing Rifle's old harness stayed by his side.

"I brought you some soup," Abby said.

Misha looked up at her, his eyes far away.

"Here, you should eat something hot."

Misha took the bowl as if he wasn't sure what he was looking at. The smell must have broken through, however, as he soon started sipping at the hot liquid. Abby had forgotten to bring a spoon, but that didn't seem to matter. He drank straight from the bowl, prodding the chunks into his mouth with his fingers. Abby waited quietly until he was finished.

"So no one has actually told me what happened here. Last I heard it was a group of humans coming to attack you guys. Can you fill me in?" Abby knew better than to ask if he was okay. Rifle wouldn't have come to get her if he was.

"They came, we fought," Misha said, nodding, looking back out over the water. "Then another tiny group of people came and told us about a mega horde coming our way. We made a truce with our enemies, let them over the wall, and then fought off the dead when they showed up."

"That explains all the faces I don't recognize."

"There were so many," Misha whispered, his face turning down toward his lap.

"Come on, how about we get out of the water?" Abby took the bowl from him and rinsed it. "You're going to get a pretty bad sunburn sitting out here and your dogs are scared."

"Scared?" Misha looked up, his pale eyes finally starting to come back.

"Yeah. I don't know them as well as you do, but this looks like some nervous behaviour to me. They're scared, I'd say, probably think something happened to you." *Something did happen to him*, Abby thought. "Come on, I'll carry your clothes and we'll get you into some shade."

Misha snatched the bundle of clothing floating beside him before she could. Abby was trying to ignore the strange clouds floating about in the water, drifting off everyone from the container yard who walked in.

"What are you doing here?" Misha suddenly asked, finally realizing who it was walking out of the water with him.

"Long story that you don't need to bother with now."

"Your face is all bruised."

"Part of the long story; I'll tell you about it later. Hey, do you have a ball or something? I'm sure your dogs will feel better once you play with them."

"Yeah, but they're in my container."

"I'll go get it. I remember where your container is."

"You have to go in through the roof hatch."

"That's fine." They reached the nearest container where Misha stood in the shade it threw, his bundle of clothes dripping a dark, blackish-red as he squeezed them against his chest. He let his machete clatter to the pavement where it was immediately sniffed by Bullet, the Australian Shepherd wearing Rifle's harness. The splotchy dog's eyes were the same nearly-white-pale-blue as Misha's as he looked up at his master.

Misha's not their master, he's their pack leader, Abby reminded herself. "Wait here, I'll go get a ball. Maybe you can throw a stick or something for them in the meantime, or show some of the people around here those tricks you teach them."

"Yeah, maybe."

Abby grabbed her shoes and socks, and returned the bowl to Lauren while explaining where she was going. She hoped she was doing the right thing. If she could get Misha to play with his dogs, it would help to bring him out of the shock in which he seemed to be mired. Also, the sight of the dogs playing might help the others she saw in the same state. She didn't need to know the details of the battle to know it had been horrible: she could see it on all their faces.

Once up the ladder, Abby had to take a moment to orient herself. Provided the container yard residents hadn't moved a bunch of stuff around, she knew the layout but had never been on top of it before. People walked about on the containers, or sat on the edges, while some climbed in and out of roof hatches. Several people were running to retrieve supplies from inside to bring elsewhere; others were bringing out pets that had been locked away. As Abby made her way across the containers, always heading for the bridge that appeared the most secure, she looked around the yard. In the container alleys, people moved the dead, clearing away the corpses from the doors. Farther from the community centre, she saw the dead were piled deeper, several heaps having managed to reach up to the top of the containers. Beyond, the wall was well manned. Men and women stood on the highest containers with large spears in their hands. As Abby got closer, with the sounds of voices, fire, and water dying away behind her, she could hear the zombies still moving and moaning beyond the protective barrier. Those with the spears were thrusting downward whenever they could take one out. Abby suspected Jon would be up there.

Walking along the container tops wasn't always straightforward. With the hatches cut into them and many with those plastic bottle lights sticking out, Abby had to watch her step. She noticed a couple of round holes where the bottle lights used to be but had already been crushed, the adhesive holding them in place letting go and allowing the bottles to fall through. The holes they left behind were just large enough for a careless foot to slip through and an ankle to be broken. It was likely some of the people receiving treatment in the community centre were victims of just such an occurrence.

Nearing Misha's home, Abby realized that getting into it wasn't going to be as easy as she had hoped. The entire row of containers had corpses draped all over it, and the ladder bridges had been drawn back or knocked over.

"Need some help?" A young man Abby didn't recognize wandered over from where he had been helping some others shove bodies off the top of the containers' ends.

"One of my friends lives over there; I told him I'd get something from his place for him."

"Sure, I can help. Come on, lift the other side of that ladder."

Together, the two of them bridged the gap, the far side of the ladder resting unsteadily on top of a dead zombie.

"My name's Elijah." He took off his glove and held out his hand.

"Abby." She shook it. "Are you one of the people who were attacking this place yesterday?"

The young man flushed as he put his glove back on. "Yeah, guess I was."

"Sorry, didn't mean to embarrass you or anything like that. It's just I didn't recognize you, and I didn't know if you came with that group or maybe showed up at some other time between now and when I was last here." Abby knew she was rambling.

"Last here?"

"Umm, yeah... I'm from another group that works with this one sometimes." Abby silently cursed herself, fearing she may have said too much.

"Is that why you're in your pyjamas?"

"Kinda, it's a long story."

"Maybe I'll learn it one day, maybe I won't. How about you hold this end of the ladder steady, and I'll go across to clear off the corpses around that end?" Elijah suggested.

"Yeah, all right."

While Abby knelt on her end, the young man carefully crossed, his arms held out to either side for balance. She watched as he shoved off the nearest bodies, the ones barely balanced on the edge of the container, then stepped off to move the one that the ladder was resting on. Once it was out of the way, he resettled the ladder, making it secure so that Abby could cross.

"So which way is your friend's container?"

"That way," Abby pointed. "I don't think you'll be able to move all the bodies between here and there."

Elijah shrugged. "The ones on the edge are easy to shove off."

As Elijah inched along the edge, kicking bodies off with his large boots, Abby followed carefully behind him. A few times the young man had to lean over and drag a body with his hands to get it to move, but he was always able to make a clear space for their feet to fall.

"God that stinks." Abby came close to retching up the soup she had eaten when a dead zombie's belly burst open like a bubble. She covered her mouth and nose with her hand, but it was still like being punched in the face, an experience of which she had a very recent memory.

"Yeah, a bunch are so dried out that they don't really smell, but the sloppy ones are rank. I think my nose has shut down to be honest," Elijah commented. "That, or I'm learning to survive without breathing."

Whenever Abby waited for a more stubborn body to be moved, she looked toward the wall, trying to identify one of the people there as Jon. Every time she failed to spot him, a knife twisted in her belly as a wordless thought fluttered through the back of her mind. She had a long time to search when they finally reached Misha's container and Elijah had to clear several bodies off of the hatch.

"I feel bad that you're doing all this work for me," Abby said trying to pull her mind away from her thoughts but unable to remove her eyes from the wall.

"Meh." Elijah shrugged as he peeled a black intestine off the hatch and tossed it aside. "All this crap has to be moved anyway, right? I don't think it matters where we start."

"Fair enough. After this I'll find some gloves and come back to help you."

"You don't have to if there's other things you should be doing."

"We'll see." Abby climbed down the hatch once Elijah opened it, wondering how it was possible that he had been shooting at her friends just the other day.

Under the hatch there was light in Misha's container, but it quickly turned to darkness at the far end. The bottle light had been knocked out and had rolled to the base of the ladder where Abby stood. Peering into the gloom, she could just make out a stain beneath the hole for the bottle caused by blackened zombie blood oozing through. Closing her eyes, Abby visualized Misha's place as she had last seen it, picturing all the things on his milk crate shelves. Hoping everything was still in the same place or near enough not to matter, she stepped out of the light and squeezed past the dripping gunk. Her hands fumbled along the shelves, her eyes still adjusting, until they wrapped around the familiar feel of a flashlight. She hastily turned it on and shone the light all around the large metal box, feeling like something was in there with her. There wasn't; she was alone as logic had told her she would be.

Figuring it wouldn't hurt to grab several supplies while she was in there, Abby first located a backpack. She filled it with some of Misha's personal food and water stores, and some treats for the dogs. She then packed their toys, a handful of items to use as masks, and both pairs of work gloves.

A shadow passed over the hatch opening and Abby froze. Her mind raced as she wondered if trusting Elijah had been a good idea. She knew next to nothing about him. What if he started tossing bodies inside, then closed the hatch and piled more on top? It would be extremely difficult for Abby to get out without getting infected dressed the way she was. With her heart in her throat, she hurried to the ladder and climbed back out into the sunlight. Elijah was shoving bodies off the sides of the containers; the shadow had just been his while walking by.

"You get what you were looking for?" he asked after picking up and tossing a corpse that was hardly more than bones covered in dried out flesh.

"Yeah, thanks for your help."

"No problem. Hey, can I ask you something?"

"Sure."

"Once this is over, like, the zombies still out there are all gone... Do you think I'll be allowed to stay here?" The way he asked the question suddenly made him a lot younger and Abby realized she was wrong to think he was a young man. He was still in his teenage years, even younger than Claire.

"That'll be up to our leaders."

"Oh. Okay." He turned away to shove off another body.

"I'll put in a good word for you though, if I get the chance," Abby offered.

"Thanks, that would be great." He didn't sound very enthusiastic about her meagre offer. "This place looks nice. Or it did before this mess covered it. Still better than out there."

Abby wondered how much he had seen in addition to this invasion. "Well, I better get going before my friend wonders where I am."

"Yeah." Elijah returned to his work, deciding there was no point in going back to where Abby had first found him and continued to clear off the container he stood upon.

Abby crossed the ladder again and headed back toward the water. Part way there she realized she should have mentioned the food to Elijah, but it was too late to turn back now. If Lauren and the others didn't need her help, then she'd put on Misha's gloves and probably a mask, then head back to help him. She could tell Elijah about the food then, and maybe get to know him better, learn more about the outsiders and how they survived.

Choosing to cross as few ladder bridges as possible, Abby took the long way getting back to the row by the water, suddenly thinking about all the written work she had lost in the Black Box. She headed toward the end of the container row where another container had been placed sideways filling most of the gap. Corpses were still piled high at the very end of the row and up against the far side of the bridging container, but there was still a path. Abby hopped the gap, but froze the moment she landed.

Something in the corpse pile had moved.

Abby stood perfectly still, her eyes locked on the location where she had spied the movement. She felt naked standing there in her pyjamas and boots without any sort of weapon on her. Just as she was starting to think she had imagined it, the movement came again. A zombie's mouth slowly opened, but there was no way it could still be functional. From where Abby stood, she could see that the top of its head was caved in, its brains leaking out. But the mouth was clearly opening. Had the virus changed? Was taking out the brain no longer enough?

A large black rat wiggled its way out of the corpse's mouth, its fur slick with gore. It looked at Abby with its intelligent, beady eyes and paused for a second before springing at her, its mouth wide to show its blackened, infected teeth.

Abby reacted on instinct. Spinning in place, she allowed the rat to land on the backpack instead of her, then slid out of the straps as quick as a snake. The rat clawed and bit at the material, not yet realizing that it had failed to grasp its prey, but that wouldn't last for long. Abby slammed her boot down on the creature, which squealed in pain but quickly twisted around to bite its attacker. Abby lifted her boot a short way, the rat's teeth hanging on, then slammed her foot down again. The rat squealed through its mouthful, but persisted. She slammed again and the rat went slack, its spine broken. Lifting her foot higher, Abby brought her boot down one last time, the force of the impact breaking anything left of the rat's bones and crushing its guts out.

While using her boot to shove it toward the corpses, Abby picked up the backpack, the fabric slightly torn, and slung it over a shoulder. She looked out over the rest of the zombie corpses and was horrified to see more small movements among them.

"Rats!" she finally found her voice to scream. "There are rats in the corpses!"

34
Nessie's Not Conscious

Nessie kept drifting in and out of the light. She preferred the darkness where it wasn't so painful. Once, however, when the light returned, it wasn't so bright. Wondering if night had come, Nessie held onto consciousness a bit longer. Her eyes focused just enough to tell her it was still daylight, but that she had been moved inside. Then she slipped away again.

***

When next Nessie awoke, she assumed she had been given something for the pain. It was still there, a terrible throbbing in her lower abdomen, but the severe bite had been taken away. Had she been able to, she would've refused the painkiller, telling them not to waste it on someone as old as she. There was also a lot of noise, a lot of raised voices. She was used to the screaming and crying that came with the light, but this was different. This was panicked orders. Something different was happening; were they being attacked again? Nessie tried to see but it was difficult to keep her eyes open.

"*Momma?*" a familiar voice whispered.

Nessie looked up toward the sound. An IV stand loomed overhead with a feathered face peering down from it.

"Hello, Dragon," Nessie wheezed, barely able to get the words out. Someone had retrieved her bird for her. This made her happy, but she wished she knew who so that she could thank them.

"You're awake," a different, far-less familiar voice spoke from Nessie's side.

She looked over and saw a face she had seen before but had never gotten to know. He was young, somewhere between eighteen and twenty-two by Nessie's estimate. She had seen him around the container yard like she had seen so many others, but had never stopped to ask for a name, or at least not remembering it if told.

"Why did you have to tell them?" he asked, his eyes filling with tears.

Tell them? Tell them what? Nessie was too tired to actually ask the questions.

"She wasn't hurting anyone. She was my friend."

Nessie didn't like the odd look on his face. Although she couldn't follow along with his words, there was something about his expression that was wrong.

"It's okay, I guess. I can make new friends. Maybe you'll be my friend."

When his hands moved toward her throat, Nessie wanted to scream but couldn't get it out in time. After one last breath, her air was cut off.

"It's okay," he spoke softly, soothingly, despite what he was doing. "You'll come back. You'll be more peaceful when you do. No pain. It's better this way."

The zombie in the container, Nessie finally remembered, but it was too late. She tried to push him off but was too weak. She dug her blunt fingernails into his wrists as she attempted to pull his hands away from her throat, but it seemed to have no effect on him. The darkness was trying to creep back, but this time she didn't want to go into it. This time she wouldn't be able to get back out if she did.

"*Rooooaaaarrrrrrr!*" Dragon screamed above them. In a flurry of feathers, he swooped at the boy's face. "*Zombie! Zombie! Zombie!*" he kept squawking in a harsh tone that Nessie had never heard before.

The boy shrieked and fell away, his hands batting at his attacker. Nessie took in a ragged breath, her throat burning with it.

"Get it off me!" the boy screamed, blood running down his face and fingers.

He finally struck a blow to Dragon's body, sending the bird careening sideways. He got no respite, however, as a human tackled him to the ground. Nessie's vision was fading again, but the cowboy hat was instantly recognizable.

"The bird attacked me! It went crazy!" the boy was screaming and wiggling, trying to buck Dakota off of him. He lost all chance of that when her friend Hope, and a boy whose name Nessie didn't know also sat on him.

"Are you okay?" A gentle hand touched Nessie's arm. "I'm sorry we didn't see it until it was almost too late."

Nessie looked up to see Dr. Riley standing over her, but she looked different. Her features were tired and weak, and her upper torso was covered in bandages. *Has she been injured too?* Nessie thought, not able to remember that Riley hadn't been at the container yard during the attack.

"Quin! Help the kids tie that asshole up!" Riley barked, but it was followed by a wince.

A man at least as old as Nessie walked over to her and gently placed Dragon by her side. "I think he's just stunned."

"I'll check him over once I'm done with you," Riley told Nessie.

"It was the zombie," Nessie croaked, her throat flaring with pain. "The zombie in the container. Him."

"Don't try to talk, you could make it worse," Riley told her sternly. The doctor looked like she was about to collapse herself.

Nessie couldn't remember what happened beyond that. She ran a finger gently down Dragon's back then let the blackness take her.

35
Riley's Pushing Through

Riley watched as Nessie slid into unconsciousness, unable to keep her awake. Her own body was fighting to stay awake, weakened as it was. Riley could only hope that Nessie would survive all of this.

"What's going on over here? Is there a rat?" Boyle limped over. Riley heard he had fallen off a container and badly twisted his ankle. She hoped that's all it was and that he didn't have a fracture.

"No, Gerald was strangling Nessie," Dakota quickly told him. She had been the first to notice that something wasn't right about the interaction between the elderly woman and the teenager. In the flurry of chaos that followed the announcement of rats, everyone else's eyes had been on the doors.

"I was helping her!" Gerald cried pitifully from the floor with his arms bound, Hope and Peter still sitting on his back and legs.

"No you weren't!" Dakota screamed at him. "You were trying to kill her, even Dragon knew!"

"That bird is crazy!"

"She said something about him being a zombie in a container before slipping into unconsciousness," Riley quietly told Boyle while Dakota and Gerald continued to yell at one another, Hope joining in and taking Dakota's side. "I don't understand what she meant."

"I understand. All right, calm down, all of you," Boyle barked in an unusually harsh tone.

Everyone fell silent, including others who were watching the confrontation from a distance and whispering to one another.

"Someone move him to a holding container," he ordered.

"But I didn't do anything!" he cried as a man and a woman swiftly stepped forward and hauled him up as Hope and Peter scattered.

"Gag him if he won't shut up," Boyle ordered.

"Please don't leave me for the rats!" he cried as he was hauled out of the community centre.

Boyle sighed and wavered a bit on his feet as he pinched his eyes shut.

"Maybe you should sit down for a moment," Riley advised.

"Maybe you should too," Boyle looked pointedly at the hand she had white-knuckle gripped around the IV pole to steady herself.

Hope, Peter, Dakota, and Quin all helped Riley and Boyle over to the seats they had occupied earlier. The kids had already learned to identify most of the medical supplies and immediately went back to their task, getting Quin to jot it all down and handing out things when doctors came asking for them. Dakota made sure a doctor with more focus than Riley went to check on Nessie.

"Not the best time to come home," Boyle commented as he sat in one chair and lifted his injured leg up onto another.

"No choice."

"I heard."

"What are we going to do about the rats?"

"Same thing we've done in the past when a bunch of the buggers showed up. Keep the containers shut, guard the walls and doors of this place, and let the dogs, cats, and that mad-ass badger go to town on them."

"It won't be as simple with all those bodies for them to hide in and under."

"The bodies will also distract them though. Infect them, sure, but even when made extra aggressive, a fat, fed rat is less likely to pose a threat. We just have to keep clearing the dead away, keep some of our animals around the pile still waiting to be burned, and bludgeon what we can." Boyle winced.

"I hear it's a twisted ankle," Riley commented on his leg.

"I hear the same, but with the swelling and no x-ray, no one can say for sure."

"What's going to happen with Gerald?"

"There will be a trial. We'll need to hold a couple actually, and the sooner the better in my opinion."

"You want to hold a trial in the middle of all this? Does Karsten know?" Riley knew that Karsten hated trials.

"I guess you didn't hear. Karsten's dead."

"What?" The words hit Riley like a punch to the gut. The German U-boat captain had been one of the first people to come to the container yard to begin setting it up for habitation. He had literally poured blood, sweat, and tears into getting this place running.

"I saw it happen. We were to fall back to another container when he slipped on some gore. Managed to keep his feet, but it allowed a zombie to get him. He knew he was done then so he didn't fall back with the rest of us. Instead, he stayed put and brought down with him as many as he could."

Riley swallowed the lump in her throat. She had lost people before, people far more important to her, but it still came as a shock. "How many others?"

"We don't know yet. That infection testing board is the best we have to let us know who's alive," Boyle nodded in the direction of the white boards and chalkboards, "but not everyone's been tested yet, and with the rats, some of those people are going to come back for a second or even third testing. We won't know who's dead for a while yet."

"Maybe someone should go around asking? Ask who they saw die?"

Boyle shook his head. "Not everyone knows everyone's name. Besides, you weren't here so you don't know what it was like. You could easily think someone was dead when in fact they're alive and well. I also won't put them through that. Too many people are still in shock. No, we'll find out as we go. It's not like any of them could've disappeared only to show up later."

Riley nodded, figuring he was probably right. "So, these trials, who's going to sit on them?"

"Me, for one. Either Crichton or Bronislav, but not both. One of them should continue to run things while we do this. I thought you might be a good choice."

"Me?"

"You weren't here so you can be considered impartial to a degree, and people respect doctors; it's not like there's much else you can do right now."

He had a point. "How many trials?"

"There will be three; we'll try to get through them as quickly as we can. I already have suggestions I'd like to put forth during two of them."

"Who else will sit? Don't you usually have five for these things?"

Boyle nodded. "I want one more person from the container yard, and one from the Black Box. We're also going to have a sixth sit with us."

"A sixth?"

"I don't know how much you've heard, but we were warned of the zombies' coming. A group of five people had been tracking them. Two of them are still outside the walls somewhere, but the other three are in here with us. If at least one of them is still alive, they might be able to give us the opinion of a total outsider."

"You trust them that much?"

"I'm not giving them the power of a vote, just an opinion." Boyle spotted Claire in the crowd that was growing and flagged her down. Since the call of rats, those too tired and weary to fight were moving indoors, as was the food that had only recently exited the building. "Claire, I need you to find some people for me. Do you know everyone on this list?" he handed her a scrap of paper.

"Yeah, I think I know what they all look like. Except for these two."

"Ask someone from the container yard: they'll likely know who they both are. Find everyone on that list and send them to me. Oh, and if you spot either Crichton or Bronislav, send them too, whichever you find first but not both."

"On it." Claire pressed into the growing throng and disappeared into it.

"I'm guessing witnesses were on that list as well?" Riley asked.

Boyle nodded. "Come on, we should clear out a small corner of this place for our deliberations."

Riley would rather remain seated, but she got up to follow Boyle anyway. Touching her bandages, she noticed a gross dampness in them, most likely from her drainage tubes. She was going need that looked at before the day was over, but first she thought she should find a jacket to hide it for the trials.

***

"Riley? You awake?" a gentle hand lighted upon her shoulder.

"Yeah, I'm awake." Her eyes shot open, but she couldn't say for sure if she was lying or not. She had been in that state between waking and sleeping, able to hear what was going on around her but paying no attention to it, her mind drifting.

Riley sat in a chair in the corner of the community centre, wearing a leather jacket with a busted zipper that hid most, but not all, of her bandages. Her seat was part of a ring of eight, all of them so close together that most people's knees were brushing. Only two remained empty for the moment. Around the ring sat Crichton, Boyle, a woman named Angela who had lived at the Black Box since before the Diana residents arrived, and Harry, whom Riley was very happy to see had survived the attack. His mind was a very valuable asset, and on top of that, his son was a good friend of Hope's. The newest addition to the ring, the reason Harry had woken her, was someone Riley didn't know.

"This is Tommy," Boyle told the ring by way of introduction. "He carries no vote, but is here to provide an impartial, outside view should we need one."

"I'm not sure I'll be much use." Tommy wiggled uncomfortably in his seat, but made no attempt to leave.

"Let's get started. Bring forth the first case."

A crowd of people stood outside the ring, watching the proceedings, but most were there out of necessity rather than real interest. Bronislav was in the process of moving people around, getting those who couldn't work just yet to safe resting places, but for now the community centre was overcrowded. As Claire pushed through them to get someone, Riley's eyes found Max, who was lying on a nearby cot and watching from between two people standing beside him.

Claire returned with a large blond man, whose pants were stiff with blood. His T-shirt was somewhat cleaner, but based on where the stains were, Riley guessed it was one he had worn beneath a longer-sleeved shirt that had been removed. Slung over one shoulder was a large sword that he didn't remove when he sat down.

"This is Evans, leader of the group who attacked our walls before the zombies came," Boyle told the circle. "We're to decide what to do with both him, and the people who followed him."

"Am I allowed a statement?" Evans asked.

"Yes, but generally we wait until after the evidence has been aired."

Evans politely gestured for Boyle to continue.

"Evidence against: there's no doubt about you leading your people to our wall in order to attack us. I saw you, as did Harry, and others in your group have confirmed that you're in charge for the most part. Evidence for: you surrendered peacefully, obeying every command we gave. Both you and your people were a valuable asset during the zombie attack and are even now helping with the aftermath. I feel it important to note that none of us were killed during your group's attack, not even the hostages you held, although some were injured. Also, when one of your men attempted to harm one of ours during your surrender, you personally aided in putting a stop to it. That man is dead. He continued to be uncooperative during the zombie assault and shot Nessie. His own people threw him to the undead hordes in response. Any evidence I missed?"

"I'd like to mention that when I came across him outside the wall during his assault, Evans didn't look like he wanted to be there," the man named Tommy spoke up, albeit somewhat hesitantly.

Boyle nodded and looked around the circle, but no one else had anything to add. "Evans, you can make your statement now if you'd like."

"I won't try to put my blame on someone else. Yes, I led my people here to attack. Most of them are innocent, however, especially those who went to that island of yours. My party was just scared, angry, and swept up in the idea of vengeance. Having talked with those I captured, and now seeing you here, I've come to believe your people had no part in what happened to mine. For all I know, they were killed by that same group who has taken over your second camp that I've heard others talking about. If there's to be punishment, apply it to me, not those who don't deserve it."

"Very well. I'd like to put forth a resolution," Boyle told the circle. "I believe we should allow Evans and his people to stay if they wish. Based on what I've heard both here and from others, this has all just been a disastrous misunderstanding, one which they've been working hard to make up for. Any objections?"

No one objected.

"Vote."

All five who had votes raised their hands. No one knew this case better than Boyle, and no one was about to argue with him about it.

"There you have it, Evans: you and your group are welcome to join us. If not, you're free to take any supplies you brought with you."

"Thank you." Up until that moment, Evans had been sitting like a large rock, a posture Riley had mistaken for a natural one. Now, he visibly relaxed, becoming less imposing with his relief. He had been far more worried about this than she had realized. "I'd like to talk about those who attacked your other camp if I may."

"Once we're done with the trials; hopefully they'll be as fast as yours. Feel free to remain seated. Second trial is against Nessie."

Riley frowned, as did others, finding this trial unexpected.

"Nessie is accused of having contraband materials, specifically grenades. Evidence against: they were seen in her room; in fact, she showed them to us. She wouldn't say when or where she had gotten them from. Evidence for: in the end, she showed them to us, knowing there could be consequences, because she believed they could help us against the zombies."

"And they did," Tommy added, speaking more confidently than previously. "We haven't yet been able to go looking for any parts of his corpse, but considering no one has seen an armoured zombie, we're fairly confident that Dean was taken out in the opening salvo."

"I'd also like to point out that Nessie gave us a lot of her good fabrics, leathers, and blankets so that we could muffle the logs we used for rolling the containers," Harry also spoke up. "And I'd heard that she took that bullet while protecting the youngest around her."

"I heard the same," Angela added. "The kids she pushed over seem to believe she saved their lives."

"I'd like to put forth a resolution," Boyle said again. "The materials she gave up to Harry and his crew will not be returned to her. If they're still good, they will be evenly distributed to anyone who wants them. Objections?"

Everyone shook their heads.

"Vote."

All five raised their hands again. Boyle had clearly thought about both of these trials beforehand and planned their outcomes.

"Now, our last trial. Claire, please go get Gerald. If he's still being difficult, get the guards to help you."

Claire nodded and dashed off. Riley shifted in her seat, attempting to sit more upright. This was the trial that Boyle didn't know what to do about, the one that would require more focus.

When Gerald was brought before them, he immediately tried to speak, but closed his mouth again after a stern look and hand gesture from Boyle.

"Gerald, have you ever witnessed a trial before?" Boyle asked the boy.

"No," he answered, more words trembling on his lips but staying put.

"You will be given a chance to make a statement *after* evidence is given. You're free to demand any witnesses mentioned against you be called forth; however, the reason they're not here now is that they're rather busy at the moment. While evidence is given, keep your mouth shut; you can argue against it in your statement. Think you can do that?"

Gerald nodded, his jaw clenched tight.

"Gerald stands accused of harbouring a zombie within our walls, and the attempted murder of Nessie. Evidence against: chains that match the description of those seen holding the zombie were found in your container. Tools that match the bolts left behind in the container were also found, as were healthy hair samples that match the colour and length of your hair. Some of your neighbours have attested to seeing or hearing you leave your container in the middle of the night and not return until hours later. No one has yet claimed to be your friend or really knows you all that well, which speaks against your character. As to Nessie, you were seen attempting to strangle her. Unfortunately, she is still unconscious and no one has yet been able to determine if she'll ever awaken. Riley says that before she fell unconscious, Nessie told her that you had something to do with the zombie in the container. For those of you who may not know, Nessie was the one to report the zombie to us after some kids discovered it and went to her about it. Freya conducted the majority of the investigation. Evidence for: no one has seen the zombie since it was moved. No one has actually seen Gerald anywhere near where the zombie was kept. Thankfully, no one's been killed so far, and only Nessie's been hurt. Several people have also attested that Gerald fought the zombies just as hard as anyone. I think that about covers everything." Boyle's announcement that a zombie had been found being kept within the container yard's wall rippled through the crowded community centre.

"I'm on trial because I have no friends?" Gerald's voice cracked. "I have trouble sleeping at night so I go for walks sometimes. I'm not the only one. I've seen lots of people out at night, and I guess my neighbours aren't sleeping either if they noticed. My hair is brown and kept short like every other guy here. Harry, your hair is the same. And plenty of people have tools in their containers, and the chains I bring outside the wall with me when I help clear containers. Sometimes we have a use for them depending on what we find. And I was trying to *help* Nessie when that bird attacked me." He gestured to the puffy red scratches on his face and bandages someone had applied to the deeper wounds that had bled.

Riley knew he was lying about the last bit, which immediately put everything else into question for her. Why would he try to kill Nessie if it wasn't related to this captive zombie?

"Anyone have any resolutions to put forth?" Boyle asked wearily. "Gerald, please don't speak during this unless asked."

"I say we execute him," Angela immediately suggested, fully believing in Gerald's guilt.

"That's too extreme: no one was killed," Crichton countered.

"Can I ask a question?" Riley spoke up. "Gerald, how old are you?"

"Eighteen, or there abouts." His face had paled at Angela's suggestion, making the scratches look almost unreal in their red contrast.

"Who's your guardian?" Harry asked next.

"I came here two years ago and you guys said I was old enough and capable enough not to need one." Gerald's voice was tight, suggesting his throat was swelling with tension. Riley felt fine with that, hoping he struggled to breathe so that he would know what it was like for Nessie right now.

"Who took care of you before you got here?" Harry continued.

Gerald shrugged. "Various people. Most of them kept dying."

"I see." Harry nodded as if something had been confirmed for him.

"I think I know what you're getting at, if I may speak," Evans chimed in.

"Go ahead."

"Children raised outside walls like these, with no one teaching them in any consistent way, turn strange. I've seen it happen. Watching so many die around them, they develop a skewed view on death and can no longer properly connect with people. Adults break out there, while children merely bend into something twisted."

Gerald's face went from white to red as his eyes filled with tears. His mouth opened and closed a couple of times, but he failed to decide what to say and kept it shut in the end.

"Tommy? You've spent a lot of time out in the wilds, what do you think?" Boyle looked to the other outsider.

"I've seen a lot of people do a lot of bad things and not even realize they were doing it. Do I think this kid could've done what you said? Sure, of course. Do I also think it could be someone who seems totally adjusted? Certainly. You never know what someone is capable of until they do it."

"Let's clear some things up. Who thinks Gerald attacked Nessie?" Crichton asked, raising his hand. Everyone else with a vote did the same. "And who thinks he kept a zombie in a container?"

Riley believed Nessie knew what she was talking about, so she raised her hand alongside Angela, Crichton, and Boyle. Only Harry didn't raise his hand, believing Gerald was, or at least could be, innocent.

"So all that remains is sentencing," Crichton confirmed.

"I still say we execute him," Angela crossed her arms firmly. "If he did it once, what's to stop him from doing it again in the future?"

"Your point is fair, but execution is too much," Boyle agreed with Crichton.

"Well, if you don't want to give him a confinement sentence, and you don't want to kill him, that leaves only banishment," Riley followed the thread to its conclusion.

"That's as good as execution," Gerald squeaked.

"You survived, what? Nine years outside the wall already?" Crichton spoke to him. "I'm sure you have the skills to survive long enough to find another shelter that will take you in. We'd give you food and water supplies, as well as a weapon. Not a gun, we don't have enough ammo for that, but a good blade. If you confess now and tell us why you did what you did, and what happened to the zombie, perhaps we'll come up with a different solution."

Gerald imitated a fish again, his mouth opening and closing silently, but he said nothing and finally went still.

"So, are we agreed on the resolution? Confinement until the next scavenging party goes out, and then exile?" Boyle looked around the circle and no one objected. "Vote."

Everyone raised their hand except Harry, but then after a moment of thought, he raised his as well.

"Exile it is."

36
Evans Is Planning

Evans watched the prisoner's face turn from white, to red, and then back to white following his sentencing.

"Can someone please take him back to a holding container?" Boyle asked the witnesses clustered around.

Gerald had gone completely limp, his eyes distant, and had to be carried from the space. Evans had been worried he might fly into a rage and attack, but he seemed to have gone the other way, at least for now.

"You had something you wanted to talk to us about?" Boyle turned to Evans. "Something about the group that attacked the Black Box?"

"Yes," Evans nodded, remembering his half-formed plan. "I don't know what this Black Box is, and I don't know the people who attacked you. It's possible they're the same people who picked off our scavengers, but there's no way to know for sure. What I do know, is that some of your people heard part of the battle from there, which means they will have heard it. If the wind is right, they're also going to see the smoke from your body burns."

"He's right, we definitely heard something although most weren't sure it came from this direction," the woman who demanded execution, the one who Evans hadn't been introduced to, spoke up. "You said you guys used grenades, so I'm guessing that's what we heard."

"We don't know much about that group, so there's a chance they'll come this way to investigate," Crichton sighed and ran a hand down the side of his face. Evans had been introduced to him not long before this odd version of court.

"I may know of a way to help you."

"How?"

"Your place here is nice, one of the better ones I've come across. I'm going to advise my party members to stay with you."

"This sounds like you don't intend to stay yourself," the woman with deep bags beneath her eyes and wrapped in bandages under her jacket cut to the point.

"I don't. I've never been comfortable staying anywhere for too long. I had planned to stay for a few days, help you clean up, but I think a better use for my time has arisen. Let me change my clothes, pack my supplies, and pick one of my horses. You take me to a safe place beyond the wall using that submarine of yours, and give me directions to your second camp. I'll go over there and make up some story that explains the noises and the smoke."

"What story?" asked the archer who'd fired two grenades with his arrows.

"I haven't gotten that far yet, but I'm sure I'll have time to come up with one. I can even take that exile with me, if you'd like. If he's with me, he's less likely to try to find his way back. In fact, I know of some camps who'd take him, even knowing what he did, provided they still exist."

"It would buy us some time," Crichton said, turning to Boyle.

"Time for what?" the bandaged woman asked, although Boyle looked like he might have asked the same thing.

"We can't take the Black Box back, not with our diminished ammo supplies and not with them knowing where the entrance is to the vehicle elevator outside the walls. But there is something we can do to hurt them. I think it's best we continue to discuss this somewhere more private." Crichton looked around at all the watchful eyes and listening ears.

Boyle agreed and the ring of people rose.

"Tommy, you're welcome to come listen in if you'd like," Crichton told him. "If we do drop off Evans, perhaps we can arrange to pick up your remaining group members."

Tommy nodded.

"I should be getting back to work unless you think you need me," the archer declared.

"Go ahead, we'll find you if we need you for something."

The angry woman went with the archer, leaving without a word.

"He may be going, but I'm coming with you," the bandaged woman insisted, although she looked ready to collapse back into her seat.

Crichton looked ready to object, but Boyle spoke up first. "Your opinion would be welcome."

"Claire," the bandaged woman turned to the young woman who had brought Evans to his trial, "could you tell Hope where I've gone? And keep an eye on her and the other kids; I don't entirely trust Quin to watch out for them any longer than I already have."

"You got it."

"You can lean on me if you'd like," Evans told the woman as they moved toward the throng of people who surrounded the ring of chairs.

"Thanks." She managed to put a lot of caution into that one word as she placed a hand on his upper arm, not so much leaning on him as using him to steady herself.

"I don't believe we were introduced. I'm Evans." He would have offered his hand, but it would have been awkward as they threaded through the crowd.

"Riley."

"May I ask what happened to you, Riley?"

"Breast cancer with an extremely poor sense of timing."

"You were able to determine that you had cancer?"

"The Black Box still has a lot of modern medical equipment, along with the power to run it."

"You're a fortunate group."

"In that way, yes."

They exited the building, stepping back out into sunlight. It seemed that as soon as the rats appeared, all efforts were diverted to clearing the dead bodies away from the structure; a space had been created around the whole building. People with handheld weapons and thick pants had formed a ring within the space, ready to smash any rats that tried to get through. A whole swarm of cats and dogs were also patrolling for the vermin. The people too tired to deal with the rats were mostly crowded into the refurbished warehouse, but a group of them seemed to have ducked inside the holding containers. More people were being instructed to climb up on top of them and the roof, where most of Evans' party members had made their stand. Evans wondered if they had accidentally broken any of the solar panels up there.

"Ki-nam!" he called out upon spotting the man.

The older man walked over and didn't bother with a greeting, even though they hadn't seen one another since before the zombies. Evans was glad to see he had survived.

"These people have agreed to let us stay here if we want. Can you start spreading the word to the others?"

Ki-nam nodded, heading back to whatever he had been doing. He'd tell people as he came across them.

Evans continued to follow Boyle, Crichton, and Tommy to wherever they planned to have this meeting. When they came across a dark-haired man with broad shoulders, they stopped briefly.

"Bronislav, think everyone can handle things without you for a moment? We're having a meeting that you should sit in on," Crichton told him.

The man named Bronislav looked around at what was going on, then agreed things would be fine and joined their little party. Boyle, limping, took them down an alley between containers that people had started to clear out, knocking on doors until he found one that was empty. They all clustered inside. Crichton found and lit a lantern on a shelf, their only source of light once the doors were closed behind them. In the fiery glow, Riley made her way to a pair of bunk beds at the back and sat down on one of the lower ones. Soon, they all clustered back there, three to a bed. Evans wondered whose home they had invaded.

"I had heard that Karsten was killed, but I'd like to confirm that before we start," Crichton spoke first.

"I saw it myself," Boyle told him.

The lack of care on Crichton's face as he heard this made Evans wonder if he was trained to do that, or if the man was like himself, unable to properly connect.

"To bring everyone up to speed, the Black Box was taken last night. We had found a boy, half-starved, and took him in, never suspecting he was actually a plant for a large group of well-armed raiders. He somehow got word to them, letting them know where the entrance to the vehicle elevator was, the only entrance beyond our fences, and likely told them everything else he had learned. Although we had sealed the entrance to the vehicle elevator, they somehow managed to get it open and get inside, allowing them to attack us from both above and below at the same time. We were quickly overwhelmed and many, including myself, were captured, while the rest barricaded themselves inside whatever room they happened to be in. They proved they were more than willing to kill hostages, so in the end, I had no choice but to give them the Black Box to keep anyone else from dying."

"That was early this morning. We then led everyone to the submarine and brought them here," Bronislav finished.

"I was one of the last people out, making sure no one was held back. Only then did my man who was holed up with the power supply open the door and let them have access to it. What people don't know, what Bronislav and I only shared with a necessary few, is about the explosives."

"Explosives?" Boyle frowned.

"Around the power supply, in the hydroponics and medical labs, and around every entrance and elevator shaft, are hidden several stable but powerful explosive charges."

"Why would you set those?" Boyle asked angrily. Beside Evans, Riley squirmed uncomfortably, pulling her tattered leather jacket more tightly around her shoulders.

"There's a reason we never told anyone what the power source is," Bronislav explained. "Having lived in a submarine, I know how nervous people get around nuclear energy."

"The Black Box is nuclear?" Riley gasped. "I always thought it was some new thing that Marble Keystone had come up with but not shared with the rest of the world."

Marble Keystone? Evans wondered how the company that released the zombie plague was related to all of this.

"It is a new technology," Bronislav told her. "I don't understand it very well myself, but the engineers we've let in there tell me that it's far more stable and efficient than anything they've seen. The former NASA engineer with us says it's even better than what they had been building for their rovers that never made it to Mars. Still, people are uncomfortable near the stuff, so we told no one. Let them think as you did."

"So the explosives are for…?" Boyle prompted them to get back on track.

"In case there was ever a leak, an emergency precaution. We'd have everyone evacuate, and then bury the place."

While Bronislav spoke, Evans watched Crichton's face. The man was solid, hard to read, but Evans thought he saw something flicker there. If he had to guess, he'd say that wasn't the only reason Crichton had planted the explosives. The man had probably guessed something like this would eventually happen, the locations of the explosives backing up this theory. Why else put them in medical and hydroponics labs?

"So you want to set these explosives off and bury the attackers," Riley came back around to the start of the conversation.

"We'd lose the Black Box," Crichton nodded, "but we'd rid ourselves of them. We could hope to salvage the farm fields, and not have to worry about them coming here, at least not in large numbers."

"How do you set them off?" Tommy wondered.

"I have the remote." Bronislav took the device out of his pocket. It was a simple thing with a twist dial to turn on the power, and a switch under a protective plastic shell. "I was able to hide it on me before they took over the command centre." He wouldn't say how, suggesting it wasn't a comfortable method of smuggling.

"I'm guessing there's a reason you haven't set it off yet," Evans figured.

"Range," Crichton told him. "To make sure all of them are set off, you'd pretty much need to be directly above the centre of the compound."

"Which we can't get to because they'll be guarding the place, and we can't storm it because of our minuscule amount of ammo," Boyle sighed.

"Did you leave anyone behind? When we boarded the submarine?" Riley wondered, an odd expression pulling at her features.

"Jamal stayed behind to watch if we were followed, and in case James showed up with the others who went out. We're supposed to pick him up in a week, why?"

"Because I might have a plan if everyone is willing, and we're definitely going to need Harry."

The way she said it made Evans nervous.

***

The sun was nearing the western horizon as Evans sat at the top of the rocky shore. He had his gear packed and was watching as the people of the container yard convinced his horse to get into a fairly small boat, a strip of cloth keeping the beast from seeing exactly what was happening. Apparently, it was easiest to just ferry Evans across the river and they didn't need the submarine for that.

Across the water, Tommy's two friends were waiting. They had been contacted using Morse code flashes and directed to cross the river via a bridge upstream. Soon, they would be crossing back over into the container yard where they would make the decision about whether they wanted to stay or not.

From his pocket, Evans removed his battered notebook. He updated his maps to include the container yard, as well as where he had been told the Black Box was located. He had just finished when Ki-nam came over and sat down beside him.

"Are you sure you want to leave on your own?" the man asked. "Not everyone will want to stay here with what's happened."

"Yes, it's time I stop leading for a while. Besides, I won't be alone, I'll have Gerald with me. And the horse. What's that one's name again? I think it's Moe but I always get the names of the grey ones mixed up."

"That's Moe," Ki-nam confirmed. "You should have picked a younger horse."

"Moe's fine." In fact, Evans had picked him purely because he was getting on in years, but he was still strong and healthy. The younger horses would be more useful to the people who remained. Besides, he knew this particular horse was easy to manage. The grey beast was well broken-in and didn't frighten easily. This suited Evans, who was only a mediocre rider himself.

"You are not leaving because you have to, are you?" Ki-nam asked next.

"No, I wasn't forced out. Just like the rest of you, I was given the option to stay. But I can't. I stay anywhere too long and I get anxious."

"Very well. I wish you luck, then."

"Thank you, friend. I'll be sure to visit." If he lived long enough to visit that was.

"Are you sure you won't stay longer to say goodbye to the others?"

Evans shook his head. "That would take too long. Today they've said goodbye to enough of their friends who can't return. I don't want to deal with their tears and their begging. Besides, I promised these people I'd help them with something."

"So you'll leave the tears and the anger to me and the others."

"Not my problem anymore, Ki-nam." Evans got to his feet, seeing the boats were just about ready for him.

Ki-nam rose as well, and briskly shook Evans' hand, wishing him luck once more. As Evans made his way across the rocks, he came upon a familiar black and white body.

"You again," Evans paused, looking down at the cat.

The cat looked back up at him with shining golden eyes.

"You're not coming this time. You're staying here and gorging yourself on rats."

The cat brushed himself against Evans' legs. With a resigned sigh, Evans actually bent down and stroked the creature, giving its ears a scratch. The cat then caught the scent of something and took off.

Down by the water, Evans carefully boarded the canoe. When the end of his sword caught the side of it, he nearly tipped the whole thing over. Only the men standing in the water, holding the canoe steady, kept him from taking a spill. In a much larger boat, the kind that Evans realized made up a large chunk of the bridge to the island, Moe the horse was lying down, attended to by a pair of veterinarians. At the mouth of the river floated another canoe, in the middle of which sat Gerald with a blindfold over his eyes that matched Moe's. Evans was under instruction to keep the teenager blinded for a while, to make sure he didn't quite know where he was. It would reduce the chances of him running away from Evans if he didn't know the location of the container yard.

"I'm ready," Evans told the paddlers. One of them was Tommy, who was crossing to make sure there would be no trouble with his two friends.

The boats glided smoothly over the water, against the current that was pushing them toward the large bay. The paddlers kept them mainly steady and on course. The river was wide and it took them several minutes to reach the far shore. Once there, Evans stumbled back out of the canoe and watched as two men carried Gerald to shore and dumped him upon the rocks. With his wrists bound behind him, he folded over his bag of supplies when it was placed in his lap. Even though the kid's eyes were hidden, Evans could see that he was frightened.

Tommy met with his two friends, and the three of them exchanged words: mostly about the super smart zombie. Apparently, the two of them had been scanning the corpse pile outside the walls from a distance, but they had yet to find a sign confirming the thing was fully dead or whether it was still moving around somewhere. They had also been searching the surrounding area, wondering if maybe it had run away, but no signs had been found to indicate that either. They seemed to take this as good news, believing that if the zombie was still moving, they would know about it by now. Evans decided they knew more about the thing than he did and also took it to be good news.

Once Moe was up and on solid ground, Evans saddled him by himself, letting the container people get back into their boats. There were no long, heartfelt goodbyes here, just a few silent head nods in Evans' direction. That was the way Evans preferred it.

"On your feet, Gerald," Evans commanded the teenager once the boats were on their way.

"Who are you?" Gerald asked nervously as Evans led him toward the horse, carrying the kid's pack.

"My name is Evans. I'm the one who was sitting next to you during the trial, the one with the sword."

"The one who said you'd seen people like me before," he responded rather bitterly.

"I know of a whole camp of people like you." Evans climbed up on the big, old draft horse and pulled Gerald up with him. The kid was skinny enough that Evans could sit him on top of their packs, which he had lashed behind the saddle. "Hold on here," he advised the kid.

"People like me?" Gerald wondered, pressing his knees into Evans' sides in an attempt to stay balanced as the horse started moving. It wasn't easy to hold on with his hands behind his back, but Evans didn't want the kid free to remove his blindfold yet.

"People who don't believe the zombies are really dead, that something can be done to save them, that there's still something human down inside."

Based on the way Gerald shivered, Evans knew he had hit the nail on the head.

"Stick with me, do as you're told, and I'll take you to this camp. They'll take you in without much trouble."

"Were you exiled as well?" Gerald changed topics.

"Yes," Evans lied, figuring it would help the kid trust him more. "I was more behaved about it than you were. I admitted my guilt for the sake of my party, and in exchange, I got to keep my horse and not be blindfolded like you are."

"Can you take my blindfold off? And unbind my hands so that I can sit better? I'm afraid I'm going to fall."

"I promised I'd keep you blindfolded and bound until we stop for the first night."

"Can't you free me now? They won't know."

"I keep my word, kid, which includes taking you to that camp I mentioned if you behave. Right now, behaving means keeping your mouth shut."

Evans guessed the kid was looking sullen right about now, but he did as he was told and ceased speaking. As they rode, Gerald wiggled around a fair amount, trying to find a comfortable way of sitting. In the end, he slumped against Evans' back, his legs tucked up with his knees pressed uncomfortably into Evans' sides. That was fine; with the sun setting, Evans didn't plan on riding for much longer anyway. Tomorrow, with the kid's arms free, they should be able to come up with a better arrangement for the two of them.

It was dark before Evans picked a place that they could stop for the night. It was some old factory, but Evans didn't take them any farther than the front office. Once he guided Gerald inside and got him standing in a corner, he carefully led in Moe. The front windows were all broken, but Evans was fine with that. The broken glass still littered the floor beneath them, along with a drift of brittle leaves. Anything trying to get in would make enough noise to wake him.

"All right, I'm freeing your wrists now," Evans told Gerald as he carefully unknotted the rope. He could have cut through it much faster, but it was good rope for which there were plenty of uses.

Once his hands were free, Gerald rubbed his wrists, which were red and raw. He then pulled the blindfold up and off his head.

"There are no windows," he commented.

Evans quickly explained about the glass and leaves. "Here's your pack. You're on your own for food right now; we're not sharing until I know you better."

"If I'm not allowed to talk, how will you get to know me?"

"Ever hear the saying 'actions speak louder than words'? I find that to be true. Now eat up and get some rest, we're starting out early tomorrow."

Gerald set up his sleeping kit in one corner of the room, while Evans kept near Moe. The horse was already asleep, possibly still getting over the tranquilliser he had been given during the zombie attack. Evans' exhaustion hit him all at once the moment he laid down. He was asleep in seconds.

***

For two days, Evans rode with Gerald, making their way around the top of the big bay and then back down. They conversed little. Evans spoke to Gerald only when necessary, and Gerald only occasionally asked about the camp to which Evans was taking him once this was over. Of course, Gerald thought they were heading to the camp directly, and

Evans thought it best that he believe that. It might make him freak out once he learned they weren't, but it kept him from orienting himself and running away at the first opportunity. Thankfully, the kid hadn't been outside the container yard's walls since he had arrived there and didn't know this area.

The days were filled with light foraging, the occasional bashing in or cutting off of a zombie's skull, and riding, always riding. Evans' ass and thighs were sore from the saddle and he found himself looking forward to their stops more and more. After saddling up after breakfast, they rode until lunch, at which point they would take the time to forage in whatever buildings were closest. Most of them had been picked to the bone, however, so their only real finds were when they came across wild vegetables, fruits, or mushrooms that had grown since the last people had been through. Evans silently thanked the man he once met who had taught him all about mushrooms, specifically which ones wouldn't kill him when eaten. After lunch, it was the saddle again until nightfall, when they would stop again, eat dinner, and sleep.

On the third morning, Evans woke up with painfully cramped legs. He decided that once this was over and he was actually taking Gerald to the camp he knew about, he'd plan for a lot more stopping and even some walking. Moe would probably like that. Although he was a big beast of a horse and was handling the weight of both people and their packs well enough, his old bones couldn't keep it up forever.

Evans got up wincing and picked some food from his pack. After returning all his gear to the large bag, he decided to walk around while he ate, checking for anything useful nearby. He hoped the walking would loosen his muscles somewhat. Gerald was still asleep. They had spent the night in the upstairs of a skinny townhouse. Gerald had decided to risk the mouldy, dusty mattress on the one bed, but Evans had brought up couch cushions to put down under his sleeping mat. Downstairs, the place had taken on a new odour since the previous night: a large pile of rather fresh horse shit steamed on the kitchen tiles. Leaving the saddle where he had placed it the night before, Evans picked up Moe's lead and brought him out back where the beast could graze on the overgrown grass and weeds. Investigating the shed, he found nothing but a busted lock and useless junk. Like everywhere else, someone had been there before him. He guessed it was people from the container yard when they still held the Black Box. Before they got their boat system up and running, it probably wasn't uncommon for groups to walk from place to place, gathering supplies as they went.

"Evans?" Gerald's wavering voice drew him back out of the shed. The relief on Gerald's face let Evans know just how hard it was going to be to do what he had to do later today. "I thought you had left."

"Did you not see the saddle where I left it?"

"Yeah, but—"

"And my pack still upstairs?"

"Yeah, but—"

"Trust me, kid, if I'm going to leave you, I'm not going to leave all my supplies and something as valuable as a horse behind. Have you eaten yet?"

"Only a little bit."

"Eat some more then while I saddle up Moe, and then bring the packs down."

Gerald disappeared back inside.

When Evans brought the saddle to Moe, the horse seemed to have a look in his eyes that matched how the man felt. The beast was just as tired of the thing as Evans was.

"At least you're not pulling a heavily laden cart anymore," Evans reminded the horse as he flipped the saddle over its back. "And hey, there haven't been that many zombies; they were probably all drawn to one camp or the other with all the commotion lately." It was probably the container yard due to the prolonged 'commotion.' Whatever the exact reason for their absence, Evans was grateful for it.

When Gerald returned, they strapped the packs behind the saddle together, then climbed up into their usual seating arrangement. With his arms free, Gerald could hold onto Evans' shoulders and no longer needed to dig his knees painfully into Evans' ribcage; he had learned to balance. With his legs protesting against the usual seat, Evans squeezed his heels into Moe's flanks to start him forward.

They reached the bridge cluttered with old ruined vehicles earlier than Evans expected, which meant they were ahead of schedule. That was fine; Evans would much rather be early than late. While they were crossing, he looked over at the railroad bridge that he had been advised was not good for horses and briefly thought about abandoning his duty. He wouldn't do that though; he wouldn't break his oath after the grief he had caused. On the other side, only trees and bushes crowded the edges of the road, but Evans had been assured there would be some sort of rest stop structure ahead. Moe continued to plod forward, following the soft, weedy shoulder that was better for his feet, while Evans continued to scan their surroundings.

"What are you looking for? Did you see something?" Gerald whispered, noticing Evans' more alert status. "Are there zombies in these woods?"

"There are zombies everywhere," Evans informed him. "That's what I'm looking for." He pointed ahead as the rest stop came into view around the bend. It wasn't much: just a tiny gas station with two pumps. Someone had spray painted the word *dry* on the pavement in front of them, the letters faded and cracked with age.

"Why are we stopping here?" Gerald wondered as Evans walked them close and dismounted.

"There's something we need to do." Evans loosely tied Moe's reins to a pump, next to where a patch of grass and weeds had sprouted up through the pavement.

Gerald hesitated getting off the horse, but he didn't have much choice when Evans started to untie the packs from underneath him. Knowing he would follow, Evans headed into the tiny station. The racks had long since been cleared off, and a few knocked over. The place was picked as clean as Evans knew it would be; even most of the wooden boards that made up some wall shelves were absent. He headed behind the counter and placed both packs on the floor, slipping something out of the side pocket of his own.

"Come over here," Evans told Gerald.

The kid hesitated again, but then walked over behind the counter.

"Hold out your hands."

"Why?"

"Just do it."

Gerald held out his hands. Evans quickly slipped the rope around his wrists and tightened.

"Hey! What are you doing?"

"Making sure you stay put." While the kid was still disoriented by what was happening, Evans kicked his legs out from under him. On the floor there was a brief scuffle as Gerald attempted to wiggle away, but Evans easily overpowered him. He dragged Gerald to a secure-looking strut in the middle of the checkout counter and tied the kid's wrists to it.

"Why are you doing this?" Gerald wailed.

"Keep quiet if you don't want the zombies to come. There's something I need to do alone and I don't want you disappearing on me."

"There's no need to tie me up. I'll be good; I'll stay here."

"Gerald, one of the first things I learned about you is that you lie, especially under stress. I don't trust you."

"How do I know you're coming back? That you're not just leaving me here?"

"I'm leaving both the packs." Evans gestured to where they sat on the floor. If Gerald really tried, he could probably reach them with his feet, but it would badly hurt his wrists so Evans guessed he'd only attempt it as a last resort. Patting down Gerald, he removed the trench knife the kid had on him and placed it with the packs.

"What if zombies come? I'm defenceless."

"If you stay quiet, they have no reason to come. There's no easy way for them to shuffle right in here, and they can't possibly see you from outside, so don't make a sound and they'll go right past."

"What if there are scavengers?"

"Would you bother with this place?"

"If I were desperate."

"If they're desperate, you won't be able to do anything anyway. If someone like that does come, and they do find you, just let them take the packs without a fight. Say nothing unless spoken to, and don't lie."

"But…what if they're cannibals? Or slavers?"

"Something you should know about me, Gerald, is that I've travelled a lot. During all that time, I've hardly ever run into any cannibals, and the ones I have, have all been up north during winter when food is scarce." A memory tried to worm its way into the front of Evans' mind, but he quickly suppressed it. After a particularly bad northern winter, he now only travelled up there during the warmer seasons, and even then, not often. He didn't have anything encouraging to say when it came to possible slavers.

"What happens if you don't come back?"

"I'll be back before nightfall."

"But what happens if you're not?"

"That would mean we're both in some serious shit, wouldn't it? Now stay here, and stay quiet."

Gerald opened his mouth to say something else, to protest some more, but Evans clapped a hand over his mouth to silence it. He didn't bother to repeat himself, just kept his hand in place, staring into Gerald's eyes until the kid nodded.

Without another word, Evans got up and went back outside, carrying his sword and his shotgun with him. He wished he had some shells for the shotgun, that it wasn't just a tool for idle threats. Moe snorted as he was untied and remounted. This time, instead of letting the horse plod along at the pace it preferred, Evans kicked it into a brisk trot. He wanted to get this part over and done with as soon as possible.

Once he had headed into the trees, Evans was forced to slow down again. He let Moe decide the best route between the trunks and branches, using the sun to make sure they were going the right way. A few times,

Evans had to keep Moe from walking over some dangerous-looking rocks or deadfalls, but for the most part, the horse knew what it was doing. On the other side of the strip of forest, they came across several warehouses or what looked like factories, and Evans knew he was close. He knew he was extremely close when a crack rang out and the pavement in the intersection up ahead puffed from the impact of a bullet.

"We can hear your horse!" a gruff voice called out after Evans had reined Moe to a stop.

"Where are you?" Evans called back, pretending he didn't know that to take a right at the intersection would have him facing down the street and looking at the fence the former Black Box residents had set up.

"How many are you?" the voice called back instead of answering.

"One, plus the horse!"

"Dismount and come around the corner slowly!"

Evans didn't dismount, but he urged Moe forward, walking them into view. He scanned the area, taking in the fence of many materials, as well as eyeballing the nearby rooftops and windows, even glancing backward just in case.

"I said to dismount!" the gruff voice shouted angrily. It came from a man standing behind the fence.

"Yeah, that's not happening." Evans walked Moe a little closer.

"Stop!" the man's rifle raised and pointed directly at Evans, so he stopped.

"I mean you no harm," he told the man at the fence.

"Sure you don't," he sneered. "Park! Come take a look at this guy! Tell me if he's one of them!"

The first man was joined by a second who looked Evans up and down. "Nah, he ain't one of them. I'd remember a big guy like that for sure. Where do you come from, stranger?"

"All over. I'm with a party of roamers."

"And where's the rest o' this party o' yours?" the man named Park asked.

"Elsewhere. I'm an outrider, searching for points of interest for the main column."

"Well, this ain't no point of interest," Park informed him.

"No? You appear to be a settlement. You're not open for trade?"

"No, we ain't."

"Very well, I'll be on my way then. May I leave you with some advice?"

Park and the other man looked at one another and then shrugged, gesturing for Evans to say his piece. Other guards were watching, fingers near triggers.

"You see that smoke over that way?" This far, the black smoke from the body fire was thin and wispy. "My column came from there. If you have scavengers out, I wouldn't recommend sending them that way for a few weeks. There's a massive horde of the dead."

"What's the smoke from?" asked the first man to have spoken.

"We managed to trap a bunch in a warehouse and light it. The flames distracted the things still outside while we escaped. Still lost a lot of good people though."

"We've been seeing smoke from there for days now. Why's it still burning?" Park glanced suspiciously in that direction.

"Didn't have time to get a proper look, but it appeared to be some sort of lumber yard, lots of stuff to burn. It's a shame really. A lot of good material is going to waste, but I'm not complaining. It should keep those rotten bastards occupied while we keep moving."

"You see any other groups out there? Big ones, not much in the way of supplies?" Park changed topics.

"No, why? Should I have?"

"You gave us advice, so I'll give you some. There are bandits somewhere to the south and east of here. I suggest you take word back to your party and tell them to head straight north."

"These bandits why you're not open to trade?"

Neither of the men answered.

"We'll head north then, thank you." Evans started to turn Moe around.

"I like that horse," the gruff sounding one called out.

Evans sighed. He had come so close to getting away clean. "I like him too." Evans turned Moe again so that the horse's head and chest could shield him from a direct shot from the fence.

"Yeah, but what if I like him *more* than you?" the gruff one said with a grin.

Evans proceeded to pull back on the reins, getting Moe to walk backward as straight as the horse was able.

"Where you going?" the gruff man laughed.

"You said you weren't open to trade."

"Doesn't mean we're not open to gifts."

"Let's be honest. We both know that if you want my horse, you'll have to shoot me, and you're more likely to hit him than me." Evans pulled out his shotgun and held it in one hand while the other stayed tight on the reins.

"I don't mind horse meat," Park commented.

The gruff one raised his rifle again, but after a second lowered it. He mumbled something to Park, and they both watched as Evans continued to ride backward to the intersection. As soon as he was in line with the next street, he wheeled Moe about and kicked him into a gallop, crouching low over the big horse's neck to make himself as small a target as possible.

With his heart hammering in his throat, Evans steadied his breathing. He didn't know what stopped the gruff man from shooting: maybe the possibility that Evans wasn't lying about having a party not far away. He was just glad that he didn't.

Taking a different route back to the rest stop, Evans ran Moe hard, making sure no one could follow. He had completed the first step of Riley's plan, and now he had to move onto the second.

37
Doyle's Uncomfortable

Living in the woods was a miserable affair. The floor of the cave was on a slight slope, which was never more obvious than when trying to sleep. Their only meat came from squirrels who got caught in the snares, several of them not dying quickly, leaving the task to whoever's turn it was to check the traps. Doyle suspected it was the small amount of meat off one such squirrel that had him outside the cave and shitting over the side of a log for most of the second night. That, or the stream water hadn't been boiled properly, although no one else was affected. Because of the boiling, the water tasted of the metal pot, while the rest of their food was hard, dry, and didn't taste like much of anything.

"To think that after the Day, this is how we lived," Doyle once commented to Canary.

"This isn't how we lived at all," she replied. "We kept moving, food was easily scavenged as it hadn't yet started going bad, the water was still running in a lot of places, and we often found couch cushions, if not actual beds, when we stopped for the night."

At least her leg seemed to be healing. Everyone in the group worried about it, but it hadn't bled for some time and the discoloration was from a bruise that had formed around the injury and not from infection. Canary took off her bandages and washed them and the injury in the ocean every day, then wrapped the long strip of gauze back around. For the most part, everyone went into the sea at least once a day. Feeling clean was possibly the only luxury this place afforded, even if it didn't take long to get dirty again.

"I miss clean underwear," Jamal said on the third day.

"Wash it in the ocean," Doyle grumbled, having barely slept the night before. He had just come in from washing his ass off and didn't need any reminders about that part of his body.

"It's not the same, not without soap."

Doyle didn't bother trying to keep up the conversation; he just curled up in his sleeping bag and closed his eyes.

On the fourth day, they had a bit of a zombie problem. A few of the dead things that lingered around the factory up the shoreline decided to come down for a visit. The zombies had been useful on the second day when one of the men who had attacked the Black Box came snooping around. He had followed the trail as far as the zombies would allow, but had to turn back when the dead noticed him. Had he been able to linger, he might have discovered the trail went suspiciously cold at the docks and figured out that the group had gone to sea.

Doyle's axe sank into the skull of the final zombie.

"That the last of them?" James asked as he looked around for more.

"Looks like it," Doyle answered. "What do we do with the corpses? A body burn will draw too much attention."

"Well, we can either spend hours digging them graves, or we can push them out to sea." James clearly preferred the sea option so that's what they did.

It took more work to remove the bodies than it did to kill them. Doyle and James had to pick up the rotting things between them and walk them to the water. Once there, they waded in across the slippery rocks, and attempted to push the things down where the undertow would grab them.

"I hope Jamal is okay." The third man was out checking their snares and getting water from the stream. Doyle tried not to think about Rose, who was today's spy, watching the Black Box from a distance, and possibly dealing with much worse problems.

"The guy's a monkey; he could be up one of these trees before the zombies even knew he was in the woods," James told him. "I just wish he'd hurry up and get back here to help us with these."

At that moment, the corpse they were carrying between them split in two, leaving Doyle holding a pair of hips and legs, and James a torso, head, and arms, with a string of guts slopped out between them. The smell hit Doyle hard, and he might have thrown up if his stomach hadn't been so empty.

"Goddamn it, why couldn't it rot like this before leaving the factory?" James hissed between his teeth. He was just as tired of their situation as everyone else. Doyle bet he would scream if that wouldn't risk their safety. He knew that *he* wanted to scream. They dragged the corpse halves to the water, the guts managing to stay attached as they slid over the rocks like some mutant squid.

At least the zombies gave them something to do. That was what was really trying about staying out there: the never-ending boredom. Outside of checking the traps, fetching water, and cooking, there wasn't much to do. The only interesting task was watching the Black Box, but only one person did that at a time. Doyle was grateful for the books they had risked their lives for, because he was sure they would be killing each other by now without them. Everyone read most of the day, especially Canary who could only do so much on her wounded leg. Nights were worse, when there was no light to read by, and even standing guard was dull and dreary. They could have used their flashlights, but no one wanted to drain the batteries, just in case.

It was the 'just in case' that no one spoke about out loud: just in case the submarine didn't come back. Doyle was sure they would wait a few days past the expected time, hoping the submarine was only delayed, but what if it wasn't? What if something happened and they never showed up? It would be just the five of them with minimal supplies, trying to walk all the way back to the container yard, with known hostiles along the way. It would be a week, more with Canary's leg, and they wouldn't know what they were walking into. If the submarine didn't come, the only reason why, that Doyle could think of, had to do with the container yard being in trouble. The noises Jamal claimed people had heard while evacuating only gave strength to that idea.

The last of the zombies was finally sent out to sea, and James and Doyle waded out of the water.

"We should wait awhile before anyone goes swimming in case those things come floating back," James suggested.

"Agreed," Doyle nodded.

"I'm going to go find Jamal." He stalked off. He was what Doyle considered a man of action, always needing something to do. All this waiting seemed to be wearing on him the most.

Doyle decided he should let Canary know that neither of them were dead.

Back in the cave, Canary was lying in her usual position, her head and shoulders propped up on her bedroll in the spot that got the most sunlight. She had clearly been reading again based on the book lying beside her, but a dagger was held firmly in her hand as Doyle came in.

"Everyone okay?" she asked, laying the dagger down once she knew he wasn't a zombie about to attack her.

"As okay as we get out here," Doyle answered. "That book any good?" He noticed the cover was different from the last one she had been reading.

"Not sure yet, I'm not very far in." She picked it up and showed him where her bookmark sat very close to the front cover. "The one you're reading get any better yet?"

Doyle found his book and flopped down beside her, glad he had thought to take bookmarks as he removed his. "No. That ending I theorized? There's been more evidence to support it. For a mystery story, it's not being very mysterious."

"Maybe it's deliberately misleading you and you'll be surprised."

"I doubt it; I don't think this writer is good enough for that."

With their conversation ended, Doyle and Canary opened their books, but he read only a chapter before he became tired with the current section of plot and ended up just sitting and staring out through the mouth of the cave, watching the spaces between the branches for Jamal or James. He finally gave up and crawled back out. Canary didn't bother to ask him where he was going: they both knew the answer would be nowhere.

Doyle wandered around for a bit, checked to see if any of the corpses had washed back onto shore, then headed over to the fire pit. Nothing had changed, and they already had more than enough split wood so Doyle wasn't going to bother cutting more. His axe had become rather dull, but no one had a whetstone with which he could sharpen it, and he wasn't about to use some random rock and risk damaging his primary weapon. At least the weight of the axe was still enough to drive the blade through a zombie's skull, even if the blade ended up being as dull as a spoon.

Since he was there, Doyle knelt down and set the fire, so that when Jamal returned to cook any meat he brought back and to boil the water, all he'd have to do was light it. It didn't take long, soon leaving Doyle with nothing to do again.

When James returned with Jamal, they found Doyle just sitting next to the unlit fire, staring off over the water. Neither asked what he was thinking about; Jamal merely handed over the three squirrels and the skinning knife. Doyle went to work separating the meat, while James put down the water pails and left to fetch the single small pot and single small pan Jamal had been left with. Jamal lit the fire, careful to keep it as smokeless as possible. They had deliberately set up their fire pit beneath the branches of a very thick coniferous along the edge of the pebble beach, so that any smoke they did emit would hopefully be dispersed and hidden by its branches.

"We'll be out of squirrels soon," Jamal commented once the fire was going.

"You make them sound like rations."

"Moving the snares isn't enough; there just aren't that many around here anymore," he continued. "Did you notice I only brought back three today?"

Doyle had noticed, but didn't want to say anything. When they first started laying snares, the forest was lousy with the rodents, which was great considering the animals couldn't be infected. Every day they brought in fewer, however. The squirrels had either learned to avoid the traps, or had left the area all together. Doyle didn't believe they could have eaten so many as to reduce the population that much, but he would also admit that he could be wrong.

James returned with the pot and pan. With nothing else that they could do, they boiled the water, carefully roasted the meat, and hoped for the best.

***

On the sixth day, Doyle found himself lying on the leaf-strewn ground of the forest floor, his eyes locked upon a rabbit. His body was perfectly still as he willed the rabbit to come just a little closer. If it came just a bit closer, perhaps only two lengths of its own body, Doyle should be able to strike out fast enough to hit it. Striking it with Canary's pointed copper pipe wouldn't necessarily kill it, but the rabbit wouldn't necessarily survive either. Both this morning and the day before had yielded no meat in the snares, and Doyle was craving protein. The rations were keeping them alive, but only just, all of them constantly hungry and desiring flavour. He had spotted the rabbit by chance and creeped and crawled as close as he dared. Now he just needed the thing to come a little bit closer to him, just a hop or two.

Somewhere beyond the rabbit a branch snapped loudly.

No! No, no, no! Doyle thought as the rabbit raised its head, its large ears on the alert as its nose twitched. Leaves crunched from the same direction as the branch, and the rabbit bolted. Doyle attempted to catch it anyway, lashing out with the pseudo spear, but he wasn't even close. The rabbit disappeared.

Doyle silently cursed and grumbled, wondering whether it was Rose or James he'd have to berate, when he realized that the sounds weren't coming from the direction of the camp. Whatever it was, it sounded big and was following the trail the Black Box residents had blazed. The flattened path was already starting to fill in with new growth, and some of the trampled stuff managed to spring back upright. For a second, Doyle wondered if it could be a boar, which excited him with the prospect of meat. Two things quickly put him off this idea, the first being that it didn't really sound like a boar, and the second being that pigs were easily infected in the same way that humans were.

Lying still, Doyle waited until the sounds passed by his location, then crept toward the trail so as to come at the thing from behind. He kept hoping that it was just a deer, something he could pretend was possible to catch, but he knew it was nothing like that. When he reached the flattened area, Doyle kept low against a half-rotted log, peering over the top of it. Along the trail ahead of him walked a big grey horse with two riders perched upon its back. Doyle would have been even angrier if his wrath weren't so tempered by his fear.

At a great distance, one in which Doyle couldn't even see the horse, he followed it along the trail that wound through the trees. He hoped no one was on the pebble beach, or if they were, they were in a position to dive out of sight.

Doyle left the path and crept through the trees in order to spy on the beach. The horse had stopped at the edge of it, the rider not risking the animal in the open. Instead, the man hopped down, leaving his smaller and younger rider up on the horse. The man was tall, broad, and blond with a large sword strapped to his back. Doyle pulled his fire axe off his back and wished he had attempted to sharpen it.

Reaching into one of the packs that the younger rider had been sitting on until he slid forward into the saddle, the big man pulled out what appeared to be a large piece of stiff paper that had been rolled and then crushed flat. A terse instruction was given to the young rider, one which Doyle couldn't hear, and then the big man walked out over the rocks. When he neared the water, he unrolled the paper and held it up toward the forest, slowly turning left and right. Even with the big, bold, black letters, it took Doyle a moment to read and understand the words.

The Container Yard Sent Me.

Beneath these were squiggles that Doyle definitely couldn't make out. Not sure what to do, the former fireman continued to lie flat. The man was probably a friendly, but why wouldn't the yard send someone more recognizable? Why send someone at all? It could have something to do with the submarine, which would be bad, or could be the Black Box invaders had captured the container yard, which would be worse. In the end, Doyle didn't have to make a decision, because James stepped out of the trees and approached the man first. Deciding he shouldn't be alone when there was that second rider, Doyle got up and approached as well, keeping firm grips on both his spear and his axe.

"Is one of you Jamal?" the stranger asked warily as Doyle and James approached.

"No," James answered simply.

"James and Doyle then. Crichton had hoped you'd found your way here. This is for you: he, Boyle, and Bronislav signed it." The man handed James the stiff paper while Doyle kept his distance, watching both the stranger and the young rider still mounted on the horse.

"I recognize these signatures, but not you." James didn't hand the paper back; instead, he rolled it back up and stuck it in his rear pocket. "Why isn't Karsten's name on here?"

"My name is Evans. There's a lot I have to tell you; it'd be easier if everyone were together. Is Jamal still here? And I heard there were two women with you, Rose and... Canary, if I remember correctly."

"Who's he?" Doyle pointed to the young rider.

"Gerald. He's part of the long story. You don't have to take me to your camp, but I'd like to talk somewhere a little less open."

"Doyle, go get Canary and Rose; we'll talk by the fire pit," James decided. "Jamal will have to wait to hear this; he's not in the area at the moment."

Not liking the idea of leaving James alone, Doyle did anyway. At least it wasn't boring anymore.

***

Evans was right when he said the story was a long one. It involved him attacking the container yard, an unbelievable number of zombies, trials, and explosives, as well as the death of Karsten.

"The Black Box is nuclear?" Canary asked as if she hadn't understood the word.

At the same moment, Rose said more angrily, "We've been livin' with enough live explosives to bury us at any moment?"

James ignored them both, although he looked equally surprised by the revelation of the explosives, and he wasn't easily surprised. "You have this detonator with you?"

"I do."

"And it's up to us to get back on Black Box land and set it off."

Evans nodded. "We're to do it tomorrow. I've been told the container yard will distract the guards, although they hadn't worked out the specifics of it yet."

"Great, so the plan isn't even complete," Rose complained.

"No, it's complete; what I meant is that they hadn't yet figured out if their method of distraction was even possible."

"And what about Gerald here? Is he part of the plan?" James asked about the exile next. The young man was sitting somewhat apart from their group.

"No, he'll stay here with my horse."

"Aren't you risking him running off with the horse?" Doyle pointed out.

"I am," Evans agreed. "But if he does, he'll never find the camp that I know will take him in. Even if he does find the exact one I'm thinking of, they'll be very suspicious of him and possibly refuse him entry. They know me, and if I say he'll fit in with them, then they'll take him in. Isn't that right, Gerald?"

"Sure. Whatever you say," he mumbled sullenly.

"Then we have to decide who gets to carry the detonator," James moved onto the next discussion. "Whoever it is, the rest of us have to protect him or her with our lives."

"I think it should be Canary," Doyle immediately suggested. "She's fast and quiet."

James shook his head. "Not with that leg. Sorry, Canary, but if you come on this mission, those stitches are bound to rip out. Painfully, I might add."

"*If?* I wasn't aware there was a chance I'd be staying here. No, I'm coming with you guys, stitches be damned." At least her hand was better.

"Rose, you're probably our best bet carrying the detonator. You're the smallest of us, the hardest target to hit."

"I'm not too fast with my prosthetic on," she pointed out.

"Which is why you won't be wearing it."

"So let me get this straight: I get to run in there holdin' the detonator, leavin' me without any weapons to defend myself with?"

"Yeah."

"Can't she just put it in her pocket?" Doyle mentioned.

"No, I want it in her hand," James told them. "I don't want to risk it being dropped without notice. And if Rose does go down, I want it to be easy for someone else to pick up."

"Sounds fun, I'm in," Rose spoke in a serious tone.

"I suspect this isn't really a volunteer mission, but I'm in as well," Doyle sighed.

James turned to Evans. "You've already done a lot for a community you don't intend to stay with."

"And I planned from the start to do this as well."

"I just want to confirm again, that it was Crichton who decided to do this?" Doyle asked.

"Yes, why?"

Doyle shook his head. He was thinking of the children he had seen with that group. While spying on them, he had seen the way the kids were being trained, taught to kill and deceive men just as much as they were taught to kill zombies. Still, they were children, and the plan didn't sit right with him when it came to them.

"I don't suppose there's a way we can get the distraction to occur at a certain time, is there?" Canary wondered. Doyle suspected she was having the same thoughts, as the children were always outside at the same time of day.

Evans shook his head. "There's no way to communicate with them. I don't even have an exact time when they're supposed to show up. We're to sit tight until they get here, then move whenever you guys think it's best."

James nodded. "The plan is settled. We head out early tomorrow in order to be in place when the time comes. Bring only weapons and ammo, with a bit of food that can fit in your pockets; something you can eat quietly if you find yourself getting hungry. Everything else we'll leave a fair distance away, somewhere between where we plan to breach and where we're to meet the sub."

Everyone agreed, even Doyle despite his twisting guts.

"Hey, did you bring food with you?" Rose turned to Evans.

"Of course, why?"

"Any of it meat? Even salted stuff."

"Yeah."

Rose grinned.

***

That night the cave was extra crowded with the two additional people. Doyle barely slept, the gentle slope never making itself as well-known as then, unlike Jamal who slept like a baby after hearing a stripped-down version of what was going on. Every time Doyle did manage to nod off, he dreamt of children screaming and crying in the dark.

The morning hadn't even arrived before James was rousing everyone. It took a while to get back to the Black Box and he intended to be there early, even if it meant they ended up waiting all day. In this instance, it was infinitely better to be early instead of late.

Doyle ate, emptied his bladder, and packed up his gear. Even Evans was bringing his pack along, despite his plans to not go to the sub afterward. Only the horse and the kid's pack were staying at the camp with Gerald.

"If I'm not back by noon tomorrow, feel free to assume I've been captured or killed," Evans spoke to Gerald in the shadows near the horse. "It may be I've just been injured and your former people are taking care of me, but it's up to you what you think. If you decide I'm dead, I suggest you follow this coast. Go around those zombies up that way, but then stick to following the water until you're sure you're far away from the Black Box. I'll most likely be back before nightfall like last time, but in case there's a snag, I recommend you wait until noon tomorrow. Do you understand?"

Doyle couldn't see Gerald but suspected he nodded.

"I want you to say it," Evans insisted.

"Wait until tomorrow at noon before I consider taking your horse."

"Good kid."

The walk to the Black Box was slow and meandering. They followed the trail for a bit, but then went off course. There was a specific spot along the fences, near the river, around which they were circling toward; a place where everyone was agreed that the guard posted there would be easily distracted. He would definitely head toward the diversion that the container yard had in mind. Passing between several large buildings at the edge of the forest, they stopped off in one to stash their supplies. They separated them in case a wayward scavenger came poking around. Everyone knew where everyone else's stuff was, in case only one of them made it back out.

"That's a lot of books," Evans commented when he learned what was contributing to the majority of the weight they carried.

"Do you want one?" Doyle offered.

Evans shook his head. "I'm not what you would call a reader."

As they left the packs behind, Doyle realized that those books, with whatever was already at the container yard, was all the books they'd have left. Their library was going to be buried along with the enemy.

The position along the fence that they had chosen was next to a field of long, yellow grass. Doyle hated crawling along his belly over the dirt, but it kept them hidden. It also helped that they were able to tear up a bunch of grass along the fringes, dirt and all, and put it on their backs as camouflage. Cut in large chunks, the dirt and grass made a sort of heavy blanket. They all moved slowly in the light of the rising sun, trying to disturb the grass as little as possible. Luckily, there was a bit of a breeze that morning, so the grass was swaying anyway. Doyle crawled with his axe ahead of him, freshly sharpened by the whetstone Evans had let him borrow.

When they were close enough, James reached out and gently touched Doyle's hand. Doyle then reached to his other side and touched Canary's, even though he could barely see her through the leafy blades. He noticed that her hair was nearly the same colour as the grass.

They waited a long time.

From Doyle's position—which he came to realize was in another part of the same field in which the boy had been found—he could see through a gap in the crap that was piled up along the bottom of the fence whenever the breeze blew the grass just the right way. He watched the feet of the guard go by through the gap, knowing that if he raised his head a bit, he'd be able to see the man's face. He didn't raise his head though; he wasn't going to risk disturbing the dirt and grass Rose had laid across him.

When the children came out for their usual outdoor lessons, briefly glimpsed through the fence gap and over the recently planted crops, Doyle tensed. He hoped and wished that now would be the time that the people from the container yard would begin their distraction. But nothing happened, followed by more and more nothing.

The children would be going back inside soon. Doyle's muscles were rock hard, praying that now was when they would show up. That now was when they *had* to show up. But they didn't.

"I have to pee," a tiny voice called back to the others. It was so near, so close to the fence! Doyle spotted small feet heading toward him. He remembered the way the kids practically begged for attention from the woman he assumed was their leader whenever she made an appearance. Doyle thought he could use that. He could whisper some lie to the kid, say he was carrying out an exercise, make him keep the rest of the kids outside, tell him that he would be rewarded with affection.

It seemed James knew exactly what he was about to do, because the moment Doyle opened his mouth, the man's hand clamped down hard across it. From the grass next to him, James' eyes burned into his, made all the more fierce-looking by the dark dirt that covered and shadowed his face. James kept his hand there until the young boy finished peeing and ran off to rejoin the others.

The children went back inside.

38
Danny's Exhausted

Danny couldn't remember ever being so tired. His wounded shoulder always ached, but there was so much to do, every day, whether it was corpse removal, rat killing, or helping with the construction project, that he pushed on through the pain. He constantly felt pulled in multiple directions as one person after another called to him, needing another able body to help out. He wasn't the only one. Everyone capable was dashing about, trying to get everything done as quickly as possible, trying to get everything back to normal. At night, Danny barely felt his bed before he was asleep, only to be woken up again what felt like minutes later despite the drastic change in light. At least that kept him from dreaming.

For a week they worked, those not capable staying on Animal Island, the bridge constantly being monitored, guarded, and hooked and unhooked as people went back and forth to see their families. Danny didn't have time to visit his nieces, Hope and Dakota, who had been moved over there the first night after the submarine had appeared. He barely had time to see his sisters-in-law, Riley and Cameron, who were busy with their own tasks. His expanded family was also running all over the place, helping out where they could. Sometimes he'd be working beside them, like helping Misha kill rats, or Abby carry a corpse, but most of the time he had no idea where anyone was.

On the last day before the mission, he found himself outside the wall, guarding people who were moving corpses to a second body burn that had been started out there. By the time they were done, they were going to be out of wood and out of the charcoal they used in their barbecues. All the bodies from within the wall had finally been thrown on the pyre; now they just needed to be monitored and turned like logs to make sure everything got burned to ash. The ashes themselves were then being shovelled into the river where the toilets were perched. Some people were hopeful they might increase the fish population, but no one seemed to know for certain. Although ash had a lot of uses, no one wanted to use the stuff leftover from such a horrible pyre.

Danny patrolled the path that had been cleared a couple of feet away from the wall, at the base of the zombie pileup. With his dented metal baseball bat in hand, he scanned the distance for roaming zombies and the ground for scurrying rats. They had lost a large number of people to rat bites already; some suspected more than they lost during the zombie attack, but Danny had never heard the numbers. He was sweltering in his heavy boots and the thick, tough leather that had been strapped on over his pants, but feet and legs were always the first points of attack for the rodents. Some would jump for the face, but unless they had an elevated position, they always fell short. Thick gloves also covered Danny's hands and arms up to his elbows so that if one did land on him, he could rip the thing off.

Along his walk, he made one stop. On one of the distant containers, the ones they hadn't yet searched through for supplies, someone had hung what was left of the zombie corpse known as Dean. Danny suspected Mark and his crew were behind it, having spent a few days searching for the thing. Hunks of meat dangled inside bits of body armour and duct tape, all of it burnt and peppered with shrapnel from roughly a dozen grenades. Even as Danny watched, another piece of something slid free and plopped on the dead below that were still waiting to be burned. Danny was glad that the thing had been hung there; it gave him a place to direct his anger whenever he wasn't so tired or busy that it numbed him. He still carried the sling Freya had taught him to use, and more than once he launched a rock in the corpse's direction but never succeeded in hitting it; it was too far away.

His eyes then wandered past the hanging body and looked at the containers themselves. The sides of the ones on the bottom of the stacks were all slimed with fluids and pieces that had been rubbed off the zombies when they walked past. They were disgusting to look at, as disgusting as everything else was this past week. At least inside the walls some people had taken to filling buckets with salt water and rinsing off what they could. Out here, they needed another big storm. Danny kept walking, not liking to dwell too long on what the future might hold or what they needed, because they needed too much.

When noon came around, Danny went to the community centre to get his ration of food. They had reduced the amount everyone was allowed, because without the Black Box, they no longer had vegetables or grain coming in, and no one was out scavenging or hunting. Normally, Danny's stomach would feel hollow most of the day with reduced rations, but he was somewhat glad for them now. Eating anything was a chore, every bite having to be forced down into a stomach that would rather vomit than digest. Danny understood he needed to eat all he was given, especially with all the work that was being done, but he found the task unpleasant.

"Danny! Over here!" Mark called out when he spotted him looking for a seat.

Danny walked over and joined the bench along the wall that his group and a few others had claimed, several of them squeezing together to make room. The community centre was always crowded these days with people cooking, eating, the injured on their cots, the cats on rat patrol. There were even people who weren't injured spending their nights in the community centre; those whose homes weren't safe from rats because of openings in their containers that needed repair and those who were too tired to cross Bitch Bridge. Danny himself had once spent a night in there after letting someone else use his bed, settling in next to Nessie who continued to knit or write in her notebook whenever she was awake.

"What have you been up to this morning?" Mark asked, wedged tightly next to his girlfriend or wife or whatever their relationship was defined as.

"Watching for rats and zombies outside the wall," Danny answered. "You?"

"Fire duty." That would explain the smoky smell. "Have you seen Jon?"

"He's probably down at the waterfront helping with the construction project." That seemed to be where Jon always was these days. Ever since the zombie attack, he had worked himself into a fervour, barely stopping to eat or take a piss. Claire often had to bring food to him as he wouldn't realize how long he had been working, how long it had been since he last ate.

"That kid's got problems," rumbled the black man from Mark's crew known only as Boss.

"He's just working through some stuff," Danny said defensively. "We all are. A lot's happened." And was still happening, what with the crazy plan to make sure the Black Box attackers didn't come here. "I'm going back to work," Danny told them, finishing the last of his meal in a hurry. As he got up, he heard Suzanne say something, but didn't catch the words or who it was directed to.

Back outside, it didn't take long for Danny to get roped into another task, this time helping to haul salt water to clean around sites that needed repairing.

***

For once, Danny found he couldn't sleep come nightfall. He lay on his back in the dark, remembering the night before the zombie assault. This wasn't so different.

"Jon, you awake?" Danny whispered in the quietest voice he could.

"Yes," Jon replied immediately.

"I assume you volunteered for tomorrow?"

"Yes."

"Are you scared?"

This time there was a pause before the answer came, but it was the same as the others. "Yes."

They continued to lie in silence for several more minutes, but Danny knew that Jon hadn't fallen asleep during that time.

"Do you think this will work?"

"I don't know," he answered honestly.

"I hope it works."

"Everyone hopes it'll work."

"Do you think things will go back to normal after this?"

"No," Jon replied bluntly.

"Boss thinks there's something wrong with you, you know, like, in your head?"

"Well, he's not wrong."

"Yeah, but he said it like there's nothing wrong with him either. Like he's not messed up like the rest of us."

"No need to get worked up about it."

"I'm not, I'm just…"

"Distracting yourself?"

"Yeah."

They lapsed back into silence, and this time Danny didn't bother to break it. He continued trying to sleep and found himself staring into the dark once more.

***

The next morning, everyone was sombre, moving at a more sluggish pace than usual. Only around the construction project were things chaotic as people tried to get it done. For several nights, people had worked in shifts to complete it on time.

Danny shovelled the ashes of burnt zombies into the river all morning until he heard that the project was finally completed. He got his lunch from the community centre and forced down each bite, wondering how many of them were eating their last meals, and whether this one was his. Either way, he couldn't taste it. Afterward, he reported to the docks.

"Thank you all for volunteering," Bronislav told them once everyone had arrived. "Could you all try to split up into groups, standing with the people you've worked with most often?"

Danny found himself standing with Jon, Misha, and Bryce, whose face wasn't looking nearly as swollen as it had, but was still discoloured.

"How's Larson?" Danny asked him.

"He's in the clear infection wise, but it's not like the finger will ever grow back."

A few days ago, Larson had been working on the construction project when a rat popped out and chomped down on the ring finger of his left hand, piercing both work glove and flesh. Luckily for Larson, he had been holding a pair of wire cutters in his right hand. Reacting quickly, he chopped off the bitten finger, with the rat still hanging off the end of it. His scream had been loud and shrill, quickly bringing the medics who found him crushing the rat flat beneath his boot while blood flowed freely from his new stump.

"I stopped in to see him earlier," Bryce continued. "He was making jokes about never being able to marry. I think he's mostly disappointed he can't come today. How's your shoulder?"

"Still hurts, although all this work has kept the muscle from stiffening and the stitches haven't popped for several days." The duct tape he had taken to strapping over the wound helped with that. A little voice within Danny begged him to back out, insisting there was still time. Danny squashed it. He wasn't going to let his friends go without him.

"All right, you four will be pullers on the front," Bronislav told their little group as he went by.

"That's the most dangerous job, isn't it?" Misha sighed.

"I think Bronislav has the most dangerous job, actually," Jon corrected him. "He's going to be on top of the conning tower shouting orders."

"Not in the sub?" Bryce wondered.

"He's got more than enough sailors who know what they're doing; they don't need him inside. Come on, let's get on board."

The U-boat rested lower in the water than it had when it first arrived. On one side of the top decks, their makeshift cranes for getting large things over the wall and lifting containers had been bolted and modified. Beneath them, half-below the water, stubby containers with doors on their sides had been welded on sideways so that their doors faced upward. On the other side, to balance the weight and offer protection, other small containers had been sliced up and welded back together to form a haphazard-looking barrier. The thing looked like a monster.

Danny scrambled across the gangplank, taking up a position with Jon, Bryce, and Misha at the front. A newly constructed and awkward wall bent at a ninety-degree angle along the forward deck, so the four huddled up in the corner where they wouldn't be seen. The rest of the volunteers came aboard as they were given their assignments. The sub's crew was already preparing inside.

"How are the dogs?" Danny asked Misha while they waited.

"They're fine. Rifle's been limping a bit more; I think he keeps overexerting himself. The rest are all delighted about the rats they've been catching. I'm glad they eat the things instead of bringing them to me like some of the cat owners have been dealing with."

"Yeah, Robin was telling me that Splatter keeps doing that," Jon added.

"Splatter made it out of the Black Box?" Danny hadn't seen the calico cat anywhere.

"Apparently, he spent more time outside the Box than in. He was already out there when the attack came. Robin doesn't know whether he followed the column to the submarine or someone found him and carried him, but he was loaded aboard and Robin came across him sometime after she got out."

"I feel sorry for those people whose pets couldn't get out," Misha spoke quietly. "They're likely still in there."

"Don't think about that," Bryce insisted. "The animals that got left behind are likely already dead. Tell me, if your dogs were in that situation, would they just accept their new masters or fight them?"

"I know some would fight, but others I'm not sure about."

"Once one dog attacks, those cunts won't trust any of the animals. They've probably shot them all already."

Danny had no idea if that was true or not, but he let himself believe it was. He needed to hate these people or he might never sleep again.

"I'm actually surprised you're coming," Danny commented in Misha's direction.

"Why's that?"

"I don't know, you've just looked...tired."

"I've been tired before."

"I've never seen you like this though."

"You didn't know me in the first twenty-four," Misha replied, obviously referring to the Day. The way his ghostly eyes pierced into Danny he knew not to ask more. Danny had been too young to hear and remember all of Misha's story when they first met; all he really knew was that the former Russian had survived with basically nothing but Rifle by his side. Danny could remember the way he used to be a bit wary of Misha, but tried to hide it, recalling the man's injuries, especially the way his cut-up feet looked, and how he was practically feral. Everyone had been weird that first day at Riley's cabin as they adjusted to what had happened, but Misha was the only one Danny found himself frightened of. That didn't take long to change, however, and they became good friends, family even.

"So why *did* you volunteer?" Jon asked. "I'm not used to seeing you without your dogs."

"Why did *you* volunteer?" Misha countered, getting a little bristly with all the questions aimed at him. "Pretty sure we're all here for the same damn reason."

The sub was finally loaded up and rumbled to life beneath them, cutting off their chatter. With all of the new additions, they were slow to accelerate. Danny watched the far shore slowly slide away as they entered the big bay. They would pass between Animal and Quarantine Islands, but the wall was on the wrong side for Danny to be able to see anyone. Figuring he should at least try, he left the huddle in the corner, jumping up and grabbing the edge of the wall when he thought they were passing the right location. Hauling himself up, he peered over at Animal Island, trying to spot his nieces. They were easy to spot, as all the kids had gathered the moment someone let them know the sub was moving. Hope and Dakota stood with their best friends, Becky, Adam, and Peter, all of them waving. Dakota had taken her hat off and waved with that, while Peter and Adam were trying to hold Hope up for a better view. Danny waved back, but then lost his one-handed grip and stumbled back down onto the sub's deck. He didn't know why the others were doing this, but he knew he was doing it for them. Danny had only been fourteen when the Day happened, not much older than Hope and her group. He had survived thanks to the help and sacrifice of others, and now it was his turn to do the same for the next generation.

"Who's watching?" Bryce asked as Danny rejoined the group.

"The kids, Becky included. I'm guessing all the adults are too busy."

"I wonder how many of them need new parents," Jon thought aloud.

Hopefully not many, Danny thought to himself. "Hey, Jon, do you remember that girl you had a crush on back before the Day?" he suddenly remembered.

"What girl?"

"The one you went all vegetarian for."

"*You* were a vegetarian?" Bryce raised an eyebrow. Jon could devour a slab of meat like nobody's business.

"Haha, right! I totally forgot I was a vegetarian once. I'm pretty sure I forgot that the moment the zombies showed up."

"Too bad *they're* not vegetarians," Bryce quipped.

The three of them continued to talk about idle matters like they usually did when going out on scavenger trips. Misha stayed quiet, clearly listening but not adding anything to the conversation.

"Quiet in the ranks, we're approaching target," Bronislav called down to everyone from the conning tower. "Get to your positions."

Misha was the first to scramble over to the line, with Jon, Danny, and Bryce following closely behind him.

"I still can't believe we built catapults on the side of a submarine," Bryce commented as they picked up the length of rope.

"They're more like trebuchets," Danny corrected him, although they weren't really that either. They couldn't manage a counter weight or the height for a regular trebuchet, and instead used various pulleys and the four of them hauling on a rope; four others did the same for the one on the back.

As they neared the barge dock, Bronislav resorted to hand signals, keeping them quiet and unseen for as long as possible. Danny didn't need to see Bronislav's signals to know when other volunteers opened the containers that held their ammunition. The stench of the corpses they hadn't burned was rather distinct.

Shouting came from the shoreline and Danny knew they had been spotted so he gripped the rope even tighter.

"Fire!" Bronislav bellowed.

The four men hauled on their rope, running together to the far side of the deck as fast as they could. Overhead, the arm of their former crane swung upward with a large leather sling on the end of it, not too dissimilar in concept from Danny's. When the sling hit the right spot, the zombie remains it had been loaded with were let loose to fly and splatter onto shore.

"Reload!" Bronislav bellowed. There was no point in telling them if their aim had been true, as they couldn't turn the devices they had built. Any aiming had to be done by repositioning the entire U-boat, and those commands were shouted down through the conning tower where Danny couldn't hear them.

There was more shouting from the shoreline as the trebuchet was lowered back down. Danny caught a glimpse of their loading team: three people he remembered living in the Black Box before they had found it. For them, this place had been their only home since the Day. Danny could understand their hatred for these people and their willingness to do anything to them.

Without being able to see the loaders while in their start position, they had to wait until Bronislav shouted the command, as he was the only one high enough to see all of the teams. More zombie guts and heads, some of them with rats carefully duct taped inside that morning, were thrown overhead. Danny and the others quickly put on their mask gear when some drips and gobs fell onto them.

Soon, the trebuchets were out of sync, Bronislav having to shout at them individually. Bullets pinged and ricocheted off their wall, causing dents, and even holes in the thinner spots. The hope was that the zombie guts and the sub would be a distraction, drawing the guards away from their posts, but since they weren't really that much of a threat, the majority of their people would stay inside. Danny knew these pseudo trebuchets didn't have much range, that they were really only messing up the barge dock and surrounding areas. The rats would be problematic, but the dead zombie parts were just gross and a nuisance. Still, Danny hoped the other team in charge of setting off the bombs hurried.

"Fore deck, fire!" Bronislav shouted and they ran across the deck again. They were all beginning to tire. Even with the pulleys taking much of the weight, it was hard pulling up that arm with enough speed and force to get it to properly fling the infected projectiles. Danny was soon drenched in sweat, his legs and arms trembling. There were two other teams huddling somewhere nearby but out of sight, ready to take over when they were too exhausted, but Danny was determined to keep going as long as the others were.

The shots hitting their wall decreased, but the cracking gunfire didn't slow down. It took a moment for Danny to realize that the shooters were now aiming at the trebuchets and pulley systems, trying to destroy the machines as opposed to those running them.

"Second team!" Jon was finally the one to call it for them.

As a fresh group of four scrambled onto the deck from where they had waited on the ammo bins, Danny and his team fell back. It was as they were slipping down the side, bypassing the ladders that had been set up, that they heard the explosion. A crack, a bang, a heavy whump and a great rumble dwarfed the gunfire from the shoreline. The submarine was rocked and Danny found himself losing his balance and being thrown overboard into the river. He wasn't the only one, but no one was hurt, and the low lying position of the ammo containers allowed everyone to scramble back aboard. As Danny was hauled out of the water by Jon, he looked into the sky beyond the submarine and saw several large plumes of dust that had been launched into the air. He tried to count them, to determine if all of the explosives had gone off.

"Rear deck fire!" Bronislav screamed into the silence that had followed, snapping everyone's focus back onto his or her task. They needed to keep launching the dead, keep the chaos going so that the team that had set off the detonator had a better chance of getting back out.

Danny breathed heavily, sitting flopped over and letting his limbs rest. He needed to prepare for the moment when the replacement team got tired. Bryce vomited once into the river, but insisted he was fine, just exhausted, and that he'd be okay soon. Misha was the only one to remain on his feet, his head cocked and listening to all the various sounds of battle, waiting for the call to return to pulling.

When the call finally came, the submarine was moving slowly backward, retreating down the river. The gunfire had dropped off drastically, but they continued to throw dead things onto shore anyway, trying to keep the enemy from following. Danny and his team had begun to scream with effort whenever they ran, although the urgency was less.

"Cease fire!" Bronislav called out. They must have reached the rendezvous point around the bend in the river where they had arranged with Evans to pick up the explosives team and didn't want to pepper the area with corpses before they got there. They were currently sitting ducks, or rather, one big floating duck.

Danny rested as he watched the two canoes that had been loaded onto the submarine slide into the water. Their four strongest paddlers were onboard in seconds, the blades of their paddles slicing deep into the river. The canoes moved fast and were quickly out of sight, heading for shore to pick up the team.

Danny redirected his gaze to the wall and saw there were more holes than he had been aware of; some of the bullets must have passed dangerously close to them.

"Bronislav!" one of their loaders called up. "Did we get them? Did you see? Did all the explosives go off?"

Bronislav was a red mess when Danny looked up. What had to be a narrowly missed head shot owing to the fact that he was alive, had left a gash across Bronislav's face, covering him in his own blood. It looked like his arm or shoulder had also taken a hit based on the way he wasn't using it.

"I can't say for sure about the deeper bombs, but all the entrances are certainly gone."

The U-boat volunteers all cheered, while silently praying the lower bombs had gone off as well. If they hadn't, then the Black Box might still have power and the raiders would be able to survive long enough to dig themselves out. If that occurred, Danny imagined an angry hornets' nest of people descending on the container yard in the coming months.

"Team safely aboard canoes, resume firing!" Bronislav suddenly shouted.

Danny scrambled up and returned to his place in the line. As soon as all four of the team members grabbed hold, they ran across the deck again, more zombie debris flung to shore. The canoes came around the back of the submarine, off-loading onto the ammunition containers. As soon as they were all aboard, the sub resumed its backward retreat.

Between shots, Danny looked over at the returning team. They were all dirty, bloody, and hurt.

"Someone replace me!" Jon shouted.

Instead, the entire replacement team took over. Jon ran over as Rose climbed up onto the sub. The two of them had been close friends ever since the Diana, and it seemed that closeness hadn't diminished despite living in separate locations. Rose was bleeding freely from a cut on her stump arm, but seemed to be the least wounded of the bunch. The injured were quickly hauled up the conning tower to be administered to by the doctors waiting inside. Danny watched as James limped his way along, finding it difficult to tell what was mangled boot and what was mangled foot on the end of his left leg. Canary was bleeding from her leg as well as several small cuts on her face, neck, and shoulder. Doyle was holding an arm across his bloody waist, but the fact that he was moving under his own power gave Danny hope that it wasn't too bad, that it was just a cut from a blade and not a hole from a bullet. The man Danny knew the least, the one he guessed was Jamal, was the worst off. He had to be carried and the bone sticking out of his leg made it obvious why.

"Where's Evans?" Danny asked as Rose and Jon released one another.

"He decided he wasn't badly injured enough to need a doctor. He's headin' his own way."

"What, he's leaving?"

"He told me to tell anyone who asked, goodbye for him, so yeah, he's goin' someplace else."

Danny didn't know how he felt about that. Evans had kidnapped him, but he had grown to like the man anyway.

"Did you get to the right spot?" Bronislav shouted down.

"Oh yeah!" Rose grinned. "My ears are still ringin' from that! Felt the land jump beneath me too!"

Everyone cheered again. Jon helped Rose up the ladder of the conning tower so that she could get her wound attended to. As they moved down river and back into the big bay, there was no need to keep throwing zombie parts, so everyone sat down to rest.

"What's next?" Misha wondered.

"We get everything cleaned up, and everyone settled in," Bryce told him. "After another week or two, we'll send some teams over to see who's left at that place and if any radiation has leaked out of the ground. If it hasn't, we'll look into killing whoever's left and reclaim our crops."

"And if it has?"

"We'll have to monitor it and decide what to do then," Bryce said, shrugging.

Danny felt confident there wouldn't be a radiation leak. They had the container yard, a place they could call home. Nothing and no one was going to take it from them this time. With blades and bullets, with teeth and nails, with everything they had, they were going to stay put this time, and damn anyone who thought otherwise.

The End

CHECK OUT OTHER GREAT ZOMBIE NOVELS

DEAD ASCENT
by Jason McPhearson

The dead have risen and they are hungry...

Grizzled war veteran turned game warden, Brayden James and a small group of survivors, fight their way through the rugged wilderness of southern Appalachia to an isolated cabin in the hope of finding sanctuary. Every terrifying step they make they are stalked by a growing mass of staggering corpses, and a raging forest fire, set by the government in hopes of containing the virus.

As all logical routes off the mountain are cut off from them, they seek the higher ground, but they soon realize there is little hope of escape when the dead walk and the world burns.

CHAOS THEORY
by Rich Restucci

The world has fallen to a relentless enemy beyond reason or mercy. With no remorse they rend the planet with tooth and nail.

One man stands against the scourge of death that consumes all.

Teamed with a genius survivalist and a teenage girl, he must flee the teeming dead, the evils of humans left unchecked, and those that would seek to use him. His best weapon to stave off the horrors of this new world? His wit.

CHECK OUT OTHER GREAT ZOMBIE NOVELS

RUN
by Rich Restucci

The dead have risen, and they are hungry.

Slow and plodding, they are Legion. The undead hunt the living. Stop and they will catch you. Hide and they will find you. If you have a heartbeat you do the only thing you can: You run.

Survivors escape to an island stronghold: A cop and his daughter, a computer nerd, a garbage man with a piece of rebar, and an escapee from a mental hospital with a life-saving secret. After reaching Alcatraz, the ever expanding group of survivors realize that the infected are not the only threat.

Caught between the viciousness of the undead, and the heartlessness of the living, what choice is there? Run.

THE DEAD WALK THE EARTH
by Luke Duffy

As the flames of war threaten to engulf the globe, a new threat emerges.

A 'deadly flu', the like of which no one has ever seen or imagined, relentlessly spreads, gripping the world by the throat and slowly squeezing the life from humanity.

Eight soldiers, accustomed to operating below the radar, carrying out the dirty work of a modern democracy, become trapped within the carnage of a new and terrifying world.

Deniable and completely expendable. That is how their government considers them, and as the dead begin to walk, Stan and his men must fight to survive.

CHECK OUT OTHER GREAT ZOMBIE NOVELS

DEAD PULSE RISING
by K. Michael Gibson

Slavering hordes of the walking dead rule the streets of Baltimore, their decaying forms shambling across the ruined city, voracious and unstoppable. The remaining survivors hide desperately, for all hope seems lost... until an armored fortress on wheels plows through the ghouls, crushing bones and decayed flesh. The vehicle stops and two men emerge from its doors, armed to the teeth and ready to cancel the apocalypse.

TOWER OF THE DEAD
by J.V. Roberts

Markus is a hardworking man that just wants a better life for his family. But when a virus sweeps through the halls of his high-rise apartment complex, those plans are put on hold. Trapped on the sixteenth floor with no hope of rescue, Markus must fight his way down to safety with his wife and young daughter in tow.

Floor by bloody floor they must battle through hordes of the hungry dead on a terrifying mission to survive the TOWER OF THE DEAD.